"Doug Casey and Dr. John Hunt's compelling novel, *Speculator*, describes the world of stock fraud centered around a too-good-to-be-true African gold discovery. Given the fact that Casey already has two *New York Times* best sellers under his belt, one would assume that this would be a page-turner. The reader will not be disappointed. Many of the important questions facing society today are also dealt with in this novel. Utilizing fiction, Ayn Rand addressed issues facing society of her day; Casey and Hunt do the same through their characters. *Speculator* is a suspenseful, well-written novel—and, more importantly, one that will make you stop and think."

— Al Korelin, Host, *The Korelin Report*

"A rousing adventure where gold mining, market mining, and corruption meet Ayn Rand in the mythical African country of Gondwana. Charles's adventures play out between real insights into human nature and greed, focused as only Doug Casey can."

**— Brent Cook, exploration geologist,
Editor, *Exploration Insights***

"Doug brings the clear writing style that made him a bestselling investment author to fiction. *Speculator* is a page-turner, full of knowledge and insights that Doug Casey and his coauthor, John Hunt, have learned from real-world speculations and travels around the globe. The book rings true because they have lived the life."

**— Adrian Day, author of *Investing in Resources*,
Chairman, Adrian Day Asset Management**

"At last! A Harry Potter for adults! Your new friend, Charles Knight, combats people with unparalleled political power, and people whose cunning and deception made them incredibly rich. He will take you with him though an African revolution, unpredictable characters with at least three sides, and a gigantic mining fraud. A double-deceptive conclusion leaves you eager for the next book to see where Charles Knight will take you!"

— Thea Alexander, bestselling author of *2150 AD*

"Who knew Doug Casey—brilliant investor, essayist, speaker, entrepreneur, anarcho-capitalist—was also a novelist? You must read *Speculator!*"

— Lew Rockwell, author of *Against the State:*
An Anarcho-Capitalist Manifesto,
Chairman, Ludwig von Mises Institute

"A well-written and exciting adventure for intelligent people. In the confrontation between the peaceful and creative persons, and those whose actions embrace violence, fraud, and other forms of dishonesty, this novel provides a microcosm of a world that reaches far beyond the African continent where it is set. It is a really good book!"

— Butler Shaffer, author of *Calculated Chaos*

"*Speculator* is a terrific book. A gripping adventure story played out in a dramatic setting. It is also a smart and thoughtful book that is brimming with interesting facts and asking important philosophical questions."

— Mark Ford, *New York Times* bestselling author,
Editor, *Creating Wealth*

"*Speculator* is a wild ride, a philosophy in action *tour de force* that both excites the reader and invites him to examine all he thought he knew about the nature of man and the state. Casey and Hunt's vivid prose draws us in, while their unforgettable turns of phrase cement themselves in our mind. *Speculator* is a must read for anyone seeking to better understand the world around them and, by extension, their own place in it. Contrarians and independent thinkers will delight in these pages— and wait impatiently for the next installment! Highly recommended."

— Joel Bowman, Editor, *Truth and Plenty*

"Finally, a work that fuses sound, consistent philosophy with a highly readable, action-packed story. And who better to guide us through the twists and turns, all the while offering us his fresh, original take on the world, than Doug Casey? Against a landscape of artless fiction and stale, trite philosophies, Casey offers a refreshing perspective as only he can."

— Anya Leonard, Editor, *Classical Wisdom*

"*Speculator* is a roller-coaster lesson on the arcane world of gold-mine investing. An African revolution, massive fraud with massive profits and losses—the novel is such fun you don't notice how much you are learning. But, mostly, it is a good read with a unique protagonist."
— **Wendy McElroy, author of *Liberty for Women***

"John Hunt—a doctor, entrepreneur, and fiction and nonfiction author—joins forces with the famous Doug Casey in the first of a six-novel series the likes of which no one else would ever contemplate. Or risk!"
— **B.K. Marcus, Contributing Editor,**
Foundation for Economic Education (FEE)

"Years ago my favorite Arthur Hailey novel, *Airport*, gave us an intimate insider look at the airline industry. Now *Speculator* gives us an intimate insider look inside mining and the world of finance. Readers of Doug Casey's nonfiction will especially appreciate his first plunge into dramatic fiction."
— **J. Neil Schulman, author/filmmaker, *Alongside Night***

"It's very rare in literature to have, at the same time, a captivating story and a potent serving of sound philosophy and free-market principles. *Speculator* does it better than anything I have ever seen. It could introduce you to a new way to look at life. I expect *Speculator* will become a timeless classic. If you thought *Atlas Shrugged* was good, *Speculator* will blow you away. As someone who deeply believes in personal and economic freedom, I can't wait to see what Charles does next."
— **Nick Giambruno, Senior Editor, InternationalMan.com**

"At last, an adventure novel about gold-mining exploration in insanely dangerous places such as Indonesia and Africa. I've debated Casey at forums, and his brilliant mind, added to his mining expertise, adds authenticity to a wild way to get rich quick: ranging from a Bernie Madoff-type swindle echoing the infamous Bre-X scandal that rocked Canadian miners, to boy soldiers and gangster mercenaries. A great read."
— **James Dines, author of *Mass Psychology*,**
Editor, *The Dines Letter*

"*Speculator* combines the fast-paced action of a Dirk Pitt adventure story with the cerebral message of an Ayn Rand novel. The authors' knowledge of how markets, mining, and governments work is impressive, yet the book reads like a day at the beach. Crisp, intelligent, and witty, this new adventure series might even out-Rand Rand."

— Jo Ann Skousen, Professor of English Literature, Chapman University

"Along come Doug Casey and John Hunt with their fantastic, riveting story, *Speculator*. Just as I could not put down *Atlas Shrugged* until I finished it, I simply was glued to my screen until I found out every jot and tittle of what happened to Charles Knight, the fictional hero of this novel. I am simply delighted that this is to be but the first in a six-part "High Ground" series of novels. If the other five are even in the same ballpark as this one, we are in for an exquisite treat. This really is a magnificent novel."

— Walter Block, PhD, Professor of Economics, Loyola University, author of *Defending the Undefendable*

"All too often in the world, fortunes are made and lost less by the genius of entrepreneurs than by the caprice of those who stifle, connive, and repress. Casey and Hunt weave a fine tale of a young man in search of success, but who must confront power and corruption along the way. The story entertains the reader while the lessons that emerge, both moral and economic, educate in profoundly important ways."

— Lawrence W. Reed, President, Foundation for Economic Education (FEE)

Books by Doug Casey:

The International Man

Crisis Investing

Strategic Investing

Crisis Investing for the '90s

Totally Incorrect

Right on the Money

Books by John Hunt:

Higher Cause

Assume the Physician

Your Child's Asthma

SPECULATOR

SPECULATOR

Doug Casey
and
John Hunt

Book 1 of the High Ground Novels

Speculator

Published by HighGround Books, LLC

ISBN: 978-0-9859332-5-8 (paperback)
ISBN: 978-0-9859332-6-5 (hardcover)

Cover design by Jim Ross

Map by Paul Woodward

Edited by Harry David and Nathalie C. Marcus (InvisibleOrder.com)

Acknowledgments

W E are grateful to Nathalie Marcus, Harry David, and Paul Woodward for their wise and efficient editing and guidance; Jim Ross for his artistic excellence; and B.K. Marcus and Jeffrey Tucker for putting us together in the first place.

We individually gained intellectual stimulation from Ancha Casey, Kimberly Johnson, David Galland, Lobo Tiggre, Joyce Curran, Mary Lou Gutscher, Jayant Bhandari, Chris Leverich, Terry Hale, Marcia Abbott, Ann and Jim Hunt, John Slovensky, Neal Sansovich, our families, friends, colleagues, co-conspirators, and the many others who add spice to our world.

Contents

1   A Resolution Almost Unresolved   1

2   A Logical Geological Theory   8

3   Secrets and Secret Societies   20

4   A Foolish Fantasy and a Gbarngeda Reality   29

5   Small-Small   51

6   A Rumble and a Race   59

7   After Action Assessment   68

8   The Floating Hospital   72

9   Sabina, Now of the IRS   80

10   A Viking Father Confessor   88

11   A Conjecture Strengthened   94

12   A Polite Urban Manhunt   101

13   Dinner with a Gamma-Type Wolf Larsen   106

14   The Heart of the Beast   114

15   A Theory of Speculation   123

16   The Bear in the Ziggurat   129

17   The Nine *P*'s in Intensive Care   136

18   A Search and a Party   144

19   Fiscal Taxes and Physical Recovery   151

20   Two Plans Are Hatched   159

21   A Walk and an Assault   166

22 Macro Theories and a Micro Lesson 177

23 Nighttime in Gbarngeda, Daytime in San Diego 184

24 An Explosive Rumble in the Jungle 198

25 Conversations in the Jungle 204

26 Discoveries 213

27 Doing Well by Doing Good 224

28 Springer Shocks Sabina 237

29 The Person in a Hot Tub 255

30 New York and Toronto 261

31 San Diego and Adamstown 273

32 Soccer and Shares 278

33 The Spider Meets the Fly 285

34 Transoceanic 294

35 The Six *P*'s Vindicated 307

36 A Dinner and a Death 315

37 Charles, Meet JohnJohn 326

38 A Secret between Old Friends 341

39 Sabina Comes Into Her Own 347

40 A Double Reversal of Fortune 355

41 A Hole in the Jungle 371

42 Rally 381

43 The Two Daughters Attack 390

44 Arms at Rest 398

45 $200 Million to the Bad 406

Epilogue 418

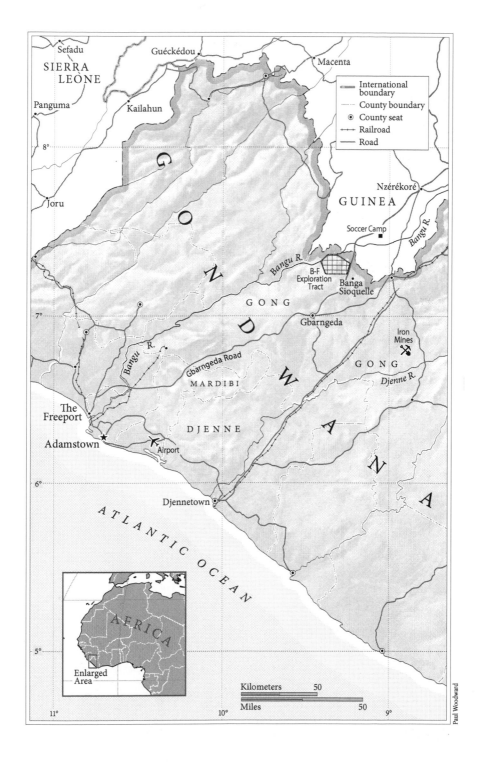

SIERRA LEONE

Sefadu

Guéckédou

Macenta

Panguma

Kailahun

Joru

G O N D W A N A

GUINEA

Nzérékoré

Soccer Camp

Bangu R.

Bangu R.

B-F
Exploration
Tract

Banga
Sioquelle

GONG

Gbarngeda

Iron
Mines

GONG

Bangu R.

Gbarngeda Road

MARDIBI

Djenne R.

The
Freeport

DJENNE

Adamstown

Airport

Djennetown

ATLANTIC OCEAN

AFRICA

Enlarged
Area

International boundary		
County boundary		
County seat		
Railroad		
Road		

8°

7°

6°

5°

11°

10°

9°

Kilometers   50

Miles   50

Paul Woodward

A junior mining company takes your money and their dream, and turns it into your dream and their money.

1

A Resolution
Almost Unresolved
(A Cliffhanger in the Jungle)

CHARLES Knight stood tall at the edge of a precipice. Far below, the tumultuous Bangu River scoured its path along an ancient fault while its roar echoed up the canyon walls it had carved over the eons. He gazed over hundreds of square miles of thick African bush.

The decades-old geologic surveys conveyed none of the continent's colors, its fragrance, the weight of its air. To the north stood steep hills capped with erosion-resistant dark-green basaltic rock—the congealed blood of extinct volcanoes. To the west, a ghostly band of gray clouds, pregnant with rain, floated at the horizon. When the rain arrived, it would come in torrents, the likes of which few people on the planet ever experienced.

The ledge on which Charles now stood had suffered the assault of such rain for millennia. Little remained of the limestone glue that had, for all that time, maintained the integrity of the rock. The additional stress of his 180 pounds simply proved too great. With a sound no louder than a sigh, the once solid rock transformed into fluid under his feet. He felt it happen. He knew what it implied. Gravity, its will defied too long, would wait no more.

He reached for anything solid and found nothing. Sadness at lost opportunities weighed upon him more than fear. His twenty-three years of life would end as an irregular stain on the jagged brecciated rock two hundred feet below, a stain that would appear only after agonizing bounces off outcrops that would mangle his body on the way down.

There was nothing Charles Knight could do but die.

And the nearest person who would give a damn was 5,000 miles away.

*　　*　　*

"So. What do you want in life, Charles?"

His Uncle Maurice asked him this with the air of a wealthy man who knew the workings of the world. They were the first words that Uncle Maurice had *ever* said to him beyond a brusque grunt that served as an initial greeting. Charles had just turned thirteen, and it was both his first trip back East and the first time he had met his uncle, his mother's mysterious—and reputedly dangerous—brother.

The boy sat in the great man's luxury apartment among a bewildering assortment of financial newspapers and corporate reports, surrounded by walls sheathed with books. He'd been assigned one of the spare bedrooms and given to understand he could stay until the end of summer, or until he wanted to go back to Montana. Or until Uncle Maurice asked him to leave. Whichever came first.

Uncle Maurice was an intimidating man. He had a big head that Charles knew was filled with brains and packed with knowledge. And a formidable body that, though bursting with fat, was full of heart. Or so his mother used to say.

Charles shifted to sit upright on the couch, pushing aside some scattered debris of his uncle's unkempt lifestyle. After a moment's hesitation he looked at his uncle and replied simply, although his voice cracked with a combination of tension and the hormonal changes of adolescence.

"I want to live a good life." He hesitated again. Then, eyes sparkling with more enthusiasm: "And an adventurous, maybe an *exotic* one."

Uncle Maurice raised the eyebrows on his expansive forehead and pursed his lips between prodigious cheeks. His expression changed from one of brief surprise to one of interest, now studying his nephew with closer attention. He then followed his first question with a challenge.

"Charles, I expected less from a boy your age. I'm impressed. So I'm giving you an assignment. You will define for me, and for yourself, on paper and in detail, exactly what you mean by *a good life*." Maurice paused for a moment and scratched at his round chin. "And tell me what you mean by *exotic*. These concepts aren't normally mentioned together, certainly not by someone your age. The one brings to mind a monastery, the other a Bangkok cathouse."

Because he was still in school—a situation that would not persist much longer—Charles was accustomed to teachers assigning mind-numbing fluff to no useful end other than to occupy his time. But his own uncle assigning him homework just wasn't fair. It was summer vacation. His mother had died three weeks ago. He hadn't come to New York to write an essay for this man. He came here because his father—consumed in grief—thought the time apart would be good for both of them.

"When is it due?" Charles asked, with just a touch of ill-concealed distaste. Based on his school assignments, he presumed a deadline for filling several pages with conventional thoughts in order to please a teacher who was herself just going through the motions.

Exploring the city from the top of the Empire State Building to the tunnels in the subway system had a lot more appeal than writing a paper. As did visiting the Natural History museum and studying the exhibits at his own pace without the distraction of other students. Or climbing into the torch of Lady Liberty—whether or not it was legal. What adventure would he have to sacrifice to write a pointless essay? This assignment would at the very least cause him to defer reading *The Count of Monte Cristo*, which he had squeezed into his travel backpack that morning before he boarded the plane.

But it turned out Uncle Maurice was nothing like those teachers. He was more like a co-conspirator.

"Charles," the great man said, "you need to explore New York for now. First things first. Your assignment isn't due tomorrow. Nor next week."

That was a relief.

"In fact," Uncle Maurice continued, "it's not due until the day you've discovered the answers. It may take years, or decades. So you have plenty of time to think about it. I know you like books; I've got a good library here. I'll give you a few to help you kick off the process."

During the rest of the day—and the rest of his life—Charles Knight's mind returned to this exchange. Perhaps it was because memories are profoundly imprinted during times of emotional stress. Maybe it was because this was the first connection with a man who loved his mother too, and who ached along with Charles. It wasn't long before this spark from his uncle had ignited into a driving quest to explore what might constitute a life that was good. And adventurous. And exotic. And more.

What, indeed, was the meaning of life?

*   *   *

Uncle Maurice had issued that assignment ten years ago, almost to the day.

Charles Knight chanced one look down, past his sweat-soaked shirt, past his muddy pants, and past the tips of his boots that were unable to find purchase on the unstable, near-vertical rock face to which his hands desperately clung. Boulders that looked like teeth littered the canyon base far below. He was attached to the cliff by little more than friction. He would have a few seconds to contemplate his life while he fell to his death.

The rush of the river's water overwhelmed all sound other than the throb of blood surging through his head. He slipped further, abrading his chin and the tip of his nose. Grit from the rock crunched between his clamped teeth. He found a dangling vine, grabbed it, and strained with ferocious intent to postpone his demise. But neither his arm nor the vine could suspend him for long.

His father had advised him against this trip, just as he had advised a skinny and ambitious twelve-year-old Charles not to build a tree house in the high branches of the backyard oak. The consequences of that endeavor included the scar near his elbow, glistening white in the bright sunlight against his dark tan.

His father had cleaned the wound, laughed, and said, "The apple doesn't fall far from the tree."

That lanky teen had grown into an athletic young man with a permanent glint in his determined yet playful blue eyes. And his uncle's challenge a decade ago had turned into a mission of ever-greater personal interest. He always assumed he'd have time to complete it.

Now, however, confronted by a plunge into a literal abyss, he regretted that his quest would go unresolved. Life really *was* short.

His eyes scanned the weathered limestone conglomerate, its quartz crystals and mica shards burrowing under his nails as he clawed with his free left hand.

He glanced up at the remains of the ledge. Through a conspiracy of fate, physics, and recent rains, the outcrop had collapsed just as he completed collecting the rock samples that now inconveniently weighed down the pockets of his cargo pants.

These rock samples represented the gold-bearing formation that had drawn him to this country. The subsurface structure lay exposed here, revealing the mineral composition of the whole area. No expensive drilling equipment was needed to gather the rock. Instead, he had impetuously risked his life for it. Two minutes ago it had seemed like a good idea.

He had twenty feet to climb, if he could move at all. But as he struggled, the vine that tried to save him released its hold on the tree far above. An unexpected serenity enveloped him as his free fall began. Maybe the overdose of adrenalin relaxed him.

Perhaps he should not have tried this particular career path, he thought.

A single root of the vine, the only one that had managed to infiltrate the subsurface rocks, proved just strong enough to jerk him to a wrenching stop. He dangled in the open air. There was nothing to swing to, nothing to push off of. His forearms cramped.

Okay, now came the fear. He let out a yell from his diaphragm to the cosmos at large. "Hold on!" He meant to encourage the root of the vine, or his hands, or nature as a whole. The yell increased his strength and courage. But his voice just echoed back at him from the shadows of the cliff four feet in front of his nose.

The vine bled through its cracking bark. It was just as near death as he was. His mind flashed to the trivial nature of his existence. He wondered if he'd feel it when he hit the rocks below. It's said that people feel little pain when mauled by bears or tigers. Perhaps his end would be the same?

It made no sense to exit his existence immersed in fear and panic. Those base biologic responses were simply too degrading to consume the rest of his life, all twenty seconds of it. At least his life would conclude with an adventure in an exotic place. But had he led a good life, to the very end? He thought Uncle Maurice should have the chance to learn.

Perhaps the cosmos agreed, because just then a thick rope fell from what could only have been the heavens. It slapped against the rock ledge above and dangled to his left. Charles's bloody fingers grabbed at the man-made miracle. He transferred his weight to the damp rope just as the vine sheared through, his left hand burning along the harsh manila. After securing his grip, he released the broken vine from his other hand and, with a passing appreciation, watched it undulate down to strike onto the sharp rocks below. Then he adjusted his grip, wrapped his ankles around the rope, and shinnied to the top of the cliff.

"Hey, kid. What were you doing down there?"

Charles looked up as wiry arms reached under his shoulders and dragged him from the edge of death and onto horizontal ground. The rock samples in his pockets dug into his thighs. He rolled over on his back and stared at the sky, exhaling a loud sigh of relief, fatigue, and gratefulness. His body broke into a cold sweat despite the humid heat of the jungle.

"Thanks for the help…." He paused for an exhausted moment, looking at his savior. "Mr. Winn, isn't it?"

The frail-looking man wore small spectacles balanced low on his nose so that he peered over the top of them. A broad-brimmed boonie hat sat low on his ears, with long strands of grey hair emerging from under it. A soft grin formed on his weathered face and in eyes as blue as Charles's own. This stooped-over, gimpy-legged, and seemingly beaten-down old Dutchman was named Xander Winn.

Charles had steered clear of the man earlier on the tour for reasons he could not quite understand. Something about Winn just didn't add up.

Winn pointed over to where the rope was tied to a Caterpillar amidst miscellaneous machine parts, spares, and other mining equipment. "If you wanted to explore the canyon, the rope was right in that pile of gear. It would have been wiser than pretending you're Tarzan." He chuckled.

Charles's heart raced, his arms ached, his chest pounded, and sweat soaked his clothes. He was covered with abrasions and bruises and blood.

6

A minute ago he had almost died. And this man joked about it. You had to respect that. Maybe Winn was okay after all.

Winn used his cane to get to his feet. "We should rejoin the others."

Charles luxuriated in the heavy air, its feeling on his skin, and the overwhelming joy of living another day. He could continue on Uncle Maurice's quest.

He would remember to treasure each minute of life, for a miracle had happened, in the form of a hunched-over Dutchman and a rope.

2

A Logical Geological Theory

XANDER Winn limped back to the path as Charles struggled to stand up on wobbly legs. Winn spoke as if he expected Charles to be right next to him.

"I thought you were a dead man when I looked over to the ledge and saw you were missing."

Charles stiffly jogged to catch up. He mopped his face with the back of his arm, smearing some blood from his chin across his stubbled cheek.

"I should have known better. The rock there is weathered and incompetent. Or maybe it was me who was incompetent...."

Winn stopped, turned, and looked at him. "To me, you were highly competent. That is, if your intent was to get yourself killed."

He expected Winn to ask him why he had gone over the cliff edge, but Winn didn't ask. Instead, he continued, "Lesson One: to succeed, position yourself to take advantage of luck. Lesson Two: bad luck happens. So plan on bad luck, not good luck. You should have taken precautions on that cliff face. But you didn't. Next time you will."

He turned and walked on.

Charles raised his eyebrows and hurried after Winn, who negotiated the irregular path with his cane. Charles was there in time to steady the man's arm just as Winn tripped over a root.

Winn acknowledged the assist with a glance. "I've done my share of stupid things that seemed like a good idea at the time. Once, in the high mountains of Sichuan, I edged along the side of a sheer rock face on a twenty-inch-wide ledge with a five hundred foot drop below me, all to see some pointless mineral formation and prove my manhood to nobody at all, because nobody was there. In Colombia I walked across a gorge on three pieces of bamboo that were tied together with cow intestine. I got lucky. Insanity is not conducive to survival."

They caught up with the main group. The other men stood near a thirty-foot-tall drill rig. The machine angled fifty degrees off upright, aimed back toward the canyon, and made a deafening racket as its bit tore into the rock.

The small group of investors—six including Charles and Winn—studied the drill rig, operated by a muscular man named Harry, who possessed a military bearing with close-cropped graying blond hair. Harry had introduced himself as from Zimbabwe when they had chatted earlier. To Charles, Harry seemed to assess each of the visitors in turn as if they were either prey or dog excrement—Charles wasn't sure which.

These investors had traveled thousands of miles to reach this mining camp, not far from the village of Banga Sioquelle in the far-northern reaches of the chronically troubled nation of Gondwana. They came not for pleasure, which was in short supply here, nor even adventure, which could appear unexpectedly in unwelcome quantity, but to investigate a gigantic gold discovery. They were latecomers; dozens of groups had preceded them, and now that the rainy season was starting, the junket season was almost over.

The other four on the tour may have known their way around boardrooms, but they knew very little about rocks and minerals, and only a little more about the companies that explore for them. They and their clients mutually urged each other to jump aboard the booming market for natural resources. Physically and psychologically uncomfortable in the jungle, these men just wanted to check off some boxes on a due-diligence list, and then hightail it back home to Europe so they could regale friends with tales of their adventures in the African bush. They were Parisian, and therefore even more out of their element in this English-speaking region of West Africa.

So these visitors didn't challenge the B-F Explorations technical team with difficult geological or engineering questions so much as engage in small talk, complaints about mosquitoes, and idle inquiries about what it was like to camp out in the middle of nowhere. Geologists, who might best be described as outdoorsy intellectuals, loved places like this. But these Frenchmen were brokers and fund managers, not geologists.

Yet each fund manager was capable of buying a private placement worth a thousand times the cost of this excursion, with the money going directly into the company's treasury. They might also buy more shares in the open market, "talk the book," and take the stock price even higher than it already was.

B-F Explorations had gone viral. Fund managers knocked down their door to give them money. It was a rare and coveted situation for a junior mining company. Most exploration companies, hoping to find the next Golconda, wound up proving that their deposit was uneconomic. Experienced speculators were aware that less than one in 3,000 prospects ever turned into a mine and treated these stocks as lottery tickets, not heirlooms.

Goodluck Johnson—the man who led this part of the tour—owned the surface land here. Goodluck liked to emphasize that fact repeatedly. "My land is quality land, because of my gold," he'd said at least half a dozen times so far. True enough, perhaps, although land in this part of the country had little value without massive capital investment, something in chronic short supply in Gondwana. Goodluck smiled a lot. After all, his expected windfall would finally realize his aspirations for his family of eleven children (over the course of three wives and a mistress). He was sixty years old, or thereabouts—Goodluck didn't know exactly when he was born.

This week's tour group followed their smiling guide away from the noisy drill. Only Winn was aware that Charles had almost died. But for Winn, Charles's body would be smashed at the bottom of the gorge, and the group might not even have noticed his absence. Someone made a half-hearted inquiry about Charles's newly disheveled appearance and the scratches on his face but was satisfied with a terse "I took a tumble back there."

The B-F Explorations driver and the French investors had ignored Charles from the beginning, stuffing him in the far backseat of the company Land Cruiser and saying nothing to him during the four-hour drive up from Adamstown, the capital city.

It seemed he wasn't worth paying much attention to.

The path was lined with boxes packed with recently drilled rock cores, three inches in diameter. Some of the cores lay intact, some in shattered pieces, depending on the integrity of the geological structures the drill had penetrated. There were hundreds of wooden boxes, each longer than a coffin, with three sections of rock core side-by-side. Standard practice dictated that half the cores would be kept on site and half shipped to a lab for assaying. Lightweight corrugated zinc roofing material lay atop some of the crates. Most were open to the elements.

"Are cores usually stored so informally?" Charles asked Winn. Charles didn't know what was normal for mining prospects that existed in the last place on earth you would want to be.

"It's just rock, Mr. Knight."

"Rock loaded with gold."

Winn shrugged.

Charles palmed a few small pieces of shattered core to add to his pockets. Maybe Harry—the white man with military bearing—turned his head at just the wrong moment and caught the motion. Charles couldn't be sure.

The men listened, with varying degrees of interest, as Goodluck discussed particular core samples in his jovial, self-content manner.

Three words are sufficient to describe the West African bush: sweat, mud, and heat. And so the men were glad to be guided back to the field lab, a somewhat cooler cinder block structure where technicians performed preliminary assays. It was a typical field lab—several computers, a large white multi-user microscope, a bench with a mortar and pestle, beakers, and a Bunsen burner running off a rusted propane tank. Equipment catalogues, some reference books, and a stack of field notebooks lay scattered about. Charles looked through a doorway into an adjacent room at rock cores placed out on a bench near a 14-inch sliding compound miter saw, situated to cut them into slices.

It was time to hear from the head geologist of B-F Explorations, Dan Smolderhof, who over the recent months had become a hero back in Canada.

Smolderhof put an arm around Charles's shoulder and said, "Great to have you here, son. I hear you had a spill—sorry about that." Then he moved to the front of the room, placed his hands down on a desk, and spoke as if Charles and the others in front of him were not even there.

"We have a very high-grade deposit here," the tall and lanky Canadian geologist stated with an assurance borne of frequent repetition. His unkempt graying hair splayed unceremoniously over large ears, attesting further to an evident lack of care as to whether or not he successfully impressed these investors.

He spoke loudly, with a flat, matter-of-fact tone. "The latest drill cores average over an ounce per ton, but the deposit could turn out to be much higher grade because of sporadic veins of bonanza-quality ore. Everyone knows about the eight-foot-thick formation with over five ounces per ton. But it's the volume that counts. We could be looking at 200 million tons of readily accessible ore."

The fund managers glanced at each other, all doing the same mental arithmetic. Two hundred million tons times, say, an average of $1,000 of value in each ton, equaled $200 billion.

After allowing time for them to calculate a predicted share price based on discounted future gold production, Smolderhof, who was also a founding shareholder of B-F, stoked their enthusiasm with a shift into a less scientific persona. "The assays are all terrific. This isn't a case of a few highly enriched veins that swell, then pinch off and disappear. This is not like some of those formations in South Africa, plunging thousands of meters into the ground—so deep that workers burn themselves on the rocks and refrigeration is one of their major costs. No, our gold is right here for the picking, essentially at the surface. Gold as pure as a temple virgin!

"You want to get in on this, trust me. Today, if you can. The maar-diatreme setup, Jesus, like nothing I've ever seen. Beautiful fracturing. Great primary and secondary porosity. Gold spread through every layer like melted butter on popcorn. And like we've been saying, extracting and processing costs will be minimal for an ore body like this. Hell, nature has done half the processing for us already. If we wanted to, we could put run-of-mine ore straight on the leach pads, and it's almost straight to bullion. Just like that! Easy pickings top to bottom of every core we've drilled."

It was an odd spiel, with half the statements appealing to a mining engineer, a geologist, or an experienced resource analyst. The other half reminded Charles of the snappy patter you might get from a carny barker. Because of his technical background, Dan Smolderhof had the rap down even more convincingly than his partner back in Canada. He could radiate either exuberance or quiet confidence, as required, because the drill cores proved that the company was sitting on the largest accessible gold reserve on Earth. It was richer than the finds that had sparked gold rushes in California, in the Klondike, in Australia, or even in South Africa's Witwatersrand. It was a discovery of global historic importance.

Charles couldn't help but smile as he calculated his own return on this stock so far, based on the day's opening price of $136 on the Toronto exchange. His 15,000 shares were but a tiny fraction of what Smolderhof held; but his shares were now worth far more than everything else he owned put together. Getting lucky with a hot stock was so much easier than trying to build a business. On paper at least, he was rich—really rich for a twenty-three-year-old high school dropout. His decision to study the world of speculative investment and embark on a career as a professional speculator, which seemed like a terminally bad idea only an hour ago, once again seemed prescient.

Mining exploration had come a long way from the days of a prospector wandering around with his mule in the boonies. Professional geologists now surveyed by air, looking for gravity or magnetic variances. Then they'd hit the ground. First, they'd go to streambeds to sample the soil: gold and other heavy minerals washed from their origins might concentrate there. The next step might be to follow the sediments upstream, sampling for soil anomalies—which in exploration language meant a measurable and preferably high concentration of gold. Digging trenches came next, to get under the surface. Only then, if the results were very encouraging, would an expensive drill rig and a crew be mustered to the area.

By this time, a company was in for hundreds of thousands of dollars on nothing more than a prospect. As hungry as the drills were to grind through rock, they were hungrier still for money to feed them, and that made the excited hyping of small hopes into big dreams a regular and expected art form in the industry. In other sectors of the economy the way these exploration companies talked to bring in investment funding might be considered "fraud in the inducement." But in this world, the investors—whether sophisticated or naïve—were expected to realize that hope, no matter how strongly worded, is often nothing more than hype. In legalese, all statements were to be considered "forward looking."

In their effort to convert hype into fact, B-F Explorations left few doubts about the quality of the ore body that they controlled below the surface of northern Gondwana. Smolderhof was a structural geologist, and he released his mapping work of the area regularly, updated whenever new core was drilled or informative new surface features were found. Reputable labs in both South Africa and Canada performed duplicate assays of the cores. B-F's attention to ensuring trust in their spectacular results contributed to the soaring share price.

Estimates climbed to 10 million, 30 million, 50 million, and now, as Smolderhof conjectured, even 200 million recoverable ounces. If they were right, the B-F deposit alone equaled nearly three times the whole world's annual gold production—although the fact that it would only be produced over decades, if indeed it was ever produced, escaped mention.

Smolderhof waxed eloquent, here in West Africa or back in Canada, to selected audiences, and especially uncritical journalists. He explained how the ancient volcanic activity of this region had produced acidic hydrothermal fluids that decalcified the limestone that buried the Archean conglomerates in this one region of Africa. And how petroleum had flowed upward through the limestone—on its way to what are now the Nigerian oil fields—leaving behind a trail of carbon. Over the eons, he could confidently state, superheated acidic water had ebbed and flowed, in and out, through the deeper, gold-rich ancient conglomerates, leaching gold and carrying it toward what was now the surface limestone, where the carbon served to reduce the gold back to its neutral atomic form, causing it to deposit in the form of nanoparticles. More magic came because the gold transfer from the older and deeper rock up to the limestone occurred in so many recurring cycles, repeatedly concentrating the gold.

The result was nanometer-scale gold particles, a thousand times smaller and even more invisible than the microscopic grains in the famous Carlin-type deposits first found in Nevada. It remained a subject of intense academic investigation back in North America. But the assays spoke for themselves. There was an insane amount of gold here.

B-F controlled the only major limestone formation in Gondwana that hadn't been eroded into oblivion. His novel geological theory seemed sound enough, and Smolderhof had the right credentials to present it. It went over the heads of all but specialists. Smolderhof encouraged people to appreciate his genius in recognizing it for what it was.

And it *was* genius, a brilliance that emanated from an academic mind that had spent years creating puzzles for the purpose of solving them. His was a theory outside any box that economic geologists considered standard. And as a result he could get no research funding when, decades ago, he first proposed the theoretical existence of such mineral deposits. So Smolderhof had left academia in frustration and sought his proof in the real world, intermittently performing menial services for established companies and then consulting for junior mining explorers just so he could pay his bills. And he kept looking.

Unique local conditions laid down millions of *visible* ounces in the Witwatersrand in South Africa and millions of *microscopic* ounces in the Carlin Trend of Nevada; Smolderhof had discovered that Banga Sioquelle was the next iteration of a uniquely formed mega deposit. He explained that previous explorers simply hadn't known what to look for. The gold was here, "lush as fungus," he said—just wasn't visible to the naked eye, or even the microscope. Even good microscopes could only detect things at micrometer level. This gold existed at the nanometer level, one-billionth of a meter. It was invisible.

It all made sense, and Charles was an early buyer.

Yet something didn't feel right. Uncle Maurice taught Charles to pay heed to his gut instincts. Contrary to common opinion, intuition wasn't mystical; it was scientific. Intuition was the ability to properly integrate many subtle pieces of information. To have good intuition, therefore, someone needs experience and data and a logical mind that can fuse them into coherence.

Smolderhof's compelling presentation continued. "Jeez, look at the assays, for chrissakes. Of course there wouldn't be placer deposits downstream, because it's all nanoparticle gold! Any gold that eroded off this deposit would stay in suspension and wash all the way out into the ocean. Early prospectors were relying on friggin' riverbed deposits to guide them. Fools! Of course there weren't any!"

All those earlier geologists would have known this, had they only read his papers. "All they had to do was drill one friggin' hole in the southeast expanse and ka-bam! they could have ripped the lid off this decades ago."

Inside the lab building, where the overworked air conditioner offered scant protection from the heat, Charles stood listening to all this, silent, as Smolderhof began proffering shallow answers to the Parisians' superficial questions. He nurtured a naïve hope that he would learn from the wise inquiries of the others. But the others weren't asking wise questions.

After the initial flurry of questions, Charles overcame his reluctance to speak up. "Mr. Smolderhof, I don't understand why it takes so long from the time you publish the start of new drilling to the release of those core results."

Smolderhof glanced at his man Harry, who stood at the side of the room. Charles noticed the tall B-F man with the striking gray-blond hair and hard face move back toward the exit.

Xander Winn stood next to Charles and added, "Dan, it seems like it takes longer and longer for each set of cores. Recently, it took three months more than any previous time for you to finally release the data."

Serious investors followed drill results and assays closely—drills were known as "truth machines." They were the main indicators of whether a stock certificate was likely to make you rich or just turn into a wall decoration. Companies therefore tended to release data—at least positive data—as rapidly as possible to help boost the stock price.

Ignoring Charles, Smolderhof answered in a manner that sounded both patronizing and judgmental. "We do it right, Mr. Winn. That's why. We think it's very important to be precise. We're enthusiastic, sure, but we don't release early, speculative guesses. We provide hard data, confirmed twice and often three times by assays from different labs. My structural maps of the region are confirmed by independent geologists, and we keep our drilling program active to further delineate what we have here. And what we have here is the best ore body on the planet. We are in Africa, Mr. Winn. Things take time here. If you want to get it right, that is."

It was a vague non-answer; South African labs operated as efficiently as those in Canada, and planes transporting cores flew at the same speed everywhere. Smolderhof's assurances rubbed Charles the wrong way; they crossed the line from confident to glib. The man aroused a nebulous suspicion in his mind, the same suspicion that had enticed him to gather the rocks he now carried in his pockets. He would have them assayed back in the US. It couldn't hurt to have his own confirmation.

One of the investors asked Smolderhof a useful question then, his English laced with a heavy French accent.

"Dan, we hear rumors about a deal with one of several majors. It must happen, no? But when?"

Smolderhof smiled. "Of course it has to happen. But we aren't in a rush. The more we delineate the ore body, the higher our valuation will be on a deal with a major. So no rush."

Winn prodded, "But you *are* in discussions?"

Smolderhof replied to Winn with evident irritation. "Of course we're in discussions."

There was more to it than that. Building a huge mine required a huge company. The government of Gondwana, desperate for development, wanted such a deal as quickly as possible. It would create jobs, and that would help defuse the very real dangers presented by a large population of impoverished, testosterone-charged young men with too much time on their hands. The government was well aware that a mine would result in roadbuilding, electricity generation, training for the locals, housing projects, and huge amounts of ancillary capital flowing into the country.

Even more relevant, it would generate tax revenue, much of which would find its way into the pockets of the president and his cronies in the form of fat "consulting fees" and liberally padded construction contracts for relatives and friends. Of course the bureaucracy's skids would also have to be greased regularly with large deposits to offshore bank accounts and envelopes stuffed with cash. There was every reason to get the mine built yesterday.

Paradoxically, while the government wanted the mine operating immediately, its numerous bureaucratic layers were delaying progress until their individual pounds of flesh could be ensured. The news of the deposit's size was like pouring blood in a river full of piranhas. The ruling class in each political district and the heads of almost every ministry required a payoff. Every low-level bureaucrat who had to stamp a form required a little *weekend money* to move it along.

In Gondwana, as in the rest of the Third World, even starting a kiosk legally required visits to a dozen different government offices and a sheaf of approvals; few people bothered. The fact that most of the myriad laws, rules, and taxes were disregarded was critical in keeping the place from mass starvation. The informal economy was the real one. But starting a major visible enterprise required jumping through all the hoops.

Smolderhof, for all his care with the sampling and the assays and the structural work, took criticism for being too lax about obtaining the so-called "permissions." His palm greasing was less liberal than officials thought appropriate. So the kleptocratic culture slowed things down at the low levels of the government in ways that the upper levels couldn't really control. The 2,000 employees of the Interior Ministry, few of whom ever showed up except to collect their paychecks, now swarmed their shabby desks, loathe to miss an opportunity to both prove their patriotism and cash in.

But while bribery was necessary in Gondwana, Western governments threatened to prosecute their own citizens if they played by the African rules. European and American companies trying to do business were damned if they did and damned if they didn't, while the Chinese padded some pockets and took over the continent.

"These deals take time, as you know," Smolderhof added. "We have a ton of suitors. All the big names. Every one of the majors. I could tell you more, but then I'd have to kill you." He gave a practiced smile, pointed his finger at Charles and pulled an imaginary trigger. A few of the visitors chuckled politely. Charles, who most often had a ready smile on his face, didn't.

Then there was a noise.

A gruesome screech followed a crack sufficiently loud to pierce through the muffling effect of a forest filled with bamboo. Charles thought he heard a man shriek in the distance. The low background clamor provided by the distant drill abruptly ceased. Some kind of accident?

The two-way radio on the desk sputtered, and Smolderhof barked at it in his dyspeptic, raspy way. An explanation crackled back, something about mud and slurry and a drill that had spasmed out of control and burrowed into an arm.

A rare bit of bad news from the otherwise-glorious southeast zone.

Limb-threatening but not life-threatening, so long as the man was quickly tended to, Smolderhof explained to the disconcerted group. After emergency first aid, they'd have to transport the victim eight kilometers down the muddy path accessing the camp to reach the semipaved road, then another sixty klicks southward to the little clinic in the town of Gbarngeda run by an American physician's assistant. Then on to the capital, if need be.

Charles imagined Adamstown's semi-functional hospitals with their semi-sterile surgical suites. Gondwana was not a good place to have a serious injury.

Smolderhof continued, "Jesus, if it's not one thing it's another. Gotta run, gentlemen. But you all get the idea. I'm sorry to leave you. Tobi and Goodluck will take you back out to the road, where the car will get you back to your hotel, eh? Any questions, any questions at all, be happy to, okay? And feel free to visit our operations anytime. The door is always open to you. Hell, you'll own part of it soon, right!"

And then the grizzled, oft-disappointed geologist in charge of over-seeing Banga Sioquelle's prospecting operations, a failure for years but a Midas at last, jerkily glad-handed them and was out the door, huffing toward the scene of the limb gouging.

While the B-F crew dealt with the crisis, understandably the ques-tion-and-answer session had to be curtailed. The fund managers were anxious to get back to Adamstown for dinner and drinks, and then on a plane to Paris, via Dakar, in the morning. It was clear enough: jump in now before the ore body ballooned yet again and the hurtling stock price approached the vicinity of Alpha Centauri.

3

Secrets and Secret Societies

THREE John Deere Gator utility ATVs waited to take the visitors up a well-worn track to the main road. Charles and Winn rode with a short, shy local man named Tobi—Goodluck Johnson's sidekick—who had known Goodluck forever.

Tobi, who was an amateur geologist, had done the first work on Johnson's land, using a borrowed water-well drilling rig to hammer through the rock, testing the pulverized effluent for gold. Tobi had made contact with Smolderhof and brought him to Banga Sioquelle. Tobi had had little to say during the tour he had ushered them through. Johnson and then Smolderhof did all the talking.

It was hard to understand Tobi's English, a creole that, among other things, dropped all the final consonants of each word. Perhaps the phrase "Ba thi happeh" meant "Bad thing happened," but neither Charles nor Winn could be sure. Tobi kept repeating it. He also said, "Dange tighs he now," which to the best of their translation ability meant "Dangerous times here now." Was he referring to something other than the unfortunate accident and the dangers of drilling operations? Tobi had a tendency to repeatedly, almost imperceptibly, shake his head back and forth, as if he were trying to negate the whole world.

Charles and Xander took the back seat and leaned close so they could speak over the ATV's noise.

"For having come all this way, it wasn't much of a tour," Charles said. They had explored a few metal shipping containers, a bunkhouse for the drill crews, some tents for the local labor, a dining hall and cookhouse, and the cinder block lab. "There were three drill rigs, but only one was running—isn't that a bit odd with so much at stake?"

Winn shouted back, "Four drill teams just rotated back to Canada. It's the beginning of the rainy season. Things slow way down here in West Africa."

In addition to the scant facilities and scant personnel, it was but a scant road that Tobi drove them along, if one could call it a road at all. Twin ruts cut their way through palms, bamboo, and scattered rubber trees. The rough undergrowth made traveling outside these paths impossible without constantly swinging a machete.

"For all Smolderhof's assurances, turning this prospect into a working gold mine won't be easy," Winn said. "If he doesn't understand this, he's a fool. But I think he does understand. That makes him a knave. It will take a major mining enterprise with plenty of money and experience to pull it off. Millions more in drilling and development expenditures, and then maybe billions to actually build the mine and finance it to profitability. Mining is no longer an industry where a couple of guys and a mule can strike it rich."

"So a deal with a major is absolutely necessary...."

"Absent that deal, this place has no value at all."

The point of this trip was to find out the truth. But the truth was starting to dull the shine on the trophy. The potential that his shares in B-F could be worthless assaulted Charles's stomach like he'd swallowed a hot rock.

The heavy-duty ATV reached what before the wars had been a paved road but now lay rutted and torn. Tobi's jostled passengers got out near two parked Toyota Land Cruisers, only one emblazoned with the company logo. Nodding goodbye, Tobi wrestled with the ATV's steering, spun the wheels, and headed back toward the prospective mine, a spray of red-brown dirt flying up from the knobby treads. The French institutional investors, newly armed with field experience and anxious to back up the truck for more shares in this promising speculation, hurried toward the company Land Cruiser. Charles was about to join them when Winn called out.

"Why don't you come with me in my car, kid?"

Something still felt wrong about Winn. But it would beat being crammed in the far back and ignored for the next four hours. One of the

Frenchmen deigned to hand him his backpack, which he then threw in the empty backseat of Winn's car.

"I don't like to rely on other people's schedules," Winn explained, leaning against his car's hood as the B-F corporate SUV skidded out of the grass and onto the road, picking up as much speed as it could before turning out of sight. "We should get to know each other better."

As the other car disappeared, Winn stretched out to Charles's height. He no longer stood hunched over. His face no longer appeared downcast, nor humble. His spectacles came off—as did his hat with an artificially attached fringe of long gray hair. Its absence disclosed a full head of short brown hair with only some gray at the temples, not the balding, scraggly pate Charles had assumed. Winn set the cane with which he had hobbled around the B-F tract across his shoulder, and suddenly looked more like Indiana Jones than a withered old man. He had dropped two decades and transformed soft flesh into muscle in a few seconds. The doddering retiree became a fit fifty-year-old.

Charles grinned in appreciation. "Nice!"

For the last couple of hours, his sixth sense had been faintly telling him that there was something askew. Was it B-F that was wrong? Or was it the disguised Winn? Or something else?

"I've got a feeling you're a good guy to know around here," Charles said. "I came here to further my education. I'm picking up a lot more from you than that whole crew back there."

"Or," Winn replied, his Dutch accent now mingled with American, "you could cut out the middle man and go right to Sun Tzu's *Art of War*. One of his teachings is to always appear either much stronger or much weaker than you are." Winn winked. "As suits your purpose."

He added, "I expect to gain something from our relationship too, kid. It's a foolish old dog that can't learn a few new tricks." Winn glanced up and down the empty road. There was no noise other than the occasional screech from a monkey in the distance. The place was thick with the scent of dry ground and humid air and impending rain. "Why don't you empty your pockets of those rocks you stole from B-F and get comfortable."

Charles smiled sheepishly, reached into the oversized pockets of his cargo pants, and placed the hard-fought rock samples into a compartment of his backpack. "Getting these almost cost me my skin."

Winn replied, "Stealing can get you killed."

"Stealing rocks?"

"They aren't your rocks, Mr. Knight. And you took them."

Charles had thought himself smart, coming up with a way to check on the veracity of B-F's drill results by finding the one place on the property where the old geologic surveys and Smolderhof's structural maps suggested the gold-bearing formation just might be exposed to view, there on the face of the cliff. It was enterprising! Yet here stood Winn telling him he was just a criminal.

Charles frowned. His gut tightened as he realized that the fact they were just rocks didn't grant a reprieve from the moral conundrum. How much of a difference did it make whether you took something worth one dollar or a thousand? Was it justified to steal a loaf of bread if you were starving? How about if your child was starving? Were rocks different from bread in principle?

Property is property, whether worth a lot or a little. What if the rock contained a rough diamond, something not uncommon in these parts? This was a mining site, where any rock could be of value just because of the information it might contain. Hadn't he said to Winn—at the very moment that he picked up the bits of core—that they were loaded with gold? But then again, he came here as an owner of the company, and surely that implied some right to investigate.

Charles could not let these questions fade unconsidered. Fortunately, Winn seemed to respect his need for a moment of contemplation. He struggled a moment longer and glanced at Winn. He understood then that it was not Winn's impersonation of a crippled old man that had set off his internal alarms. It was his *own* intentions that had disturbed him. He had behaved like a thief and thought himself clever for doing so. He was a guest, yet his actions were hardly consistent with those of a guest.

Then another suspicion, equally inconsistent with that of a well-mannered guest, crossed his mind.

"Is there any chance we could stay here for maybe fifteen minutes or so?" Charles asked.

"I'm not excited about hanging around here," Winn replied. And then, with a faintly dramatic flair, he added, "This is secret-society territory. It's unwise to be white here without local men for company. It's a little like being white in South Central LA after an unwelcome verdict, or black in places where the Klan is strong. I like my pieces and parts where they are, instead of dried and tied on a string around somebody's neck."

Charles, with eyebrows raised, turned toward Winn.

Winn looked back at him, and continued. "It might be better than in the Solomon Islands, though. A wandering geologist was crucified there not so long ago. Not sure if it was an atavistic religious thing they picked up from the missionaries, or if the locals just resented his trespassing...."

Voodoo originated in the secret societies of West Africa before being conveyed across the Atlantic in slave ships. These organizations retained the unmentioned cultural power in this region. Everyone stayed involved. Lawyers, farmers, servants, beggars, politicians. Females had their *Sande*, and males their *Poro*. The wisdom and authority of a *Poro* leader would no more be questioned than that of the pope. He possessed divine insight, amplified by the power of traditions passed through centuries of a bush indoctrination steeped in taboo. The secret societies for now allowed the government to exist. But there was no mistaking whose laws were important, and whose were not.

The imaginations of outsiders run free in efforts to envision the goings-on of the secret societies. Some say their purpose is to seek out and destroy evil. The terrifying fetish garb of the Poro Devil during the rarely observed rituals suggested that these people had witnessed evil firsthand. They knew what evil looked like.

Sometimes evil looked like a deformed newborn infant, sometimes like an epileptic. And sometimes like a white man on a dirt road deep in the bush, unaccompanied, disappearing, never again to be seen.

Winn swung into the driver's seat of the Land Cruiser with the agility of a trained athlete. Charles climbed up into the passenger side, his muscles now fully recovered from their earlier strain, although his blistered hands would hurt for days.

"Why do you want to hang around here?" asked Winn as they each closed their doors and locked them.

"To see if the B-F team is going to take a trip to the hospital with their fallen man."

Winn nodded. "You think they were putting on a little Kabuki show back there?"

"Well, it didn't look like we were worthy of their time."

Winn started the car and flipped the air conditioning on at full tilt. His voice, no longer raspy and weak, carried easily over the fan. "There are still no helicopters allowed in Gondwana. It's a no-fly zone enforced by the UN; when the natives get restless, the big boys like to take away their toys. So the B-F medic will have to drive right past here"—he waved his hand to indicate the road—"if they're really going to take that poor man and his arm to the clinic in Gbarngeda.... So let's wait a while and see. And while we're waiting, can you tell me, Mr. Knight, why you decided to travel all the way from the USA to come see the Banga Sioquelle operation for yourself and steal its rocks?"

Charles felt a need to be candid. "Gold. Adventure. Excitement. Someone I respect said Africa is the best place left in the world for a young guy like me to get rich."

"If you don't mind heat, insects, disease, and poverty, that's true. It's much improved from the days when the early explorers faced death every day, but it can be pretty miserable."

"I like roughing it."

Charles's lack of chronic misery in his life so far resulted from little more than an accident of birth; he had, in effect, won the cosmic lottery by being born a white male in the US. It was a situation guaranteed not to last.

Winn nodded. "Good for you. Get your hands dirty. But you have a better answer than just coming here to get rich, don't you?"

"It was about time for me to start swimming in the deep end of the pool."

"Where was your shallow end? Where did you go to school?"

"Montana. But I skipped a lot of classes." He was proud of that, and suspected that Winn might approve. "Spent most of my time roaming around the woods or in the library."

"I see. A real education at the School of Truancy. Bet they never thought of looking for a truant in the library. What did you do after high school?"

"I didn't finish high school." He looked at Winn, searching for evidence of concealed disdain or outright admonishment.

But Winn nodded his head in wry approval. "How did that work out for you?"

"I learn fine on my own." Charles shrugged. "I just read something, and it leads to something else interesting. Montana has fossils all over the place. What kid doesn't love dinosaurs? Reading about paleontology took me to biology and geology. I wanted to understand how rocks are formed, so I had to learn some chemistry—plus I was like most normal kids and wanted to learn how to make gunpowder. I started playing with model planes, and then model rockets, and got interested in physics. You need math for that. I loved all of the popular science magazines, so ended up just following my nose from one thing to another. But I didn't grow up rich. You need money to put theory into practice. I needed money, so I started working."

"And that's how you learned economics.…"

"Yeah." Charles replied as he reached into his backpack, extracted two bottles of water, and handed one to Winn. "Science made sense, but the economics books I first got my hands on made no sense at all. It all rubbed me the wrong way."

"What do you mean?"

Charles turned his neck to look along the road, hoping he would not see a Poro devil emerging from the thick bush. "I don't know. I haven't figured it out. It was mostly opinions on what the government should do with their *human resources*, disguised with a lot of math. It was all about how they'd use people and their property."

A series of tiny muscles in Winn's face expressed nearly imperceptible amusement. He said, "Economics and finance revolve around money. But the professors that teach these subjects never define what money actually is. Money is important. It's not just hunks of metal, pieces of paper, or computer entries. It represents all the time you spend earning it. It represents all the good things you want to have, and do, and provide for others. It really represents life itself, in concentrated form. Money isn't a thing. It's a moral concept. That's one reason—there are lots of others—why I'm not a Christian. Their traditional concept of money being the root of all evil—although the actual proscription is against the *love* of money—has set mankind's moral and economic advancement back many generations. It's perverse. A lot of concepts that aren't only wrong, but indeed are the exact opposite of the truth, have taken claim to the moral high ground."

26

Winn also looked up and down the empty road as he chugged down the water with relish. He spoke slowly. "We're on the same page, you and I. There was little in school that was going to help me succeed in life. It's like the teachers expected everyone to join a union, like theirs, and collect a salary for the rest of their lives."

"My school credentials aren't going to get me into a high-salary job."

Xander acknowledged that with a nod and said, "Salary. That's trading life for subsistence. Did you know that the word *salary* comes from *sal*, which is Latin for salt? And *pecuniary* comes from the Latin *pecus*, for cow? Both cows and salt were once used as money. That legacy has persisted in our languages. But salt can wash away in a rainstorm. Cows can get sick, they need to be fed, and each one is different. So metals—gold, silver, and copper—became preferred as money. It's why we're here."

"And now it's paper money," Charles added.

"Yes, the preferred money of government, because it can be printed with no work at all—but only by governments and banks. That's why they have so much power. Everyone else has to work hard for money."

"They don't teach any of that in school."

"Not even to university economics majors."

Charles grinned—a smile that concealed a bit of anxiety. "Maybe we should open a paper mine. We can dig up lots of paper out of the dirt and sell it."

"That's called Wall Street, kid. And it will result in a real economic catastrophe at some point. These people don't understand the economic fundamentals. Now tell me more about how you wound up here."

Sitting in a Land Cruiser far in the bush with his hands still throbbing, Charles wondered about that himself. He told Xander, "It's an opportunity to learn by doing. I combined my old interest in geology with my new interest in discovering economics, and put together a few bucks. One thing just led to another. I got introduced to a broker who specialized in mining stocks, and he steered me to B-F. I liked the B-F story and started buying. With a little push from my uncle, I started learning about mining, and then mineral exploration. From what I could see, the stakes have gotten big enough that I needed to get my boots on the ground. I wanted to see this property, see the people in action, and get a grip on the politics here."

Winn smiled and held up his fingers in succession, counting from one to three. "People, Property, and Politics. The three most important of the Nine *P*'s. You can only be sure of them by being on site."

Charles nodded.

"The Nine *P*'s aren't something you heard about on a CNN financial show. You learned the Nine *P*'s from someone who knew something about resource investing?"

It was his Uncle Maurice again. "Yes. Phinancing, Push, Paper, Promotion, Price, and Pitfalls." Charles held his own fingers up in succession.

"Pretty smart for a young guy."

"I hope to get wiser faster than I get older, Mr. Winn," Charles replied diffidently.

"Call me Xander. If you live long enough, I suspect we could have a lot of fun together."

They waited. Not a single vehicle went north on the road despite it being the main path from Gondwana to the Guinea border, which was just a few kilometers away. No vehicle from B-F Explorations whizzed by southbound, trailing blood on an urgent ambulance mission to Gbarngeda. And no Poro Devil materialized from the bush.

As the two men waited on that narrow dirt road, it occurred to Charles that he still knew nothing about Xander Winn. The flow of personal information had also been a narrow road, all in Winn's direction.

4

A Foolish Fantasy and a Gbarngeda Reality

THE vice president of the United States despised being the vice president. He had been much happier as a governor, for then he could control things. The vice presidency offered no direct power, other than a mostly irrelevant tie-breaking vote in the Senate. Even the soapbox it allowed him to stand on was low and ignored. He needed authorization from the president to do anything meaningful, and the president liked to keep his subordinates on a short leash. The vice president regularly tried to rip that short leash apart with his teeth.

"Dick, what's on the plate for today?" It was 8:30 in the morning. With so little to do, why not sleep in?

Dick Stafford, his chief of staff, had crawled with him all the way up. Dick was a partner for life, a remora that had long ago attached itself to a political shark that looked like it was going somewhere. They had remained best friends since tenth grade. Six inches shorter than the VP, Dick had less hair on his head and more on his back. Unlike the VP, he lacked the physical characteristics needed to garner the booboisie's votes. But whereas the VP interpreted reality with a reptilian part of his brain evolved for aggression, dominance, and reproduction, Dick Stafford consistently processed the world with his cerebrum's neocortex. Dick had the brain of an engineer, practical and calculating. The VP's predatory goals were clear. But the means of achieving them, now that men lived in offices rather than caves… not so much. The VP needed Stafford to tell him how to get where he wanted to go.

Stafford pursed his lips judiciously. "Not much is on the schedule for the day, Mr. Vice President. Are you thinking of anything in particular?"

The VP closed his eyes, annoyed that the world was passing him by as he awaited the end of the president's tenure. "Dick, what's going on with my Government Efficiency Enhancement Initiative?"

Stafford grunted. "The government isn't very efficient at initiating it."

The irony of the remark passed without note. "What do you mean? It's been, what, three months?" The VP had sent out a memorandum asking every agency to begin a program of temporary personnel exchange with every other agency even remotely connected to its mission. Everyone agreed it was a good idea.

"Six months, actually. Unfortunately, sir, as yet only one person has been assigned across agencies as part of your pilot program."

"Only one." The vice president said this with a combination of frustration and resignation.

"What did you expect, Chris?" Stafford frequently regressed to the familiar. When Christopher Cooligan became president in six years, Stafford would refrain from using his first name. "Look, there's nothing in it for the cabinet secretaries or career agency heads. If they transfer out someone good, they've got to break in a newbie. And they're afraid his replacement will just be a loser, an Old Maid card somebody else is trying to get rid of. And most of the bureaucrats eligible for transfer don't want to go, since they'd lose the power base they've built. They know the people in the new agency will try to freeze them out as potential competitors for promotion and disruptors of the status quo."

The VP of the US compressed his lips as he acknowledged how little effect his wishes had on the bureaucracy. Back home he had been the team quarterback and the best player in the school. Here in DC, everybody had been the quarterback at home, and some from much bigger schools. Players here had all proven their skill at manipulating their way to the pros. So now he competed with the most ruthless politicos, all protesting how their cockamamie ideas would improve the world.

He was playing in the political major leagues, it was true, but like almost every vice president, he was sitting out the game on the bench.

He barely even used his West Wing office. Why bother? The staffers in the White House stayed generally polite, and particularly polite when informing him that the president kept their calendars too full for any additional assignments that might come from the VP. So he and Dick tended to spend their days at the Eisenhower Executive Office Building in the vice president's ceremonial office. His position was ceremonial anyway, so it fit.

Stafford said, "On the bright side, the initiative got you a lot of press."

"Yeah, but the news cycle only lasts a day or so."

"It really is a good idea, Chris. Your initiative should bring in more revenues. Cross-pollinating the agencies should make them more capable, more aware, more able to accomplish their purposes. But almost nothing is going to happen until Congress passes the bill setting up an agency-interchange commission, mandates action, and funds it."

Presidential executive orders were followed as if they were law. But vice presidential initiatives were treated like a little girl's wishes for a pony. If the VP got a pony, he might hurt himself. And he might get ideas and decide to run off and join the circus. Where was the upside?

But he had friends in Congress, so his bill was being debated in both houses. In contrast to the VP's assertions, the opposition claimed his program would just further strengthen and centralize government—and then turn into another of the hundreds of brain-dead bureaucracies, mainly interested in its own survival and growth, at a cost of hundreds of millions, or perhaps many billions, every year.

Still, Congress might throw him a bone and pass the bill in the next session. Although it was schizophrenic in many ways, Congress rarely turned down an opportunity to spend money; it showed they were "doing something" and "taking bold action." And the members who pushed it through would have a favor to call if the VP made good on his ambition to be the next president.

"If I'm going to move into the Oval Office six years from now, I need to have some successes to stand upon… 'Less waste, more revenue!' How's that for a campaign slogan? It's short, snappy. People can remember four words."

Who could argue with that, the VP thought. It was the opposite of "More waste, less revenue," a somewhat better descriptor of reality.

"More waste, more revenue" was even more accurate. A few libertarian cranks, who would be dismissed out of hand by the mainstream, might say that "Less revenue, less waste" made the most sense. The question was, which four words would sell best?

It was a detail for his PR staff and the pollsters to sort out.

The two men quietly sat across from each other at the VP's desk, so close and yet so far from the real locus of power. The VP thought he might as well have just stayed at home. Even the First Lady, the country's unofficial National Busybody, could get more traction in her efforts to fight obesity in whales, buy everybody a puppy, and mandate national sensitivity training—or whatever.

He shook his head. "So... who's the one person in my pilot program?"

"A young woman from the SEC has been at the IRS for almost four months. Her name is Sabina Heidel."

"That's it? SEC to IRS? Not State to Defense? Not NSA to Justice? Not FBI to IRS at least? I mean, Dick, hardly any of the voters have ever even *heard* of the SEC!"

That was certainly true. Hundreds of agencies and departments existed that few outside of government had ever even heard of, unless they were being prosecuted by them or receiving money from them.

"True, but they *have* heard of the IRS. And it's all we got. Just low-level SEC to low-level IRS. That's all that's happened as yet. But this Sabina Heidel is something else."

"What do you mean?"

"I mean she's a Miss America, but with brains. Stunning. Beautiful. So I hear."

"Well, that could be something then." His reptilian mind started thinking on a different level. "We need a promotable personality to get attention. Let's keep an eye on her, Dick. Maybe bring her in here, and set up a meeting.... And as for today, I want some top-level agency heads on the phone to tell me directly why they haven't begun what I ordered them to do. They're appointees, and we do the appointing."

Stafford picked at a fingernail. "Sir, we both know they'll give you lots of good intentions, and tell you they're working on it. But I can tell you right now why they haven't done it."

"Yeah? Why's that?"

"Because they don't give a shit."

*   *   *

Two hours after leaving the drill site at Banga Sioquelle, the two foreigners relaxed in a tiny zinc-roofed restaurant in Gbarngeda, the seat
of Gong County, where they kept an eye on the town's medical clinic.
Still no injured man from B-F appeared. They passed the time drinking
a strange concoction of eggnog and gin, a local specialty. It went down
Charles's throat with a burn, while clinging to his teeth like glue.

"It makes you bigger, man. It makes you so much bigger! Hah!"
The jolly proprietor took pride in his creation, known far and wide
for its ability to enhance the proudest possession of the region's male
population.

Charles couldn't help but smile at the proprietor's confidence in the
drink's advertised qualities.

His ready smile was an advantage, although not likely one bestowed
by the Yahweh he learned about in Sunday school; the God the Father
they taught about lacked a sense of humor. Certainly, Sister Mary
Joseph—who ran the parochial school where his mother enrolled him
in fourth grade—rejected good humor. She equated his persistent smile
to impertinence and a challenge to authority. Indeed, there was often a
fine line between insolence and his innocent amusement at the absurdity
of the cosmos. When he approached too close to the line, Sister Mary
Joseph took a sharp crack at his knuckles with the cane she brandished
like a swagger stick.

Most women, the nun excepted, found his provocative and disarming smile appealing. It displayed both his intelligence and a sheer delight
with life. But Charles also smiled when anxious, and even, sometimes,
when angry.

The restaurant—really more of a shack—offered either the cool eggnog, which had first dibs on the bar's tiny fridge, or room temperature
beer, at a balmy ninety degrees and rising. There was little breeze outside.
The screens around the eating area stopped the airflow entirely and the
mosquitos only somewhat. The lack of circulation through such screens
discouraged their use among the population in these climates, and even
the use of mosquito nets over beds. Any limitation to airflow simply
made it too hot to sleep. Malaria prevention took a back seat to restful

slumber, no matter how many mosquito nets international health agencies provided.

"So I know this is your first trip to West Africa, kid. Also your first out of the States?"

Charles shook his head in a noncommittal way. "Kind of. I've been to Canada. But there's a lot less difference between an American from Montana and a Canadian from Alberta than there is between an American from Montana and one from Alabama. Yet we can't cross the Canadian border with just a driver's license anymore. I wonder when we won't be allowed to cross the Montana border."

Winn prompted him. "So what exactly made you buy into B-F? There are thousands of little wannabe mining companies all saying, 'Look at me.'"

"At first it was just that one purchase," Charles admitted, "advised by a broker in Vancouver. I didn't know much about this sector other than that I was interested in it. I really didn't know what I was doing. I guess I still don't."

"Well, you jumped into the deep end coming way out here, first time out. How much did you buy at first?"

"B-F was trading at about a buck, and the guy promoted me into five thousand shares, initially. Five thousand bucks is real money, for me at least. It motivated me to start taking this stuff seriously."

The dressing-down he had received from Uncle Maurice served as the even stronger motivation to learn the field. He could *hear* his uncle's grimace right through the telephone line when he had told him of the purchase. Maurice, sure the promoter had suckered him, did nothing to hide his anger and disappointment. Charles had concentrated his limited portfolio in garbage. Worse than risky, it was thoughtless. But instead of invalidating and discouraging his nephew, Maurice had helped Charles turn coal into diamonds.

"My uncle hooked me up with a friend at a boutique investment house that specializes in natural resources, to give me some mentoring. In the process of debunking B-F, my uncle's friend actually started getting interested in the company. I've moved to San Diego so I can work with him. We called B-F's office. They said if I could get here on my own dime I could join you all on this tour. So I came."

Winn nodded.

"Once we started researching it, I knew I'd gotten lucky. I bought more of the stock along the way up."

Winn failed to conceal a cracking smile and scratched his ear. "It's said that luck materializes when preparation meets opportunity. It certainly seems that luck can be more than just an accident, more than a roll of the dice. Maybe it's a reflection of good karma. Maybe it's the universe's reward for being well prepared. There was a reason Napoleon didn't want smart generals: he wanted lucky ones."

Charles swatted a solitary daytime mosquito and gazed around the small muddy town. Dozens of tiny shops lay within sight, selling various foods and wares. A boy across the road laughed and kicked a ball with his friend while waiting for passing motorbikes to stop for fuel he would sell them from gallon-sized mayonnaise jars. A group of men ate a picnic atop a giant container truck as it trundled past. The tinged sweet scent of burning charcoal lay thick in the air.

"Nobody tells these boys they can't sell gasoline in mayonnaise jars," Charles mused. "Without them, Mr. Winn, I don't know how you would have fueled up your Land Cruiser."

"It's not Xander's Land Cruiser. It's mine."

Charles twisted his neck around to see who had said this. He caught a quick grin from Winn assuring him that his new friend wasn't worried about this sudden interloper.

"T.J. Wandeah, this is Charles Knight. He's been up to Banga Sioquelle with me."

"We will get to know each other, Charles Knight." TJ's eyes smiled and his voice was full. He held out his hand, and Charles grasped it in a failed attempt to accomplish the complex local handshake. "I will teach you how to shake hands like a true Gondwanan."

TJ was a handsome, heavy-set man whose precise age would be hard to assess except that his eyes betrayed his youth. The man settled down on a plastic patio chair and leaned way back with a comfortable smile on his face as if he had known Charles for years.

"What have you been up to, my friend?" Winn asked.

"I had to fill my time with something while you wasted your day, Xander." No man would mistake the glint in TJ's energetic eyes and the elevation of his eyebrows for anything other than the intended message:

TJ had enjoyed the companionship of someone of the female persuasion. And he was still reveling in it.

Xander said to Charles, "It took me five years to figure out this man. You see, TJ is modest."

TJ shrugged.

Xander said, "This man here next to you is the son of the most famous man in Djenne County. That's southeast of the capital. Djennetown has the most beautiful beaches you will ever see."

"So true!" TJ said.

"Everyone in Djenne knows and respects the name of TJ's father. As TJ is the first son of the first wife, he shares his father's name. How many brothers do you have, TJ?"

TJ shrugged again. "That depends on how high you can count. Everyone is my brother!"

"And his brothers turn to him, after his father of course. T.J. Wandeah Senior is the senator from Djenne."

Charles asked, "Were you here during the wars, TJ?"

"Some of the time. My father took us to the States at first. We spent years in Minnesota."

Xander said, "As a kid, he worked at a radio station there."

"And I'm planning to set one up here soon."

"TJ has his finger in many pies here. I doubt there is anything that happens in this country that TJ doesn't hear about in half an hour. Everyone is a friend of TJ, and I can tell you, that can come in handy."

"If I didn't know important people, how could I keep you out of jail, Xander?"

"True, my friend."

As was the case for many in Gondwana's higher society even during peacetime, TJ had attended college in the US, and, before that, lived in Germany for a couple of years of secondary school when that was the way the political winds blew. Despite the persistence of the civil conflict, after college graduation he came back to Gondwana, where he started building businesses, hoping for peace, while making do during war. He was a dreamer—but also effective at giving reality to his dreams. That entailed driving from town to town all over Gondwana to keep tabs on his ventures, which in turn gave him the opportunity to enjoy his greatest indulgence: high-quality single malt imported to serve the demands of those with good taste. "Scottish tea" kept him awake and comfortable on the harsh drives that were so often punctuated by blown tires, washed-out roads, and marauding rebels.

TJ had gained some advantages by starting his businesses when he did. Running businesses during wartime offered both pluses and minuses. One plus was that profits were very high. So TJ had made excellent profits. They would have been spectacularly higher had he imported weapons as a primary business venture. But the high profits from selling weapons in war could well end up a minus. Buyers, fully armed, might resent those high prices. And the people at whom the muzzles aimed tended to be especially unsympathetic. Arms dealers existed in the paradoxical position of being much in demand and yet detested. TJ knew how to play that game but decided not to. Moral and practical arguments could be made for getting weapons to various groups. But wars end. He chose to invest in activities that didn't automatically trigger antipathy and that thrived in peacetime too. So TJ survived the wars and now the peace, accumulating capital along the way.

Xander looked at TJ. "Thank you again for coming up with me and for letting me use your car."

"I hope it was worth the trip for you. For both of you." TJ languidly signaled the proprietor, who, without needing any further instruction, provided him with both a warm beer *and* a moderately cool eggnog.

Charles said, "I'm not sure yet."

"Do you have money invested in B-F?" TJ asked, after he threw half the beer back in one long gulp and grinned with contentment.

Charles gave TJ a level look. "Too much of my net worth! More than I should."

Winn said, "That's right. Diversify, Charles. Who knows what can happen in a country like this? Ebola could knock this place for a loop. A warlord wannabe could light up a revolution here, take over the capital, chop off the heads of the cabinet ministers and stack 'em up on the beach. And then cancel all mining leases and contracts. Your new fortune would evaporate...."

Charles looked at TJ, who nodded. But what TJ said didn't match his expression.

"Xander exaggerates," TJ said. "No one wants war here anymore. No rebels in the Gondwana bush. Not anymore."

"Where are the rebels now?" Xander prodded TJ for Charles's benefit, obviously knowing the answer.

"*Former* rebels," TJ replied, with a swing of his thick arm. "They are grown up! They are all around: teaching school, directing traffic, running this restaurant… who knows? Many rebels are amongst us, but they aren't rebels anymore. All of them were forgiven in the general amnesty. Now the government doesn't bother people much, so few people get mad. And the crazy men who led the rebellions are mostly dead."

"Mostly?"

"One is a senator. He has the seat next to my father."

"They got rid of the last major criminal who ran Gondwana during the last war," Winn added. "The new guy doesn't seem to be a hardcore sociopath, although maybe he just hasn't grooved to the possibilities. The last guy had his secret police disappearing people in the night. It was crazy to even think of putting money here then, and nearly impossible if you tried. No tourists, no business—nothing. The place is still a shithole." Winn gave TJ an apologetic shrug that TJ acknowledged with a confirmatory shrug of his own. "But it's improving. The current government has too little money to really bother the regular folk with much beyond the usual shakedowns. So the people here are starting to do most everything that needs doing."

TJ interrupted. "That's about to change."

Winn nodded. "The World Bank is coming to Gondwana to teach the government how to tax its citizens, revamp its central bank, increase the government's security forces, build a more impenetrable bureaucracy to push paper, and, as they say, 'help Gondwana join the international community.' But until all that happens, these are a happy and free people, despite the poverty."

Charles had spent a few days on his own in Adamstown and had been impressed by how little fear there was in the capital city. No one seemed scared of the few cops he saw. Two uniformed men approached him once, but only to politely ask for some *cold water* or *weekend money*, both terms Charles learned meant a transfer of money from him to them. When he declined, they wandered off. The community pretty much policed itself, the way even major cities in Europe had done until early in the nineteenth century.

Winn continued. "The World Bank will loan a bunch of money to the government, supposedly to build roads and such. The politicians will siphon off most of it."

Charles turned to TJ. "What does your father think of this?"

"That's *why* he's a politician, my new friend." TJ raised his eyebrows.

Charles laughed, but was left to guess whether TJ's father was leeching blood himself or working to stop the hemorrhage.

"What about the Chinese?" Charles asked.

Winn deferred to TJ, who replied, "The Chinese don't care who runs the country. Here, they lease the iron mines. Part of their lease payment is to pave some of the roads—primarily the ones leading to those iron mines. They bring in Chinese contractors and Chinese machines to do it."

Winn interrupted. "So less World Bank loans that the politicians can siphon money from."

Charles said, "I bet the World Bank doesn't like that one little bit."

TJ shook his head. "That is too bad for them. The World Bank just prints money to loan us, but the work we Gondwanans have to do to pay it back is very real. The Chinese give us a better deal. We sell them some of our ore instead of selling ourselves." TJ swallowed the rest of his gin-infused eggnog, looked expectantly down at his crotch, then shrugged.

Charles did the same.

The two younger men laughed while Winn shook his head, a faint smile emerging through his feigned disapproval.

Sweat soaked through Charles's oxford that he kept tucked into his pants. His feet felt on fire in his boots. TJ was dry. Maybe that was to be expected of a native. But Winn kept dry too. Winn's thin, white fly-fishing shirt fell untucked; the top three buttons he left undone, and his collar flapped open to reveal graying hair on his chest but little perspiration. Charles noticed Winn's unsocked feet, which were coated with a thin layer of dry Gbarngeda dirt. He had replaced his boots with open sandals. The airflow through Winn's loose clothing kept him dry.

Charles untucked his oxford, freed the buttons below his neck, and wished he weren't wearing boots.

The men sat quietly, sipping at their drinks.

Winn said, seemingly for TJ's benefit, "Charles, what have you actually learned today?"

"Beyond what you and TJ are teaching me, not much. Johnson and Smolderhof just mimic each other and repeat what I've read in the analyst reports and their press releases. I could have stayed home and played beach volleyball."

"But then you wouldn't have met TJ and me."

"And you two are worth every dollar I spent to get here." Charles raised his drink. "The B-F folk didn't seem to care about us today. Maybe they're putting all their effort into making that deal with the major."

Winn shook his head. "TJ has been helping me look into that. Smolderhof isn't pushing hard. And that troubles me."

"Is he standing up for honor and integrity? Not greasing palms sufficiently because he feels it's wrong?" Charles asked.

"Does Smolderhof give you the impression that he's an ideologue?" Winn shook his head. "Every junior mining company is in a rush for a deal as soon as they get lucky enough to delineate an ore body. It's their best exit. Grab the money and run. I don't understand this delay. And although you never asked, kid, *that's* one of the big reasons why *I'm* here."

Charles said, "The bigger the ore body, the better the deal for B-F, right? Maybe Smolderhof wants to drill more to see how big this thing really is. Why leave extra money on the table?"

"They're already past that point. Increasing the reserves even by another 50 percent won't have that much effect on the deal. Even with all the infrastructure established, a major operation can only mine this deposit at a certain rate. Let's say they actually have a hundred million ounces in the ground. Even if they mined at, say, three million a year—which would be by far the biggest gold mine in the world—it would take over thirty years to get it all out. Discounting the future, 50 percent more ore mined beginning three *decades* from now doesn't add much to present value. And that's assuming the government doesn't try to steal it all next year by nationalizing the whole operation. At this point, it's the nature of the deal, not some possible extra gold, that will determine the peak stock price. They are playing with fire with the government in lots of ways. The government might decide to restrict how much of the ore they can take, or maybe bring in a competitor from China. Then they can all get their palms greased again, right?"

Charles said, "Given the significance of that risk, Smolderhof should be pushing with everything he's got to get a deal with a major."

Winn raised his finger and his eyebrows as well, acknowledging Charles's point, and said, "Yet, he's not."

The men stayed quiet, trying to sort it out in their minds.

A train of logical thought brought Charles to comment, "You say the government here serves no useful purpose. They just line their pockets, raise costs, stop things from happening, and corrupt society. You'd think it would be worthwhile for a mining company to just get rid of them. It would be a big win for everybody...." And the same was true in the US. Perhaps it could be made to happen. "Maybe a proper revolution would replace them with... nothing."

TJ smiled. "The capital city here is almost as full of useless mouths as the one you have in the US."

Xander nodded. "I like the way you think, kid. It makes logical economic sense. They tried doing that in Katanga province in the Congo, in the '60s. It should have worked for a bunch of reasons, not least that Congo is an artificial country with a completely dysfunctional government. Like most here in Africa. But the UN quashed it." Xander got a faraway look in his eyes, as if he'd been there then. "No matter where you are, the powers that be don't like change, especially when it breaks their rice bowls. Perhaps someday it will happen, but not here, not now. Parasites die only after they've killed the host."

Charles sipped at his eggnog, seeking clarity. It wasn't coming easily. The B-F shares were riding a wave upward, reflecting investor confidence in the B-F operation. But Winn did not share that confidence. Smolderhof might be acting against the shareholders' interests, and Charles wanted to understand why, especially because his own gut still told him something wasn't right.

Winn must have been thinking along the same lines, for he said, "When something doesn't make sense, question your assumptions. B-F may be lazy or incompetent or just making bad choices, but that's no excuse for us to do the same."

"What are you getting at, Mr. Winn?"

"Only that due diligence demands that *you and I* cannot afford to be lazy, incompetent, nor make bad choices. This stock's already a long-ball home run for you—a hundredfold win. And that's extremely rare. Maybe it can *double* again, and a double from here will put a lot more change in your jeans. But you best keep your eye on the exit in case the theater gets too crowded and somebody yells fire."

Being rescued from death by a man who could disguise himself as a rickety old gimp was a fair start to any day. But Winn, clearly an old hand when it came to the business of Africa, was interested in teaching him exactly what he most needed to learn. And that was more valuable than gold.

Winn again read his mind. "Lucky we bumped into each other. Maybe together we can figure this thing out."

Charles's face lit up. He sensed adventure. "Count me in!"

Winn then turned to TJ. "There was an accident up at the B-F tract today. Some poor guy let out a scream as he didn't get his arm cut off."

TJ said with assurance, "They were trying to get rid of you."

Winn scratched at the rough stubble on his chin. "If they're willing to fake a medical emergency, maybe there are other little cheats here and there. Like Mark Twain said, 'a gold mine is a hole in the ground with a liar at its entrance.' Mining exploration is all about hope, and draws more than its share of hustlers. It has a lot in common with the religion business. They're both based on belief in the improbable. And the prospect of instant salvation, financial or spiritual.

"In technology deals, you can generally see if a widget works or not. In manufacturing, you can count and measure the widgets coming off the assembly line. In oil exploration, you put a hole in the ground, and the oil either comes up under pressure, or it doesn't. But in mining exploration, it's much harder to be sure what you have."

Eric, the owner, chef, bartender, and dishwasher of the hundred-square-foot establishment, had been providing them special attention. He handed Winn another gin-and-eggnog concoction before the Dutchman had emptied the previous.

Charles felt more concern as this conversation proceeded. He was rich now, and didn't want to lose his paper wealth. "The stock price is damn high for a site that hasn't yet produced a single ounce of gold, and possibly never will, considering everything that can go wrong."

Winn nodded once. "It's one hell of a speculation. Almost everyone in North America and Europe is talking about this place, right here, where *we* are. And where, quite notably, they *aren't*."

"Precisely. I wanted to learn more than I could from newspapers." Charles's felt a pang of nostalgia. His father owned and edited a small newspaper in Montana. He had spent many happy years dropping by the press after school. The aroma of the ink became the scent of home. He learned as he got older that many articles—especially the financial columns—were little more than plagiarized transcriptions by cub reporters using wire services and press releases as their only sources of information. They sat at their keyboards not recognizing that they were the last person in the game of telephone, with no ability to interpret the garbled profusion of propaganda and planted stories that emerged. Most people who relied on such sources of information didn't even know what they didn't know.

"Have you ever visited a gold mine before?"

Charles nodded and reflected back on that trip, just a few months earlier. "In Nevada. An open pit like they say Banga Sioquelle is going to be. It was much lower grade than here. But at least there were power lines in Nevada."

Winn chuckled. "Here they'll have to build a power plant big enough for a small city, in the middle of nowhere—and bring in fuel for it. It's going to take time to train the labor here. And lots of expensive workers will need to be brought in. Security is going to be a problem, with this mine producing something like 20 percent of the GDP after it's operating. Nevada is a desert; there's not enough water. But this place has way too much water, and that's an even bigger problem. The old phrase 'like owning a gold mine' doesn't mean unlimited wealth anymore. It's more like unlimited amounts of risk and hard work. Were there any vindictive blood-soaked drill bits out there in Nevada and bits of limbs scattered all over?"

"Not that I noticed...."

"I wasn't surprised by today's melodrama," Winn said. "It's happened before." With his right index finger he made a little circling motion representing the idea of eternal recurrence.

"What do you mean?"

"Oh, a few days ago, TJ went up to Banga Sioquelle alone, not as part of a junket."

TJ chimed in, "I was given a brief tour and allowed to ask some innocuous questions. But then I asked about the core processing, and..."

Charles interrupted. "Killer drill!" He said it too loudly.

The restaurant owner swooped in. "Everything okay?" He poured some more water.

"Yes, sorry," Charles said.

"Killer drill," TJ agreed, more subdued.

Winn said, "Maybe our friend Smolderhof likes to put on acts."

Charles replied, "You like to act too, Mr. Winn."

Winn placed his unnecessary cane on the table and smiled. "Sometimes you want people to think you've got a pair of aces, and sometimes you want them to think you're an idiot trying to get lucky with an unsuited two-seven." He shriveled into the withered appearance he had maintained during the B-F tour, and then in a flash grew large with a confident laugh.

Winn said, "Here's something else I find interesting. Do you remember from your reading what B-F found in the first two holes drilled in the central zone?"

"Um... those two holes were empty. Nada. Zilch."

"Correct. But every other hole B-F drilled has served to prove their scenario of gold, gold, and more gold. Now, what happens if you find no gold whatsoever in the rocks you stole from the formation that supposedly has gold spread like butter?"

"If there's no gold at all in my... stolen rocks... it would make me wonder."

Winn looked directly at Charles and said, "Sure it would. But these days, it's a whole lot easier to fudge books than to alter rocks. So now scammers congregate on Wall Street, not in the jungle."

Charles scrunched his eyebrows, grasping at the positives. "So it seems pretty unlikely that B-F would be anything other than what it seems to be."

"It does."

"Multiple assays from trusted labs, all in agreement."

"Yes."

"Even parallel holes. Same results."

"I know."

"And all the people who have looked at this, and with analysts writing detailed reports?"

"Well, be careful there, Charles. Remember: garbage in, garbage out. Analysts look for mistakes in company reports, but who suspects a brazen fraud, with everything fabricated out of whole cloth? This is a region with a history of gold production and the right kind of rocks; it could pass a geologist's smell test. I know lots of people in this business. Most of them are stand-up guys. I asked around about Smolderhof and his partner, Washerman. I got mostly shrugged shoulders, hands balancing like scales. These are a couple of guys well into middle age who have never had a real success. Now that doesn't mean they're bad guys. But it's a yellow flag. I don't know...."

"So...?" Charles prompted.

Winn continued, "You were the one who was suspicious enough to crawl out onto that cliff face."

"I just thought it can't hurt to check for myself. Firsthand knowledge trumps other people's say so."

TJ interjected, "I agree. It's the difference between *Erfahrung* and *Wissen* in German."

Charles made a mental note to look the terms up later. "My sophomore history teacher taught me to question authority."

"Sounds like a good teacher."

"Nope. The opposite. He was the authority I learned to question. He constantly misled us about history."

"Misled, Charles?"

"He tried to skew our thinking by presenting good guys as bad guys, and bad things as good things. Some things are just matters of opinion. But not an entire worldview. I don't think anybody else in the class even noticed what he was doing."

Winn leaned back and pushed forward with the thought. "Fraudsters can be smart, charming, and inventive. Sociopaths are generally smart enough to know they have to camouflage themselves to resemble normal people. When I was young, I spent a year with the circus. I've met guys that could take your watch off your wrist, then pick your pocket, take twenty dollars out of your wallet, and use it to buy you a drink so you think they're a hail-fellow-well-met. It taught me not to trust what I'm told unless I see it myself—and most of the time not then either."

Charles calculated how much wealth he would no longer have if B-F were really a fraud and let out a breath. "Yeah. Once a man tried to sell me a beat-up old piano by claiming it was one of the finest custom-made pieces ever, commissioned by the king of Siam. He was a practiced and enthusiastic liar. But I know about pianos. I don't know much about mining."

Winn said, "Egregious fraud is rare in business—but it's always possible, and I like to rule it out. This bull market in gold and gold stocks has been going on for a couple of years. People are looking for reasons to *buy*, not reasons to sell. Fear is out, greed is in. It happens every decade or so in tech stocks, or in oil stocks, or in real estate, or bonds, or in something. Easy money makes investors optimistic to the point that any normal criteria for judgment are suspended. They think that this time it's different. The black line of a stock chart does their thinking for them. It turns into a momentum play. Then they reach a tipping point in mass psychology. After that happens, even people who usually go by facts start following the crowd."

Charles admitted, "I sometimes follow the lines on charts...."

"They give you context. They let you see the trend. They let you see whether something is cheap or dear relative to where it's been in the past. But they don't predict the future any more than tea leaves or Tarot cards. And there are a couple more red flags getting waved at us at Banga Sioquelle."

"For example?"

"Let me ask you." Winn emptied a bottle of eggnog and slumped back in his chair. The restaurateur glided in with another old beer bottle filled with more of the tasty thick yellow-white goop. "Is there anything else that has popped up in your research, no matter how small, that strikes you as peculiar?"

Charles was beginning to realize the value of a long brainstorming session over drinks. In some ways it was more important than more conventional forms of work. "Look, you know I'm new at this...."

"New doesn't make you stupid."

"Okay. Well, I wonder about a geology that doesn't exist anywhere else in the world, and that can't be explained by any previous theory—that's a bit of a red flag to me. Then, the very use of the term 'nano' always bothers me in any company—it's a buzzword. Like 'organic' in the food industry. People lose their wits when they hear magic words; they cloud the mind."

Winn chuckled. "Yeah, things don't change much. Back in the '60s bull market, people would buy any company whose name ended in *onics*, *ex*, or *tech*. I have to agree, there's a lot of fabulous and first-ever about this B-F prospect. But excessive promotion is the norm in this business. It's one reason a lot of experienced investors hold this sector in low regard. What else?"

Charles had not yet had enough time to mature his new suspicions, so he grasped at something. "I read somewhere that there was a PhD chemist at Banga Sioquelle. That's not typical, is it?"

"Not for an operation this size, no. All they would be expected to have is an experienced technician, but a chemist is a plus. Ollie Shifflett is the fellow's name. I presume he's doing the local assays before shipping material off to South Africa and Canada for the formal assays. B-F is just making sure that everything is beyond question."

Charles tried to put pieces together. Mining-exploration stocks were always, by nature, risky and promotional. They had no income and by necessity spent their time raising new money just to stay solvent. Their existence was akin to a treasure hunt in a vast ocean, an Easter egg hunt with one egg hidden in a thousand square miles. Their burning matches flared brightly when they first went public. But, if you held them long enough, they'd singe your fingers before going out. B-F seemed to be one of the exceptions that kept the punters coming back to the betting window.

Charles said, "There was something about cyanide leach tests.... A write-up in the *Northerly Miner* talked about how rapidly the B-F gold dissolves. This is the highest-grade ore known that has so little visible mineralization. You can't see a thing, even with a microscope. I suppose this all supports the theory that this nanoparticulate gold is the dominant deposition. They say there's no way to salt that."

Beyond stories about shooting gold dust from a twelve-gauge into rock, or scattering gold flakes onto a stream bed, Charles knew almost nothing about how results might be falsified—how supposed "ore" could be manufactured from useless rock in a process called *salting*.

"Yes, yes. That's what we are told, and it's logical that there's no way to salt nanoparticulate gold." Winn now leaned forward. "That's it, that is *exactly* it. Very good, kid. But it's strange. I've been doing this for thirty years, since I was your age, and I haven't ever come across this before."

"New theories. New technology. It happens. It doesn't mean fraud."

"True. Geology as a proper science really only started to come of age at the beginning of the twentieth century. Even plate tectonics only became accepted in the 1960s. New theories are the essence of science."

Charles's skepticism took another turn. He said, "New science and new technology might also provide new ways to *commit* fraud."

Winn nodded. "In the nineteenth century, platinum was cheaper than gold, and it was used to counterfeit gold coins. Computer technology and xerography gave currency counterfeiters a big leg up for a while starting in the '60s. Little shiny things called Wellington stones came out in the '70s and were nearly indistinguishable from diamonds; a lot of pawnbrokers and jewelers got taken for a ride until the knowledge leaked out. It's like in a war: the offense always has the advantage when they come up with a new way to attack."

Charles shook his head as he kept processing his inner thoughts. "How about the assay labs?"

Winn shrugged. "I called Slimmer Labs, their primary assayer in Jo'burg. They didn't want to tell me about the B-F assays—confidentiality and so forth. There's no percentage for them to talk, and that's quite correct and proper. But it never hurts to ask…."

"What's your feeling about Slimmer?"

"I've dealt with them before. They're trustworthy and know how to do an assay. They're not going to be part of any scam. No point in it for an outfit in their position. But it's important to know the lab. I remember one fraud that took place in Nevada. Fantastic assays were reported by 'THS Lab.' Turned out the initials stood for Tonopah High School, and they had the chemistry teacher on the payroll. That was pretty bold."

"So we both are skeptical, but based on essentially nothing. We need to get more information."

"Yes, we do."

The glint in Charles's eye increased, and he lifted an eyebrow. "Goodluck Johnson invited me back anytime. I don't know if he was just being gracious, but it's his land. So I think I have a standing invitation. And I think you both are included on that invitation."

"That's convenient, kid. And Smolderhof reminded us we owned some of the project. Sounds like an open door beckons."

"If they were somehow salting, where and how would they do it?"

Winn scratched at his chin. "Kid, if it *is* happening, with the consistency and reproducibility they are getting, then they are somehow doing it to intact cores, before they are split and sent off to various labs. I have no idea how they would be able to do this."

"That last building we were in, the concrete one where Smolderhof sang and danced for us—that was their assay-and-shipping facility, wasn't it?"

"So we assumed." Winn's consternation was evident. "What's the problem?"

Charles replied, "There wasn't enough dust."

"What?"

"They are supposedly cutting cores in that place where Smolderhof did his burlesque. And it isn't like they cleaned the place up for us. Where was the rock dust? It should have been on everything, right? The cores on the table in there should have been covered with dust. Dust should have filled the corners. Maybe there's another place the core is being carved up, away from what we've seen."

"I've never once been at a drill site where their assay, storage, and shipping facility wasn't a centerpiece of the tour." Winn looked into the distance for more than a minute. "Let's assume they *are* salting. They wouldn't want their contract drillers seeing that. Only a few of the staff could be involved. They would need to do it offsite."

TJ had been sitting quietly, listening. But he provided the most important comment now. "Right here in Gbarngeda is the nearest major trucking point from B-F. Their samples all have to come through this town sooner or later."

Winn smiled. "Then maybe this is where they would salt them, right here. Offsite. Before they split the cores and ship them off."

Charles took another swig from his gin-filled eggnog. "Right here in this town. Maybe you and I should hang out here in Gbarngeda for another day, poke around, and see if B-F has '*ein* secret lab' somewhere near town." Charles imitated an atrocious German accent.

"You mean '*Ein geheimes Labor*!'" TJ again offered the German, with a laugh. One of the few advantages of having spent time in Germany for high school was picking up the language. But, since so many Germans spoke perfect English, the knowledge served little useful purpose—except to surprise people who didn't expect a West African black man to speak German.

TJ then frowned. "But I cannot stay to help you find out. I have business in Adamstown tonight." He looked at Winn and then at Charles and frowned some more, involuntarily it seemed, for suddenly he recovered and said with a smile, "But you can keep the car, Xander. I will borrow a motorbike to go home."

Winn held his bottle up in a toast to TJ. "Then I'm in, Charles! One day spent looking for a hidden laboratory could be worth millions of dollars to me. That is one helluva return on investment! And, kid, if you live through tomorrow here in Gondwana, you can make a ton of money too."

Yesterday the possibility of not living through tomorrow would not have occurred to Charles. This was the second time today the specter of imminent death had arisen.

Maybe Africa *was* a dangerous place, after all. And maybe he was out of his depth.

5

Small-Small

THE people of Gbarngeda stood tall, proud that their town was the capital of the great Gong County. In their minds, Gong was the strongest, the best, the greatest of all counties. With the wealth from their timber industry, prestige from the most respected university in the country, and now the expectation of the world's largest gold mine, the people of Gong had more reason to be proud than ever before.

Of course the timber industry consisted of little more than a couple of men with a crosscut saw, slicing down every tree with any market value on public land, trucking them off, and bribing forestry officials to look away. Only privately owned land, conserved by owners who generally wanted to leave something of value to their children, retained old-growth trees. Perversely, the publically held preserve of primeval forest would erode to scrub in less than a generation.

But in Charles's view, the illegal-timber-industry men just might know where in the surrounding jungle a *geheimen Labor* was being kept *geheimen*.

Even with their university, the timber, and the nearby iron mines, Gbarngeda was a town of only 7,500 people, hardly a metropolis. Adamstown, four hours away by car, had two hundred times the population. As in every other third world country, there really was no alternative to the capital for anyone who wanted to get ahead. Trying to scratch a living from poor jungle soil in the middle of nowhere offered limited possibilities for upward mobility.

Two boys kicked a ball in front of the one-story concrete Gong County office building. Three scrawny chickens picked among the pebbles at the entrance stairs. The ball got past the younger boy as Charles headed to the building. He picked up the mostly deflated ball and tossed it back to the boy, who flashed him a smile.

His inquiries inside regarding the location of B-F's facilities were a waste of time. He had learned nothing with his careful probing at the local bars the night before, identified nobody who admitted to being in the timber industry, and now had nothing to show for his efforts scouring through the scattering of unsorted, mold-ridden county real estate records. The uncertainties of who legally owned what land in this wartorn nation, where few paper records survived, could only add another layer of confusion and despair to the psyche of any Gondwanan war refugee returning home. He hoped Winn had had more luck finding evidence of a secret B-F lab. If it even existed.

Charles had time before his scheduled lunch with Winn back at Eric's restaurant. As he emerged in frustration from the county office building, he found the same boys, now done with their soccer ball, sitting on the stairs. He sat down near them and considered what to do next.

The barefoot teenagers were lean, with wiry arms and short hair. They wore long clean pants, but their shirts were ragged and dirty. Perhaps this afternoon would be shirt-washing day at the river under the bridge leading out of town. Charles had earlier seen a dozen or so men and women scrubbing clothes on washboards and laying out pants to dry on the rocks. It was not considered acceptable to wear shorts except when playing soccer, for some cultural reason unknown to Charles. Perhaps it was like many of the other customs and beliefs brought to the continent, first by Muslim imams, then by Christian missionaries. They were all accepted as part of the natural order of things.

Boys everywhere can be remarkably shy. But a young white man sitting so close to them was just too interesting to leave be. The younger boy kept looking at the older, moving his head, encouraging. He pushed his elbow into the bigger boy's side and made a face, the equivalent of saying, "Talk to him, stupid."

"Mah name is Saye. Saye," the older boy said, without looking at Charles.

Charles's ears were not yet attuned to the accent, but this clearly was an introduction.

"I'm Charles."

"Charles. Charles," the boy said.

The door to a friendship now open, the younger one chimed in with a broad smile. "Mah nay is Nyahn. Nyahn."

"Ni-ann?" Charles tried, accenting the first syllable as he thought he had heard it.

The boy smiled again, bigger. "Yes, Nyahn. Nyahn."

"Nyahn Nyahn?" Charles asked.

"No. Nyahn… Nyahn."

Charles chose to stick with just one "Nyahn."

They sat silent for a minute, then Nyahn asked, "Whe' you fra'?"

"America."

Nyahn and Saye both seemed to get closer, without really moving. "Ah, America. I li' America. You tek me deah?"

Charles smiled uncomfortably. "Take you there? I wish I could. I'm sorry."

The boy's dejection lasted only a second before he smiled again. "You wan eah?"

Charles was not hungry—the heat and the dehydration kept hunger low. He hoped to walk a tightrope between friendliness and concern for intestinal integrity in this far-from-sanitary neck of the woods. There was nothing truly safe to eat here except prepackaged imported foods, most of them long past their expiration dates. He had heard about bush-meat and palm wine and fufu. None of it sounded very appealing. He hoped the boy would not try to supply him with any.

But not to worry; it's hard to put those foods in a pocket. Instead Nyahn pulled out what looked like a sticky clump of sesame seeds wrapped in plastic, tied at the top.

"Dis is good. Ver' good. You try." Nyahn held the local treat right up near Charles's face. Charles's wish to be polite and his curiosity trumped his desire to be prudent. In it went. And it wasn't bad, slightly sweet, with a pleasant texture, and moist enough to go down easily.

"Thank you. It's nice, Nyahn."

Eric's Place was only across the street. Charles thought, why not? and invited the boys to come over for a real meal. They could get fed and be on their way before Xander arrived.

It didn't take much encouragement; a free lunch at a restaurant was an extraordinary treat.

The two boys joined Charles at the same small, round metal table he, Winn, and TJ shared yesterday. Silence was acceptable in Gondwana; small talk was not required to be sociable. The boys were excited just to be in the presence of a foreigner while they quietly awaited the delivery of three warm Cokes. After a few sips, however, Saye allowed that he was sixteen and Nyahn twelve. Charles remembered being their age, not all that long ago.

At age twelve he had lived in Red Lodge, Montana, where his father published—and mostly wrote—the *Carbon County Gazette*, and his mother worked as a nurse in a local clinic. The newspaper always hovered on the verge of failure, but the family's needs were modest. He worked on the neighbor's ranch as well as their own. He swung from a rope into the swimming hole on the river near where he fished for trout. He hiked every mountain in the region. And, unlike these barefoot boys, he had several pairs of shoes.

"Are you friends, or brothers?" Charles asked. They looked like brothers.

"Nyahn is my younger brother. Same ma, same pa. Pa killed in the war. Not know where Ma is. She gone, far away, many years. We live wit Auntie Leah."

By the time he was Saye's age, Charles's mother was dead, but he was not alone. Although his father was aloof and performed his paternal tasks more out of duty than out of love, he was always present. His father had reluctantly agreed to his leaving school and taking on self-education. Charles built an office out of the room above the garage, with its own outdoor entrance accessed via a wooden staircase. He set himself to earning money and studying whatever he thought was important to further that objective, anxious to build a real business from scratch.

He spent most of his spare time with his books—that and taking his dirt bike on wild rides through the woods. One day, on the way home, he stopped into a martial arts studio and decided to add that to his schedule. Whereas his father was no athlete, Charles had always been quick and agile. He loved and respected his father, but his genes must have come entirely from his mother, for he had almost no traits in common with him. So after his mother's death, he found other models for his own life, from television and books.

He was raised with opportunities, despite the hard loss of his mother. There were far, far fewer opportunities for these boys in Gondwana and, he suspected, no one to encourage them to read the very few books available.

"Are you in school?" Charles asked.

"Yes. School," Saye said, absentmindedly. "I am in tenth grade."

"I am in sixth grade!" Nyahn's pride was clear. "I get all *B*'s and *C*'s."

Saye chastised his younger brother by poking him gently in the ribs.

Charles had a brother, also four years his junior. He felt his stomach give a turn then, as it did whenever he thought of his brother. Perhaps if he had been more available to him after their mother died, instead of working in that upstairs office and in the garage so much, distracting himself with computers and books, perhaps then things could have been different.

His business here in Gondwana disappeared from his mind. It was just these boys and him now, sharing three Cokes and earning friendship. He asked them, "What do you like to do? When you are not in school?"

"Soccer!" Nyahn said, jumping up from the table and spilling some of his Coke.

Saye pushed him firmly back into his seat and pointed to the Coke. "See! You make mess, Nyahn. Now clean up!"

But even as he harshly spoke, the older brother was already brushing it off the table with his hand. Nyahn ran over to the bar and asked for a rag. Napkins were a rare and valued commodity in Gondwana, usually supplied in the form of two or three sheets of toilet paper. He came back with six sheets of toilet paper and did his best to finish cleaning the table with it.

At their age, Charles never had occasion to question his supply of napkins or paper towels. Poor in the US and poor in Gondwana were two entirely different concepts. The poor in the US were often obese. Nobody in Gondwana who had the resources to become obese would possibly be considered poor. In the US, McDonald's hamburgers were lambasted as low-quality food, and rice magically considered high quality. A McDonald's in Gondwana would have been the most nutritious food in a country where polished rice was just a stomach-filling source of cheap, but nutritionally bereft, calories.

"Where do you play soccer?"

As Charles's ear adjusted to their dialect, he didn't have to pause as long to interpret Saye's response. "We play at school sometimes. But there is a soccer camp, not too far away." He indicated the road and pointed. "Just up north, not too many miles. We are going there after sawing wood in the bush."

Their side profession meant they probably knew the local bush well. But for the moment, he focused on their obvious enthusiasm. "Yeah? Soccer camp sounds nice. When do you go?"

"Dis week. We leave at end of dis week. After we work. Many boys, many men. Thousands. They say the soccer fields are nice. Big fields, and everyone gets uniforms and shoes and food for free."

"I'm glad you're going. Your school won't mind?"

Saye and Nyahn both looked down in shame.

"No money to pay school fees."

So they were quitting, at least for now. Charles considered asking how much it would cost to pay their fees. Although he was inclined to help people who deserved it, the fact was that even if he cashed in on B-F stock and gave all the money away, he would run out of capital long before this country ran out of poor people. Besides, when he was this age he was about to quit school too, although for different reasons.

Quitting school had turned out to be a wise move for him in the US. There, school had amounted to wasted time with babysitters and propagandists. And faster and better means to a solid education were possible. But here in Gondwana, maybe school was the only way to get any form of education. School and education were two very different— but often confused—concepts back in the US. But here, well, he just did not know.

"Do you earn money sawing wood?"

Nyahn, the younger boy, replied, "Yes, yes. Much money."

Saye corrected his brother, "We earn small-small money."

"Do you know this area well?"

"Yes, very well. We know all this area."

It couldn't hurt to ask. "Are there any secret laboratories around here?"

Neither boy understood. He wasn't going to try German.

"Are there any buildings where men use saws to cut up rock?"

Their response gave cause for hope.

Nyahn nodded his head quickly while Saye frowned. Nyahn began talking in an excited and rapid pidgin that Charles could not understand at all, combined with pointing and scribbling with his finger a fleeting map made from the sticky residue of spilled Coca-Cola on the table.

Saye said, "Nyahn remembers better. He thinks there is dis place up de Guinea Road." Saye followed his finger along a line of Coke. And then he pointed to the bridge that led across the river.

It was the road to, or from, Banga Sioquelle. If the boys were referring to the B-F prospect site, that wouldn't be helpful.

"How far up that road?"

Saye looked at Nyahn, who shrugged.

Saye answered for him, although Charles couldn't be sure of his accuracy. "Not far. Two or three miles past the river bridge."

That was encouraging. Banga Sioquelle was much farther away than that.

"On the left or right?"

"Left side, left side," Nyahn said. "Very near. Small-small walk."

"Can you see it from the road?"

Nyahn took a moment to try to understand the question before replying hesitantly, "No."

"How far off the road is it?"

Again Nyahn hesitated. Charles asked the question again, a bit slower.

"Deep in da bush," Nyahn replied. "But there is a path. Trucks go in deah wid da rocks to be sawn."

Nyahn's eyebrows furrowed and his face looked, if anything, concerned. Charles could not guess why. He thought he would give the boys a break and maybe later ask them more about this secret place where rock was sawn. He and Winn could go there this afternoon.

He asked Nyahn, "How long is soccer camp?"

"It has been there for months. Many boys there."

The answer wasn't to the point, but the question wasn't important.

"How will you get there?"

"We walk. Two days, maybe three if it is too raining. Soccer camp is in Guinea." Saye pointed to the road again and then at the receding bits of the Coca-Cola map.

"I know that road. I just came from Banga Sioquelle."

Nyahn looked at Saye. Nyahn did not know where Banga Sioquelle was.

Saye said, "I know the Banga road. That's where you were. That's where Banga Sioquelle is."

The Banga road was forty miles north. "How much farther will you have to walk *after* you get to the Banga road?"

"Oh, small-small. Twenty more miles. Small-small."

Charles replied with some awe. "Twenty-mile walk. Small-small." It sounded like "small-small" could mean anything from next door to a country away.

At Nyahn's age, Charles had a bicycle to take him to the local middle school two miles away. By the time he was Saye's age, in addition to his dirt bike, he had his own two-thousand-dollar pickup, and the truck even ran, as long as he spent a few hours each week under the hood or inside the transmission. He shook his head, too faintly to be seen. These kids didn't even have a sure source of food—and no shoes.

Yet they smiled. He sensed calmness. They were typical brothers in what Charles considered a highly atypical place.

But this wasn't atypical. No electricity, chickens pecking the dirt, wafting charcoal smoke, torn clothes, laughing children playing on the empty road in bare feet: this all typified much of the world, just not the world where he grew up. These two boys might be able to teach him just as much as Xander Winn could. They had accomplished much just to live long enough to be teenagers in a place that had so recently emerged from a brutal civil war.

Through a screened wall Charles peered upward at clouds that approached—dense, dark gray, burdened.

"Yes," Saye said, "it will rain soon. Very much and for a very long time. You will see."

6

A Rumble and a Race

THE boys had been right about the location of the lab. And about the rain.

Sodden clouds veiled the afternoon sun. What little light trickled through barely penetrated to the jungle floor.

Charles had only caught a brief glimpse of the bizarre machine in the long zinc-roofed structure; it was like nothing he'd ever seen before: metal, wires, pipes, all illuminated in flashing purple sparks. Now he would pay the price for his nosiness. He had walked up to the place and knocked on the door. Apparently he wasn't supposed to be there, for he was now running for his life, ducking through the jungle path, trying to find his way back to where Xander watched from a distance. Squalling blasts of rain muffled a gunshot as the trunk of a rubber tree exploded, hurling shards of milky wood, one of which embedded itself into his shoulder. Charles dropped down, his fresh wound immersed in the muck of the swamp; white latex of the rubber tree and the red blood flowing from his arm mixed with the meandering current of mud.

"Keep your head down!" Xander ran up to him.

Charles spit out a mouthful of the foul muck as he shouted back at Xander. "Smolderhof said we were welcome anytime!"

"Guess not!"

"So much for walking up and introducing ourselves." Charles groaned. Pain arced through his shoulder.

"I did suggest that was a bad idea."

The repetitive crack of automatic rifles cycling through entire magazines filled their ears. But for the rain washing the air clean, the gun smoke would have blown their way and filled their nostrils with a scent that reminded Charles of his childhood.

"Are you okay?"

Charles called back, "My shoulder. Think I was shot."

Winn pulled himself around a copse of bamboo, staying low. The cold rain reduced the danger presented by the abundant snakes that populated this place just a few miles outside of Gbarngeda. Winn rolled over to Charles. His face revealed sharp concern, at least until he had examined the wounded shoulder. Then he smiled, just for a moment. "Ugly. But it won't kill you. Hold on...." He grabbed the four-inch splinter in one hand and Charles's shoulder in the other and yanked.

Charles gasped and did not breathe for what seemed an age. Then he grunted through clenched teeth. "Okay, *now* I feel like I'm shot."

"Not you, kid. That tree was shot. Let's get the hell out of here before they learn how to aim." Winn raised himself up on his hands and knees and crawled.

Charles pushed up and forced himself to ignore the pain. Another hail of bullets tore through the bamboo and the rubber trees, scattering razor-sharp rods of bamboo into air already laced with suspended globs of milky latex. The bent-over rubber tree that had moments earlier erupted pieces of itself into Charles's shoulder took the brunt of another barrage, enough to carve through the five inches of its nine-year-old trunk. The tree would not make it to ten: it came down hard as the last tendrils keeping it intact bent like boiled noodles. It crashed down on Winn's head.

Winn lay face down in the muck; the tree pinned his head and neck. His arms moved to pushup position, elbow deep, his back muscles defined through his soaked white fly-fishing shirt as he strained to lift himself and the five-inch-diameter tree upward. He collapsed face-first, drowning in the muck of the swamp.

Charles tried to lift the tree with his hands, but it was too heavy and the rain made it too slick to keep a grip. On his knees, he wedged himself next to Winn and drove his arms down under the tree like a forklift, heaving with his back. His wounded shoulder screamed in protest. Winn, blinded by the muck, sensed the shift, for up he came out of the mire, and with a herculean effort pushed himself from under the tree. Both men collapsed on their backs, Winn swearing as he hit the ground.

A well-timed wave of water rained down on them like surf breaking against a seawall; the colossal drops struck their faces and chests with the impact of paintballs fired at close range. An additional unwelcome beating, but at least their pursuers couldn't advance toward them, or properly aim their weapons. Pulverizing rain saved them even as it tried to drown them.

After crawling, rolling, and squirming down a slope that was half waterfall and half mudslide, they stood, but stayed low while bullets fired at random flew overhead. Charles followed behind Winn, weaving along a path unsuitable even for animals. He glanced over his bleeding shoulder toward the ridge behind: invisible, grayed, and obscured by the whipping water that pounded into his eyes. The rain was severe and substantial and it displaced much of the air, so much so that it was hard to breathe.

Up one hill, and then another hill, the rain subsiding, they coursed, never slowing down—running, stumbling, sometimes falling, with pain and armed men driving them on. It took twenty minutes to come in sight of the road and TJ's Land Cruiser. Spackled with brick-red dirt, it beckoned, wheels one-fourth buried. The road was semi-functional in dry season. But now the flood from the sky unveiled the true capacity of the rainy season by transforming the road into a lethargic mud river. It was too thick and shallow for a boat, but optimal for embedding a car.

Winn threw himself into the driver's seat.

The car's four-wheel drive gained traction before Charles's pulled his right foot inside. Mud sprayed up from the tire into his face. Fire-hot shocks screamed through his shoulder as he reached and then pulled the door closed. It was just pain—not a good thing, but a reassuring proof he was still alive.

"What did you see in that building that was important enough that they came at you shooting? Did you find the smoking gun?"

The Land Cruiser bounced so radically that Charles could not grasp the unbuckled seatbelt as his head smacked against the roof. "Lots of smoking guns. All aimed at me!"

"Hey kid, I was there too."

Charles grimaced, embarrassed at not having asked if Xander was okay.

"I'm fine. Except for a hole that I didn't have in me this morning."

"You got shot?"

The car bounced over a series of rivulet-flooded ridges. "Yep. In the ass. Hurts like hell every… time… we… hit a… bump."

Charles saw him wince with each impact. "I'm sorry, Xander. The way you were moving, I had no idea."

"It's just pain, and adrenalin is a pretty good anesthetic for a while. Pain isn't fatal." He sucked in his breath as the car barreled down a slope not meant for any vehicle at this time of year. Charles managed to buckle up just in time. Even the trail-rated suspension of the large Toyota complained loudly as it hit bottom and flattened out its springs. For all his stoicism, Winn groaned even louder than the car. He turned hard right as they intersected the road to Gbarngeda. It too was unpaved, but its surface of compressed rocks was silky smooth compared to the trail's muck and ravines. He floored the accelerator and played the steering wheel as the truck fishtailed.

"Now you're just having fun," Charles shouted over the scream of the engine and the pounding rain as he grabbed the vehicle's oh-shit handle above his head even tighter, despite the pain that it caused.

"Must have fun.… It may be the whole point of life." Winn smiled, with crow's-feet making his eyes gleam with devilish intent. He winked, but he winced at the same time.

Charles asked, "Where are we going? We'll need to get stitched up."

"We'll go high end. We're going on a cruise ship."

"Say what?"

"You'll see." Winn squirmed in his seat and winced again.

Charles twisted, reached into the back seat, and wrenched a greasy towel from under a box of tools. He gave it to Winn, who wiped the mud off his unshaven face and then the back of his head. As he handed it back, Charles saw that it was covered with more than mud and grease. There was blood, and a lot of it.

"Umm, Xander? You're bleeding."

Winn looked at the towel, his hard face perplexed. He reached his hand up to the back of his head, rubbed around for a moment, winced again, pulled it away, and looked at his shining red fingers. "Skull fracture, kid. Damn tree."

"Neck okay?"

"Neck is fine. Skull fracture this deep though means my brain got squished. That explains things."

"Explains what?"

"Why I have a screaming headache. Why I need to vomit and want to pass out."

Indeed Winn looked like he was heading downhill fast. From what Charles saw through the muck coating his skin, Winn had lost all color from his face.

Winn pulled the car to a stop, the tires sliding and skidding in the mud, the car not far from falling off the road.

"Kid. You drive. As fast as you can." He opened his door and staggered around the car, meeting Charles by the hood. "There's nothing the physician assistant at the Gbarngeda clinic can do for me. Stay on this road. It will take us to the Freeport, just west of Adamstown. The *Africa Grace* is there. American surgeons. If I pass out, they'll need to operate on me. In this country, that's the best chance I have."

He stumbled. Charles, heart pounding, grabbed his new friend under the arm and guided him toward the passenger seat. Winn pulled his feet into the car. Then, with his last strength and the last of his consciousness, he embraced Charles before slumping forward. Charles pushed Winn's limp torso back against the seat, buckled him in, and moments later hit fifty miles per hour on a road safe only at twenty-five. He dodged water-filled potholes that, if hit, could flatten a tire or break an axle. He slammed on his brakes to avoid flowing streams of uncertain depth that crossed the road. He sped though Gbarngeda, ignoring everything and everyone. He sped through the rural villages, rudely spraying mud from his tires onto the thatch-roofed huts and anyone who was out during any break of the rains. He drove on and on, for hours. He raced through the late afternoon, hoping he was still on the right road. The rain did let up, but Winn never stirred.

Charles recoiled at the thought of losing a friend before knowing much more than his name. He realized once again how little he knew about Xander Winn. Nothing at all, really.

Before sunset he approached the outskirts of Adamstown, a trip accomplished in perhaps a record time. He flew down the only road he knew, hoping he would recognize the entrance to the port he had only seen in passing once, a few days before. There was electricity here. He saw a billboard that had previously caught his eye because it proclaimed a remarkable message: "Do Not Rape. She could be your mother." This spoke to the displaced boy soldiers, now adult males, who were taken to war so young that they might not recognize their own mothers. The impact was potent and sick.

A high wall surrounded the whole of the Freeport. The single visible entrance had a barrier and a guardhouse. He had no pass, no letter, no official documents. But he had money. He looked at Winn, out cold still, hopefully breathing. "I hope they let us in—but we're going in one way or another," Charles said to him, wishing he would get a response.

He stopped the Land Cruiser, rolled down the window, and appraised the thin black guard dressed in camouflage utilities. He had a scowl, but no gun.

"What you want?" the guard demanded.

"My friend is badly injured. He's unconscious."

The guard stooped to peer through the window at Winn.

"Where you go?"

"The *Africa Grace*. He needs an operation."

"Why you no go to hospital?"

"*Africa Grace* is a hospital. American doctors."

"Are you American?"

"I am. He's Dutch."

"You cannot come into the port. No access."

"We have to or he will die!"

The guard shrugged.

Plan A wasn't working. Time for Plan B. Charles pulled out a twenty-dollar US bill. "I have to bring him to the *Africa Grace*."

The guard glared into Charles's eyes: his face twisted, stern, angry. Frustrated, annoyed, and even angrier, Charles didn't relish the thought of smashing through the gate, but he dropped the shifter into first, about to execute Plan C. Then the guard's face relaxed and a broad smile appeared, displaying a set of perfect, evenly spaced white teeth, as he appraised the small fortune he'd just come into. "My friend. My friend.

Go on, then. Hurry to help your friend. Pier 3. You cannot miss it. The ship is red. Hurry."

A wave of relief. The gate lifted, and Charles accelerated up a broad, flawlessly paved road between metal warehouses. He couldn't yet see the bay or ships, just never-ending corrugated steel walls.

He smashed the brakes in order to slow in time for a turn marked "Pier 3." His destination appeared: white superstructure, red hull, a huge old ferry converted to a hospital ship. Financed by a foreign charity, they provided free care in countries with few doctors but plenty of sickness.

Night hits quick and hard near the equator. The red hull now reflected the setting red sun as it cast a dark crimson patina on the gray clouds above and the white skins of the three people pushing a stretcher down the gangway. They rushed to greet Charles and the unconscious Winn as Charles brought the car to a halt. Charles sent a mental note of gratitude to the guard at the gate, who must have called ahead. Twenty dollars was probably more than he earned in a week. So much for money being the root of all evil.

A young woman in light-green scrubs with long blond hair yanked opened the passenger door and reached in to unbuckle Winn. "Sir, sir, are you awake?" She squeezed his shoulder firmly and took his pulse at his neck. Winn groaned. She pried open an eyelid and shined a flashlight into it. "He's barely responsive. Pulse is slow." Then to Charles without looking, "What happened?" Charles could not place the accent of her fluent English.

"A tree fell on his head," Charles answered, still in the driver's seat. "And he got shot in his backside... his butt." Saying he had been shot in the ass did not sound Christian, and the *Africa Grace* was a Christian hospital ship.

"Need a C-collar here!" she called over her shoulder. In thirty seconds the device was supporting Winn's head upright.

She weighed about half of Winn's two-hundred-pounds, but nonetheless managed to pull his unconscious body toward her small frame and lever him onto the stretcher as the male orderlies moved to help.

"Bring him up head first!" the girl commanded the men. "We don't know what is going on in his skull."

The men started running him up the gangway, the woman in scrubs and Charles just behind.

Charles wanted to supply as much helpful information as he could. "He's about fifty years old, I think."

"Is he otherwise healthy?" she asked, not looking back.

"As far as I know. But I might not know. He's fit though."

"How long ago was he injured?"

"Over four hours ago. He lost consciousness about thirty minutes after the tree fell on him. Not right away. Then it was a long drive out of the bush."

"What's his name?" She reached the ship proper with Charles two strides behind.

Charles hesitated. She heard more than saw his hesitation.

"Okay, well then, what's *your* name?" she tried, irritation evident.

Charles didn't answer.

"Well, I'm Caroline." She led him through to the room that served as a sort of emergency department. Four orderlies transferred Winn to a stronger and less mobile bed. It wasn't a smooth move—almost a throw, really, but it was professionally accomplished. Several medical personnel took their positions and began working Winn over—cutting clothes off, sticking electrodes to his skin, someone near his head setting up to perform a procedure.

Caroline repeated what she had learned from Charles to the man standing by Winn's feet, also in scrubs, but sporting a long white coat and a stethoscope. He was the only one attired in the highest symbols of medical authority. He watched his team perform a drill they knew well. Two infused fluids and medications into Winn's arms, another pried open his mouth and inserted a breathing tube.

"Let's let the team work," she said to Charles.

Caroline led Charles out through another door, down a hallway, and out to the other side of the ship. The sun merged with the horizon. Only crimson light penetrated the thick atmosphere. Blue and green paint on the buildings and containers looked black as the night consumed the port, one color at a time. Caroline's blond hair now glowed red, the only color of the spectrum not stolen away from the sinking sun.

She looked at Charles, probably for the first time. Charles watched as her face transitioned from an indifferent professional competence to something more delicate and feminine while the evening breeze moved through her hair. A few strands brushed against Charles's bare arm. Her eyes fell first, then she turned away, toward the rail. Charles did the same. They said nothing as they watched the sun sink into the water. The top rim of the orb met the sea and turned a bright green, just for a moment, before slipping below the waves. Darkness overwhelmed Gondwana.

After Action Assessment

"WHO the hell was there, Harry?" Smolderhof shouted through clenched teeth. The rain fell hard, a deafening cacophony on the tin roof of the shack.

"A white man. We don't know who. Sure as hell not that old cripple or one of those Euro-weenies. We got those Frenchmen back to Adamstown—already on their plane home. It must have been that kid, Charles Knight. He was creeping around in Gbarngeda, asking questions, yah. And I thought I saw him pocketing some of the drill core."

Harry's accent and penchant for slang developed as a consequence of growing up on a Rhodesian farm and then joining the country's military during its long, and ultimately futile, war against its rebels in the '70s. His physique resulted from the combination of genetics and spending months at a time in the bush, humping an eight-pound FAL and a sixty-pound pack. His was a hard, rope-like body, not the smooth, sculpted, and bulky musculature many US Marines sport from hours of pumping iron in a gym. He kept his attitude taut and muscular as well, accentuated by a mouth distorted with a tortured grin: not a congenial smile, but the rictus of a death's head. It had appeared that way for much of his almost sixty years. African bush wars impart a certain outlook.

"Who was on guard, Harry?"

"Not my men. Two of the locals Ollie found. Trigger-happy kaffirs didn't even ask what the guy was doing there. They peppered the place. Emptied three mags each." Harry, through long experience, was a one shot, one kill type of operator, and often preferred a well-placed knife blade because it could be equally effective while silent. But more to the point, he would have politely asked who the interloper was and what he was doing on their hidden property before shooting them.

"Shit, the gunshots will have been heard by everyone in town!" Smolderhof shouted. "Must have freaked everyone in Gbarngeda out of their gourds. How are you gonna deal with that?"

Ollie Shifflett always wheezed, but he found the breath to say, "It was a raging downpour, and it's three miles from town. No one heard anything."

"Well, that's a small positive," said Smolderhof without any evidence of being pleased. "So how the fuck do they miss a guy when they fire a hundred and eighty rounds?"

"Who said they missed?"

"They missed the vital parts, or we'd have a body! You look around real good?"

Harry didn't like what that implied about his competence, and his expression reflected that fact. Over the years, he had learned to stay calm in the face of ignorant people who were foolishly angry. "You know what it's like this time of year. Flooded everywhere, so it's impossible to track anything. But no. There's no body."

Smolderhof punched the steel wall of the shack. "How much time did he have at the machine?" He glared at Ollie Shifflett, the sickly designer of their top-secret device.

The balding little chemist shook his head and replied with evident confidence, "Not enough time for anyone to figure out that it's a colloid infuser, Dan."

Smolderhof dropped his shoulders. He sat down on a moldy canvas director's chair and stared at his knees, then shook his head. He looked up at Harry. "We can't count on that. There's too much at stake to take chances."

"Any others scheduled to come through?" Harry asked.

"God I hope not. Maybe with the Burke deal finalized, Washerman will finally stop sending investors."

Shifflett said, "Who knows who could sneak in with one of those groups."

Harry agreed. "Make sure no one else comes."

Smolderhof spat back, "I don't control that. Washerman's been focused on the Burke deal for the last month, and the junkets have been on autopilot. Hell, he says yes to everyone who wants to come. He said yes to that damn kid."

"Having visitors was always a bad idea."

"Dammit, I know that. But Washerman doesn't know it, and it's got to stay that way. What happens in Banga stays in Banga."

Washerman could give a much more compelling presentation, with no chance of a misstep, if he was entirely sincere in his belief that Banga actually had more than a hundred million ounces of high-grade gold.

Harry reiterated his point sternly. "But no more investor jaunts, Dan. You make sure of it."

Smolderhof replied, "It won't matter soon. Now it's Burke, and *their* timing, that matters."

"When are they going to get here?"

"I don't know. But I can't imagine they'll move too fast, if that's what you mean. We've got time." He said this uncertainly. "We better have time." Smolderhof turned to Harry. "What about Knight?""

Harry shook his head slowly. "People don't go tramping through the jungle in the rain unless they're after something."

"He's just a kid. He's a penny ante investor. Doesn't know his ass from his elbow."

Harry held both his hands up, palms down. "Don't count on that. We don't know who he is, or why he's here. Things often aren't as they seem...."

Smolderhof sneered then, a bitter grin, acknowledging the irony of Harry's observation. Their whole current existence, their whole operation, was based on nothing being as it seemed. "Do we know anything else about Knight?"

Harry replied, "I just know what he told me when we were talking yesterday. Twenty-something years old. American. He says he's a new speculator. He called himself that—a speculator. Like he was proud of himself. This is his first trip to Africa. He's here alone. An American his age is in over his head in this shithole. I bet he is full of shit himself too. *Speculator*, hah! He just learned how to wipe his own ass."

Unlike most people, Harry wasn't put off by the idea of a speculator. Most people saw a speculator only as someone who profits from crises and financial upsets, who ruins life for the average person. It seemed like the financial equivalent of his own profession. Perhaps this Charles Knight thought of a speculator like Harry saw himself—as a moral hero, doing what everyone needed when no one else was able or prepared. Speculators might set aside food before a famine, so they could make it available—at a significant profit—to those less prudent. They carefully set aside money to buy property when others desperately needed cash. A speculator only took advantage of chaos in the same way as a doctor might take advantage of a sickness or an injury, earning a living by healing a disease he didn't cause but had the foresight to know was coming. But, for some reason, the public saw doctors as always good and speculators as always bad.

Ollie Shifflett shook his head. "That kid may not know his ass from his elbow. But whether or not he's full of shit, he's the first person to come near the colloid infuser."

Smolderhof took a moment to reply. "He's probably just a kid who's read too many adventure novels. The problem is when he gets back home, all bloodied and cocky and talkative. I don't want to risk any rumors."

Harry shrugged. "Well, then there is only one option."

Smolderhof replied quickly this time, without hesitation, decision made. "I agree. At this point, it's better to be safe than sorry. Find Knight. Find out if it was him. If it was, disappear him."

8

The Floating Hospital

DESPITE being dog-tired, Charles would barely sleep that first night on the *Africa Grace*. He tried to rest, but his thoughts overflowed, racing through a combination of the recent trauma and distant memories.

He saw his little brother, full of naive hope the way kids are, smiling as he cast his line into the river bordering the far end of their ranch.

He saw his father: young, still with ambition, emulating a Jimmy Stewart character, trying to ensure that only truth graced the pages of his newspaper. His father's idealism faded as he came to realize that truth was often both hard to determine and dangerous to know—and not necessarily very profitable. Hearst had built an empire based on titillation and entertainment, where truth endured only as an arbitrary and optional addition.

He saw his mother, still joyous and youthful when he was a toddler. The dream twisted into a nightmare, as tentacles of darkness crept across the sky, smothering the mountains and the river like ink from a squid and suffocating her. It was like listening to a country-and-western singer, crooning in ultraslow motion over the years, a litany of disappointments while entropy wore her down.

He finally emerged from the half-sleep in midmorning, washed up, and found the emergency room where he'd left Xander. Caroline told him that Xander was out of surgery and stable. She looked at him, indicated he should sit, and cleaned his wound again, finding another shard of tree bark that had worked its way to the surface during his fit-ful attempt at sleep. There was no way to fully anesthetize the area; the damage was too high up to use an intravenous block with a tourniquet, so everything was done with local anesthesia, and each shot of the stuff not only burned, but seemed only marginally effective against the pain. When she hosed out the hole in his shoulder with saline, it felt like a chainsaw.

"Sorry. Your body is all inflamed from the latex that was stuck in the wound. The stuff is sticky; it was hard to remove last night. It'll be nasty if we don't keep the wound clean."

"Thanks," he said through gritted teeth.

"I'm going to sew this up for you, but I can't guarantee it will work. If this gets infected, it'll have to be opened back up again to drain. You'll end up with some manly scar either way."

"Can you tattoo on top of a scar?" Charles said in jest. Growing up in Montana, he primarily associated body ink with identifying livestock.

"I don't know," Caroline replied, not seeming to care. "Do you have any tattoos?"

"Not yet. I'm not sure I've done anything to warrant them." Charles thought of a man he had met less than a week ago, whose short-sleeved shirt disclosed a discrete tattoo on his forearm. It looked like a feathered arm holding a short sword. A conversation over a few drinks revealed that this Polish man, whose name was Bazyli, formerly served as a French Foreign Legionnaire. Charles had never understood why someone would want to advertise his group affiliation for life, until he saw the pride on this man's face and heard of the camaraderie and of the dangers that he and his fellow Legionnaires had faced together. Bazyli's identity had become closely tied to those of his fellow soldiers. Perhaps that's why tattoos were big with the military, prison inmates, and outlaw bikers.

Bazyli was passing through Adamstown on the way to a freelance contract in Guinea. He took a couple of hours out of his day and accepted seven drinks to share his seemingly endless accounts of humor and horror. "If you had any prior military experience, I'd invite you to come up with me. We're just training people, and I know they could use a few more instructors." A few years back, Charles had considered joining the US Marines as he listened to their recruitment ads, which promised adventure and travel. He enjoyed war movies, which also amounted to recruitment ads. But he was put off by the brutality and the prospect of blindly taking orders to kill possibly innocent people for some politician's concept of the "greater good"—or for some trivial, undefined purpose.

Caroline engaged in her conscientious work, a process of closing the gash with two layers of sutures. "I'm telling you, this is a risk, closing it at all."

"Okay. It's my risk, and I'll take it. You're off the hook." It sounded less grateful than he felt, so he added with an appreciative smile, "I trust you."

"It's really up to your immune system. But you'll need to take the antibiotics we give you."

"Yes, ma'am." He tried again to place her accent. European somewhere. Even as she bent over her work, her posture was perfect. It did not look forced. She simply held her body naturally in a position that seemed... what was it? *Regal*, perhaps.

Royalty: the inbred progeny of successful marauders. Kings and princes were rarely benevolent but rather were thugs who lived only by stealing from their subjects and making war against adjacent kingdoms. Yet so many people still placed them on pedestals. It seemed a flaw in human nature that they were even tolerated, much less revered. Charles caught himself in his thoughts: don't judge them all together. Whether born a prince or a pauper, it was all luck of the draw. An accident of birth. One's character, however, was largely one's own creation.

He asked, "What's your story?" with his smile the result of faint anxiety.

"My story? I don't have a story. I just work here."

"You're not a doctor, though."

"No."

"Why are you here?"

"I'm here to sew you up." She pulled on the thread, causing a wince, and deftly flipped her needle driver. She began twisting the suture through her fingers repeatedly, a cascade of knots magically appearing.

"How long have you been on board the *Africa Grace*?"

"About nine months. They give me a lot of responsibility here. It's fun." Fun to many women Caroline's age meant buying clothes and flirting in bars. This woman was different, and Charles liked different.

"Where were you before?"

"The ship came in from Togo. We were there for four months. Now here for the last couple of months. There's no shortage of work. Every morning, we get a busload of people from a clinic we set up at the government hospital in the city."

She told him about that hospital, about the halls filled with cots, the lines of people camping overnight in the usually vain hope of seeing a doctor. Most of the Gondwanan doctors had fled the country during the wars to seek safer and greener pastures. Even now the few doctors who graduated from what passed for a medical school in Adamstown had to leave the country to get their postgraduate training. Most never returned.

In the city, there was only one x-ray machine. It only occasionally worked. And although the operating rooms were screened off from the outside, wind and dust blew right through, along with an occasional cat.

"There's this one government hospital that gets all of the United States' foreign aid because it's named after one of your recent ex-presidents, but I can't see where the money goes. There are other hospitals around that do better despite getting no money infusions. But they are private. Anyhow, it's better on the ship here. The patients come, our surgeons operate, our dentist extracts teeth, the nurses make sure everything goes smoothly. I help out with whatever needs to be done." She padded his sutured wound with a soaked gauze sponge, cleaning off the blood and the yellow iodine sterilizing fluid. "And for the moment, that is you."

"It's kind of you to do all this. Do you mind if I ask again? Where were you before?"

Caroline sighed. "Four years in the US, at Princeton, majoring in political science. I learned some things, I suppose. But I wanted to learn something more valuable, go someplace unusual, do something different. My family always has done things a bit differently than most. So I came here."

"What's next for you?"

"I've been thinking about medical school."

"More school, huh? How did that work for you before?"

"I see your point. I probably do more lifesaving medical work here on this ship than most doctors do back home. But you need a piece of paper...."

"You've helped me without the piece of paper." Charles sat up on the stretcher, moved his shoulder gently around and winced again. "Okay, this is going to hurt for a while, huh?" The adrenalin had long since worn off.

"I'll get you something to keep your arm comfortable. A pain pill and a sling. You'll be fine."

Charles followed her with his eyes as she moved over to a set of steel drawers. She was very slender, but not the thin of a malnourished heroin-chic model. She had one of those metabolisms, or genetically determined body forms, or the right microbes in her gut, that would always allow her to stay slim. Her toned arms did not exhibit the fine chicken-feather hair of anorexics. She had a persistent poise and calm about her, and walked with effortless grace.

She crouched down to look through one drawer after another. He wanted to watch her as her scrub shirt lifted up to expose lightly tanned skin, an enticing dimple on either side of her lower back. But it felt awkward, almost like trespassing. So he reluctantly looked away, allowing her the modesty she was too busy to worry about.

She turned and walked back, smiling. "I found one finally. Here's a sling." Her eyes gleamed a shimmering blue, the eyebrows mostly blond like her hair, freckles across her nose. An angel. No, he didn't believe in angels. A Florence Nightingale.

She reached around his back with the sling, her face close to his cheek. Then her eyes caught his, curious, neither challenging nor cowed. She glanced down at his arm, and then briefly at her own hands. She positioned the cloth of the sling under his elbow, and then reached both her hands behind his neck, as if she were dancing with him. She adjusted the Velcro of the strap so his arm would be free of any strain. Her breath enticed him. Did she touch his neck more than she needed to?

"Are you going to tell us your name, and the name of your friend?"

"I'm sorry. I can't tell you his name."

"Is that because you don't know his name?"

"No. I think I know his name. But it's for him to tell you, not for me."

Caroline nodded. "His name is that important?"

"I don't know. But it may be. It may be dangerous for anyone to know who he is."

76

"Someone was shooting at him, so someone doesn't like him."

"Actually, they were shooting at both of us."

"Is that how this tree got into your shoulder?"

"Someone shooting at me hit the tree."

"Where *were* you? What are you involved in?"

Caroline stared at him hard, the way his mother used to when his independence tested dangerous boundaries.

He didn't answer right away; he kept his eyes downcast. He wanted to tell her, to trust that she would keep it quiet. But doing so would place Xander at risk too, and he had no right. His head popped up and he looked intently into her eyes. "I saw something I shouldn't have seen."

"Can you tell me what it was?"

"I don't know for sure, but I have an idea."

"What do you think you saw?"

"A machine. A machine out there in the bush. A machine that may be worth three billion dollars."

*   *   *

"Three billion dollars? That's what the guy said?"

"That's what he said." Caroline picked up a piece of bread with peanut butter and took a small bite. Despite the fact that peanuts grew everywhere in West Africa, the peanut butter was made in the US; it seemed nothing was manufactured in this part of the world other than email offers from Nigerian princes to share millions of dollars with anyone who would advance them a few thousand. She sat across from a shorter, somewhat-stocky woman, also in scrubs, whose face, though pretty, reflected the rough wisdom obtained by making the best of a roller-coaster life that featured hardship. Caroline had grown to love Louise, twenty years her senior. She was discreet by nature, a worthy confidant for a young woman in Caroline's position. Women born and raised in Boston tended to a skeptical outlook that is perhaps better described as *shrewd*.

"Look, princess, what is there in this place—other than you and I of course— that could possibly be worth three billion dollars?" Louise kept her voice low, a street-smart habit she'd picked up for when money was involved. No one would overhear. "This whole country isn't worth that. You must have overdosed him on pain meds."

77

"I don't know. He hasn't told me much. Not even his name."

"He's in trouble with the law?"

"What law? The law of the bush?"

"Guns aren't allowed in Gondwana. Not even the military has many. And yet his friend was shot. Only the Special Police Unit has guns here. Maybe they're after him. Maybe he's wanted by the SPU?"

Caroline thought about that for a moment before saying, "Being a fugitive from the police doesn't mean he's a criminal, certainly not here in Africa."

"Not anywhere anymore," Louise added. "Maybe he's into drugs? He's a young American after all, hanging out in West Africa. What's he doing here, Caroline?"

"I'm a young European in West Africa. What am *I* doing here?"

"Not trafficking drugs, I hope. Your mother wouldn't be too thrilled about it if you were."

Louise wasn't trying to sound righteous. She had tried lots of drugs over the years, including cocaine, heroin, and LSD, and had openly told Caroline that any concern she had was not that they were illegal. She knew from personal experience that drugs left one open to unpleasant interactions with both the local police and the various miscreants with whom they would incarcerate you. People in the drug scene tended to either lack, or lose, self-control, commonly to the point of destroying both themselves and everyone around them.

Caroline understood that Louise's concern arose out of fondness for her. She was the youngest child and accustomed to the role of black sheep. Her family expected her to behave herself, at least in public, but she didn't always comply. She had narrowly avoided the tabloids on one occasion, saved only by a combination of promises and threats her mother made to the publisher of the relevant rag. It was probably the only reason her parents had not objected to her trip on the *Africa Grace*. On this ship, she was out of sight, out of mind, and she might even, her mother thought, grow up.

She said, "He is no more a drug dealer type than I am."

"Yes, but people aren't shooting at you."

"There is that difference...."

"Okay, so either he's a fugitive from the police, or he's escaping someone else who wants him dead, and he doesn't want word getting out that he's here. Being near him is dangerous for you, Caroline. You know that."

Disappointment briefly clouded Caroline's eyes. "I know."

"He'll tell you soon enough why someone was trying to kill him," Louise said. "Boys can't keep secrets very well. At least not about things they're proud of."

"Let's make sure word about him doesn't get out." Caroline held her expression firm.

Louise shook her head with a smirk. "Caroline. An injured, bleeding, unconscious white man was driven through the main gate at the Freeport, in the middle of the blackest city in the world. And you think people won't hear about it?"

That bit of obvious logic had escaped her. Caroline's face took on a look of concern, tinged with fear. "We need to tell the captain, don't we?"

"Umm, yes, girl. We, and by that I mean *you*, certainly need to talk to the captain."

9

Sabina, Now of the IRS

SABINA Heidel's worn black armchair squeaked as she spun around. The Internal Revenue Service had purchased the thing along with ten thousand others. Perhaps some powerful committee chairman awarded the contract to a friend or relative. Or to a big donor to the current occupant of the Oval Office. It's how things had been done since the invention of government in ancient Sumer. But it was not her job to find out how the government cheats the people. It was her job to find out how the people cheat the government.

Some snide bastard in a bar had recently asked her if the victim of a robbery should be accused of cheating the thief if he successfully hid his valuables. The guy had actually compared the IRS to a common thief! Sabina had used her well-practiced smile to acquire his business card, and then arranged an audit for him: people with unpatriotic views should be punished. Her new agency existed in part as a convenient tool to harass political or ideological enemies. Why confront them directly when you could destroy them covertly?

Sabina was partway through her year at the IRS under the vice president's Government Efficiency Enhancement Initiative, his pet project to raise his own visibility. She had been a first-round *volunteer*, actually the very first interagency personnel transferee. The vice president suddenly seemed interested in her: she would be a fine poster girl for what everyone mockingly referred to as the "VP's GEE, I…"

Prior to this temporary transfer, she had worked at the Securities and Exchange Commission—an excellent place to meet useful and powerful people. But that could also be said of the IRS. She would make good use of this year, and turn the lemon she'd been handed into lemonade.

Her SEC boss, an envious witch, had nominated her as a clever and convenient way to get rid of her. Sabina, who readily adapted to the ways of the bureaucratic snake pit, accepted the assignment like a practiced opportunist: after all, her own father sat right near the top of the IRS bureaucracy. Sabina performed her insignificant work at the IRS with the same arrogance that characterized her exemplary performance at the SEC. She did not think in terms of right or wrong. The object here was results, by whatever means necessary. Few IRS employees acknowledged that their purpose was to "get" people, to take something from them rather than to create any value for them. But the subconscious reality nonetheless spawned a defensive attitude among them. Sabina, however, embraced the intrinsic nature of the job and disdained those who didn't.

The IRS tended to draw a certain personality type: in-the-box, self-righteous, and anxious to cut others down at the knees. The psychological ambiance of the Service agreed with her. She resented those who rose to wealth or power on their own terms. They seemed crass, bourgeois, and illiberal. There *should* be a hereditary elite, cultured and refined, above the fray of manufacturing or trading. It was why she liked what she'd read about feudal Europe and the caste system in India. Wealth and power should naturally accrue to the right kind of people. She excelled at being the right kind of person.

Power, in Sabina's world, came from contacts, people already in power, people she could use to gain more power. Assisted by her unequivocally good looks and unrestrained by anachronistic morality, she was in her element here.

The crony system worked well for those on the inside. It would work well for her, as it kept expanding forever. She felt comfortable among people skilled in controlling and manipulating people more than things. Some compared the world to a giant circle jerk where everyone tried to live at the expense of everyone else. But Sabina knew life to be a triumph of the best and brightest over the little people.

She ignored the stale arguments made against regulatory agencies, and lauded the industry that had arisen to capitalize on the largess of the state. Books taught you how to apply for free cash. Filling out government forms was much easier than supplying the needs and wants of others. It's only natural for organisms to seek sustenance in the easiest way. The ever-enlarging government trough provided the easiest chow. Voting accomplished nothing other than to increase the size of the trough.

So many groups, businesses, or associations constantly cashed in on the expanded power of Washington. So why shouldn't she? The Washington magnet attracted all those who lived off the hydrant of money gushing from the Treasury and the Federal Reserve—and those who wanted to have as much say as possible over the flood of regulations gushing forth from the agencies assigned to control every aspect of life and the economy. Pity the poor working fool in the hinterland who only got what trickled down after the Washington insiders drank their fill of money. The working fool received accolades consisting only of volumes of regulations and obligations.

Still, obviously, a select few had the control, and should be rewarded by this juggernaut. The indirect and delayed consequences of this system, however severe, were problems for the future, for the children. Sabina focused on her own prospects, her own future. After all, she actively disliked children—even after they grew up.

Sabina intuitively understood the way the system worked, and had preternatural skills to navigate within it. She concerned herself only with the tactical, not the ethical: should she choose a path that might augment her position and power over others, and therefore later lead to more money? Or should she direct her attention primarily toward money, which would help her later acquire more power and a higher position?

The people she was tasked to "get" were small fry. So far her brief period of work at the IRS seemed unfathomably pointless, menial, and below the qualifications of an Ivy League graduate. Her coworkers— mundane loafs all—were easily sated by the security and fat benefits of a government job to be held only until their early retirement. She didn't understand them. Didn't all their student loans constitute a social contract, assuring graduates prestigious, as well as high-paying, jobs? Didn't her expertise in social justice and gender studies entitle her to more authority? Had it not been for her dad's pull, she might not even have acquired her first job at the SEC. She might be waiting tables, tricking for an outcall service, or playing video games while living in her mother's basement like so many of her former classmates.

It wasn't like she was a princess with the world given to her for free.

At the SEC, she targeted dozens of rich people dealing in millions of dollars. At the IRS, the targets assigned to her consisted of millions of poor people dealing with dozens of dollars. But the IRS offered other advantages.

Most of the Service's hundred thousand employees just shuffled paper and added numbers, but some got tasked with enforcing the tax law in the field. The revenue was important, but tax laws also engineered society and coerced desired behavior. The US Code contained thousands of contradictory laws that the FBI could selectively enforce, enough that anyone could be indicted as an inadvertent criminal. But the IRS excelled even beyond the FBI in regard to pressuring politically unreliable groups and individuals, because almost everybody filed taxes. And the IRS not only tried you in their own administrative courts but considered you guilty until proven innocent. The IRS provided an important component of the Beltway ecosystem, and Sabina could see the organization's value and usefulness, even as she chafed at the trivial tasks assigned her.

She shook her head and glanced down at the piles of thousands of nearly identical falsified tax returns that littered her desk and floor. People once denied revenue to the government by *not* filing tax returns. Now tens of thousands took it to the next step by filing tax returns to request a refund of taxes never withheld. With 200 million returns filed every year, it was easy to file returns for a nonexistent person—or a real person, for that matter—and receive a "refund" check. Many variations on the theme existed, and one-time efforts by careful individuals were impossible to track.

But these returns on her floor were cookie cuttered for convenience in mass production. A stolen Social Security number with early filing to beat the real filer's return to the IRS computer systems consistently served as one common denominator, although an identity created out of whole cloth would work equally well. All had a similar set of income and exemption numbers—a relatively small income, a big family, a big mortgage, and two kids in college.

The tax credits, exemptions, and deductions added up. These returns all ended up with a tax situation in which the filer, whether real or imagined, was entitled to a five- or ten-thousand-dollar refund, and sometimes more. She rolled her eyes at the utter incompetence of both the writers of the tax code and her fellow bureaucrats who enforced it. The code was designed to manipulate the voting population with government's supposed largess, but instead groups had turned the system on its head, using government as a source of income by filing false returns on an industrial scale.

While criminal groups and freelancers perfected variations on the false-return scheme, the IRS staff had trouble getting the computer to send even a harshly worded notification, instead of a check, to the relevant PO box. Millions of dollars spent to capture these small scammers filled the coffers of temporary hires, who accomplished nothing; the Service caught up with only the most careless amateurs. But, on the bright side, the desperately needed new IRS hires, temp or permanent, improved the national employment figures and therefore proved the efficacy of the president's jobs program and enhanced his power base. More directly relevant, extra IRS employees augmented their supervisors' importance and pay grades; the IRS needed such justifications to bolster their pleas to Congress for more personnel.

She averted her eyes from the piles on the floor and returned to her computer to deal with another subset of small people committing small crimes and violating arbitrary rules. Her first task today involved approving hundreds of notifications that the IRS would then send out to small businesses, each demanding immediate payment for back taxes on pain of asset seizure.

Some of the recipients would call to argue the matter, shouting through the phone at an IRS clerk. How pointless. Neither the Service itself nor any of its thousands of gray bureaucrats manning the inbound phone banks could possibly care less who lost their house or business. Of course most of the callers pleaded, bleating like whipped slaves, pointlessly appealing to the powerless clerks. Later, building up some after-the-fact courage, some callers might blow off steam by plotting retribution and revolution over drinks at the bar. But in the end, almost all the serfs paid what they were told they owed, plus a fat penalty, plus the above-market interest rate. In the universal sign of distress, they might adhere a postage stamp—an American flag with the word *Liberty*—upside down on the envelope that held their check to the IRS. If a bureaucracy were capable of amusement, the IRS would certainly laugh at such pitiful protests of little people.

Some protesters and jailhouse lawyers believed that the IRS, absent a court order, had no legal authority to compel them to do anything. But they lived in a legalistic dream world; the Service could levy wages or seize financial accounts with as little as an internally generated administrative summons. Some claimed that the constitutional prohibition against seizure of property without due process applied to the IRS. Some claimed that tax returns violated the Fifth Amendment prohibition against self-incrimination. Some claimed the Sixteenth Amendment, legalizing the income tax, was never properly ratified. Some claimed the income tax was illegal because the Constitution specified dollars, and Federal Reserve notes weren't true dollars. Some argued that only gain is taxable, not labor. Dozens of arguments of this nature circulated, all of which resulted in the IRS labeling the filer a tax protester, evader, a potential enemy of the state, and assuring that he would be subject to special attention, if not a jail term. Their protests wouldn't stop the IRS from seizing their bank accounts.

Only fools bent on martyrdom painted targets on their backs by confronting the Service directly, especially by using quaint arguments based on a constitution that over time had become profusely moth-eaten.

Sabina sighed, picked up her phone and dialed her father's line. Her father had made a career out of the Service, and now sat atop the totem pole. They did not share a last name, so no one knew that she was the daughter of the big man himself.

"Dr. Lichen's office," his administrative assistant announced.

"It's Sabina Heidel. Dr. Lichen, please." Her father had received his PhD in social justice without the benefit of either courses or dissertation. It was a favor from the president of a university that needed a very large contribution to their endowment. The gift materialized from a man whose investigation—and likely indictment—for tax evasion got quietly dropped at the same time Lichen received his PhD from the appreciative university. That event had occurred not long before Dr. Lichen became the Deputy Commissioner for Services and Enforcement, and the prestige the degree conferred helped him get there.

Services and Enforcement provided the razor sharp cutting edge as well as the bludgeon. In an Orwellian twist reminiscent of love being hate and war being peace, taxpayers became "customers," and the agency pretended to be a business providing services. But despite its name, the department was only about enforcement.

Although taxes were theoretically voluntary, threats of force assured that most customers paid them. The word *services* in the name provided a psychological effect that some thought essential. Expecting hundreds of millions of people to give up a large portion of their income strictly at gunpoint would be foolish. But if the payers believed it their duty, the right thing to do… if they received lifetime programming to think taxes are not only just, but unavoidable… then their cooperation could be assured. Elephants can be restrained with little more than twine, when taught as babies that ropes can't be broken and they'll be punished if they try.

But fear remained the two-by-four used to hit the taxpaying donkey between the eyes to get his attention. Her father taught her this explicitly, through his impromptu lectures at many a recent dinner, but also implicitly, through the control he exerted on her mother, whom he never married yet dominated. Her father himself seemed to feel no fear—rather strange for a short, slight, soft man. It was as if his brain did not have any pathways for fear. Nor did he suffer from guilt, shame, or empathy. Her father's brain was wired like that of a reptile. She admired him.

"Ms. Heidel, I'm happy to put you on his schedule," his secretary said. "Is it urgent?" She knew that the deputy commissioner tried to make space in his schedule for the attractive Sabina Heidel, although her lascivious suspicions as to why he did so were entirely incorrect.

"Yes. It *is* urgent." It wasn't urgent. But Sabina's desires should compel urgent responses from everyone.

"This afternoon at 4 p.m., he will have fifteen minutes free. Is that enough?"

"Yes, that will do. Thank you."

More papers to flip through, more notices to approve. Peon work. And she had had enough of it. At four o'clock she would insist on a promotion, a change of duties. She would demand to be a field agent. Although unusual at her level, a Form 8354 request to approve and fund an undercover operation could be made to the director of field operations, and would likely be granted. Particularly if her father insisted. An undercover field agent. Perhaps carrying a gun. The thought was sexually titillating. And if her father said no, she would throw a fit. The tantrums had always worked.

Sabina flipped her blond, almost platinum hair out of her eyes and started clicking "Approve" over and over again, as each accusatory "demand for immediate payment" letter to each taxpayer popped up on her computer screen. Even if the form letters were inaccurate, so what? Everybody was guilty of something if you looked hard enough.

Examining the letters wasted her valuable time. So she clicked "Approve" again without even looking.

10

A Viking Father Confessor

CAPTAIN Anders Freberg sported a gray beard, a pipe, a short-sleeved white cotton uniform, and a black Danish cap. He was the model of a sea captain from a long-gone era when they might have featured in tobacco or aftershave ads: tall, strong, straight, and with four gold bars on each black shoulder board. He could equally well have been the poster boy for any product marketed to women.

But Captain Freberg never considered his looks, because they were irrelevant to who he was: the competent and responsible captain—perhaps a bit too serious—of whatever ship he commanded. He had commanded the *Africa Grace* for just over a year. The ship spent most of its time in port, which grew dull, but on this expedition someone very important had entrusted him with a particularly precious cargo.

Long periods of time in African ports, alongside piers no less, came as a new experience for him. His ship tied to a pier usually meant exorbitant port fees every day, a situation anathema to a captain whose bonus depended on net profits. But the government owned this port and gave the *Africa Grace* free use of the pier for as long as they were willing to stay and provide medical care to the destitute locals—unless the port authorities needed the berth for a paying commercial vessel. His challenges now paled compared to navigating the high seas in a storm, but this slow time in port, with no cargo to load or unload, left him at liberty to read from his substantial onboard library, stocked heavily with ancient classics, light on current best sellers. Although people had learned much about how the physical world functioned over the last 2,500 years, few had learned very much about how their own minds functioned. The ancients may have lacked modern instruments, but, on the other hand, they could contemplate reality without modern distractions. Although the quality of material life had risen tremendously since ancient times, its spiritual, psychological, and political aspects stagnated.

Ample proof of that opinion, as well as some limited proof against it, lay just outside the protective hull of his ship.

Gondwana, like most African colonies, had gained independence in the 1960s, confident that democracy would guarantee prosperity and liberty for all. Bongo Bufahleh, the first of the presidents-for-life, was democratically elected; he was a great believer in the principle of "One man, one vote, one time." In the end Bufahleh was replaced by a man who believed in another dictum: "One shot. One kill." The next president-for-life led the little country's dozen or so mutually antagonistic tribes down the "Gondwanan Path to Social Equality and Prosperity." It worked out reasonably well for his own tribe but not so well for others, after a decade of what evolved into an increasingly tyrannical dictatorship. It was an inevitable progression; maybe only a strong man could keep the place from flying apart from centrifugal force. Gondwana, like every country on the continent, had been cobbled together in European boardrooms, its cultural and tribal boundaries ignored. Whoever seized control of the government used it as a personal piggybank.

Some army colonels saw an opening while the second president-for-life was visiting his money in Europe. They installed a new government. Before long, after agreeing to execute the remaining ministers and their cronies, but unable to divide the spoils peaceably, the colonels had their men fight it out in a tripartite battle that constituted the first round of decimation of the capital city. The winner crucified the two losers on the beach, one of them—it was a strictly personal grudge—split open at the breastbone and eviscerated, but not before his genitals were stuffed in his mouth. It served as a good warning to what was left of the opposition.

This next president-for-life had his priorities in order, setting up a new secret police force, drawn from his co-tribalists, who had more than a few scores to settle. Unfortunately for the new president, he was one of the scores that needed settling. Poison, served by one of his loyal followers, proved a painful death. Then came more years of civil war and yet another president-for-life. The intrusion of regional peacekeepers separated the warring tribes for a while, but the peacekeepers took advantage of their out-of-towner status to loot, rape, and pillage. The place turned into a free-fire zone; every building in Adamstown suffered multiple hits from small arms, RPGs, mortars, and light artillery. The wars devoured the infrastructure, almost all of it built in colonial days, and prevented its rebuilding. Looters disemboweled the hydroelectric dams for their copper, leaving electricity production to small private gas-powered generators. The sewage system failed. Effluent overflowed from congested septic tanks into miasmatic rivulets worming downslope into the rivers. Captured rainfall and dug wells provided typhoid-ridden water. The old asphalt roads reverted to bush.

Then the United Nations inserted itself to provide a new Pax Romana. Even though, in reality, it was mostly just an expensive club for aspiring government officials, the UN had a patina of moral authority: orchestrating world peace through cocktail parties and occasionally intervening in a failed state. The UN spent the next years ensuring that Gondwanans would secretly bury their armaments in the ground to avoid confiscation. That left little more than the ubiquitous machete as a means of routine mayhem. The people began to rebuild local infrastructure spontaneously, and businesses reappeared. The Chinese bought the mining, timber, and fishing concessions from the politicians, and some of that money trickled down to street level. The United States came in with hundreds of millions of dollars to build new bureaucracies. Free food depressed farm prices, bankrupting the farmers and driving them to the city to beg for the free food that made farming uneconomic.

Despite all this, the locals, at least on the surface, appeared happy and peaceful. You might think that decades of intermittent wars, brutality, and criminal mismanagement would have ingrained a myriad of bad habits in them. But the human animal is nothing if not adaptable to current conditions. Maybe they were still in shock from a lifetime of calamities interspersed with disasters and the occasional catastrophe. Maybe the regional gene pool had been temporarily depleted of the violent.

Contrary to the opinions of the UN and NGO types who overran the country in their SUVs, it wasn't a lack of sufficient government that led to all this dysfunction, but rather the cutthroat competition for control—ownership, really—*of* the government, followed by its exploitation....

Captain Freberg turned his mind from these thoughts to confront the ship's concerns. The watch officer had informed him of the emergency arrival of a jeep the previous evening, with its two gunshot-wound victims.

The chief medical officer's report indicated that the older patient—name, nationality, and occupation unknown—arrived close to death. They'd had to drill through his skull to remove blood from the surface of his brain, then put him into an induced coma to keep him from seizing or getting a fever, either of which, the doctor reported, could be devastating for him. After stabilizing his head trauma, they planned to repair a bullet hole later in the day. Despite the severity of the injury, barring infection, they expected a rapid recovery.

The captain sipped a latte from the onboard Starbucks café, built and donated by the Seattle-based company as part of an international marketing campaign. The American coffee, which no civilized European would normally dream of consuming after breakfast, consisted of milk flavored with cheap robusta beans. No gourmet's delight, but it made the ship's many American volunteers feel a bit more at home. Some of the volunteers never even left the ship when in port; they'd heard tales about roving bands of boy soldiers and the grisly massacres that were staples of African bush warfare. Those things had faded away, but fear persisted.

At slightly shy of five hundred feet, the *Africa Grace* was not as big a ship as he would have liked, nor as new, but she was appointed with more creature comforts than any vessel he had ever sailed on, short of a cruise ship. How different from when he had sailed aboard her in Denmark as a boy, decades ago, when she ferried trains in a cavernous hold, long before her conversion to a hospital ship.

He stood on the starboard bridge wing, overlooking the activity on the piers, wondering if he would receive instructions to anchor in the bay to free this pier for container ships from China. Beggars couldn't be choosers.

"Captain Anders?" called a soft voice from below and astern. The volunteer medical staff addressed him informally using his Christian name. He turned around and looked down to the deck below, his gaze falling on the young woman whom, above all others under his command, he swore to protect.

"How are you today, Caroline?"

"May I have a word with you?" Caroline replied, her expectant face smiling up at him, her eyes squinting against the glare of the morning sun.

"Come on up."

She appeared on the bridge a moment later.

"Might I speak to you *in private*, sir?"

He guided her out onto the other bridge wing, set out over the water on the far side from the pier. In passing, he closed the ports that allowed the breeze to flow through the bridge.

He changed to Danish once no longer among the multilingual crew. "What is it, Caroline?"

People presumed a sea captain to possess superior wisdom in all matters. He was accustomed to it: humans needed a father confessor. Caroline joined the ship ten months ago, and stood out as one of the most stable, thoughtful, and confident young folk among the 442 volunteer crew currently on board. Her problems aboard the ship remained minimal, but given who she was, any problem could blossom from something Denmark-sized to something Africa-sized. What might have her looking so perplexed at the moment?

Caroline hesitated, and then her words came out in a nervous rush. "The men who came aboard—the emergency last night. You know about them?"

"Of course."

"I spent time with the younger man who drove his injured friend in from the bush."

"Ahh… yes?"

Her face reddened to the shade of a setting sun, like that of an embarrassed schoolgirl. "I mean… I was cleaning his wound. He had a shoulder injury."

"I am told we do not know the names of these gentlemen? Have you better information?"

"No, sir. He would not tell me either of their names."

"Do you have any insight as to why that is, Caroline?"

"No, but it is worrisome, do you agree? Gunshot wounds, secrecy, and all. And there seems to be a lot of money involved. Billions."

"That is all a bit out of the ordinary. What do you think about it? What do you think of the young man? What do your instincts tell you? Is he a good man or a bad man?" He should not trust a young woman's instinct in this matter; she might be smitten with the bad-boy type. He must meet this young man soon as part of his normal duty to his ship, but now also as part of his duty to her.

Caroline smiled quickly and her face brightened. Her words said something different than her face, something more rational. "I do not know, sir. I do not know."

Freberg scratched his beard again. "Some things are not our business. We heal who we can, and it sounds like these men need healing."

The girl smiled sheepishly. "Of course."

"But if you are going to see more of this man, be wise and find out what you can. Africa is replete with men who come here either looking for trouble or running away from trouble they found somewhere else. They are not subject to normal constraints. Their intentions and motivations—their backgrounds—are not those of men you have met before, Caroline." He would watch closely.

"I am supposed to have dinner with him tonight." She smiled again, somehow even more sheepishly. It was disarming.

This girl had always been endearing. He felt protective toward her, as if she were his own daughter. "Then I would like you and this anonymous young man to join me for dinner at my table this evening."

"I would be most pleased to do so." She looked as though she were about to salute.

"Oh, Caroline, one more thing before you go. Don't worry. I am paying very close attention both to what you told me, and the fact that you were worried enough to draw it to my attention. I take your concern seriously."

And indeed Freberg took it seriously enough that he called both his ship's security officer and his master-at-arms for a meeting. It was time to brush up on some rusty security procedures.

11

A Conjecture Strengthened

DURING the day Charles checked several times on his comatose friend but spent most of his time in the ship's library—a dank room equipped with several thousand dog-eared paperbacks. Sitting in an aged armchair, he looked out at the ocean and considered B-F's history in light of the theory that he and Xander had concocted, with the help of TJ and gin-infused eggnog.

Their unpleasant visit to the hidden lab reinforced the possibility of fraud. But maybe the B-F guards were just protecting their property from an invasion? Precisely to eliminate that concern, he had chosen to approach the place openly and knock on the door. Why would they feel so threatened as to immediately respond with violence?

With a newly jaundiced eye, he pondered B-F's stock price and press releases and the various analyst and media commentaries.

Charles noted that commentators conflated the word *resource* with the word *reserves*. It was a critical distinction, but one often skated over, especially when someone wanted to spin fiction into fact. A mineral resource could exist anywhere, as long as it was *potentially* extractable given unlimited funding. Something could be counted as a resource even if it was in the core of Jupiter. But it only became a reserve when it could be extracted feasibly and, most importantly, *profitably*.

The junior exploration companies and the sell-side brokerages trying to access a broader and less sophisticated investment base lacked motivation to clarify terminology. Nobody in the media made a clear distinction between the two words, partly because it detracted from the titillation and entertainment value of the story, and partly because it was a strictly economic distinction to which the public was oblivious—but mostly because the members of the press themselves wallowed in a state of sustained economic ignorance.

Of course reporters in the popular press were easy prey. Few had any background in either economics or science. Academic geologists—educated in both—might be skeptical, but rarely had the combination of audacity and incentive to speak up and question nanoparticulate gold. It's risky to either support or deny a new scientific theory. Sure, it might be the next string theory. But it could also be the next cold fusion.

Uncle Maurice had delighted in drawing Charles's attention to times when the public fell for the most absurd nonsense presented by someone with charisma and an ability to project certainty. Little more than a winning smile and a shoeshine were required to garner both votes and money. It was a cynical view, but there was precious little difference between cynicism and realism, especially in matters of mass psychology. Investors, like voters, were often drawn to sociopaths who combined charisma and guilt-free narcissism in a way that made the most egregious lies palatable. Indeed, the most dangerous men were often the most charming. In business, they could pull in financial capital and burn it faster than rocket fuel; in politics, they could draw in the masses and then waste or enthrall all that human capital. Hitler, Stalin, and Mao were the most extreme recent examples, but history was replete with politicians who specialized in the use of emotive but imprecise words. What could they lose in building hopes with a promise of change? Uncle Maurice had long ago taught him that those who most wanted power could be trusted with it least. Africa had more than its fair share of such folk.

Charles needed to call his uncle.

*   *   *

No one would have thought that Maurice Templeton and Charles shared even a quarter of each other's genes. Maurice had become a very large man indeed, now pushing three-fifty and still expanding. A homebody, although not an agoraphobe, he liked his couch. He liked his bed. He liked his pizza, his Chinese food, his Thai food, potato chips, beer, and scotch—and practically everything else that contained calories. He ordered out for delivery for all four meals per day, five on Sunday. For a fat tip, the maintenance man ascended daily from the basement of his ritzy Upper West Side building and stopped by his commodious eleventh-floor apartment to haul out giant trash bags, usually arriving a few hours before an advance patrol of the cockroach cavalry could discover the ripening opportunity. The apartment was untidy but never dirty.

As a consequence of his lifestyle, Maurice suffered from a horrific case of obstructive sleep apnea; he only slept for a few minutes at a time, and occasionally he succumbed to those restless minutes in the middle of a telephone conversation. It was a disability, but his focused intelligence more than made up for it. He was wide awake for the moment and began the conversation with a lecture.

"My dear boy, you're dealing with a business that turns your money and their dream into their money and your dream. It's an industry populated by geologists using nebulous scientific theories and patchy data to explore for hidden treasures under moose pasture held by a company that, more often than not, is run by promoters. You can't tell they're lying unless their lips are moving."

Charles smiled as he listened to his uncle, confident the man would always have his back. "You told me the same thing when I first bought B-F stock, and then again just before I came over here, Uncle Maurice. The same exact words."

There was an awkward delay in the connection.

"Oh, yeah? Well, they're words worth repeating, especially when you don't seem to listen to them."

"Do you have anything for me, Uncle Maurice?" His uncle somehow always had the latest information from somebody.

The deep voice crackled through his phone. "Burke International Mining and B-F have signed off on a deal whereby your B-F friends will receive a large influx of cash from Burke up front, and a sweet royalty deal, among other considerations. The news will start leaking soon."

Charles replied, "Okay, so Burke is the victorious suitor, then. We've been thinking B-F must be close to a deal. It was one of our theories why they didn't want to waste their time with us."

"Who's us?"

Charles equivocated. "A new friend I met here."

"Yeah? Be careful of new friends, Charles. Especially the kind you find in places like the one you're now in. Watch your back."

"He's not the one who's dangerous to me right now."

"What do you mean?" Maurice asked, slowly.

Charles began to describe his recent adventure, but by the time he mentioned the hail of bullets, a long loud snore came through the earpiece.

"Hello? Uncle Maurice? Are you awake?"

The response consisted of another loud snore that ended in a gag and a gasp. A most annoying characteristic, it limited Templeton's circle of friends. The man was best compared to a supercomputer that experienced sporadic power outages.

"What, what, what? Who's there?"

"It's me. Did you hear anything I said?"

"Sure. No, not a word. It's ten o'clock in the morning here, Charles. Naptime." Then Maurice shifted back into fifth gear. "Look, tomorrow the stock's going to rise even more. Everybody will expect Burke to confirm the ore body with their own drilling. I talked to a friend from Burke. Burke is moving faster than I've ever seen a company move. Geologists will come in from Canada and Togo. The ink isn't dry and already ships are chartered and flights booked. In a couple of weeks, Burke's men will be all over Banga Sioquelle, drilling new holes and commissioning their own assays and repeating the assays of B-F's control cores."

"Burke may not like what they find."

"If they don't like it, neither will the market." Maurice stayed silent for a moment, digesting either food or Charles's words. "So, do you know something, my boy? Something I don't know?" Again a pause. Then: "Are you thinking B-F has some problems?"

Charles said, slowly, "I don't know. I'm beginning to think so."

"I hate quoting old saws of the market, but there's some truth in the one about how you can't go broke taking a profit. Especially since you're up—what—a hundred to one on this one? "

"It may soon be time to short this stock, Uncle Maurice."

"Right now, the curve is going parabolic on the up side. Ain't nobody shorting B-F. Nobody. Forced buying to cover early shorts will keep driving the price higher. Meanwhile every mooch with a brokerage account is trying to back up the truck for more shares."

"But none of those people are here on the ground! They haven't seen what we've seen. They don't suspect what we suspect. And they won't until all those new geologists fly in from Burke. I think we've learned something that nobody else knows.…"

"Hmm… you might recall what happened to Gordon Gekko when he was in that position."

"Greed *is* good," Charles quipped, quoting from Gekko's superb speech in the movie *Wall Street*.

"Although he wasn't a nice guy, he was the only character in the movie who kept his word. Few of the hoi polloi think greed is good anymore, Charles. Everybody's been taught to hate the idea of Gekko. To the average guy, he's the modern equivalent of Fagin in *Oliver Twist*. Except the average guy hasn't read *Oliver Twist*. Be careful if you do decide to short this stock, Charles. Make sure you know *exactly* what the truth is. I don't need to tell you that you can lose an unlimited amount of money with a short. Assume the B-F story is all real. Then imagine if the day after you short B-F there's a global currency collapse and gold shoots up to $10,000. You'd be more than bankrupt."

"I wasn't born yesterday, Uncle Maurice."

"Yeah, just the day before yesterday. You've not been caught on the wrong side of a short yet. It's something men don't always recover from. I still feel responsible for your education, my boy. And I can't remember what you've learned yet and what you haven't. You are off in GaGaGu Gondwana, probably under the influence of some beautiful witch, bullets flying, and I doubt you have your head screwed on tight right now."

Charles replied, "All true."

"What are your next steps? How long is it going to be before someone else figures it out too? How long are you going to sit still? If it *is* a fraud, the longer it takes before the cat's out of the bag, the more money the criminals stand to make, and the more money the boobs in the public stand to lose. And the bigger the crash will be."

"I'm not the one lying to the public. And I'm not sure about it anyway. I'm not sure enough to risk getting sued if I say something without proof."

"So what is it you've found, Charles? What makes you even wonder?"

"We've found a machine that has no business being anywhere near B-F. And a pretty clear indication they don't want anybody to see it."

"What machine? What does it do?"

Before Charles could tell him he didn't know, Maurice was stridently snoring again, sawing through two expensive minutes during which Charles tried yelling and banging the phone against one of the ship's bulkheads in a fruitless effort to awaken his uncle.

Charles rolled his eyes and finally cut the connection.

He spent the next hour contemplating, plotting scenarios. B-F could make him megarich if he made the right moves now. But he needed more solid information.

Getting that information might lead to one other possibility: B-F could, perhaps, make him dead.

*   *   *

"I stopped by the ICU a few minutes ago," Caroline said. She stood next to Charles, who looked out into the bay over the high bow rail of the *Africa Grace*. The late afternoon heat made the sea breeze especially welcome. Caroline wore her scrubs. Charles now dressed in a manner Xander would approve of. He sported a thin, loose, buttoned shirt—untucked—lightweight long pants, sandals, and no socks.

Charles saw her appraising his attire, and he glanced down at himself before speaking. "I stopped by the ship's store. Now I can pretend I'm an old Africa hand...."

"You look nice," she said.

There was no hesitation in his response, as he smiled warmly. "You look nice too."

She laughed lightly, looking down at the blood-spattered scrubs hanging loosely over her trim frame. "I look horrible! I always do on this ship!"

"How wrong you are.... How's our patient?"

Caroline breathed deeply, with a concerned smile. "As you know, his head injury was pretty serious. It's still going to be touch and go for a while. Dr. Ellison has him in a medically induced coma."

"For how long?"

"A day, maybe two. The swelling has to ease."

Charles nodded slowly and looked out over the water.

"Are you close friends?"

He thought a moment. Then, quietly, he said, "Not yet. But I think we share something"—he hesitated a moment—"uncommon."

"What's that?"

"Core values. I feel that he's a kindred spirit."

Caroline looked up at his face as he stared into the distance. "The captain has asked us to dine with him tonight. At six, in the captain's mess."

"Dress code?"

"You're fine as is. Except tuck in your shirt, okay?"

"Got it. Thanks. What are you doing for the next couple of hours?"

"I thought perhaps I would spend some time with this mysterious American I met," she replied. "What am I supposed to call you? Are you going to introduce yourself to the captain by name?"

"When I can."

"You are into something, aren't you? Something pretty big?"

"Yes. Something that someone wanted to kill us over. So, pretty big."

"Are you sure you can handle it?"

Charles chose not to reply.

Caroline moved closer to him. "What in this impoverished country can possibly be worth three billion dollars? Did you find your own private gold mine?"

Charles smiled ruefully. "Actually," he said, "we might have found the exact opposite."

12

A Polite Urban Manhunt

THREE men, middle aged, fit, and severe, drove through the capital in a large black SUV. It was covered with mud, of course, but stood out from the decrepit trucks and rusted-out junkers cramming Adamstown's potholed streets. When a new SUV with blacked-out windows drove through downtown, people got out of the way. Whoever it conveyed was assuredly a Big Man.

The charitable NGOs also used large, expensive SUVs as their transportation of choice, but they used *white* SUVs. Everyone knew that no Big Man sat inside. Sure, it was worth keeping an eye on where those white jeeps went, for the NGOs provided a great source of free money. The hearts of the people in those vehicles were tender, while their heads were often soft and their wallets fat—an ideal combination for the upwardly mobile Gondwanan to chat up. But inside a *black* SUV would ride a top government official, a successful local businessman probably related to the president, or a wealthy foreigner, who of course would also be hooked up with the president or one of his ministers. The traffic police, with their trademark green T-shirts under their well-ironed blue uniforms, would stop all other traffic when a black SUV came through, assuring the VIPs easy passage in their pursuit of important matters. The police saluted, and all eyes turned toward the passing vehicle and the passengers concealed by the darkly tinted glass.

In this country, the people called all SUVs "jeeps," regardless of what company manufactured them. This particular black jeep pulled up against the curb, and the three large white men emerged. They wore what might be considered their Class B uniforms—two wore tan bush shirts, and the leader a blousy flowered Hawaiian sport shirt. These were favored, partly because they were friendly looking and disarming, partly because they made it easy to both hide and draw a concealed weapon.

A man selling cell phone scratch cards from behind a tiny podium watched the men carefully.

"Hey," said the driver, coming over to him. "You watch the car, yah? I pay you when we come out."

The street vendor could tell they weren't Americans by the man's accent. Maybe South African. Maybe Australian. "Sure. I will," he said. "You want your jeep wash? I can get your jeep wash for you."

"Sure, get it washed. One dollar. No more. Make sure they know that."

"I will, bossman. Your jeep will be shining soon."

There would only be a brief break from the rain and mud, but the men with buckets and dirty washrags would pay attention to the vehicle, and that provided some protection. Concealed in the back of the SUV lay more weapons than had been seen in one place in the capital for years.

Harry wore the Hawaiian shirt. He took his bearings on the street as his associates reflexively scanned the area for threats. Evening was coming, and the large white men stuck out on the crowded streets like lighthouses in a dark sea. A thousand people had line of sight to their location, which was both a strength and a weakness. Today, he hoped it would be an advantage.

He headed to a bar-restaurant, strictly a locals' hangout and well stocked with prostitutes. His intent was to find the man who had rashly intruded on his turf and remedy that man's mistake. The cost of failure could be huge. Harry himself sat on ten million dollars' worth of B-F shares that, if he did his part, could be worth twenty million in a few weeks. He looked forward to retirement but had no intention of running a bar like this to support himself—the fate of so many ex-soldiers whose financial-management skills were not on a par with their combat skills.

"Joseph," he said to the bartender, "I need a cold beer and information."

"Mr. Harry. It is good to have you back." The barkeep reached into the barely working horizontal freezer and pulled out three green bottles. He placed one in front of each man, with a piece of toilet paper covering the tops, and popped them open. The outside of the bottles, a welcome bit colder than the humid bar atmosphere, condensed water out of the saturated air. "What information do you seek?"

"I need the location of an American tourist, a white man. His name is Charles Knight. He is young. Tall. Blue eyes. Light-brown, clean-cut hair, but not as short as mine.

"Who does he work with?"

"No one local; he is here on his own."

"I will inquire. Do you have any idea where he would be?"

"I don't. Probably the standard places where Americans stay."

"I will see what my friends and I can learn."

"Thank you, Joseph." Harry handed him a twenty-dollar bill that paid for the beers six times over and then said, "I will pay you well if you find him. But it needs to be very quickly."

"I will try."

"You find me and tell me right away when you hear anything, yah?"

"Yah, bossman. I will."

Harry nodded to the other two men, who looked strikingly like himself: experienced mercenaries long in the tooth, a bit too old to be fighting others' wars, since war is famously a young man's game. And too jaded and experienced to be paid peanuts to line up in formation and follow orders like automatons. They were smart, tough, and essentially independent.

They walked out of the bar and down four long city blocks to the main office of Standard West African Bank, where a similar exchange took place with the branch manager. The next stop was the city office of SN Brussels, the only European airline serving the country.

"Do you know people here too, Harry?" the new man said. He had been working with him for a month, although, decades before, they had fought together for over a year in Biafra, knee-deep in gore most of the time. Harry knew Roscoe hated being in West Africa even back then. He hated the heat. He hated the sweat. But he was no complainer.

Harry shook his head. "No. But it is the most likely way Knight would leave the country, unless he is staying in Africa. If I were him, I'd be looking to flee."

The office was supposed to close in five minutes, but the swinging doors were already locked. Harry cut off the reflections with his hand as he leaned against the door's glass and peered through. A young and shapely Gondwanan woman attired in the fancy jacket and red skirt common to all female SN Brussels staff noticed him and, after a little hesitation, stood up and walked to the door. She smiled sheepishly, then unlocked it. Harry signaled with his head to the other men, who caught his message and retreated back away from the door to wait by the street. Harry walked in, saying, "Thank you. I won't take but a minute."

He looked around the place. There were three desks with aged, dirty computers and a half-dozen cheap, mismatched chairs in a small waiting area. No video monitors secured the place. Harry and Laetitia—as her name tag revealed—were alone.

"I'm sorry," Laetitia said, "I was trying to close up a little early today. But it's okay. How can I help you?" She seated herself primly behind a desk, showed him a chair, and pressed a button on the computer. "It will just take a moment to boot back up."

"I'm grateful. I'm rather stuck. My friend and I went separate ways for a few days. He was supposed to book our flights to the US. But I can't find him. I was hoping you might help." Harry took no pride in his ability to lie. He considered it cowardly. And it was hard to keep lies straight, which was potentially dangerous. Once you were known as a liar, both opportunities and relationships disappeared.

"Perhaps we can. Let me see what we can learn. What's your name?"

Harry did not hesitate. "Starnes. S-T-A-R-N-E-S." It was the name of the first man he had ever killed, many decades earlier. He used that alias frequently because it's wise to have a familiar name at the forefront of your mind to avoid an embarrassing hesitation.

"Let me see. Hmm. I don't see any reservations for you. What is your friend's name?"

Harry smiled inwardly. People were so trusting. "Knight. K-N-I-G-H-T. Charles Knight."

She clicked away and waited for a moment. She looked up into his eyes and smiled invitingly, and then looked back at the screen. Many of the educated people in Gondwana had learned their English from mission schools, and her excellent diction, along with her good looks, had probably enabled her to land this prime job. Harry would not have been surprised if little Laetitia on the computer was thinking of Harry as a long-shot but possible ticket out of this godforsaken hellhole. Suddenly her eyes lit up. "Got him."

He smiled at her, this time not inwardly, as he sensed she found his smile attractive.

"He is booked on the Sunday evening flight, which, because of Thursday's cancellation, is our next flight out to Belgium. Leaves at 7 p.m. Shall I book you on the same flight?"

Harry pretended to vacillate before saying, "That's a day or two early for me. I need to talk to Charles. Do you have his contact information there by any chance?"

"I'm sure we do. Yes. I don't know that I am supposed to give that out, though."

"Yes, I understand about that. Is there anything you *can* tell me that will help me get in touch with him?"

She looked back at the screen. "There is no hotel listed. No contact information other than a mobile phone." She looked at him closely. He mustered his sincerest mimicry of humility and trustworthiness, and the impression was sufficient to endear him to the young woman. She smiled conspiratorially and whispered, "I can give you his number. Just don't tell anyone."

Had she not been good enough to offer it to him, Harry would have been forced to drop back to Plan B. Like most experienced operators, he avoided violence when possible. There was always a chance of getting hurt, always a chance of drawing unwelcome attention, always a chance of unwanted complications down the road. He spoke gently. "He'll be grateful, and so will I. Thank you so much."

She gave him Charles Knight's cell number—as well as her own.

13

Dinner with a Gamma-Type Wolf Larsen

"GOOD evening, Caroline!" Captain Freberg beamed as he stood up from the table to greet the two young people politely entering his mess. He added, looking at Charles, "And good evening to you, too, young man. It is my pleasure to meet you."

Charles tried to size up the man. The captain stood tall—a model of the modern Viking. He was handsome, naturally intimidating, and possessed a strong but unthreatening voice. He looked like he could be the king of Denmark—to whom he might be related, considering the small total number of Danes.

The man had the aura of an alpha male, but something about Freberg's smile made Charles wonder if in fact he was a less common gamma—like Charles himself.

Charles knew that scientists experimenting with rats discovered that there were leaders—alphas—and followers—betas. A small number of alphas staked out the best mates, the best territories, and ruled over the passive betas (the large majority). By nature aggressive, alphas had their confidence amplified within the confines and culture of a pack; they needed the betas to pay them homage. Pretty obvious; no Nobel Prize for figuring that out. But Charles never felt like either an alpha or a beta.

But then scientists found that another type existed—gammas, who were relatively rare. Gamma rats possessed all the capabilities of alphas, including garnering the best mates and territories, but gammas felt no need to lord over the betas. Gammas did not demand the pack culture to validate their feelings of self-worth. And the alphas didn't intimidate them. They lived, if you will, as get-along-go-along, libertarian rats. The pattern held true throughout the higher animal kingdom, and the higher a species' intelligence, the more pronounced it was.

Charles's felt that warmth in the center of his chest that occurred when he encountered someone who could become a friend. "It is an honor dining with you, sir. Thank you for including me."

The captain nodded. "My name is Anders Freberg. I understand you are reticent to share your own name. That verges on unacceptable, but I will give you some leeway for the moment."

Unlike Charles's first mental image of a ship captain—Jack London's vicious Wolf Larsen, who was also of Danish decent—Freberg's quiet authority rekindled Charles's self-reproach at being less than candid.

Shake it off, he thought.

The captain indicated a seat to his right for Caroline, and Charles helped her slide into it. Then he took the seat opposite the captain. Breathing came easier here as a sweet dry conditioned air replaced the heavy scent of grease that permeated the atmosphere around much of the ship. The table was anodized steel bolted to the floor. It had a raised edge to capture any wayward dishware that would make the mess... eponymous... when the ship was underway and the seas ran high. Charles rubbed his hand along the ridge, feeling the roughness of the surface coating of zinc oxide that protected the cold metal underneath.

A short Filipino man, probably over seventy, attired in a white uniform, stepped through the door carrying glasses filled with ice water. He deftly arranged some dishes, handed the napkins from the table to his captain's two guests, placed some bread and butter in the middle of the table, and bowed slightly as he departed.

Freberg said, "In the US Navy, Filipinos were once only allowed to work in the galleys as kitchen staff and as stewards for the officers. We welcome qualified retirees who volunteer in exchange for accommodations and a small stipend, and they treat me far too well, far beyond what I would ever expect."

Charles's father had been in the Navy and was a particular fan of the Philippines, at least its northern islands. The indigenous cultures had blended well with the Spanish in the four hundred years since Magellan had started the conquest of the islands. The Spanish had imposed Christianity in the north. It was a more relaxed religion than the Islam imposed on the southern islands by the Arabs and Malays in the Middle Ages. The American patina of the last hundred years was, like the previous conquests, a mixed blessing. The Americans may have killed as many as two hundred thousand locals in quashing their bid for independence after the Spanish-American War, but that insult had been mostly forgotten. The people of the country had a tradition of warmth and tolerance.

"It seems like a good arrangement," Charles offered.

"Reciprocity is a good basis for a relationship," the captain replied.

Charles recognized then that his own presence on the ship would be subject to the same basis of judgment. Unfortunately, he was providing nothing to the people of this ship other than danger.

There was silence for a minute as Caroline offered the bread basket around.

"What is it you like to do in life?" Freberg asked.

The vague question concealed another question altogether, one that Charles was not ready to answer.

"I'm very sorry about imposing my situation on you. And I'm grateful for your assistance, both to me and to my friend. You and your ship have literally been lifesavers for us." His response was the best answer he could yet give to the concealed question, but it was nothing more than an excuse and an apology.

"I hear your friend is stable now. Stability on this ship is a very good thing. Or, for that matter, on this planet, where it is a rarer commodity. Here's to stability!" Freberg raised his glass in a sincere toast and looked into Charles's eyes with… what was it… a trace of empathy, perhaps?

Caroline chimed in, "Yes, he's stable at least, and most likely improving."

"Good, we shall all expect his recovery then." The captain turned back to Charles. "Young man, I won't press you, but it would be entertaining to know what you enjoy doing, when you have time and freedom to do it."

It was the same question, and maybe this time he was meant to take it at face value.

108

The captain encouraged him. "Your hobbies, your joys, your interests. Even your profession—of course only if it is unrelated to the current events that brought you to us: events you do not yet want to discuss, I realize." An excessive formality in sentence structure occasionally betrayed Freberg's otherwise perfect English.

"Ah. I understand." So this was the captain's twist on a standard interview technique. Perhaps the captain asked every aspiring crew member or dinner companion some form of this question. Ordinary banter at the captain's table. With that realization, Charles answered without further hesitation. "Well, I play the piano. I like to play chess. And I like to spend a lot of time reading."

"What do you prefer to read?"

Charles's tastes were eclectic but possessed a consistent thread.

"I'm a big fan of most science fiction, because it shows how the world might be, once we've mastered the physical world. And Westerns—particularly the movies. They're… morality plays—the world stripped down to its bare essentials."

He looked at Caroline, and then the captain. Would it be polite to discuss philosophical views? Or should he keep the conversation light? Well, why not? So he said, "My uncle has always impressed upon me the importance of *soundness.*"

"Soundness?" Caroline prodded him.

It was a term that had specific meaning to Charles, but not one that could be effectively presented in a brief phrase.

Charles tried anyway. "As my uncle defines it, soundness means having integrity."

Caroline asked, "So you choose authors who are sound? Sound thinkers? Sound novelists?"

That wasn't quite right. Charles felt awkward. He tried to clarify. "Well, it would be more fair to say that, when I was younger, my uncle supplied me with books he thought I would learn important lessons from. He called them *sound* books."

Captain Freberg nodded. "A strong figure, your uncle."

"Yes. My uncle… well, he and his library… influenced my tastes. I was thirteen then, when I first met my uncle. Just after my mom died. I guess I was already of like mind with him without knowing it. Starting when I was little, I used to creep downstairs late at night to watch *Have*

Gun—Will Travel with my little brother. It's an old Western. The lead character, a gunfighter named Paladin, became my first hero. It was years later… really only recently… that I figured out that what made Paladin such a hero was precisely what my uncle called *soundness*."

Charles studied the captain. Would he appreciate heavy conversations along these lines? Charles became impatient and lost interest if he had to do more than five minutes of small talk—weather and the state of the roads and such. But most people weren't like him. Impatience was no virtue, but he was stuck with it. Would the captain exchange views on practical and applied philosophy? Politics and religion: the two things you were never supposed to talk about in polite company. Perhaps this social prohibition materialized by intent—instilled to limit critique of authority among high society.

Caroline said, "There are lots of characters with integrity you could have chosen."

"Yes," the captain added. "What made you choose Paladin over other heroes?"

Charles tried to express a concept he still grappled with himself. "I think, umm, soundness has other meanings too. People who are *sound* don't live in contradictions. They're… internally consistent." He had never tried to explain this to anybody before. Hell, he had never wanted to. There was something about this Captain Freberg that invited a meaningful conversation. He'd be an easy man to take into one's confidence.

Captain Freberg added, "So it is more than just honesty?"

Charles nodded. "Oh yes. I think so. It's being honest with yourself, for sure. Caring enough to seek the truth is part of it."

"Ah, Truth. Young man, now let me tell you about *my* uncle!"

"I'm listening, sir."

"Like you, I had an uncle very influential to me. He was a ship's captain also, raised before the mast. Fifty years at sea, almost to the day. I remember sitting on his knee up until I was too big to do so. To this day, I remember him teaching me that *truth never contradicts itself*." He turned to Caroline and said in Danish, "*Sandheden aldrig modsiger sig selv*."

"Ah yes," Caroline said.

Maybe it was a known precept in Denmark.

Charles said, "Now I'm motivated to learn Danish."

110

"Are you good with languages?" Caroline asked.

"I don't know." He had thus far focused on learning other tools of life, relying on the universality of English and postponing learning other languages. "I studied French for a couple of years in school. It was the only choice they gave us. But I'm afraid I skipped class a lot."

"I'll teach you Danish. You have to know Danish. It's the language everyone in the galaxy shall speak someday!" She grinned mischievously.

"If you had your way, my dear!" the captain laughed.

Charles picked up on something then. The way the captain talked to Caroline. Protective, almost like to a daughter. But that couldn't be the case. Perhaps Danes all acted among themselves in this fashion? A small, close-knit people.... It was pure speculation. He really had no experience with other cultures. He pulled himself upright suddenly, fixing his posture. Uncle Maurice had insisted it was past time for him to become a man of the world. Caroline spoke five languages for chrissake!

"And who were your other heroes in childhood?" Captain Freberg asked.

That was easy. "Edmond Dantès," Charles answered. "Fictional, of course. But what a man!"

"I hope," Caroline said, "you don't have to spend years in prison in order to learn everything that Dantès learned."

"I'm trying to skip the prison part. But you know, prison was a necessary part of who he was. Without that time in prison, there would never have been a Count of Monte Cristo." Charles had read the book for the first time just after his mother died. His emotional state at that time cemented the character of Dantès into his mind poignantly. Life for each person is such an individual mosaic of randomly assembled experiences, he realized. The death of Charles's mother was a necessary part of who *he* was. That old pain in his chest emerged, a hollow ache that he assumed would haunt him forever. How different would he be had he not spent that summer with Uncle Maurice?

"It seems you have found good role models."

"I'll have to see how well they work out for me in the real world. But they're certainly part of me, for better or for worse."

Captain Freberg looked hard at Charles. "Would you *die* for your principles?"

It was a question Charles had not previously confronted. "Do you mean *live* for my principles? Because that I certainly try to do."

"Well, good for you, my young friend. I don't yet know what your principles are, other than that they don't contradict themselves. But that's a damn good place from which to start. An honest man you seem to be. But I do note that you are still anonymous."

"It's of necessity, I assure you, sir."

The captain rubbed his hand along the edge of the table, the way Charles had done earlier, and said, "This raised edge on the table. It's called a *fiddle*. A *fiddle* is also a word for a fraud or scam, am I right?"

Charles's adrenalin surged and his heart rate increased. Was this the way a ship's captain might accuse him of being a scammer? Or did the captain know what Charles and Xander had only just begun to suspect about B-F? Was he a part of it? How could the captain otherwise have any clue about what was going on in Charles's mind?

The pause lasted too long before he said, "I haven't heard that term in American English. But the Brits, perhaps?"

The captain said, "Yes, I'm sure you're right."

Charles watched the captain closely.

"In any event, young man, if you can stay on your track and stay *sound* in your life, you might become quite skillful at identifying fiddlers. A fiddle, a fraud, would be internally contradictory, don't you think? And therefore particularly perceptible to someone who abides by your values?"

Charles exhaled in relief. "Perhaps."

Caroline teased him. "It would make you good at poker."

"I wish I were better. It's a strange game: it's all luck *and* all skill, both at the same time. I don't get bluffed very often; I can pick up on that better than most. But it sorta evens out, because I can't bluff *others* as well as I'd like."

"You *want* to be able to lie better?"

"Not lie. Bluffing in poker isn't dishonesty, it's a skill. A bluff is a negotiation where the parties establish the price of more information." That was a verbatim quote from his father.

The conversation halted for a moment as Charles considered how pleasant it might be to have a game of poker if Caroline were among the players.

"Are you in further danger?" Captain Freberg interrupted his thoughts.

Charles nodded. "If they realized who we are, then yes. There's a whole lot of money at risk. That's why I've kept our names secret. They may be looking for us."

"Can you tell me who *they* are? Perhaps we should be on the look-out for them."

"Perhaps soon, sir. I don't like not being able to level with you."

"Tell me," the captain rubbed his bearded chin, "tell me why you did not just provide to us a couple of aliases? Would that not have been safer? Being secretive with your name certainly arouses suspicion, and suspicion spreads on a ship, like a fire."

"I'm sure. That may have been a tactical error. But, at least outside a poker game, I try not to lie to people who have caused me no harm."

Freberg nodded. "Very hard to argue with that. It is a position I agree with, although it seems most people are capable of lying to themselves and to others, when the incentives are sufficient."

"My uncle would agree. Lying to oneself is a serious crime, from his point of view."

"Maybe as long as we aren't lying, we don't owe anyone except ourselves the truth? Truth isn't a free good."

Charles internalized that. *Truth is not a free good.* This idea provoked thought. He was the possessor of a possible truth—gained at great cost and, if accurate, of immense value. It was like knowing where the wreck of a Spanish treasure galleon lay. There was no obligation to share the information with the world.

"Let us agree among the three of us," Captain Freberg proposed, "to not ever lie to each other, then. Shall we?"

Charles hesitated. "How about this. I will *probably* never lie to you, sir."

"Probably?" The captain had a grave expression.

"Right," Charles replied sternly. "*Probably.*"

"What do you mean?" Caroline's face, too, creased in concern.

Charles raised his eyebrows as a playful glint came into his eyes, and his smile broadened. "Is there a regular poker game on this ship?"

14

The Heart of the Beast

A ONE-HUNDRED-PERCENT conviction rate! That was the new goal. If he could get there, then no one would even bother to put up a fight. He had come far since he had joined the IRS.

Thirty-eight years ago, Theodore Lichen had been a poet manqué with a black cloud hanging over his head and his soul.

Thirty-six years ago, he endured a listless wife, a relentless mortgage, and a brainless job at an Amtrak ticket counter. Everything in his life had served to remind him of what a luckless loser he was, one step above a toll collector on a highway or a guard in a prison. All the gilded triumphs he had dreamed of had dissolved through a sequence of inexorable steps into muck and rust—and a void with no exit. But there was a way out. He just needed to pick up the key.

Ted Lichen had thrived in college, where the professors supported his worldview. Let others strive to be drones in the world of production: chemistry or physics, engineering or computer programming, agriculture or medicine. He would fly high in the world of literary masterminds, where he would influence what people thought and valued. Master the masters, get some poetry published in the little magazines or the pulps, move on to the slicks, a publishing contract, a novel, two novels, three novels, then the release—with rave reviews—of a whole volume of his enigmatic poetry. Maybe there would be a few mixed-but-nonetheless-respectful critiques from commenters who Just Didn't Understand What He Was Attempting, but that was *their* weakness. Then the lecture circuit, cocktail parties, collegial hobnobbing with other influential sophisticates. Then a movie contract. The stars—excepting oddballs like Clint Eastwood, Charles Bronson, or Kurt Russell—would lionize him, and starlets would make themselves available in lascivious ways. Why not, indeed? Graciousness would be Theodore Dugway Lichen's stock in trade. He would be the soul of liberality.

That is, if only he could have gotten the fucking typewriter to *work* properly! Two years into it and not a single item published, not a dollar in his wallet, and a wife painted with cellulite nagging him to bring home more bacon. If food was lacking, why was she packing on the pounds?

Okay, so maybe he didn't have it in him to be a Writer with a capital *W*. But neither was he going to settle for some self-stunting advertising job, a cog in some pool of interchangeable copywriters. He was meant for something better than *this*—better than all the things his life had ended up being, including the temporary gig at a Penn Station ticket counter that, by meaningless drift, had become, inconceivably, a soul-sucking permanent gig at which he spent all day every day helping people he despised get to Rochester or Chicago.

So when he saw the classified ad, two days after the bank said "Very sorry, but we cannot restructure your loan," he was ready. Ready to attend the IRS employment open house. Ready to transcend himself. It was a far cry from being a literary lion, but it offered a possibility of control. At least control of other people, if not control of his own life. Become All That He Could Be, rather than the nothing he was. Instead of the ninety-seven-pound weakling constantly getting sand kicked in his face, he would be the one doing the kicking. A generous government paycheck combined with a dollop of arbitrary power would be steps in the right direction.

At first he was nervous and tentative about barging into a stranger's life the way he was being trained and expected to do. It seemed impolite, even unnatural. What if the taxpayer resisted, or even took a shot at him? What if the subject spat in his face? But then he realized that the people he was so stupidly afraid of were almost always deathly afraid of *him*. And they would do what he told them to do! All he had to do was show his ID. They would bow and scrape, even roll over like whipped dogs and wet themselves, once he flashed his IRS credentials. He and his threats were backed by the might and power of the entire United States government.

So yeah, he could do that. It ended up being the ultimate power trip, and he never looked back. He devoured the various courses the Service offered to its employees. He gained a CPA by attending night school. He ingratiated himself with everyone higher up the ladder, and surreptitiously slathered grease on the rungs below him. Over the years he became the perfect man to fill the role of Deputy Commissioner for Services and Enforcement. When he indeed did ascend to that post, he began a long, slow process of lobbying to change his title: cut out the *Services* entirely and simply be the Deputy Commissioner for Enforcement. He understood the PR angle for the *Services*, but the word made him feel as if he were back at the Penn Station ticket booth.

Both the White House and the Congress liked to present the IRS as a service organization dealing with "customers" as if it functioned as a commercial enterprise. Its employees encouraged each other to recognize that theirs was the only branch of government that "earned" a "profit"— although a sound economist would laugh at the preposterous misuse of either of these words.

Since the agency was older than any living taxpayer, people didn't see it as an arbitrary creation but as part of the eternal firmament. As the government's consistent deficits took it closer to bankruptcy, it became increasingly apparent that only a very thin layer of velvet covered the mailed fist. The root and substance of enforcement was *force*, and the enculturation of fear was important to that end. The public relations messages, the smiley faces, the rhetoric about service and customers, the advertorials engineered to push the public's patriotism buttons—these operated as helpful adjuncts to the effort. But the essence remained the steel fist, not the velvet glove that covered it.

Few others toiling at the IRS recognized its means and its purpose. But Lichen did. He respected the brass knuckles, the barbed hooks, the heavy clubs.

Presidents came and went, and usually changed little besides the rhetoric. Lichen favored the current White House; on the whole, they seemed to understand the basics. And now that he was in the upper ranks of the Service, he was gratified to be increasingly surrounded by people like himself. The government in general, and the Service in particular, attracted his kindred spirits. He sat back and smiled.

In retrospect, it was a godsend his excellence in poetry had never been recognized. He might have ended up teaching at a small college, wearing a tweed jacket with elbow patches.

His assistant buzzed him. "Ms. Heidel is here. Your four o'clock."

He grunted, "Give me two minutes."

Sabina would have been the product of his fourth marriage, had her mother carried through with the marriage plans. But the pregnant bitch had run off at the last minute, leaving him humiliated and alone. He concluded that the woman was evil. He'd become aware of her numerous faults early in the relationship, but continued on, both because she was very beautiful and because those same flaws made her easy to manipulate.

Whatever her mother's faults, Sabina had reappeared at the right time of life for him. Sabina had found him six years ago when she was about to enter college. She was perfect. And clearly his daughter, although perhaps not in terms of physical appearance, which was a gift from her mother. He was glad to have missed the tedium and expense of her childhood and adolescence. But she was in his grasp now, and, as a bonus, that galled her mother.

A knock and then the door swung open. He didn't get up. "Sabina, my dear. It's good to see you. Working in the same building with you is a father's dream come true."

"Hi, Dad." He liked the title, and it hadn't taken her long to figure that out. "I don't think I'm taking sufficient advantage of the VP's Government Efficiency Enhancement Initiative. They've got me in a peon job. It's time I move up."

"What, you've been here at the IRS how many months?"

"Dad, it's boring. I'm a quick study. I need to broaden my experience. We have to impress the vice president, show him we can make his initiative work. It'll keep his attention on us, and he's likely to be the next president. So I need to get out in the field. Do something exciting. Undercover."

"What, you want some James Bond stuff? You ever do that at the SEC? We don't do as much of it here at the IRS as we used to. We don't sneak around so much anymore. At this point we get what we want just by clicking keyboards. That's what most field agents do, you know."

"Whatever," she said petulantly. "But I want to be out in the field. Can you make it happen?" She had regressed to being a teenager, as young people so often do when interacting with their parents.

"The vice president's chief of staff called me about you. Did you hear about that?"

"No."

"It seems they're interested in your career. I'm sure your looks don't hurt in making sure this little personnel exchange they concocted gets positive press. So I'm confident I've got substantial flexibility. I'd like to see you move up, and it's important to me that the VP be happy. But, as far as fieldwork is concerned, there are all kinds of people out there, and some of them take it personally when you show up asking for money. You'll need more training."

"That's fine by me."

"Okay, but you won't be working in this building anymore. You won't be able to come and get what you want, whenever you want, just by knocking on my door."

"I'll have a telephone."

The deputy commissioner considered which locations might offer his daughter the best combination of safety and upward mobility. He automatically ruled out rural communities in places like Wyoming and Idaho: she didn't like boring, and those places were full of armed rednecks with anachronistic independent ideas. Forget about the big cities. It wasn't *just* the ghettoes and barrios and the too many armed and bad-tempered men unlikely to treat a cute white girl with the respect she deserved. In the cities there were also too many IRS careerists who would try to crowd out a rookie. A file folder caught his eye. "How about a place outside LA called Laguna Niguel."

"It sounds tropical. That's where I wanna go. Laguna Niguel."

"It isn't tropical. It's LA."

"LA has palm trees. And movie stars and film producers. Send me there."

"Okay, Sabina. Whatever you want, but let's do it on a trial basis, agreed? Don't give up your apartment here in DC just yet."

"I'm good with that."

"You've never conducted an investigation. As far as I know, you've never even shot a gun." Then a thought occurred to him. "Ever threatened a taxpayer?" This last question made Lichen wince as, despite himself, he relived a flashback.

He recalled a field audit he'd performed early in his career on a manufacturer of steel fittings in the eastern suburbs of Chicago. The audit revealed evidence of clear intent: a criminal case. Standard operating procedure was to file the criminal case first. It intimidated the citizen and softened his will to resist as his defense attorney's fees mounted. Even if the IRS lost the criminal case, the civil matter of taxes due was a separate action that invariably followed. If the IRS won the criminal case, which usually meant a jail sentence for the accused, that would act as a warning to others who might be defiant. And they all wanted to defy—although most were such whipped dogs they wouldn't dare take action. Most important of all, a conviction would be a huge feather in his cap, and a commendation in his file.

He had set up an appointment with the company's CEO and majority shareholder, Ron Marelsky. He had planned to ask Marelsky a battery of questions formulated to get the man to incriminate himself. As he entered the CEO's office, he noted that Marelsky didn't have his lawyer with him. Fool. Many taxpayers, in a false sense of economy, tried to save money on attorney's fees and took the interview by themselves.

During the meeting, it became clear that Marelsky had sized him up as a lion might a wildebeest on the African veldt. Marelsky stepped from behind his somewhat cluttered desk, approached the seated Lichen, and grabbed him high on his lapels.

"Lichen, I don't like you. And I don't like you coming in here and disrupting my business. Now, I know you probably feel safe because you work for the IRS. I've got news for you...." Marelsky flipped Lichen off the chair and onto his stomach, making no effort to prevent his face from smashing down on the floor. He placed his knee on Lichen's back and extracted his wallet. He opened it and withdrew Lichen's driver's license.

"Is this your correct address?"

Lichen grunted an affirmative.

"I asked one of my buddies from the old neighborhood to tail you. I had you followed home. You didn't lie to me, so I won't lie to you.

119

I know you've probably found a few things that might be somewhat inconvenient for me. I'm not interested in doing the legal dance with your employer. So here's the drill. You close this investigation now, and we get a clean bill of health."

"Or what," Lichen had grunted in what he remembered as a pitiful effort at trying to maintain his feelings of manhood.

"Or I will burn your house down. And then I'll kill you."

Marelsky let him up.

Lichen stood, uncertain. Marelsky reached into his desk drawer and withdrew a .357 revolver, its hollow-point rounds visible on each side of the cylinder. Tears dripped down Lichen's cheeks.

Marelsky put down the weapon. "I'm not gonna kill you yet. Disposing of a body during the business day isn't easy, let me tell you." From the same drawer, he withdrew an envelope over two inches thick and handed it to Lichen.

"Here's $25,000. I don't ever want to hear from you or see you again. And make sure nobody else comes around. If they do, you're a dead man."

Lichen stood still for a minute. Prior to this experience Lichen had no concept of the depth of terror he could feel. Justifications flew through his mind: a bribe offered, even if rejected, would taint his file forever; Marelsky stood there forcing him at gunpoint. But the reality was that he wanted—he *needed*—the money. It was a classic offer that couldn't be refused: an effective use of both the carrot and the stick. So he made his decision. He reached for the white envelope

Lichen hesitated to put his daughter into similar danger, but she was demanding it. And she was right: the vice president would want to see her in some newsworthy action that he could take credit for.

Sabina had to repeat her statement to be heard through Lichen's thick reveries, "I work at the IRS, so I threaten taxpayers every day, Dad," she laughed. "Been doing it for months now. And I've been learning all the material, taking all the classes. I've even been on the pistol range. Every week too."

That was a surprise to Lichen, and it drew him back to the present. "Good for you," he said. "But absent formal training, you're at a disadvantage. And you can never be sure who you might run into. Some of these people can take it personally." He wondered how many other agents had met people like Marelsky. Even as chief of enforcement, he'd never know that. It wasn't something anyone would ever talk about.

"I'll handle 'em."

Lichen insisted. "You need to train alongside someone who knows what they're doing. I'll put you in with Special Agent in Charge Frank Graves at Laguna. I was just about to contact him about a guy I'm interested in. Matter of fact, this case might be perfect for you. It could have implications for the SEC someday, a synergy that would make the VP especially happy."

The relevant file folder was right at hand. "This is the guy that caught my eye. Charles Knight. Not much more than a kid. Roughly your age. Seems he chooses not to pay taxes. The guy's already been involved in a handful of small businesses and a bit of consulting but has never held a salaried job. He took a hit from the Service with his first business, when he was sixteen years old. Something about the Internet. We nailed him for back taxes, penalties, and interest. Crybaby closed down. Ever since, he's not declared enough income to be taxed, but he has a lot of revenues and expenses moving around. His tax returns are always done at the last minute, and he always has a zero tax burden. To the penny. The chances are excellent that he's a tax rebel."

"A tax rebel?"

"Yeah. The patterns in these returns tell us he's more than just an evader. This guy is out to make a point. He's young and probably thinks he's immortal. He has the balls to think he would get away with this. His zero-dollar returns paint a nice target on his back. Ever since all the talk about tax rebellion started appearing, we've been watching for these types. The money amounts are small. But the White House wants us to target rebels and protesters particularly and make examples of them. They want to see some heads on pikes in front of the castle walls. And we want to show the White House we care about what they want."

Sabina idly flipped through the file. "I'll make sure the vice president will care. *And* the president, for that matter. Charles Knight sounds like the job for me."

"And the vice president will likely be the next president. We score points with two presidents—that's potentially fourteen years to turn this to our advantage—if you succeed in nailing this bastard. Moreover, it's good PR."

Sabina smiled. "I presume he writes everything off as a business expense. Has he been audited recently?"

"We can only audit 2 percent of returns, and his wasn't one of them. I don't want a regular audit. It needs to be juicy. Something the news media will pick up on; label him as unpatriotic, not doing his fair share. Push the envy button: it's guaranteed to get the chimpanzees hooting and panting. Joe Sixpack likes it when he can see we're cutting down the tall poppy."

He pulled out a water bottle and took a sip. He didn't offer one to Sabina.

After swallowing, he said, "People need to know we're on the job. We need a proper poster boy, and you're the cover girl to get him." Lichen smiled, seeing that his inner poet could still turn a phrase. "Take every dime this guy has, and make him into an enemy of the people. We need a handful of these cases to publicize every year around April tax time. It keeps them lining up and saluting. But you need to find something solid on him. Or at least something we can make look solid."

"How do you want me to do that?"

"*You're* the field agent. Figure it out. The file says he's just moved to San Diego. That's in Frank Graves's region. But, Sabina, this is important: the IRS has a 90 percent successful prosecution rate for criminal tax fraud. It's my stated purpose to bring that to a 100 percent. The bastards should have no hope, and that's what 100 percent means. So don't screw that up!"

"I won't."

Lichen's face darkened. "If you can't be absolutely sure of a criminal conviction on Knight, and I mean 100 percent sure, then I don't want to see any indictment at all. Do you hear me? This is a matter of 'Go big, or go home.' Our batting average is critical. This isn't about a few extra bucks in tax. It's about the effectiveness of fear and the inescapable power we wield. This is your big chance. But since you don't know shit about investigation, you'll have to convince both Graves and me you've got the goods. I will not let anyone risk messing up my record!"

Not even his own daughter.

And with that, he dismissed his daughter.

She was a selfish little bitch. But he was proud of her for precisely that reason.

15

A Theory of Speculation

XANDER Winn's prognosis was improving. That morning, Dr. Henderson—an anesthesiologist from Texas—had discontinued the intravenous medications that had induced his coma. The hospital ship's CT scanner revealed no brain damage. As Charles visited his bedside, he began to move a bit.

A bolt, a device used to measure the pressure in his skull, protruded through gauze sponges. Caroline told him this tool would sound an alert if the pressure in his head rose. By the time Xander could get up and about, it would be gone, leaving just a small scar on his now-shaved head. The shave made Xander look intimidating, and the effect might come in handy soon. If only he would recover before their window of time closed....

"They will probably get him off the ventilator today. He should be talking soon enough. With epidural hematomas, when the patients live, they usually recover completely."

"Great. That's great, Caroline."

Charles sat next to Xander in the ICU. He felt alone and out of his depth. He needed his new partner back. Time passed, Xander slept, and Charles occupied his mind with a quixotic effort to place into context the world in which he was now immersed—a world that was not business, but something else.

The stock price of B-F had jumped yesterday; no doubt Uncle Maurice wasn't the only recipient of the leaked news of B-F's deal with Burke. Over $160 at the close in Toronto, an increase of $11 on the day. Once publicly released, the announcement of Burke International Mining's joint-venture partnership with B-F would supercharge the market. With most remaining doubts quelled, institutions and sophisticated individuals who'd been waiting on the sidelines would become active buyers. All that remained was for the big-name mass media—which rarely even acknowledged the existence of mining except as an ecological hazard—to feature stories on the world's largest gold discovery. The media's optimism and enthusiasm would soon rival that of Washerman and Smolderhof themselves. The newcomers would tell their friends, conspiratorially, of the great tip they had received. B-F was going to pop, they would say. Get on it now!

There was no rush like a gold rush.

The lemmings piling into the market fancied themselves investors. Some might be traders. Some thought they were speculators. But in fact, Charles realized, they were really just gamblers.

An investor, according to Uncle Maurice, puts capital into a business in order to create more wealth. He plants a seed that, diligently nurtured, results in a corn stalk yielding hundreds of new seeds. In an ideal world, everyone produces more than he consumes and saves the difference. That surplus is capital.

But it's easier to suckle off the government teat. So money finds its way to enterprises that know best how to suck. Companies direct evermore resources to lobby legislators and regulators so that the teat gets bigger and they get more of it.

Whether a side effect or the intended primary effect, the central bank's monopoly on money together with the government's regulations inhibit the efficient flow of information, effort, and capital. Regulations waste labor in a myriad of ways, and make things especially difficult for smaller companies to compete with the big boys. Fiat currency causes malinvestment, as free money is misallocated. Who cares how free money is spent? Whole economic sectors boom or bust with the whims of the politically powerful and the coked-up exuberance of testosterone-laden suits.

In a politicized environment, it's easier to make money by betting on how and when government-caused economic distortions will unwind, than to figure out how best to create new value. It becomes, as Uncle Maurice taught, more profitable to be a speculator than an investor.

But Charles's motivation went beyond profit. He felt morally justified betting against the government. And he liked rooting for and helping out the underdog. And that's what speculators do. Speculators improve market liquidity by buying something when no one else wants to buy. Speculators often attempt to profit from the inefficiencies caused by government intervention in the market. Because they don't focus on creating new wealth but instead capitalize on dysfunction and disasters, speculators have developed a bad reputation in the mind of the public.

A trader tries to profit from fluctuations in the market; he's philosophically agnostic. A gambler just uses the market as a legalized casino, placing bets and hoping to get lucky. Investors, speculators, traders, and gamblers are very different—but often confused.

Charles's own brief experience in the investment world confirmed that much of it was highly uncertain. He concluded that it made little sense to risk 100 percent of his capital on conservative investments that might give him a 10 percent return—if he was lucky. It made more sense to allocate 10 percent of his portfolio to speculations that could yield 1000 percent gains. If a speculation panned out it would, alone, double total starting capital, regardless of what happened to the other 90 percent of the portfolio.

The key, of course, was to find things with both big potential and low risk. That usually meant looking for deals that were severely beaten down. Not because they were bad, but because of irrational panic on the part of the public or foolish action on the part of the government.

Charles was further enticed by the idea of speculation after Uncle Maurice had pointed out an important downside of starting businesses: was it worth building a business when the tax authorities took 50 percent of the profits but zero percent of the risk? They were a shadow partner who used the business as their piggybank, contributing nothing except counterproductive rules and pointless prohibitions. Starting a company took dedication and sweat and capital, most of which inured to the benefit of a parasite.

He found himself increasingly attracted to contrarian views, out of the mainstream. Most people, navigating the waters of life, seemed sonar directed, setting their course based on what the rest of the school of fish was doing. These sonar-directed types spent their days pinging their surroundings, turning—often suddenly and without understanding

125

why—when everyone else turned. Perhaps if they turned fast enough the ones on the edges would get eaten, instead of them. It was safer, but the crowd, necessarily, always got average results. And occasionally the entire mass got swallowed whole.

Charles preferred to set his course with an internal gyroscope that largely disregarded where the others might be going.

Forgoing college was neither the first nor the last time he would break from the school.

Charles reached up and rested his hand on Xander's arm. After a bit, he rose, braved the heat on the ship's deck, and found a bench.

His cell phone rang. A local number, not the States. That was strange. Who had his number here? Nobody did. Probably a wrong number. But he answered it.

"Hello?"

An accented male voice came on the line. "Hallo, sir. I am with Diacom Cellular Communications. I am calling to tell you about a new service Diacom is offering its valued clients in West Africa. You can save much money. Would you be interested in hearing?"

"No, thank you," Charles replied, and pressed the END button before there was time for a response. It didn't feel right. He muttered, "You wouldn't think they'd make sales calls here in Gondwana." He turned off the phone altogether. He should have done that earlier.

Caroline found him moments later. A welcome waft of sea breeze moved through her hair on the way toward cooling his skin.

He wanted to greet her with something witty or brilliant but could only think of, "I just got a sales call on my cell phone."

Her voice was soft and amused. "Sales calls, lottery tickets, paying athletes and lawyers far too much money… it's all coming to Gondwana. There ought to be a law.…"

Charles responded with a wry smile, "I'm okay with salesmen, lotteries, and athletes. But there was a reason Shakespeare recommended killing all the lawyers. In my ideal world there would be only two laws: don't initiate force or fraud, and do all you say you're going to do. Beyond that, everybody has a right to go to hell in his own way."

"For a guy who smiles a lot, you're so serious." Caroline sat down next to Charles, closer than she needed to, and then turned her knees

126

toward his, the cloth of her scrubs touching the crease in his pants. "Are those the only laws you would make if you ran a country?"

He laughed. "I'm as likely to run a country as I am to deal drugs, go on a killing spree, or start a religion."

"That's good, because if you can't lie, you can't rule. Or so I hear."

"Well, you know I don't like to lie."

"But you do keep secrets." She nudged him playfully with her shoulder, but then did not pull away.

"As Captain Freberg said last night, the truth is valuable, so it's not free. I don't like lying, but at the same time I don't owe everybody the truth."

Their words primarily provided cover for the slight but increasingly provocative contact of their knees.

Charles continued. "Lying to others is bad enough, but lying to myself is actually worse. I don't have to live with other people, but I have to live with myself."

Caroline reached up to his face with her hand, and turned it toward her own.

"You're such a man of mystery," she said teasingly.

Her eyes were so close to his. Her scent excited him. He was uncomfortably aware of the oppressive heat of the sun on the metal of the bulkhead behind him. He wanted to tell her much more than his name.

Time passed and neither cared.

His rational mind overcame temptation. "If I tell you my name, you won't be safe. Besides, in a couple of months this will all barely be a memory, and then it won't matter if you know my name."

Caroline pulled back quickly, her hands falling away from his face, and her expression falling with them. She looked away, and quietly said, "I hope you don't believe that."

"Oh god, Caroline. I didn't mean it that way." He laughed. "Not at all! We men are sometimes socially autistic. I hope you can forgive me. What I meant is that the whole thing that led to us getting shot at will be long gone, and no one will care who I am. No one will feel a need to find me. Being near me won't be dangerous."

It took Caroline a moment to recover from the emotional hit of the misunderstanding. She didn't bring her hands back to him. Instead she said, "Three billion dollars justifies a lot of paranoia. When you said 'billion,' did you mean that?"

"Actually, as of today, it's quite a bit more."

They sat in silence then, but their bodies—through the closeness of their knees and shoulders—kept talking.

*   *   *

"Did it sound like Knight?" Barney asked Harry. They stood next to a Gondwanan man who sat with a telephone headset adhered to his scalp in the operations facility of Diacom.

Harry replied, "Yah… it probably was him."

The telephone operator studied his computer screen. "He connected through the tower on Bushton Island. Between Kpelltown and the Freeport."

"Is that a big area?" Roscoe asked.

Harry grunted. "Big enough, mah friend. But it's a good start, yah?" He handed the operator a hundred-dollar bill. "Let's go see what we can see and hear what we can hear."

16

The Bear in the Ziggurat

THE Chet Holifield Federal Building at Laguna Niguel is a broad seven-tier step pyramid built upon an asphalt parking-lot plateau. The architect intended to convey the impression of an impenetrable fort capped by rows of cannon and sniper ports. That made sense, for Rockwell International commissioned the building to service a major defense contract. When the deal failed to materialize, Rockwell traded the building to the federal government for some other property. Intellectual precedent for the architect's design included not only Mesopotamian ziggurats, but also the description of George Orwell's Ministry of Love. It served as an ideal headquarters for the IRS Regional Criminal Investigation Office.

Few would approach this building uninvited. And nobody liked the idea of an invitation.

The IRS shared the building with the Department of Homeland Security—an apt juxtaposition, for the one fueled the state with revenue, and the other justified the state's existence by identifying real and imagined threats. The two massive agencies integrated ever more effectively as the IRS's vast files on US taxpayers networked into those of Homeland Security to feed its appetite to know everything about everybody.

The building rose above the surrounding neighborhoods: endless middlebrow housing subdivisions, inhabited by the agencies' prey. Sabina strode toward the main entrance, about to begin the next chapter of her career. But first she had to walk across the moat that surrounded most of the building as if it were a fortress. It was Jabba the Hutt's palace in *Star Wars*. It was the evil medical building in *Coma*. It was a science fiction objectification of a dystopian future.

Belying the exotic façade, inside it was just an office building as dehumanizing and depressing as one in Moscow.

Cubicles the size and shape of tiny prison cells existed for the menial laborers, not for someone like Sabina. The power Sabina sensed she could obtain in the place made it fresh and exciting. It aroused her. As soon as she entered the hive, she found herself involuntarily evaluating her surroundings for a potential sexual partner, even among the unappealing drones and worker bees she passed.

Perhaps Special Agent in Charge Frank Graves would make the grade.

She worked her way to the admin suite and stood before the greeting secretary, Sue, who looked up at her pleasantly and introduced herself.

Sue was overweight, her round face like that of a grown-up Gerber baby. With porcine eyes scrunched between generous cheeks, she served, at least to outward appearances, as the archetypal jolly lady. Sabina surmised everyone in the office at least pretended to love her, not because she had any particular virtues, but because of her bubbly and inoffensive nature. Perhaps her personality developed as a defense, to ward off verbal barbs about her size, like those that had plagued her youth. Sabina immediately despised her.

"Hi, Sue." Sabina's voice flowed like syrup. "I love that scarf you're wearing."

Sue beamed back. "Thank you so much. Scarves are so pleasant, so full of life." The corn-fed girl had a Minnesota accent. It came as a surprise, for Sabina assumed that the Midwest would only export its best-looking stock to LA, where the competition was notoriously severe.

"Aren't they?" Sabina oozed. "You know, sometimes I wrap myself up in a favorite scarf and fall asleep. They smell so good, don't you think?" Sabina spoke the words as if she cared.

"Oh! I think so too, but I've never heard anyone else who felt the same."

Bingo, thought Sabina. Alliance assured. Office drones, however distasteful, provided a necessary service. No amount of yelling could reverse the behavior of a passive-aggressive administrative assistant who wanted to make your life miserable. Nor did any way exist to fire civil servants without an agonizing year-long process, and they all knew it.

"Sue, I'm Sabina Heidel. A new SA."

"Oh, Special Agent Heidel! I'm so glad to meet you. They just told us about your assignment here this morning!" Sue's exaggerated smile complemented her heartland accent; the playful lilt in her words tortured Sabina.

"I just found out myself a couple of days ago."

"Oh, wow. That's fast. We're all thrilled to have you here." Like everything Sue said, the words were accompanied by a pointless giggle.

Sue walked around the desk, saying, "Let me take you to Special Agent Graves. You'll like him. I like him. Everybody likes him." She ushered Sabina through a door after passing an ID card across a security pad, and started down a long hall. "You haven't had time to settle into your new home here, I suppose?"

Small talk constituted about 98 percent of Sue's conversational repertoire. Such banter was a chore for Sabina, but a necessary evil. "Actually, I've literally just arrived. I'm staying at a hotel until I get my bearings."

"Oh, you'll want a home soon, Special Agent Heidel. You folk spend a ton of time in hotels as it is. We cover the whole of the western US, including Alaska, Hawaii, and the Pacific possessions, all from this office. There are never enough SAs to deal with all the tax cheats, money launderers, drug dealers, and terrorist types. There are so many now." An air that combined confidentiality and disapproval permeated her bouncy voice.

"Well, I'm going to help cut back on their numbers, Sue."

"You keep up that energy, Sabina, and you'll settle in here just great. You'll like Frank Graves. Everybody does."

Everybody likes Frank Graves. Sue had said so repeatedly. A man of the people. Such news made it substantially less likely that Sabina would like Frank Graves. But her father seemed to respect him, so no judgments yet.

Sue stopped talking for a moment and knocked on a closed door.

"Come in." The response came as if from a distance. Perhaps the office behind the door was enormous.

Sue opened the door for Sabina and ushered her in formally. "Special Agent in Charge Graves, this is Special Agent Sabina Heidel." The flush of her face exposed her delight in her proximity to the administrative elite.

The office was not so large. What had muffled his voice was a large banana, half swallowed, half stuffed in his mouth. His cheeks puffed out like those of a squirrel. After what seemed like an interminable period, he swallowed, twice, and shook his head.

"Caught me at a bad time there, Miss Heidel." He said it with an easy smile. "I keep getting stuck with food in my mouth. Better than with my foot in my mouth though, ain't it?"

Sue laughed. "Oh, Mr. Graves. Behave yourself. This is your new agent!" She left the office, smiling and giggling as she closed the door.

A picture of Graves and his bride, from years earlier, hung on the wall to the side.

Graves came from around the desk to greet her. His hand was firm, dry, confident. So this was Frank Graves. He didn't make a great visual impression, that's for sure. But, again, her father liked him. Everyone liked him. Sabina wondered what sort of meat she would find under that fat.

He had a big head, full cheeks, not unlike Sue's, and uncontrolled thick wavy black hair that made no sense to comb. He was a grizzly bear: fat, but muscular and tall, like an ex–football lineman. That was it. He was a big, cuddly grizzly bear.

She would never cuddle with Frank Graves. Cuddling was an insufferable chore.

Sabina possessed confidence in her looks, and in her practiced style. She made easy work of men of all sizes, shapes, and colors. It was like playing with dolls. They would do exactly what she wanted, as long as she pushed the right buttons. Sabina found that most men had the same set of buttons.

Sometimes she sought out a man who could be molded like a wad of putty. These men stuck out from the crowd even while they tried to fade into it: depressed, tired, and damaged. She could spot them without exchanging a word, by the lines of their face, the look in their eyes, the slight stoop, and so many other signs that created an ambiance of defeat. They emitted pheromones that attracted a predator, and she was proud of her predator's sixth sense for such weakness. The tools muggers use to target their next mark, Sabina adopted to target her next toy.

How she could influence these men to *feel* almost anything! Guilt when *she* had sex with another man; fear that she would get bored with them. Love, such love for her! And they would *do* almost anything for her too—betray their friends, empty their bank accounts, even commit crimes. Sabina smiled at the thought. Her relationships were perfect: profitable to her and rarely lasting more than a month or two. Like rapidly turning tables in a restaurant.

She kept her eyes out for the appearance of a rich or powerful one.

But the man in front of her did not trigger her sixth sense. In fact, she felt... *intimidated?*

"So, this is a bit of a strange request from the deputy commissioner. He wants me to mentor you, one-on-one...."

"I'm an experiment, actually, as the first exchange of personnel to the IRS from the SEC, under the vice president's Efficiency Enhancement Initiative," Sabina replied. "Deputy Commissioner Lichen wants the program to be a big success, and thinks partnering new agents with the best experienced agents, right from the start, might be a better education than group classes and training. Perhaps new agents can learn more quickly directly from the masters. And since I came in from outside the organization, it's less likely anyone would get worked up about bypassing normal channels as the idea gets tested."

"Never thought of Lichen as a man who cared much for the individualized treatment of people."

"Huh?" She really had no idea what he meant.

Graves seemed to brush it off. "Well, it impresses me as a good idea, perhaps the best idea ever to come out of that office. And it would appear you and I, Heidel, are the first test bed."

She could have jumped on his bed reference, initiating the verbal foreplay, setting the stage for sexual tension, hope, desire, possibility. But she didn't sense an opening. This was going to be a challenging relationship: this man seemed to lack the normal buttons.

"First," he said, "and I am doing this off the cuff here, first, I think you should simply shadow me. Work here in this office. We'll set up a spare desk for you over there. When I'm in meetings, you'll join me. You will report directly to me on any fieldwork I assign you."

She reflexively risked a teasing query that she knew she shouldn't. "Won't your wife get jealous?"

Graves's eyes went dead for a second, as if he were recalibrating his brain, but then perked back up with a little laugh. "Um. I'm sorry. That simply never crossed my mind. And by the way, Special Agent Heidel, it never will." At the end his tone was completely flat, as was his face.

She stood there, dumbfounded.

Graves smiled. "Okay, that's behind us. Let's get to work."

It was not behind them for Sabina. To her, a challenge had been issued, a gauntlet thrown down. For the first time, she had no idea how she would do it, but she would not be satisfied until she found a way to bed this man.

Graves added, "The deputy commissioner said you would have a file for me."

"Yes." She reached into her shoulder bag. "It's pretty thin so far. We don't have much to go on. A young guy who doesn't like to pay taxes, has some small business entities, and moves cash about."

"What's he do?"

"Right now, he's listed as a speculator." She did not try to contain her disdain.

Graves shook his head. "Why do you say that with such bitterness?"

"My time at the SEC has made me jaded. And suspicious."

"Hmm." Graves sat back in his chair and leafed through the folder. "Okay, well, he's not rolling in dough, according to this. But, let's start looking and see what we find. Let's get all the pieces we can get through the usual channels. Start easy. Put it all together. Sue will help. In a couple of hours, you tell me if you think you have anything at all worth pursuing."

"Special Agent Graves, the guy is too young to be dealing with this many businesses. He's self-employed. He's had trouble with us before, and he winds up paying zero tax every year. My guess is he's hiding lots of his income offshore somewhere, thinking he's going to get away with it. He's a tax cheat. I can smell it in him."

"May I ask how old you are?"

"Twenty-four." She held her chin up, proud of how far she had come in her twenty-four years.

"Charles Knight is about your age, but he's already been on the ground floor of four small enterprises, three of them active, the other

134

one killed by us." Graves sat back in his chair and examined Sabina, who had really done nothing of value in her life, and sized her up.

He pursed his lips for twenty seconds and said nothing, thinking to himself, "It makes me wonder how *you* might smell to *him*."

Aloud, however, he said, "No more than three hours." And he turned to the papers on his desk by way of dismissal.

17

The Nine *P*'s in Intensive Care

XANDER awoke with difficulty. He had the appearance of a recently defeated bar fighter. The doctors had removed the tube from his throat and the bolt from his skull, but an IV still dripped barbiturates into his arm, and so he drifted in and out of consciousness. Charles wanted to be there when Xander's brain resynchronized with his senses.

"Mr. Winn. I'm glad you're awake." Charles put his hand on Winn's arm.

"Mr. Knight." His speech came weakly. Winn ran a dry tongue over cracked lips. "Thanks for saving me."

Charles smiled and shook his head gently. It was good to have him among the living. "You were in pretty bad shape. We got lucky."

Xander wriggled in the bed, pushing himself higher. He grimaced. It was not just his head, but his butt, too, where the bullet had torn through a lot of flesh, but fortunately no bone. A bullet damages the body mainly by transferring its high kinetic energy to the tissues into which it travels. If a high-mass or high-velocity bullet slams to a stop inside of a bone, the destruction conveyed by that much energy on the tissue is profound. In contrast, if a metal-jacketed bullet spirals right on through the body and is not stopped by bone, then less energy is transferred and less damage occurs. In target shooting, a paper bull's-eye receives a clean circular puncture wound as the bullet flies through it, while the tree behind, in which the bullet is stopped, splinters and shakes as chunks of wood explode out of it.

Fortunately, the bullet that hit Winn had gone straight through his muscle tissue and lay in the jungle somewhere outside of Gbarngeda. The trauma to his head was a much more dangerous injury.

"Can you catch me up? How long has it been?"

"A couple of days." The place smelled of rubbing alcohol and bleach, improved only by a faint perfume that a nurse nearby wore.

A pause. "We're on the *Africa Grace*?"

"Yes. They fixed you up, and here we are."

"I'm glad you aren't dead, kid."

"Kinda happy about that myself. But I wasn't in danger. You were."

"We both *are* in danger. And lots of it."

Charles knew that. But he felt secure enough here on the ship, anonymous. "I haven't left the ship. I haven't called anyone. I haven't even told TJ where his car is. The doctors and the ship captain don't know our names. They're keeping our presence here quiet."

"That's smart of you. But you'll have to tell the captain, if you trust him. It's his ship." He took a deep breath and winced. "Any chance they expect we're still in country?"

"I suppose. If they're even looking for us. They may have assumed we were just thieves, don't you think?"

Xander grimly said, "A white thief in Gondwana? I don't think so. Anything suspicious happened since?"

"Nothing." Except maybe that cell phone call, he thought.

"Good," Xander said, sleepily. "There's nothing more boring than lying in a hospital bed. I need conversation and some help clarifying my thoughts on B-F. My brain is still scrambled. Let's see if we can figure out B-F Explorations by thinking carefully. Cover all the bases. Let's do this logically. Use the Nine *P*'s. You talk, I listen."

The wounded and drugged Xander did not look like he would want to engage in such a conversation, but his appearance might belie his acuity. And anyway, Charles reasoned, the conversation might indicate how well his brain was working within his damaged skull.

"Certainly, Mr. Winn. The Nine *P*'s it is." Charles began. "The first *P* is the *people*. It's the most important thing by far, more important than all the others put together. Do the people in charge have experience and past success? Smolderhof wears many hats in the field: prospector, geologist, mining engineer, and on-site manager among them.

Banga Sioquelle seems to be Smolderhof's jealously guarded turf; he's the technical end of the business. And we have some indication that he has something to hide."

"What about Washerman?" Xander's words slurred and his eyes closed.

Charles replied, "Ben Washerman is the financial side of the operation. He's founder and president of B.F. Washerman Associates." He paused and waited to see if Winn was still with him at all.

"Mr. Winn?"

Charles stayed by Xander's bed in case he might wake soon. But his thoughts turned to Washerman, whom he had met when he first became interested in B-F. Charles had studied up on him, the public face of the company. Washerman had founded B-F Explorations as a corporate shell in Canada—where 75 percent of the world's mining-exploration capital was raised. He took three million shares at a penny for himself, and then raised another $500,000 from the usual suspects at ten cents on the assumption that he'd be able to find a viable asset and—based on his ability to tell a good story in a good market—take it public at a buck.

Through the grapevine—everybody in the small world of exploration knew everyone else, if only indirectly—Washerman hooked up with Smolderhof, who had this prospect in West Africa and was willing to vend the asset into the shell for three million shares. It was, at the beginning, a typical, garden-variety deal.

Washerman stayed relatively innocent of real knowledge of geology or mining, although over the years he had absorbed enough to talk the talk. Washerman was not a micromanager, but a big-picture guy, a promoter, an impresario. Tall, fit, handsome, charismatic, and just past sixty, he focused on how to put people and deals together. He was in charge of bringing money in the door. Washerman spent his days bouncing around Canada, the States, and Europe making his pitch, talking up the share valuation for the next round of funding. B-F Explorations was the latest and, especially at his stage of life, probably the last of his efforts in a record mostly unblemished by real success. Previously, when his luck coincided with a bull market or two, Washerman blew out his shares, giving him just enough capital to reload for the next round.

After twenty years of scrambling from one enterprise to the next, of failure followed by small success followed by failure, the natural pitchman's savvy and chutzpah were finally paying off—he'd hit a genuine mother lode. Now he wasn't promoting just another parcel of moose pasture, as were thousands of other tiny exploration companies trading in Canada, the US, Australia, and the UK, almost all of them long on hope and hype, and short on money and worthwhile properties. He no longer had to ask for cash to keep the lights on: people now begged him to take their money.

Winn's eyes half opened. "Talk to me, kid."

Charles nodded. "We were talking about the people. As an academic geologist, Smolderhof is well-enough respected. Washerman has had success and failures. Goodluck Johnson, the Gondwanan owner of the land, is an unknown. None of them are known conmen. So, up front, the B-F people are maybes. I wouldn't necessarily gravitate toward them, but neither—excepting our experience of the other night, of course—would they cause me to run and hide."

Winn nodded and his voice strengthened. "I agree. Washerman and Smolderhof are two struggling professionals in different sectors of the mining business. Both have been around the block many times, hoping for lightning to strike, hoping they find the next Treasure of the Sierra Madre before the mule dies or the pick breaks, so they can retire in the manner to which they'd like to become accustomed."

Apparently cynicism was not blunted by barbiturates.

"What's next?" Winn sounded impatient.

"*Property*. Is the place an ore body or just rock? Has it been examined with drilling, or just by sampling surface rocks and trenching? Only drilling is trustworthy. Based on the results so far, Banga Sioquelle is as good as it gets. Ultra high grade, consistent, and truly enormous."

Xander asked with his eyes closed, "What else about property is important?"

"How easy it is to mine, to process, to ship."

Xander opened his eyes and said, "B-F isn't a winner there, but not too bad either. Their property isn't under water. Their ore isn't thousands of feet underground; it's right on the surface. They claim the nanogold is easy to recover. The market believes them about that, but based on what? That may be a weakness. So far, B-F is mainly about great drill holes and amazing assay results. But that puts them a country mile ahead of 99.8 percent of the competition. What's next?"

139

"*Phinancing*, with a *P-H*. Will a company have enough cash to do the necessary exploration, and will they then be able to get more money? As for B-F, they struggled at the beginning, but then with the third core the money started flowing. Dilution had a negligible effect on share value once the price soared. There's no debt. They've now got about $30 million in the bank. B-F gets an A+ for phinancing."

"Next?"

"*Paper*. What is the company's share structure? Will management give sweetheart deals to friends and dilute the current investors unfairly? Are there lots of cheap options and warrants out? Did the founders take a huge amount of performance shares at one cent each?" Charles shook his head. "Company structure is essential to the man who runs the company I'm now associated with in San Diego."

"Good for him. Elliot Springer is no idiot."

Charles looked at Xander thoughtfully. "I never told you who I worked with."

"You think I didn't know? What's next?"

Charles shrugged it off for the moment. He knew there was more to Xander Winn than the average Dutchman wandering around in the jungle. "Next is *promotion*. If the promoters hide their light under a bushel basket, a stock price might not rise even if they hit the mother lode. These companies are in constant need of more money, so a higher stock price is critical to minimize the effect of dilution on the existing shareholders, and that only happens if there are more buyers than sellers. No promotion, few buyers. For B-F, there's been no shortage of promotion. They've got half the industry media of North America and Europe pumping them up."

"And then there's *politics*," Xander said.

Here Charles felt he had a bit more to offer. "Yes, the politics can make or break anything. A country's politicians may welcome or despise the miners. If they were elected by being green and hugging the environmentalists, then the whole periodic table of the elements will be their enemy. The most developed countries are probably the biggest risk today, because they'll just stop development cold. On the flip side, strong men and dictators will let you build the mine, but then they want to use it as a piggybank, turning an economic ore body back into a moose pasture. For B-F, they have a country that seems stable for the moment, if only because it's exhausted. At least it's not in an active war zone. Still, politics is probably the biggest single wild card."

"You're right. You build a multibillion-dollar mine, all that money is an up-front investment. And the politics can take it all away with the stroke of a pen. Next?"

"*Push*. What's going to push the stock higher, and when. A catalyst to get the show on the road now, as opposed to ten years from now. Perhaps underappreciated information, something that nobody else properly understands. That's a good reason to get boots on the ground."

"Yeah, we're not here for the weather or the food."

"There's a ton of push here. The stock keeps going up."

"Yet momentum can reverse. Bubbles built on hype invariably burst."

Charles nodded. "The next *P* of the Nine *P*'s is *price*. If the ore body is barely economic, barely able to return a profit, and then the price of gold falls, poof goes our money. If the price goes up, worthless land can become an economic ore body—risky, but an ore body nonetheless. I don't know what the price of gold will be in a day or a year, but I've got to be a long-term bull."

"What you say is all pretty much the way I see it. At least until the world's monetary and financial fundamentals get sorted out."

"And the final *P* is *pitfalls*. In essence, what can go wrong? How many black swans are getting ready to land? I suspect there are many that B-F has to face, including drill rigs spasming out of control."

Xander's eyes narrowed. "Or the two of us spasming out of control."

"Right."

Xander shifted his position with an unavoidable wince. "There's nothing like taking a look yourself to sharpen the mind. I'm not sure you could get a better education than being right here in the thick of it. Plus you got shot at. Now *that* is the way school is supposed to be, not sitting in a classroom looking at the clock. You owe me tuition and a beer."

"Maybe I'll pay you with one of those magic eggnogs."

"Remember, I don't have any spare blood right now, so that stuff might not work."

Through his closed eyes Xander warned Charles. "Be careful. There is a hell of a lot on the line here. The fact we're both wounded is fair proof these B-F guys aren't your typical mining-exploration folk. Remember, there aren't supposed to be any guns here in this country. Life sentence."

"I know."

"You didn't contact the police or the embassy about the other night, did you?"

"No. No way."

Charles suspected that the police in almost all of Africa were ineffectual at best, and might unpredictably become a direct danger to Charles and Xander if they made the local headlines. Any investigation would mostly be about how to extort money based on some real or fabricated violation of a Kafkaesque law. A visit to the embassy or consulate would just get his name into another government data bank. At most, they might refer him to a Xeroxed list of lawyers, likely compiled based on the quality of their smiles at embassy cocktail parties.

"Good." Winn nodded faintly. "Have you sold your position yet? Are you going to put on a short?"

"Short B-F? No. Well, not yet. But I've started selling what I own. I figured we would short together. Right now the price is still shooting up. Burke International has signed up with them."

"Interesting. It'll come to a head soon. Thanks for waiting." His speech slurred and slowed. "The share price will keep going up for a while still though. It's the biggest and richest gold mine in the world, after all. No one but you and I suspect otherwise. And they won't until Burke drills its own holes and does its own assays."

"Can we be completely sure it's a fraud, Xander?"

"That's what my gut tells me."

"Yeah, mine does too. Just what was that machine they didn't want me to see?"

But Xander didn't answer. His brain had depleted its available supply of neurotransmitters. He would sleep for the next sixteen hours.

A nurse came by and whispered in Charles's ear, "You need to let him rest."

After a potential brain injury, thinking can cause more damage as the cells struggle to process neurotransmitters. Neurons that have been shaken, squeezed, or deprived of oxygen or nutrients don't function smoothly until these cells have recovered. The process of thinking is itself a transfer of chemicals between billions of interconnecting brain cells, and the creation and transfer of those chemicals is work. That's why the brain demands more energy than any other organ in the body and receives the most blood flow.

But when brain cells are sick or injured, their metabolism is unbalanced and they use oxygen poorly. Free radicals, ions with spare electrons spinning around, are created. Free radicals cause oxidative stress—the equivalent of an ongoing slow-burning injury to cells that are already struggling to heal themselves from the first traumatic insult. Oxidative stress in the brain adds injury to insult. The best situation for healing is for the brain to have no stimulation and no stress until its ability to metabolize food and oxygen normally is corrected.

Yet Xander would soon be out of the hospital, experiencing more stress in a few days than most men experience in a lifetime.

18

A Search and a Party

THE cool rain washed the sweat out of Harry's eyes as he walked down Kpelltown's broken sidewalks, weaving around haphazardly parked cars. Every block or two he stopped to talk to a cell phone scratch card dealer, leaving his mobile number with each one. "If you see a brown-haired white guy, young, alone, then call it." He would have to toss his SIM card after they found Knight, because these African boys would keep calling him forever, not to ask for money, but just to say hello. They wanted a connection. They recognized that new contacts could lead to new opportunities.

He had received a dozen calls already. He ran some down; Roscoe and Barney took care of some others. Apparently there was no shortage of young white men popping through Kpelltown and the Freeport these days.

Things had changed considerably in just two years. Back then potholes made the neglected roads nearly impassable; now traffic clogged the streets—although many of the potholes loomed even larger. Electricity—non-existent then—now ran sporadically, at least in buildings that had their own Chinese-made generators humming in the back. People made fires in front of many buildings at night, sitting in small smoke-scented clusters of poverty with little to share except community and tales of the recent war. The country worked to revive itself, bit by bit. And the white Europeans and Americans—*Uhuru jumpers* as they'd come to be known—were arriving, some looking to recreate value from the wreckage, some looking to hook up with an assistant deputy minister who could help them steal what value remained. It made this current job of finding a specific white guy just a bit harder.

Harry stopped by another little cell phone scratch stand that was protected from the pounding rain by a nine-foot round blue-and-white umbrella emblazoned with the Diacom logo. Ten thousand of the shiny new umbrellas had recently landed from China at eight dollars apiece, and they covered almost every vendor in Adamstown while advertising the only competitor to Gondwana National Telecom. Although Diacom was a Gondwanan corporation, it was actually owned by an Israeli company and run in country by Lebanese. The Lebanese seemed to control everything in West Africa, the Indians everything in East Africa. Soon, however, the Chinese might be eating everybody's lunch.

"Hallo. How are you, my friend."

This vendor, small and thin, wore a round blue hat and a tight-fitting red shirt and sat on a wooden box. He was perhaps in his early teens. He smiled at Harry and replied with the standard West African lingo, "Body fine oh!"

"Right. I don't need scratch cards. I need to know you will call my cell phone right away if you see my good friend—a young white man with brown hair—if you see him walk by. If your call brings me to meet my good friend, then I will pay you one hundred US dollars. Here is my number." Harry started to turn away, out from under the umbrella and into the rain.

The boy looked at Harry's back and the small card with the scribbled phone number on it. He shouted, "Pay me fifty dollars now and I will tell you where I think he is. Then fifty more when you meet your friend." Harry understood the creole English, but most visitors would not, especially when the children spoke. What the boy said sounded like "Deh fiftymo wheyoumeeyofeh."

Harry turned around and stood up tall. He did not appreciate being hustled by a squirt. His large size didn't intimidate the boy, however; the kid just shrugged and turned to talk to a friend sitting on an upside-down wooden box behind him. Water ran between his bare feet, heading down the street. Rainwater management did not exist here, other than that provided by gravity and erosion.

Harry came back under the umbrella. "Hey, my young friend. What do you know?"

145

The little vendor turned back. "My brother works as a security guard. He say someone come into his place four nights ago, dat man you describe. Drove through in a jeep."

"What kind of jeep?"

"A white jeep."

"Anything else?"

"Yes. Your friend was in big hurry. Another man with him, hurt."

Okay, that was worth the fifty dollars. He reached into his wallet, pushed aside a wad of dirty Gondwanan dollars, and pulled out a new fifty-US-dollar bill. He watched as the boy's eyes lit up. This would be a huge day for the youngster.

The boy took the money. "My brother is a gate guard at, at, at the Freeport." He said it with pride. Again, it actually sounded like "Mabrah-daeegaygah a a a defeepo." But Harry understood.

The *Africa Grace*. Knight had gone to the *Africa Grace*. It made perfect sense, and he felt the fool for not having checked it first thing.

*   *   *

The ship felt lighthearted, for it was the evening of its monthly social. Caroline convinced a reluctant Charles to go, even though she was on duty and could not attend it herself.

Xander still slept. Charles again bought suitable clothes at the ship's store. It made no sense to risk returning to his hotel downtown.

The party, such as it was, had already started in the ship's international lounge. A few people stood around a piano in the corner, chatting quietly; others sat at linen-covered tables, sedately socializing. As a Christian charity ship, no alcohol was allowed aboard. So the red punch in the big glass bowl on the table by the wall remained unadulterated by the very thing Jesus was said to have made at Cana or to have drunk at his last supper.

At this rate, Charles thought, nobody would test the 10 p.m. cut-off for being alone in a cabin with a member of the opposite sex. No hanky-panky late at night on a Christian ship. *Except for a three-way*, he mused. He could always find some loophole. Indeed, his tax return preparations each year consisted of an extensive search for loopholes—it was his patriotic duty to deny revenue to the beast. After all, the government did not own him.

In contrast, the ship had an owner, and that owner had a right to set its rules. Could he avoid breaking the rules when it came to Caroline?

Sixty people milled around in small groups, pouring punch, chatting. Charles recognized a few of the ICU staff. The puritan party marched on, stilted and quiet. A piano in the corner offered some possibilities. Pianos had always beckoned to him. His love of music began with a player piano—one of those antique foot-pumped, air-driven automated pianos into which you placed a twelve-inch-wide roll of hole-punched paper and then pressed the pedals up and down as hard as you could. The harder you pressed, the louder it played as it read the perforated paper. Even when he was a child, most people had only seen them in a black-and-white movie, if that. But rural Montana had many remnants of a bygone era.

At age three, Charles would stand next to his father's legs as his dad pumped. It was his first memory of his father. Charles would try to predict which white or black keys would be pulled down and sound their notes under the influence of the player piano's great vacuum pump.

He stood there every night, eyes barely above the keys, memorizing those movements. His brain connected the moving keys with the music, much as a toddler correlates words with thoughts when learning a language. He learned how to press the keys before the player piano itself sucked them down. Three hundred music rolls came with the piano, and his fingers memorized them all. At age six, Charles found that if he sat on the very front edge of the bench and stretched his legs as far as he could, he was finally tall enough to pump the old instrument himself. His father then bought him a music roll a week from a mail order emporium. His fingers would have it mastered before the next roll arrived.

On the day the piano broke, it wheezed instead of played; one pedal ran free, putting no air in the bellows. The nearest person capable of rebuilding it worked in Maine, two thousand miles from Montana. The antique piano would be gone for a year, but to relieve Charles's deep dismay his father replaced it with a small upright, which Charles played without the rolls. With hundreds of songs under his belt, his fingers knew how to move with the confidence of muscle memory formed since he was three. He simply needed to learn how to read music, instead of read the punch holes in a roll of paper. So he did. By the time he was ten, listeners were sure he had been trained by an expert.

Only later did he realize that he had an exceptional ear. But even as a child, he knew firsthand the value of autodidacticism, long before he knew what the word meant. At sixteen, he performed in the Billings Symphony, and at twenty, with the New York Philharmonic—albeit with their Young People's Concert series.

He made his way over to the piano and, standing, plunked a few keys. It was just a spinet but in reasonable tune. That surprised him, for he imagined a shipboard piano in West Africa would be filled with critters, with its innards bent in half from moisture. He positioned himself comfortably on the bench and tested the pedals. He flexed his fingers, still slightly sore from the rope burns, and let fly with a piano version of Chuck Berry's "Johnny B. Goode."

Within a minute, as he had hoped, half the people gathered near the piano. It never failed. By the time he began playing "Oklahoma," everyone in the room crowded around. Someone started singing, a dozen others followed, in good voice. Many missed the lyrics for the verses here and there, but the choruses were solid.

Charles's fingers darted over the keys, his broad range of tempo and dynamics revealing that he was no ordinary pianist. His fingers sometimes flew too fast to see the keys being depressed, but they all rang out obediently. His aching shoulder and scabbed palms stopped complaining after the third tune.

A half-dozen songs later, he pushed the bench back. They clamored for more, laughed and enjoyed the punch, which now had the effect of an alcohol placebo. With the ice broken, the muted evening turned into a fun party. He would play twice more, once after a long conversation with one of the older nurses, and the next time after chatting with a couple of ship's crew—the master-at-arms and the ship's security officer.

The two men had minds wired very differently from those of the medical personnel. Years at sea had taught them to love the vessel that kept them alive when Poseidon wanted them dead; they seemed to care more for the metal ship than for the humanitarian services it provided.

Charles apologized for his anonymity and did his best to assure them he was not a criminal hiding from the authorities.

"It's strange talking to someone whose name you don't know," Pullings, the master-at arms, said pointedly. Charles hoped to never find himself on his bad side. Formerly British Navy, where he served as an armorer in charge of caring for a ship's weapons, he now managed surgical supplies on the *Africa Grace*.

They chatted for a time about bullets and rifles, a conversation that allowed Charles to ask, "Does the ship carry any weapons?"

"Yes. It's not general knowledge among the crew and medical staff, but yes, the ship has arms. When out to sea in pirated waters, our policy is not to turn the other cheek, as many commercial vessels do."

"So you could defend yourselves?"

"We could if we needed to. We've stayed in West Africa, except for refitting in South Africa. There is some pirate activity here, and it's growing more off Nigeria. Would pirates try to take a hospital ship? Probably. They could get a lot of attention that way. And they'd figure it would be a soft touch to ransom."

"But we'd be ready for them." The ship's security officer winked.

"What have you got in the way of arms?"

Pullings shrugged. "Can't tell a nameless man something like that. It'll have to remain a mystery, at least until *you* are no longer a mystery."

"That's fair. I plan to tell the captain about myself tonight; it's not my intention to play the international man of mystery. It seems like things are settling down. I may be out of the woods."

That was an unwise thing to say because it was an unwise thing to believe. Charles knew this before the words came out of his mouth. Being surrounded by the ship's steel bulkheads should provide him no comfort. There were doors. And there were only a few people on this ship who knew how to avoid shooting themselves if they were handed a weapon.

The captain arrived late and made the mandatory rounds. He approached the piano just as Charles played his final encore.

"Let's talk." It was a gentle command from a man used to compliance.

The open air on the fantail became the captain's office for the purpose of this conversation. The smoke of charcoal and the scent of yeast thickened the air. Charles thought of the upside-down, stripped-out refrigerators that the resilient residents of Gondwana now used as ovens. Charcoal burned in the freezer section in order to bake loaves of bread placed in the larger space above. The refrigerator door became an oven door.

Captain Freberg said, "Your friend may be up and around tomorrow."

"Yes, and we should probably make plans for leaving."

"I am not asking for that," the captain replied. "I am concerned about what danger you may be in, and what danger that presents to my ship and people."

"I understand. I'd ask for whatever confidentiality you feel you can offer...."

"Certainly."

Charles nodded. "My name is Charles Knight. I'm American, obviously. The man in your ICU is Xander Winn. He's Dutch. I just met him the day before we came on board. But, for a variety of reasons, I trust him. We both speculate in precious-metal ventures. We're here to check out a gold-mining venture that has a high-flying valuation."

"B-F Explorations?"

Charles cocked his head. "You've heard about it?"

"One of their men picked up typhoid a couple of months ago and stayed on board with us for a few weeks. B-F made a generous donation to the ship. It is the only gold-mining operation I know anything about."

"It's not the only one in the country, but it's the only booming one."

Captain Freberg nodded. "I know. I bought a few shares when the sick man told us what they had found. They are very excited. Largest gold mine in the world. I have already made several thousand euros on it."

"You may want to sell your shares after what I tell you."

19

Fiscal Taxes and
Physical Recovery

SABINA assumed she would find abundant receipts and documents to account for Charles Knight's zero-sum tax returns. He was active in the stock market and increasingly successful, although it was all small potatoes. A few stocks he had written off as worthless, but most of his positions became winners, and he still owned them. Apart from that, she found only modest business ventures with small amounts of legally depreciated assets, fairly normal deductions for travel and entertainment, a small amount of consulting fees, and just enough salary income.

There were a number of short sales. When Sabina had started at the SEC, it had taken her a while to figure out how short sales worked. She disliked the idea of making money by buying and selling things in the first place—but selling shares before you even bought them, in the hopes that they would go down, seemed… unpatriotic.

Barry, a former trader who had joined the SEC and then fallen hard for her, had explained how profitable shorting could be. Even with good people and a good product, most businesses failed for a hundred different reasons. When management had poor skills or bad character, the chance the stock would eventually go to zero approached 100 percent, unless the government stepped in to bail the company out. And once the collapse got underway, the final blows came quick. Shorting bad companies could be much more profitable than owning good ones.

It all rubbed Sabina the wrong way. It took no effort for her to discount what Barry told her about the beneficial aspects of short selling. He pointed out that shorting kept a lid on stocks during a mania, preventing them from going as high as they otherwise might and thereby saving naïve speculators from themselves. He explained to her how, when they "covered," or bought back, the shares they'd already sold, they might be the only ones to offer bids for collapsing shares. Those positives didn't fit her viewpoint that short sellers drove stock prices down and thereby damaged confidence in the economy. Confidence—real or imagined—was the coin of the realm Sabina was working so hard to be a part of.

Knight had started early. His first investment, at age fifteen, turned $3,000 into $9,000 in three months of buying and selling Internet domain names, and he had built on that success.

Knight had a holding company called Paladin Investments for minority positions in private companies. He owned part of a local transportation company. He owned a fraction of a gas station and part of a small Coca-Cola bottling plant, and had just bought a partial stake in a new wholesale liquor business.

It looked like there were several modest loans out of his companies to unnamed overseas entities. This definitely raised a red flag and an opportunity.

Frank asked her in a formal tone, "Do you have reason to believe Charles Knight made loans to overseas tax haven companies to fund undeclared activities, with the willful intent to evade tax?"

She nodded and sneered at the same time. "Isn't it possible that he capitalized overseas companies with those loans, and now they're making money, but he's keeping the profits offshore, secretly, out of reach of the government? There's no way we'd know if he did...." Going offshore was an ideal way to evade taxes, at least if people steered clear of the increasing number of countries that signed on to tax treaties with the US. "I bet he figures out a way to take a loss on those loans later, for an uncollectable debt."

"But you have no evidence of wrongdoing yet."

She continued, "Not yet, perhaps. But on his personal tax return, he claims to own no overseas companies. That's a sworn statement. I'll bet that's where we get him."

"That's not what that question asks. It asks if he has personal control of 50 percent or more of an overseas company or overseas bank account. Maybe he doesn't. Maybe he owns 49 percent."

"It's a poorly worded question."

"Yes it is. It's a loophole, but perhaps he has climbed through it. I appreciate your enthusiasm, Agent Heidel, but in this office we enforce the law as it's written."

Sabina didn't hide her irritation. "The deputy commissioner suspects he may be an evader, and quite possibly a tax rebel!" A reference to Deputy Commissioner Lichen was a trump card she could play any time.

"We can examine all the possibilities, as long as we keep in mind that he may not have done anything illegal."

"If he's avoiding taxes by technicalities and loopholes, I'll find a way to nail him! We can't let people like this get away with stealing from the government."

Sabina exemplified a new approach to the law that had developed in recent years. Historically, government agents enforced the letter of the law. But now, Sabina could go after what she viewed as violations of the *spirit* of the law.

Frank asked, "Have you ever bought alcohol in a duty-free store?"

"Sure."

"You didn't pay taxes that others, who aren't traveling abroad, have to pay. A loophole."

"But it's legal!"

"So is having ownership in an overseas company. The key element is to see if he's declaring their earnings when it's required, and paying taxes on them, when required. For instance, if he only owns 49 percent of a foreign company that doesn't distribute the earnings to its shareholders, it may well be that no tax is due to us."

"And how do we find out if tax is due? We rely on *him?*"

"Actually, the real question is, how do *you* find out."

"I get to go James Bond, don't I?" She managed an ingratiating smile.

"It will take fieldwork. At the very least I expect this to be a safe educational process for you."

"Safe?"

"Yeah. Safe. He's small potatoes. Maybe he's a tax rebel, okay. But it's not like Charles Knight is the type of man who's going to kill anybody."

*   *   *

Xander awoke after sixteen hours, thoroughly done with being stuck in bed. He studied the intensive care unit, like a prisoner plotting his escape. Three other patients lay nearby, all sleeping. With no scheduled surgery, most of the staff were off duty, and calm permeated the place except for the monitors that went off every few minutes for no apparent biological reason. Could it be so hard, Xander wondered, to make a medical alarm that alerted the staff without waking the patient?

He filed the thought in case an opportunity arose to capitalize on it, although he was disinclined to invest in medical technologies. Regulatory insanity overburdened the field, and, if the bureaucracy ever granted approval to sell, then product liability hung around an entrepreneur's neck like a yoke. Medical devices tended to treat lawyers much better than they treated either inventors or investors. When success came, it was as often a result of cronyism as innovation. Xander had no stomach for cronies.

He pulled the IV tubing from his arm. Then he checked for a urine catheter to make sure that he would not experience deep regret if he got up.

Xander swung his legs over the side of the bed and gave himself plenty of time to make sure that adequate amounts of blood would get to his brain before he risked standing up. The nurses had not yet noticed him. He stood, turned off the cardiac monitor, and unclipped the leads attached to his chest. Then he walked out of the ICU in his hospital gown.

He found scrubs on a metal shelf outside the door. He grabbed a shirt and pants marked extra large and put them on. Going barefoot was fine. He cautiously climbed the stairs in a companionway, opened a door, and stepped into the rising sun of an early African morning. The daylight hurt his eyes; he closed one and shielded the other.

He stood alone on the still-cool deck. His lungs filled with an air steeped in nostalgia and rich in flavors so welcoming and natural, especially compared to the plastic and alcohol that had permeated his every pore during the past several days. After a few minutes, he wandered over to the side. He gazed out on the bay toward a small regional container ship, perhaps two hundred feet long, hoisting anchor, the clanking of the windlass audible as it wound through its rusty chain. There was something pleasant about that sound; it spoke of freedom and adventure. The ship carried containers headed northwest to Jamesport, or perhaps southeast to Harker on the border. If heading southeast, it would pass by Djennetown, only a few hours away, where his good friend T.J. Wandeah lived. Djennetown had once been the busiest port in the region, but the war left those facilities in ruins. Rumor had it that there were plans to rebuild that port—someday. Then TJ's home could perhaps thrive again. Of any place he had been in Gondwana, Djennetown had most seemed like a home.

After sixty hours in bed, his legs felt like boiled noodles. But they would recover, and, he assumed, the pain in his head and the pain in his gluteus would eventually ebb away. He tried to ignore the discomfort, treating it as a temporary nuisance, not a warning to get back in bed.

Xander obeyed pain no more than he obeyed authority. If an authority could persuade him that they were right, Xander would cooperate. If they did not try to convince him and instead just tried to compel him, then Xander ignored the directive, or fought it, depending on how he assessed his relative power.

He preferred to avoid contact with authority in general, and the police in particular: too many of them were insecure bullies, drawn to the job by the power a badge and a gun gave them, combined with a fair measure of legal immunity. Most of them were just law enforcers, rather than peace officers. He had been jailed seven times in his life, once at a particularly inopportune time. He anticipated more such incarcerations. But preferably not in a Gondwanan prison.

"Ahoy!" The voice came from above him. On the starboard bridge wing stood a man in a white uniform looking down at him.

Xander waved an arm upward and said, "Halloo, sir. Thank you for your hospitality!" Xander's deep voice carried easily. Even his whispers seemed too loud. His inability, or at least occasional reluctance, to communicate in a proper whisper had resulted in one of his incarcerations. Sensitivity to any real or imagined disrespect caused many cops to develop exceptionally good hearing.

Captain Freberg invited Xander up to the wing. "We have fresh coffee," he called down.

A minute later, the captain presented him with a hot cup of liquid happiness. Another few minutes later, Xander bent over the side of the railing and vomited, the coffee splashing into the bay five stories below.

Captain Freberg stood next to him. "Mr. Winn, have the doctors given you permission to be out and about?"

"Permission?" Xander, somewhat taken aback by the word, realized Charles must have trusted the captain enough to provide his name.

"Approval."

"I haven't seen the doctors since I woke up."

"How about the nurses?"

"I've seen them."

"And they said it was okay to come out?"

"I didn't actually *talk* to them...." He grinned, at once mischievously and apologetically.

"Ah." Captain Freberg stroked his bearded chin, then retreated into the bridge, and a moment later came out offering a cup of water. "I'm wondering if you have had anything to eat in the last four days."

"Not a thing."

"Then starting off with coffee was probably unwise, do you not think?"

"Actually, it was rather stupid." Xander sipped at the water. "This makes more sense."

The officer of the deck stuck his head out through the door from the bridge. "Captain, a patient is missing from the ICU." The officer paused. "Oh, I guess you know that."

Freberg shrugged at Xander, turned to the OOD, and replied, "Please let them know he is safe with me and that I will accompany him back to the unit directly."

"Aye aye, Captain."

Freberg abruptly said, "There is a car over there, at the head of Pier 2. Do you see it?" He indicated with his head the correct direction, but did not point overtly. A steely edge replaced the warmth in his voice.

Xander scanned the area and identified the front end of a black Land Cruiser tucked in behind a wayward container. "I see it."

"And I have seen some white men walking back there. They are watching the ship."

"I see. For how long?"

"Yesterday afternoon until now. The car has not moved. Friends of yours?"

"I expect so," Xander replied.

"Your young friend, Charles, asked me to be on the lookout."

"He must trust you, then."

The captain reflected a moment. "I think so. We played chess and talked last night.

"What plans did you two devise?"

"How to get you off the ship safely."

"And?"

"We have some ideas."

"I don't suppose just contacting the port authority to expel the unwelcome vehicle was one of them?"

"No. If we did that, then they'd know for sure that we are aware of them. Then they would just stay outside the gates, watching. Or sneak back in again, different car, different people. It takes just a little bribe."

"Then perhaps we can sneak out in a container."

"Yes. That is one option. But let's assume they have paid off some men on the wharves here to keep an eye on any white men who get loaded into a container. It seems likely they may have."

"And option three?"

"We sneak you on a launch from the *Africa Grace* onto a regional steamer, perhaps that one at anchor there, that will take you out of the port and drop you off at their next destination. We can get you onto a launch relatively invisibly, pop around the far side of that ship, emerge a few moments later a bit lighter with no one the wiser." The harbor hosted a dozen old tramp steamers dating from the '40s and '50s, before container ships took over: ships that were still loaded by hand and packed with miscellaneous bits and pieces of cargo, vestiges of a rapidly vanishing era.

"And then we're on a slow boat to China."

"Hopefully just a slow boat to Sierra Leone or Ghana or Nigeria. But you'll be safer."

"I'll need to catch up with Charles. Before I leave, there are some things in country that I have to clarify."

"Life, Mr. Winn, is more important than any investment."

"True. But I'm not talking about exchanging my life for a little information. I'm talking about exchanging a small risk to my life for a massively valuable piece of information."

"Is it worth it?"

"When you go to sea, Captain, you risk your life for some goal, do you not? When an office worker commutes in his car, he takes a risk, just so he can get to his job. This is no different, except here it's a somewhat bigger risk for a vastly bigger reward."

"What valuable piece of information do you seek?"

Xander looked at the captain. "I need to know exactly what's going on way up in Banga Sioquelle. And just how far they'll go to keep us from finding out."

20

Two Plans Are Hatched

IT was 2 a.m. and Sabina could not sleep. It happened sometimes after a night of prowling for a mate of the moment. She did not need a particularly handsome man as external validation of her own appearance. What made a man attractive to her was whether she could get what she wanted out of him.

Married men offered significant advantages. The simple fact they were at risk made them easier to manipulate into giving her the element of dominance she wanted.

She sat on the edge of her hotel bed. The man sleeping nearby was handsome enough, but that's all she could say in his favor right now. He'd lost control early and meekly apologized with a lame excuse about her being too beautiful. She had rolled off him unable to hide her disgust, and he fell asleep. She wanted to kick him out now, but he was an attorney, and he could come in handy someday. Perhaps one of his clients would become a target of the SEC or IRS. And perhaps in a few hours he would be more useful sexually—less sensitive, more able to meet her needs. She picked up her phone and snapped a few pictures of him naked as he slept.

Her long legs carried her first toward the bathroom and then to the closet, where she pulled a short, thin silken bathrobe over her naked body, and then stepped into the suite's living room, closing the door behind her. She sat on the couch, opened the heavy, obsolescent laptop the Service had assigned her, and placed it on her thighs. The edge pressed against her pubic bone, and she felt its vibration as the hard drive

159

spun up. She tried to develop some enthusiasm for the man in her bed. He would just have to do.

She scanned through yesterday's unopened emails, mostly banal administrative items. Two bureaucracies now burdened her with messages. Human Resources at the IRS decided to compel her to go through, once again, those tedious sessions on sexual harassment and diversity awareness. The torturous process spread two hours of platitudes and bromides over two full weeks of classroom time. Her agency classmates wouldn't care; they were the types that studied for driver's license exams, and were willing to be paid to be bored.

She had called her father and left him a message about it, sweetly pleading with him to intervene, but her old man had not replied.

There was one interesting email among the pieces of bureaucratic chaff.

"Dear Ms. Dresden," it began. She had chosen the name of her father's cousin as an alias in the undercover game she had started playing. "I received your note, your resume, and your networking information. I think it best if we next meet in person to determine if there is synergy to be found. Might tomorrow work? If so, I am available at 3 p.m. Best, Elliot Springer, Alchemia Resources."

The boutique San Diego money manager had recently started providing Charles Knight with a small amount of income; it was a good place to start.

She had sent Mr. Springer a backgrounder on herself—it was titillating to fabricate a resume. The only real item was her picture, which was probably responsible for gaining her the interview. She granted herself an undergrad Harvard psychology degree, including a year of modern literature at Oxford; these were subjects easy to bluff. She had considered changing her first name, but decided that the immediate reaction her first name evoked in males outweighed the minimal risk. She rejected adding conversational Chinese to her skill set, only because the risk of embarrassment outweighed the transient exhilaration of the deception.

She reviewed the imaginary Sabina Dresden's resume to anticipate likely questions. Although confident she could make the ruse work, the fact she had no legal liability made her especially bold. It was official IRS business, and she was untouchable. Becoming a special agent would be an excellent career move. She felt like the always-successful lead role in a television drama about government investigators solving crimes.

Her resume reported that she was twenty-five years old. A graduate of Harvard Business too. She had a nice letter of recommendation from a professor, on sabbatical and unable to invite a personal call, however. Another from a former mentor who was, so sadly, now dead. Her cover note conveyed a desire for an "in the trenches" position in the investment world because she was disappointed in the paper shuffling she was involved in and wanted to gain experience in something more hands-on. From the little she knew of Charles Knight, this was her best angle for getting anywhere near him and whatever offenses against society he was committing.

She quickly typed a response to Elliot Springer saying she would be there at 3 p.m. Then she went to work on the irrelevant emails, pounding on the keyboard of the slow computer in the effort to make it do what she needed it to do at the pace she wanted.

She connected to the IRS database and pulled up the files on Springer. Married, two dependent children. More charitable and business deductions than most people with his income, although his adjusted gross income was a bit low for a man in his position. Lots of business losses from his side ventures accounted for that. He either wasn't a good businessman, or he excelled at finding ways for businesses to lose money. A lot in common with Knight, in this.

But a business can only lose money for so long before it needs to take on debt or get an equity infusion. Where was the money coming from for these businesses of Springer's and Knight's? It would take, at the very least, an audit to find out, and that could be arranged. She searched for his criminal record. Nothing. There was no record of political donations. This guy kept a low profile, a further indication he might be hiding something.

There was little more information on the Internet: a school-newspaper article mentioned his presence at the local farmer's market; his wife made comments at a school-board meeting; brief comments about his company sponsoring a middle-school YMCA basketball team. That was it. There were many people with his name, including an artist, an attorney, and an old jockey.

She had worked for an hour when she heard rustling through the bedroom door. The rapid-fire man in her bed aroused. Sighing, not really in the mood, she put the machine aside and rallied for a second round, hopeful of an improved outcome.

*   *   *

"The States won't be a particularly safe place either," Charles stated somberly, after weighing all their options.

Xander Winn sat on the edge of his hospital bed and nodded. "The market capitalization is in the billions. Outside of B-F folk, you and I are the only ones who suspect that its true value is quite a bit less. If we're right, neither of us is safe right now, not anywhere in the world. "

"What *is* the true value, do you think?"

Xander shrugged. "If this is a giant fraud? Well, those first two cores—the ones that came up empty when they first started drilling—may be the only truth we have. It's possible that there's lots of gold at Banga Sioquelle. It's more likely that there's *some* gold in Banga Sioquelle, but only small high-grade pockets, good for artisanal miners, but not the kind of volume you need for an industrial operation." He poked a finger up under the bandage wrapped around his head and scratched.

"That's the usual modus operandi of fraudsters," Xander continued. "A tasty stew of lies has to be seasoned with the truth—even if just a pinch—lest the palate rebel. It's possible there's nothing economically extractable there at all. But I doubt it. That sort of fraud is much more risky. This may be one of those companies that started out with good results, then they overpromoted them and let both expenses and expectations get out of control. The market starts demanding results, and they decide to fabricate them—just until they can find the mother lode. Then the market cap of the company starts soaring, and the founders realize their money will come from the stock, not from the rock."

Charles said, "So, why don't we act now? Let's dump our holdings, sell short with the proceeds, release the information, and the market will take care of the rest. We've made a killing on the way up. We can make almost as much again on the way down."

"Oh, hell, kid. We can make a hundred times more on the way down! When you figure out how, you tell me what you've learned." Xander looked at him with a frown, and added, "We're already in a lot of

162

danger. They think our little outing discovered the fraud. Walking away now will capture a few million we've already made, sure. But it doesn't keep them from wanting to kill us. We might as well make the rewards worth the risk we're already in. If we play this out we can make a once-in-a-lifetime score."

"If we do make a killing, I suppose some bastard will claim we were given inside information. We'll end up in jail."

"Right now, that's the least of our worries. If this is indeed a fraud, then I don't think we'll be allowed to live long enough to make any money from it; life is cheap around here. With billions of dollars now on the table, these guys have no tolerance for anyone mucking up their game. They've got to realize their profits. And, unless they're more stupid than I think, they have some plan to avoid spending the next decade behind bars."

"Then, shouldn't we act now? There's no point in trying to kill us after the damage is done. They'll have other things to worry about."

"Aren't you getting a bit ahead of yourself? You saw something in the jungle and got shot at, and you think that's evidence? We could be wrong. Who is going to believe a couple of guys who are throwing rumors around, in the face of so much evidence to the contrary? The market is full of short sellers who mount black PR campaigns against companies after they get caught with a bad short position. But you're right about the insider trading. They'll call us Gordon Gekkos and report us to the SEC for trying to defraud and manipulate the market, and sue us personally for defaming the reputation of B-F and its principals."

"*We* aren't the frauds!"

"Welcome to the world, kid. The whole world's financial system is more fraught with fraud and bogus economic theories than most people can imagine. Point that out and you'll be labeled a malcontent, or a crank. Worse, you can end up accused of being a criminal. To paraphrase Voltaire, it's dangerous to be right when the government is wrong, and very dangerous to tell the truth when they're lying."

They both fell silent for a moment—Charles thinking, Xander distracted by the pain of his wounds.

When Xander spoke again, he said, "Entirely apart from that, we need real proof, not just suspicions."

"So, what do you suggest?" Charles asked. Winn had thirty years of experience he lacked.

"Well, I'm going to head back to Gbarngeda to take some pictures and gain some confidence about what that machine you saw does. Hard evidence will provide the answers."

"What? Is that blood from the accident clouding your mind?" Charles was challenging a man he respected as both older and wiser. But Winn would see the concern on his face and could take no umbrage.

"The hail of bullets cut our investigation short. We didn't have enough time. We need photographic documentation."

"Xander, we almost spent the rest of our lives there. All three minutes of them!"

"True. So we have to be more careful this time."

"We?" Charles confronted the unpleasant implications of the word. But there was only one correct response. "Absolutely. You sure as hell can't go on your own. Sign me up. And you're right. We have to be sure that when Burke's men drill their parallel cores they'll come up empty."

"Unless they never get to drill."

Charles looked quizzically at Xander.

"Look, these guys don't want to go to jail. And they will if we prove they're swindlers, or if the Burke team comes up empty. So they have to both shut us up and delay the Burke deal."

"But if the Burke deal is delayed, the price will still come down.

"They can explain away a Burke delay. This stock has a lot of upward momentum. B-F could inflate their exploration results even more; they have more drilling results to release. It's true no tree grows to the sky, but this one looks like a giant redwood."

"Without Burke, sooner or later it will fall," Charles insisted.

"But as my friends say: the market can stay irrational for far longer than you can stay solvent."

"So, you think they have another plan in the works? Or are they just fools?"

"Although there are many fools, only a fool would assume everyone else is a fool."

"Xander, you're a philosopher."

"Let's think about this. If you were in a highly unstable African country that had just finished a civil war, and you were a sociopathic liar, didn't care about collateral damage, and had a billion dollars at your disposal to cover up a fraud of this size, what could you do?"

If B-F was a fraud, what *could* they do to cover it up? It was an intriguing hypothetical, although Charles felt a little like a vegetarian trying to eat a steak. An outrageous but perversely logical idea struck him. He wanted to discount it out of hand, but he couldn't. Shock spread across his face as he considered B-F's exit strategy. He looked up at Xander with no effort to hide either his pain or his disgust, his head shaking. "No. They couldn't possibly…"

Xander nodded, with a wry twist of his mouth. He reached out and put his hand on Charles's shoulder. "Sure they could."

21

A Walk and an Assault

SAYE and Nyahn trudged along the muddy road, at the beginning of their long trek north toward a paradise of soccer. The long, untraveled road made them feel lonely and exposed.

They were a little hungry, sure, but there was always something edible hanging from a vine. Failing that, they could dig up a root or a tuber. The hunger was neither acute nor chronic; it was not something that ruled their lives. What did rule them was a desire to be near other people. That had caused them to wait to leave until after their auntie had come home. She hugged them tight, scowled at them, advised them to be good, and hesitantly sent them on their way, her cheeks wet.

A tear carved a swift channel through the thick dirt on Nyahn's cheek, as the boys crossed the bridge over the small river on the edge of Gbarngeda. Each step took them farther from their friends and the school they attended when they had money to pay the tuition. He missed the school even more now that they were walking away from it. Nyahn wiped his cheek before his brother might notice.

Nyahn saw uncertainty in Saye's eyes at first. But then his older brother's face softened. Saye reached out and wrapped an arm around him and pulled him close as they walked along, hobbling for a moment as Nyahn tripped on his brother's foot. Nyahn laid his head against his brother's chest and then pushed away, and ran on ahead, now laughing.

Saye laughed too and ran after Nyahn as he jumped and skipped up the road.

"You no can scowl and skip at same time!" Saye shouted. "Try it!"

Nyahn turned around and started skipping back toward Saye. He tried to frown, turning his mouth down at the corners and making a mean expression in his eyes, but when he did, he lost coordination and could not skip. He rolled down on a dry bit of ground laughing and laughing. Saye was there then, sitting on him and rubbing his hand across his short hair.

A few minutes later they both tried it, and both failed; indeed, it was impossible to skip and scowl at the same time. They either couldn't scowl, or they couldn't skip.

They wouldn't get far that day. With the clouds overhead, it would soon be too dark to walk safely. There would be bad things about—at least in their imaginations. And it would rain for sure. They needed time to build a shelter.

Saye said, "We should have left earlier."

"Maybe we should have stayed in Gbarngeda?"

Saye looked back down the road they had walked. It was only a few miles. "We be good."

If it wasn't possible to be safely among people they knew, then he would at least rather be nowhere near the road at night. Saye led his brother down the elevated middle of the road for fifteen more minutes until, in the fading daylight, he recognized a possibility for shelter. Nyahn saw it too and, without exchanging a word, took the lead. To their left was the path to the secret laboratory that their good friend Charles had sought. There was a place a ways down that path where they could sleep for the night.

They walked ten more minutes into the thickening bush along a path just wide enough for one vehicle. The place they chose to sleep would have been invisible if they had not been actively looking, camouflaged as it was by the vegetation. The boys knew about the hidden shipping containers only because Nyahn had bumped into them when looking for wood to saw a month earlier. Someone had assembled plants, leaves, sticks, and browning palm fronds to conceal two forty-foot shipping containers, but the mass of vegetation formed an unnatural pattern that Nyahn could see through. The containers were about twenty yards off the path over some trampled ground.

Saye and Nyahn pulled a few dozen of the not-yet-desiccated palm fronds from the camouflaging pile and within ten minutes had rigged a shelter against the side of one of the containers. The palm fronds, designed by millions of years of evolution to capture the rain and channel it toward their central stalks, were an ideal material for an instant roof. Properly overlapped, as every Gondwanan child knew how to do from repeated observation and practice, the palms would provide full protection from even the most forceful onslaught of water, as long as the winds stayed low.

With their shelter set, the boys went wandering in two directions, seeking something to eat. Nyahn came back first with a coconut. Saye returned with several large plantains. He handed Nyahn his big knife, which Nyahn used with a skilled hand, peeling off the husk and then sharply striking the coconut five times in a circle around the top of the big nut, which popped off. The boys drank the thin coconut milk inside and ate some of the white meat; it was much tastier than the plantains, which, uncooked, were like bland, woody bananas.

As the sky darkened completely, the boys lay down, each with a pillow of sticks with some broad leaves on top, and were soon asleep. The sounds of the insects, the birds, some lost chickens, frogs, and an occasional monkey filled the night sky for a couple of hours, noises that were closer and therefore louder by far than the hum of a distant generator. But then there was quiet. Nyahn knew what that quiet meant. He rolled over to his other side so he could face his brother, who slept there in the blackness.

The rain came next. It came hard.

*   *   *

Darkness fell on the Freeport.

Harry had watched the comings and goings on the ship through the previous night and the better part of the day. There was surprisingly little evidence of any medical activity. Perhaps the ship did not operate its clinics and operating rooms on Saturday, giving the staff some downtime.

Many white people, dressed in light tropical clothing, had disembarked into the noontime sun, moving down the broad ramp that came straight off the ship's side. Several took umbrellas to guard against the afternoon rains. Almost everyone covered their heads—some wore baseball caps, but most wore stereotypical broad-rimmed hats, as if they were heading off on safari.

Vehicles belonging to the *Africa Grace* had awaited the disembarking crewmembers on the pier. From a discreet distance, Harry had examined with care each male who emerged from the ship. Too far away to make out their faces clearly, he sought out the anxious gait, the way a head was held, the fear that would be telegraphed from the mannerisms of a young kid scared out of his gourd. There had been no tall good-looking kid with sharp features and brown hair among them. Knight must still be on board, or he had left before they arrived.

The cars, all white Land Rover and Nissan four-wheel drives, had driven out of the Freeport gate to explore whatever the country had to offer. The tourists would keep their cameras busy documenting miles of dirt roads with people walking long distances, women carrying heavy loads balanced on their heads with infants tied with brightly colored lapas to their backs. Mud shacks, endless bush, and the occasional frame of a vehicle—totally stripped of everything—that hadn't measured up to the rigors of the country's roads. Smoke from charcoal heating up the rice and roots. Classic Africa.

Late in the afternoon, the medical-personnel-turned-tourists returned from their day of driving around looking at poverty and the polluted streets of the city and its environs.

Soon, the sun set.

Harry signaled to Roscoe to stay concealed. He and Barney walked behind a long series of containers, and then around a building to emerge at the vessel's stern. The darkness would allow them to climb aboard the way rats had been doing for millennia. They watched the illuminated stern of the ship for ten minutes. Harry did not like their chances of getting aboard unseen. Surely there would be men stationed there, people milling about.

Barney asked, "Should we wait until everyone is asleep?"

Harry's response was firm. "Activity is good cover. We go now." His mind wandered briefly, yet again, to how much money was on the line for him. Each time he recalculated it, the more he wanted Charles Knight dead. The kid might be standing between him and a real retirement. He would dispatch Knight the moment he had a chance.

Harry grasped a thick hawser that served as one of the lines holding the ship to the pier. He swung his feet up to wrap around it. Hand over hand he inchwormed away from the edge of the wharf, the thick rope rising steeply to the hawsehole into which it disappeared. Barney followed behind him; they moved in synchrony, ascending quickly and silently. Harry threw his hand up into and through the hawsehole, and used this added purchase to lever himself over the stern rail. So far, so good. But there was too much light. He reached his hand down, glancing at the twenty-four-foot drop to the dark water, and grasped Barney's wrist to pull him up and over with a mighty but silent heave to land on the stern deck. Then Harry turned.

"Hey!" was all the man had time to say before Harry took three quick steps forward and silenced him with a punch to the head hard enough to crack cement. They found an entrance to a stairwell, and it took less than a minute to drag the unconscious deckhand all the way down to the bilge of the ship and into a dark corner. Barney placed a heavy metal grating on his head and neck. To anyone who happened along, it would appear to have been a bad accident. He smiled wryly; it was a good thing they had a nice hospital on this ship.

They now stood inside a massive hold aft of the ship's engines. Train tracks still ran through here, going nowhere and accomplishing nothing other than to reveal the vessel's pedigree as a Danish train ferry. During its redesign, the shipyard lowered the overheads. The sixty-million-dollar overhaul that turned it into a hospital ship included multiple new decks to make room for surgical suites. Boxes and wasted medical supplies lay scattered around. The men paid them only passing attention. Their eyes sought out possible threats: actual people and remote cameras that might warn those people.

They crept forward down the port side of the ship in dim light, breathing musty air laden with the smell of bunker fuel. The stark metal interior exaggerated every noise. Sounds that began elsewhere in the ship spread through the steel and down the passages, to concentrate in this giant reverberation chamber. The noise of their footsteps and the levering of a stuck handle on a watertight door went unnoticed.

They headed up a stairwell—a *ladder*, to sailors—that should take them to the bridge if their estimates were correct. They would start at the command center.

They emerged through a companionway and moved briskly along the open foredeck for a dozen feet before finding the route up to the unoccupied bridge wing. A quick climb and they stood on the bridge itself.

The bridge structure spanned even beyond the width of the ship's hull, with the bridge wings standing out over the water to both port and starboard. A uniformed duty officer—dressed in a white shirt and black pants—stood in front of a set of illuminated instruments on the starboard side.

The middle-aged officer with a full paunch smiled through the dim light and said, "Good evening," and continued about his examination of the data streaming through the instrument.

Taken aback, Harry had to reassess the situation. His initial plan was simple and straightforward, as the best practical plans tend to be: take control of whomever he found on the bridge, and beat them until they told him where to find Charles Knight. It helped that this officer expected no foul play.

"Good evening, sir. How is the night?" Harry said.

"Lovely," the officer replied, turning away and walking toward them. "I am Timothy Mullins, the ship's purser. I have the watch tonight. You are new."

"Yes, I am," Harry stated candidly. "Name is Tim Starnes. And this is Addy Brooke." For Barney, he used the name of a grade school classmate.

The purser said, "I can hear from your accents that you are from Zim. I'm from South Africa myself. How long are you with us? Are you doctors?"

"No. Radiology technicians." Harry guessed at a good answer, and it seemed to fly.

"Oh, good, you are very much in demand here. So much head and neck surgery is guided by the CT scans. Who's paying your way?"

Harry did not know how to respond to this. He assumed the people who worked on the ship were paid by the ship. He guessed again. "No one."

"Ah, volunteer. That's good of you. Most people here at least get some help from their churches. But some are like you... paying their own way. Lots of good people in the world, aren't there?"

"For sure." Harry looked around the bridge slowly, as if just a curious guest. "Anything exciting lately?" Better to ask questions than try to answer them.

"Not really."

"Ever feel like the ship is in danger? Ever worry about pirates? Criminals getting aboard?"

"Not many pirates in this harbor, eh? We keep a good watch. Haven't had a problem yet. I've been with the ship for years. The only way aboard is via the gangway, and that is always guarded, and of course security has its metal detector machine there at reception. It's hard to get much past that."

Harry did not expect to sneak the information they needed out of the officer. He decided to push forward. "Right. Well, *we* got past, didn't we? We are running low on time. It has been nice, yah. But see, my friend and I need to find one of your guests. A man named Charles Knight. Where is he?"

The officer caught Harry's change in tone immediately and moved with shocking speed toward a device on the wall that Harry assumed was an alarm. Barney leapt toward him and threw the man against the bulkhead, three feet short of his target. The officer collapsed on the floor, not unconscious, but his breath knocked out of him, struggling for air through a larynx spasmed closed by the impact. Harry squatted down next to him and rested a hand on the man's shoulder.

"My friend. Relax. You will breathe easier in a moment. Relax."

Over the next few minutes, the officer did relax some. Harry remained patient.

"You are starting to feel better. That's good. Now, sir, I need you to tell me, where is Charles Knight?"

Still gasping, although now controllably, the officer croaked, "I don't know who that is."

"A man came aboard five nights ago. Injured."

The officer shrugged with evident defiance and tried to stand. Harry denied the attempt. Blood oozed from the resulting bruise that appeared on the purser's face.

"We are a hospital ship. Lots of people come on board injured."

"Not lots of white people." Harry grabbed the man's pinky and began bending it backward. "If you scream, I will kill you. Make no noise except to tell me the location of Charles Knight."

Pain caused the officer's lips to curl back around his teeth. The finger snapped with a sickening crack and he made an involuntary muffled groan. Harry took the next finger in his fist and edged it backward.

The officer was no slouch. He could take the pain. Harry figured this was not going to be an easy man to break. But then, quite unexpectedly, the man said, "Okay, okay, hell, what's the point?"

With renewed optimism about the evening's prospects, Harry replied, "Yes, what is the point, indeed. You were about to tell me something?"

The officer looked defiantly into Harry's eyes. "I don't know a Charles Knight. They never told us their names. But two injured white men left the ship. They are long gone."

Harry stared at the man's eyes. There was no fear there. But also no deception. Knight was gone. And he wasn't, in fact, alone. "One of them was a young guy, tall, right?"

"Sure."

"Who was the other man?"

"Told you. No names. They didn't say."

"An old man, hunched over? Walks with a cane?"

"Hunched over? No. He had a head injury." The finger bent back tighter. The officer said, "I saw him walking. He limps from getting a shot in the butt. He's not an old man though. He's my age."

Knight's partner was an unknown. It would complicate things.

Harry asked, "Where did they go?"

"I don't know. They were secretive folk."

Barney prompted him. "Airport?"

The officer said, "Look, that's all I know. I'm the purser, not a fucking information agency."

"Where is the captain?"

"Off duty."

"Call him up to the bridge."

The officer slid upward against the wall, moved over to a phone, and dialed.

"Be very careful," Harry advised, a gun now at the man's temple.

A moment later the officer spoke into the phone. "Sorry to disturb you, sir. You are needed on the bridge." The pistol pressed harder against the temple. The officer shrugged.

Harry listened in on the earpiece of the phone as the captain asked, "Mr. Mullins, what's the situation?"

"Just needed on the bridge, sir."

"Understood," came the reply. "I will be there immediately."

The phone replaced, the officer shrugged again. Then Harry smashed the butt of the pistol on the back of his skull, and he crumpled to the floor. Barney dragged the purser back and tried to tuck him under a long wooden desk covered with maps, manuals, and navigation instruments that extended much of the width of the bridge. Mullins's unconscious body did not fit well.

Harry and Barney stood back-to-back in the center of the bridge, assessing the various entrance options. They heard movement, a rattling of a door, and a slam, and then the captain appeared, coming through the starboard bridge wing, walking rapidly toward them. Barney swung around.

Captain Freberg moved quickly. And he was large. Harry immediately raised his pistol and said, "Far enough, Captain."

"What do you want?" the captain demanded.

"Information. Then we will leave you be."

"Where is my officer?"

"Alive for now. But he will need your doctors soon. I suggest you give me what I need."

"And what is that?" the captain yelled.

"The location of two men: Charles Knight and his companion."

The captain's deep voice exploded with a series of exemplary expletives, with no break for air, and no opportunity for interruption. It was a series of invectives likely never heard before on this Christian medical ship, at least not in sequence. The Danish captain's command of salty language impressed Harry, who was something of a connoisseur of barracks vocabulary. The words distracted Harry from hearing two men slip through the port bridge wing door, one armed with a pistol, the other with an AR-15 semi-automatic rifle with a thirty-round magazine.

"Drop your weapon!" Pullings, the master-at-arms, shouted, holding his pistol with a two-handed grip while walking straight toward the two men.

Barney whirled around, crouching down, and fired his gun from near the floor. The first bullet went through the glass on the bridge door. The second flew wide of the ship's security officer, himself now crouching while aiming his AR-15 and pulling the trigger.

The high-velocity .223 NATO rounds came out of the gun one trigger pull at a time, but the officer knew how to pull that trigger quickly while, more importantly, aiming accurately. Three bullets went into and through Barney's chest and neck. Barney stopped firing and began running toward the officer, evidence that, however deadly, the lightweight, high-speed 60-grain bullet lacked immediate stopping power if it didn't impact bone or a solid organ. Blood flooded from his wounds. The officer fired two more rounds at his head, and only then did Barney stop forever.

The captain meanwhile had leapt forward toward the windowed front of the bridge, to avoid the hail of bullets fired by his own officer and to gain speed and leverage. He nimbly ran partway up the window and, as if spring-loaded, propelled himself back toward the center of Harry's chest before Harry could aim around Barney's collapsing body and fire his pistol at the two officers. The captain knocked him hard against the back wall and crashed his fist into Harry's wrist, trying to knock the gun away. His finger spasmed and the gun fired but he held on. The captain struck at his wrist again and again in rapid succession. Each time the gun fired, but then Harry's hand opened, and, after one more brutal smash on his wrist, the gun fell to the floor in a clatter. He lunged down for it, smashing his palm against it, sending it scuffling across the deck toward the dead body.

Harry pried himself from under the captain's heavy legs and ran for the starboard bridge wing door. The AR-15 fired from behind him three times. He smashed through the glass door and out onto the wing, through the open sliding door to the grated deck. He leapt over the rail, his hands pushing him out like a pole-vaulter. For a moment he hung in the dark night, nothing below him, and then he plunged down past six decks into the oily water below.

175

Captain Freberg ran to the wing and looked down into the murky waters. "Light up the ship!" he called out to anyone able to move. If he called the crew to quarters, there would be a large number of untrained and defenseless medical personnel buzzing to their stations imagining it to be a lifeboat drill, unprepared for any number of uninvited men who might be on the ship. Those who had heard the gunshots would be running around soon enough as it was.

Pullings flipped switches in the bridge. He barked into a phone, "Crank up the second generator if you need to! We want every light on."

The captain came back to the security officer, who leaned down over Barney, shaking his head. He found Mullins then, moaning under a bench, just regaining consciousness.

Freberg reached for a phone and rang the on-call doctor. "One of the officers has been knocked unconscious. We need a stretcher on the bridge immediately." He then picked up an intercom line that broadcast announcements throughout the ship. He had never made an announcement quite like this one.

22

Macro Theories
and a Micro Lesson

DARKNESS fell upon the miserable road as Charles and Xander drove in TJ's Land Cruiser toward their destination outside of Gbarngeda. It would be pitch-black by the time they arrived in the vicinity of the B-F core-processing facility. Thick clouds blanketed the moon and stars, and promised another rainstorm. The two men in the car, both now with entirely bald heads, one with a headache, talked sporadically along the way.

"I figured if the surgeons had to shave your head, I could lose my hair too, for solidarity."

"Mighty kind of you, Charles. But I suspect you only did it to avoid being recognized."

"Caroline worried it would make me stand out more."

"Maybe on a ship full of white people, sure. But out here? You're going to attract attention no matter what. Best to not look like you."

"That's what I figured. But my feet are still itching from the nuts you told me to put in my boots."

"There's no better way to change your whole appearance than to walk differently. You can't walk like a cocky young man when you have peanuts in your boots."

"I'm learning from a master."

"As did I."

"I worry about the people on the ship," Charles said.

"Me too. But they're not going into a shooting gallery. We are."

The miles came and went, and the SUV groaned and squeaked as the mud insinuated itself into the struts, the wheel bearings, and every moving part. The bolted connections in the truck bounced a thousand times per hour, expanding the bolt holes while eroding the bolts. Over time even welded parts would crack apart with metal fatigue under the onslaught of Africa. What passed for roads in Africa were the enemy of the vehicles that traveled on them. And the vehicles, in turn, scarred the roads with ever-deepening ruts. Roads and cars here were involved in never-ending mortal combat, with entropy always winning.

Xander's wounded buttock was not as strong as a welded part and indeed enough weaker that he felt he needed to stop talking to focus on obliterating the pain.

Most of the trip passed in silence. Charles's mind drifted from the risk that they drove toward, to thoughts of Caroline. Then to his mother and off into childhood memories. Most mental images from formative years drift by like clouds on a summer day. But without remembering all the places where he had learned them, or from whom, lessons remained intact inside him. Most lessons were positive. But some had the effect of a bee sting: they made a real impression, and you tried to not experience them more than once. He was nine when he learned a lesson that became a core value. He was younger even than that young boy Nyahn, who lived somewhere hours ahead in the bush.

It was a lemonade stand on a street corner.

His mother had offered to supply free lemonade powder, free cups, free ice, or free labor—all normal components of a kid's lemonade stand. But his father insisted that Charlie's enterprise stand on its own merits, unsubsidized by parents. And so he learned lessons about profit and loss. A net loss meant he had wasted both time and money. Profit, although not the only thing that mattered, proved that other people valued his efforts. Otherwise, why would people pay him money? He learned that profit was something to be proud of.

As time went by, Charles matured and he realized that profit—as long as it arose in a truly free market, without force, fraud, cronies, subsidies, taxes, or regulatory compulsion—afforded the best objective signal that he wasn't wasting his life on counterproductive work. Honest profits increased the global supply of wealth. The creation of new wealth was the single best weapon against poverty. Profit was worth fighting for.

His lemonade stand proved a success. He positioned it on the corner of an intersection where people walked, not just where cars whizzed by, and close to the town's park, where the frequent strollers became a convenient market. It opened when the summer heat peaked. The voices of the boys in the stand were loud enough, the cups big enough, and the ice cold enough. They charged more than they should and received their premium as a payment for their cuteness.

Their cup overflowed with quarters toward the end of the first day. And again the second day. Their early success encouraged them to market new drinks—mint-, lemongrass-, and honey-flavored lemonades. More quarters and now dollars. Charlie and his friends did well.

He remembered when the boy had first appeared. The fourteen-year-old kid had an attitude. He was not just a misguided boy from a dysfunctional home. To the contrary, he came from a home with nice parents. Despite his background, he had no understanding of right and wrong, and no concern about his lack of it. He was a walking argument in support of the contention that alien reptilian creatures inhabited some human bodies.

"Hey," the boy said. "Nice lemonade stand." And then, in a tone that implied it was supposed to mean something, "My name's Danny."

Charlie took it as the compliment it seemed to be. A much older boy giving him praise was a boost. "Thank you. I'm Charlie," he replied. But something inside him felt uneasy.

"Is your lemonade as good as it looks?"

"Would you like a free taste? If you like it, a full big cup is twenty-five cents."

"Seems fair."

Danny drank the sample and said, "It's good. How much of this do you sell each day?"

"Over two hundred cups a day."

"Wow. That's great. Twenty-five cents a cup. That's like a hundred bucks of profit a day."

Charlie frowned, quickly calculating a much lower profit figure. But older boys were smarter. And it didn't make any sense to argue with a customer.

Danny didn't buy a whole cup. But he came back the next day.

"I've been thinking," Danny said. "I'm concerned for you. This is a dangerous corner. Aren't you worried about your stand getting knocked down, your money getting stolen?"

That was a disturbing, and unanticipated, possibility. He'd built the stand of nice wood and plastic, and no one seemed to mind it being there. It was supposed to be a safe area. The man who owned this corner lot got free lemonade, and he, amused by the boys' offer to barter with their product, considered that sufficient rent. No one had bothered the stand in the two weeks it had been operating so far....

"I don't know," was all Charlie said.

"Well, you should worry. You might want to ask the cops to keep an eye on the place."

"They come almost every day to buy some lemonade. I can ask 'em."

"That's a good idea, Charlie. Definitely ask them. But don't forget, the cops may be the ones who bust up your place. You can't trust anyone these days."

The police came. They said he shouldn't worry. They would keep an eye on the place. But they lost credibility when the next morning Charlie found a damaged stand, his carefully constructed sign missing, and dog poop smeared on the little wooden counter.

It took them all morning to fix it up, and even then, the sight of the disinfected counter provoked lasting distaste in Charlie. So he improved it, with a covering of tin foil over plastic, transforming it into a more modern facility.

Danny didn't come by that day.

But he did the next day. "Everything going good?"

"Yeah, but someone stole our sign and broke the stand."

"Oh, Charlie, I'm sorry. That sucks." Danny flipped him a quarter and sipped at the lemonade he was given. "Hey, I got an idea. How about this. You're making money doing what you know how to do. But I'm bigger and can stay up later. How about I keep an eye on your place and prevent any more damage?"

"Would you do that?"

"For the right price."

180

Charlie again felt ill at ease, not quite sure what it meant. It would take a few more years before his brain would be trained to understand the subtle warning signals it detected.

"I don't know. How much?" Charlie asked.

"A nickel a cup. I keep your place safe. You would still be making fives times as much as me."

"Four times. But the lemonade and cups cost me too...."

Danny stopped to think, gave up, and said, "Yeah, four times. We can get rich together. What do you say, Charlie? Want my help?"

"Maybe. I'll think about it."

"Okay, Charlie, but I may not be able to offer you this service at this low price tomorrow. Can't promise."

Charlie shrugged. That night someone threw a dozen eggs at the stand. The sticky egg white stained the paint and attracted dirt and bugs. Danny came back the next day.

Charlie did not tell him about the eggs.

"So what do you think, Charlie. We have a deal?"

"Well, I don't know. Maybe whoever stole the sign is gone."

Danny said, "What about the eggs?"

"What eggs?"

Danny made a face of condescending disbelief. "Look, Charlie. I think you're gonna need help with this place. I really do. I hear things, you know. From some of the bad kids. They got it out for you. Jealous, y'know. What's your problem? A nickel a cup. It's only 20 percent of your income. It's a good deal! If you don't take it, Charlie, you're gonna end up hurting. I want to help you. I really do."

"Danny, I don't need any help. Please don't come by unless you want to buy a lemonade."

The vandals came that night and tore the stand to shreds.

Charlie did not rebuild it. He closed up shop. Thereafter he stayed away from Danny, who was at least twice his size. And he did not start a business again for years.

And when he finally did start another business, several years after his mother died, a similar threat came from a different and unexpected source. Whereas with the lemonade stand everyone would have said he was in the right and Danny in the wrong, with this next adversary—the United States government's Internal Revenue Service—everybody thought he was wrong, both morally and legally. How dare he fail to pay what they demanded! If he'd been bigger, he could have fought Danny, and perhaps won. But with the IRS, even that was out of the question. The IRS threatened to shut down his business, and they confiscated his bank account because Charles failed to pay them the withholding tax on his contractors. His contractors—the IRS had reclassified them as employees—lost their jobs.

The dictionary defined theft as "the taking of another's possession by force or fraud, with the intention of depriving him of it." It didn't go on to say "unless it's the government."

The fourteen-year-old named Danny ran a protection racket, plain and simple; he was a thug threatening destruction unless he got paid. The IRS did precisely the same thing. Did it make a difference if Danny wanted the money for himself, or to give to some friend to pay some debt? No, it was still theft. Suppose everyone in the neighborhood had voted, and they'd agreed to force Charlie to pay five cents a cup to them so they could use the money for something that seemed like a good idea. How about then? No, it would still have been theft. And no end ever justifies such means.

As Charles drove along the African road, his mind slipped into a half-awake, half-dream state, his hands on the steering wheel but his eyes and mind far away in space and time. He fell further into a fugue, the SUV became one with his mind, and he was heading directly into the path of an enormous menacing truck. The truck was the IRS. Danny—smirking with dead eyes—drove it. Its headlights blinded Charles. He was on a collision course with extortion. The IRS truck aimed right at him. If he didn't risk death by swerving off the road, the IRS would crush him.

"Hey, kid, you're falling asleep!" Xander Winn prodded him back to the present and out of his deepening hypnotic state. No enormous truck streaked toward them along the black road.

Charles rubbed his eyes. "Thanks, Xander. I was half asleep. How the heck did I avoid potholes?"

"I don't know. You were doing okay until you started driving sideways. We're almost there, I think."

Only scattered trickles of light percolated through Gbarngeda. Generators provided electricity for a few dozen buildings where people congregated. Candles and small fires burned under the roof overhangs of the houses, with doorways open, people just sitting around. The rain would come. The passing by of the Land Cruiser—the event of the hour—would be Gbarngeda's subject of conversation for a few minutes, eclipsing even soccer and the weather.

Charles drove carefully, avoiding the occasional dog, chicken, or toddler, and headed out the far side of town and back into the bush. This road would take them to Banga Sioquelle if they kept driving, but they were not going that far. The road to B-F's satellite processing facility lay just a few more miles farther on. Ten minutes by Land Rover, an hour by foot.

Nightime in Gbarngeda, Daytime in San Diego

"LET'S pull off here. Down there. Yeah, get far off the road."

Charles tucked the car into a copse of low trees. Xander eased out, mindful of his injuries, grabbed a machete from the back of the jeep, and hacked at some palm leaves. Charles took them and lined them up against the part of the car that might be visible from the road.

"We're gonna get nailed by the bugs. Are you taking malaria meds?"

Xander shook his head. "Remember, you're only here for a few days, then you're gone. Me, I'm in and out of places like this all the time. I don't like the side effects of long-term usage of those meds. Maybe what you're taking will work against whatever variety of the malaria is here, and maybe it won't. But I've seen guys hit by nasty side effects. I take a lot of vitamin B supplements and eat a lot of raw garlic; mosquitoes don't seem to like either in your sweat. That may sound like an old wives' tale, but there's usually some truth to folk remedies."

"My doctor gave me a little lecture before I left. He said the new meds worked pretty well...."

"Against malaria, sure, they keep improving. But don't get cocky just because some doctor gave you some expensive medication. It sure as hell won't work against dengue or filariasis. Mosquitoes especially love type O blood." Xander tapped his chest. "I try to keep the bastards away from me, but if I get malaria I'll deal with it then, when they find out what kind it is. At least we're a lot better off than in the days people just drank quinine water and hoped for the best."

"How's your head?"

"Doing great."

Charles glanced at him, half in disbelief. How could a man thirty years his senior, afflicted with two major traumas less than a week earlier, say that? It didn't seem like bravado. Perhaps it was evidence that a disciplined mind could dominate undisciplined matter. Maybe Nietzsche was right: strength of will could conquer the weakness of the body.

The mosquitoes homed in on them, attracted by the carbon dioxide from their breath. The anopheles don't make much of a buzz, even near your ear. They're little things, smaller than the average mosquito, quiet carriers of a tiny parasite that lives within the bug's saliva and then transfers into the human bloodstream and liver, and, when things go badly, into the brain. During the next few minutes, each man got bitten a dozen times, despite Xander's garlic and Charles's bug spray, which trickled off in rivulets in the heat. The malaria parasites found their way inside them for sure.

"Show time," Charles said, turning back toward the road.

"Let's get on with it." Xander slapped at a mosquito.

They both would have been better off if they'd been natives, preferably born with the sickle cell mutation in their blood. A single gene for sickle cell inherited from one—and only one—parent offered strong protection against malaria, and it was one reason why malaria didn't make the region's natives as sick as it made visiting white interlopers. However, those unfortunate folk who inherited two sickle genes—one from each of their parents—lost the evolutionary crapshoot, and many of them fell to painful and debilitating sickle cell anemia.

The night was moonless, and heavy clouds obscured the stars. The only light in the area drifted upward from B-F's secretive facility in the jungle. A glow filtered through the trees and bounced off the low clouds just enough to make walking a bit easier. The men undertook a long slog along a narrow track until they reached the edge of the clearing where a fifty-foot-long shed housed the mysterious machine. The closer they approached, the more the sound of its gasoline generator dominated the jungle with a discordant wavering pitch, its struggling carburetor failing to find the right balance between dirty fuel and thickly humid air.

This time, they would not approach the building like inquisitive shareholders trying to complete a mining tour. This time, they expected to be targets.

They held low to the ground. Dim light escaped through holes and cracks in the shed walls. They watched carefully, alert for any hint of someone else in the area, but there was no motion. Charles threw a stone hard against the shed's corrugated-zinc wall; it crashed loudly enough to overcome the generator noise outside—and assuredly loudly enough to spark interest from anyone inside—but there was no response. Nobody peered out from the shed's door.

There were no guards.

It started raining.

"Just our luck.…" Charles whispered to himself.

But Xander heard the whisper. "Our *good* luck… rain will help keep roaming guards away."

Charles indicated with his finger that he was going to scout the periphery. Ten minutes later he returned and gave Xander the okay sign.

An open area of trampled-down undergrowth lay between them and the building.

They darted to the solitary entrance, about the size of a garage door, on a short side of the shed. A keyed padlock secured the door. Xander swatted a mosquito on his cheek and breathed something obscene in Dutch, directed at both the mosquito and the lock. At least the lock confirmed that no one was inside. Charles motioned for Xander to follow him along the dark wall, where he'd noticed what looked like a weak spot on his scouting foray. A piece of the thin corrugated zinc protruded at an odd angle, and Charles pried at it. The material bent easily, making a hole in the wall just big enough for them to crawl through.

The interior of the building resembled Frankenstein's laboratory without the human parts. The only light came from a row of five-gallon glass jars, each filled with a purple fluid that glowed from a series of high-voltage electric arcs submerged within it. Constant bubbling of the fluid filled the shed with the sweet smell of ozone, created by the electric arcs as they cast their violet glow.

Dusty brown bottles of chemicals lined one wall. Their labels declared danger warnings designed to be unmistakable even centuries in the future. In the center of the building stood the bewildering machine

Charles had seen briefly through the doorway just before a guard had appeared, hollering and shooting. Eighteen feet long and five feet high, it looked like a hyperbaric chamber hybridized with a still. Two air pumps, each the size of a V-8 engine, were attached to it. Set into the casing, at multiple locations, were thick metal valves attached to pipes, each leading to one of the giant pumps in a manner reminiscent of the buoyancy-management system of a submarine. Heavy-duty pressure gauges monitored the pumps. The thing had the appearance of a one-off device, cobbled together by a crazy inventor.

Winn lay on his back examining its underside. Charles knelt at the end. It was fitted with a heavy metal door featuring a massive lever lock, rather like...

"A torpedo tube!" Charles said it louder than he should have, though the generator and the rain would cover his voice to anyone outside.

Charles moved around the far side of the tube. An amateur had welded it closed with a poorly beaded overlapping seam.

Winn climbed back to his feet to examine one of the jars of liquid with the bright arcs of electricity coursing through it, a process that consumed much of the power from the overly large generator. Each jar had small gauge filaments coming out of it, or going into it, emerging from a coil and traversing through small geared motors that, if watched patiently, could be seen autofeeding the wires down into the fluid. The electric arc consumed the wires, a fraction of a millimeter at a time. Winn studied the tiny wires above the jars as they slowly disappeared into the fluid.

The wires appeared to be gold.

"Jesus."

Charles stood next to him. "Yeah."

Winn took dozens of pictures, risking use of the flash to improve the exposure. Charles moved back to the lever-locked door of the tube.

Winn glanced over at him. "Check that pressure gauge if you're thinking about opening that thing."

The gauge claimed to be at zero pressure. Charles tapped on its thick glass, assuming that doing so would be as useless as kicking tires on a car before purchasing. But in this case he was very glad he had: tapping the face of the gauge caused its needle to jump all the way up the dial to 1,500 psi, the equivalent of over 100 atmospheres. Had he lifted the lever sealing the cylinder, the door would have blasted open, thrown him against the shed wall, and probably eviscerated him. With that much pressure inside the machine, steam from a tiny hole in a welded seam or connected pipe would be powerful enough to cut off a limb.

"This thing could burst its seams anytime," Charles said. "It's a pressure chamber. At high pressure, too." Then one of the pumps came on, quite automatically, and the gauge started rising. The pump had a servo connection feeding back from the pressure gauge.

Winn pointed to the floor at a stack of about fifteen hard rock cores, cracked and disjointed in places, each piece labeled with letters and numbers with a Sharpie marker. They lay beyond the machine, tucked in the shadows against the metal wall. Winn documented everything in the building, as fast as the flash on his camera would cycle.

Charles felt his own pressure building. "We need to leave. We've got what we need...."

Winn nodded but kept taking pictures.

Charles tapped his hands on the machine while wanting to wave like a wild man at Winn. He spoke under his breath, "C'mon, c'mon, c'mon!"

Winn said, "Yeah. A few more minutes."

But that would be too long.

* * *

Elliot Springer was a handsome man. Wrinkles appeared around his eyes as he smiled, which he often did. He was fit and healthy, and radiated optimism. He projected respectability, and wore clothes carefully tailored for his diminutive height—he was just over five feet tall. He exuded style and elegance, set off by a hand-tied bow tie.

Sabina Heidel, with her long lithe legs atop high-heeled shoes, towered over him when they shook hands. Yet she felt smaller.

"You have quite a resume," he said to Sabina.

Something about the way he said it suggested to her that her fake Harvard education did not impress him much. Maybe she should have chosen Princeton—her real alma mater.

"I never finished high school," he added.

No, Princeton would not have impressed him either.

"Yet you seem like a successful man."

188

"In ways that matter to me, at least."

Pictures of horses and racetracks covered one of the walls. Some attested to his past as a jockey and showed him standing beside much bigger men: the trainers and owners.

"Do you still ride?"

"For pleasure only. I've been retired for many years. Riding a race horse is exciting, but not relaxing; it's like piloting an AA Fuel Dragster through the quarter mile."

The animals trained to go flat out, and their diets were tailored to supercharge their performance. Thoroughbred racehorses needed months of detraining and retraining to serve any other purpose; some never made the transition back to civilian life. Horses were as different as people, in both their temperaments and abilities.

"What an interesting career," Sabina said.

"It was. As is this one. How did you come to send me your resume, Ms. Dresden? Alchemia Resources is not a household name."

"A friend of a friend mentioned you at a party I attended a few months ago. I'm not even sure of his name. Charles something." The ploy was anything but subtle, but Springer wouldn't know that.

Springer's mind seemed momentarily in the distance. He then said, "Sometimes things work out through a series of seemingly random happenings. The butterfly effect."

She knew nothing about chaos theory, so she simply nodded knowingly and said, "Absolutely!" with what she hoped was the right amount of enthusiasm.

"What sort of real-world experience are you looking for, Ms. Dresden?"

She had relied on her impressive fake resume to imbue him with confidence in her intellect and energy. She intended to use this meeting to provide him evidence of her other values.

"I want to learn from people in the trenches. I'm capable of most anything, and open to most anything." She added a lilt to her voice that would have the intended effect on almost any man. She delivered the double entendre with an experienced subtlety, to allow a man to think what he wished, to have whimsical notions right then as well as later, and have those notions not necessarily stay whimsical.

189

"Well, we are certainly in the trenches, Ms. Dresden." He cocked his head. "What sort of name is Sabina?"

"Latin. It means 'from another religion,' or so I'm told." Her name recalled the famed Rape of the Sabine Women from Roman mythical history. It was as if her mother chose her name solely to reinforce a certain type of imagery in the mind of a well-read man.

Springer appeared to have no other response than to say, "Interesting."

Sabina wondered if she was facing another one of those rare men who, like her new boss Frank Graves, could not readily be manipulated. Encountering two such men in as many days could throw her off her game. She was accustomed to a position of dominance, the sexual alpha. He needed to provide her with an unambiguous opening, soon. Then she could feel good about herself again.

He said, "I bet you gave your Harvard professors a run for their money."

"I'd like to think I gave them their money's worth." She intuitively paraphrased his previous words, with a bit of innuendo, practicing the important elements of seduction: the mimicry of words, breathing, tone, posture—as precise a reflection as possible to make Springer feel he was dealing with a kindred spirit, or maybe even a soul mate.

His warm smile would be infectious to most people, although its sincerity irritated Sabina. Still, she reminded herself: keep an eye on the goal. While she excelled at pretending to agree with others, Sabina stood internally firm in some of her beliefs. When, for instance, she first heard the expression "The end justifies the means," it resonated not as warning, but as an intelligent and workable approach to effective action. She kept the end she desired in mind and accomplished it no matter what was required. It was her version of moral certainty.

"So, Ms. Dresden, what sort of person are you? What is your central motivator?"

This was the interview. So she told him fables about herself and her ideals. He asked deeper questions, ones she had never considered before and didn't quite understand.

"What do you think about the problem of poverty in this country?"

She fumbled momentarily for an answer before deciding. "Well, I think everybody should give back, and we shouldn't leave anybody behind, and everybody should contribute his fair share." She stated this with some bravado. Then, noting his lack of interest in the answer, she feared she sounded like an idiotic beauty queen stringing together buzz phrases recalled from the evening news. Better cover all the bases. "Of course we have to be fair about these things. And it's important to pay attention to bigger issues, like how we educate the underprivileged."

As the interview progressed, she noted Springer's face lose animation. His eyes grew duller and less focused on her, occasionally wandering in the direction of the clock on the wall to her left.

"Ms. Dresden, I have asked you many questions, but do you have any questions for me?"

It signaled the end of the interview. It wasn't working out. She had failed in her first effort at being a field agent. She had to rescue this.

"Yes, I do," she said. "I know you manage money and are experts at investments. I don't know much about the area. But it's exactly what I'd like to get involved with. Can you tell me more about Alchemia?"

"Alchemia speculates in troubled times and troubled places, as well as investing in companies focused on creating wealth. We tend to ignore currently popular sectors, and try to focus on areas that are out of favor. We are inclined to concentrate on energy, food, minerals, and potentially disruptive innovations. The most basic needs and ancient businesses on the one hand, and the newest and most cutting edge on the other. They are the two most volatile sectors of the market. As a general rule they move in opposition to each other, which offers market-timing opportunities. And, of course, we play each from both the long and short side, when appropriate. That's the sum of it."

"How do you do this?" She prodded him, a bit lost. She felt the way she had in trigonometry in high school. The subject was irrelevant to her native instincts and interests—although the teacher gave her a passing grade for other reasons.

"We make small radical entrepreneurs into successful bigger radical entrepreneurs. We try to bring something extra to the party that they may lack. That may be capital. It may be management skills. It may be introductions and connections. The object is to create new wealth, true wealth. A lot of what we do is private equity."

"True wealth? What is true wealth?" she asked, with a trace of cynicism that she failed to hide.

Somehow her question seemed to resonate with Springer.

He turned it back to her. "What is wealth to you, Ms. Dresden?"

She laughed in the nervous manner of one caught pretending to know an answer. "Money, and lots of it," she said flippantly, expecting that he wanted to see evidence of greed.

"Is that it?" His expression didn't change, but he expected more.

She reverted to the standard tripe that seemed to work so well for people who held forth on these things in the media. "Wealth is money. That's what it is. But obviously we need strong policies and decisive leadership to make sure that wealth is used wisely."

"You learned that at Harvard?"

She shrugged. "Well, it's important to be socially responsible to the community...." Who could disagree with that?

Springer frowned. "That view distorts reality."

"So you think wealth is more than money?"

"Certainly," Springer replied. "My definition of wealth is quite a bit broader. You'll need to figure out your own, with your mind instead of your ears, Ms. Dresden. In your schooling, I expect you spent a good deal of effort learning how to parrot back to your professors just what they wanted to hear. That's not the way we operate around here." His voice was firm and impatient. "We want people to think for themselves. I understand the pressure to conform at Ol' Crimson. I am not interested in conformity here."

"Neither am I," Sabina weakly parroted back.

Springer sighed perceptibly. "Ms. Dresden, you should be able to tell that you have not impressed me as yet. But for reasons of my own, I will give you an opportunity for redemption. Your assignment is to define for yourself what wealth means. Then we will compare notes. I will give you an hour."

His tone stayed neutral, not insulting. But she had never before been spoken to with such evident lack of respect and appreciation for her obvious talents.

She stared into his eyes for longer than socially normal.

Springer showed her into a nearby empty office. Sabina sat down at the bare desk and resented the fact that he didn't immediately accept her candidacy. Her revenge would be to get the job anyway and use it to bring the man down—along with this Charles Knight, for whom she felt a growing, and visceral, dislike.

She opened her computer.

* * *

"What? What the hell are you talking about?"

"They were more prepared than I expected."

"A hospital ship? A goddamn Christian hospital ship crew defeated you?" Smolderhof was ready to step off into a raging abyss.

"Don't push me, Smolderhof. Sometimes a lucky shot from a .22 can bring down a lion." Harry barely controlled his temper on the cell phone. If the man had been in front of him, he might have broken his nose.

"Dammit. You know how much is on the line here. What are you going to do now?"

"Where are you?" Harry demanded.

"On this goddamn pitch-black Gbarngeda road, driving through the rain, to see Ollie again. Then I have to head to Toronto for a couple of days."

"Who is left at B-F now?"

"The last drill operators. Johnson and a few of his goons. Same guys as before."

"And at the processing shed?"

"I don't know for sure. Can't get a straight answer. That's why I'm going to Gbarngeda. You know you're supposed to be managing all this, Harry, not me!"

"I've been trying!" His uncharacteristically whining voice angered even Harry himself. "Ollie said the two additional local guards are working out."

The available local help had little training or education. Hiring a couple of new competent mercs, Europeans or South Africans, to guard the processing shed would be safer. But they'd be sophisticated enough to ask questions, and perhaps tell tales later. It was a balancing act.

"I'm gonna check it out myself."

Harry said, "Good. We need more security there. We need to get—"

Smolderhof interrupted him. "Don't say it. Rupert needs everyone we have available with him up in Guinea."

"You already sent to my brother the last good man I had left."

"He was wasted on guard duty in Gbarngeda. No one ever came near the prep shed. Everything is secure."

"Apparently not! You took my man, and all of a sudden we had a breach! Do you see the connection?" Even with billions at stake, Smolderhof had skimped on security.

Smolderhof scoffed. "Pure coincidence. A fluke that you will remedy when you take care of Knight. We've always known that Rupert would need almost all our men with him by this point. He needs a strong force to maintain any control. Your brother's deep in shit up there."

Rupert was about the only living person Harry trusted implicitly. He knew his brother's situation was unstable. Rupert updated him on the situation almost every night at their scheduled call at 11 p.m.

"Still, Dan, we can't let anyone near that place again." No one should have ever found it. "My brother has four other men with him in Guinea. I have only two here in Gondwana. Shit, now only one here. Just me and Roscoe." He didn't count the locals. They could be effective if held under constant command and control. But their lack of proper training and experience made them almost a liability, evidenced by the other night when it was "spray and pray" with six magazines peppering the jungle.

Had he and Barney or Roscoe been there, Knight would never have peeked inside the shed. And if he had, they would have pursued him into the bush and finished the job at close range.

"I'm telling you, we *need* your brother and all his men in Guinea. Rupert would benefit from having *you* up there too, so finish your job quick."

Harry didn't reply. The silence lasted.

With evident exasperation, Smolderhof said, "Look, Harry, don't you worry about security up here right now, and don't worry about Rupert. You get Charles Knight and we'll be back on track again. He's the biggest danger. And there's no reason for him to come anywhere near Gbarngeda or Banga Sioquelle again. My guess is he's somewhere near you, right there in Adamstown, waiting for the next plane out."

"We should intercept Knight at the airport tomorrow. He's booked on an SN Brussels flight to Belgium."

"Where are you going to bag him. The terminal?"

Harry didn't appreciate Smolderhof's continued attempts to micromanage him but kept his temper. "He won't even get into the terminal."

"I hope not."

The signal died.

*   *   *

Five minutes later, Smolderhof bounced his jeep around a sharp turn on the main road toward Gbarngeda. He drove too fast for such a dark night, especially in this rain, which came hard now, pelting his windshield faster than the wipers could keep up. Finally he reached the area where he needed to turn to get to the processing lab. All these little side roads looked alike, especially in the dark. Was this the right one? At the last second, he decided it most likely was and swerved to the right onto barely more than a path. A few hundred meters down the path, his headlights caught a reflection off some exposed surfaces on the two containers, incompletely concealed by their attempted camouflage. Those very important containers confirmed he was where he intended, but they sure as hell should not be visible. Damn Ollie. The man was sick all the time and could not even make sure that those crucial containers stayed properly concealed.

To his right, the processing shed—the key to the whole operation—was nearly invisible through the darkness and rain.

He saw some light between the roof and the metal wall. The plasma arcs were active. Good. Shifflett at least kept the big machine operating.

Flash, flash, flash. What the hell was that flashing in the processing shed? The plasma arcs did not flash that way. Something was broken. He had no time for this. This last set of cores *had* to be finished tomorrow night at the latest. Analysts awaited the results. He had gone to great effort and expense to charter a plane to carry the split cores to the lab in South Africa, and he had paid triple to have the assays prioritized and rushed. Every one of the contract lab's fusion and cupellation furnaces would be commandeered for these samples. But assays take time, and time would be tight.

195

He needed this grand finale—the most impressive assay results yet—to inspire massive buying volume from new buyers. He still had a couple of million shares left, worth several hundred million dollars, to blow into the market.

Burke had started moving far more quickly than he had expected after the deal was inked. They planned to arrive in twelve days. Twelve days! The unwelcome presence of their drilling crews and on-site labs mandated a sudden and unequivocal end to the party at Banga Sioquelle. And here in Gbarngeda, the machine in the processing shed required disassembly, with its components buried where they would never be found.

But, if all went as planned, Burke would never arrive at Banga Sioquelle. Twelve days from now, this whole place would be immersed in chaos and covered with smoke. Then he could fly toward the beaches and into the sunset with close to a billion dollars, and a good long time to cover his tracks.

He drove past the processing shed, pushing the accelerator down even as he came up to the tent in which Ollie kept house near the facility proper. He slammed on his brakes and slid to a stop in the mud.

It was 10 p.m., so Ollie would be asleep. There was nothing to do out here in the bush other than sleep and work. But why no security guards? The rain, of course. The locals figured that if they didn't want to be out in a storm, neither would anyone else. The guards would be inside the processing shed or back in the little shelter that stood next to Ollie's tent, playing cards.

Indeed, four men sat quietly in the shelter, two with guns in their laps. They weren't drinking and gambling. Perhaps they were mellowed out on ganja, for they seemed unconcerned about anything. Of course, they had no reason to be stressed. They knew nothing of the plan, and how close the whole thing was to final fruition.

Smolderhof leaned into their shelter, his eyes burning yellow in the dim light. "Why are you not guarding the processing shed and the containers? Two men at the processing shed, at all times. ALL TIMES. Right? And regular checks, every half hour, on the containers too. And keep those containers concealed. I could see them on the way in!"

An older man looked up and said, "Is raining."

"This facility needs to be guarded night and day, rain or shine. Do you understand?"

"Yes, bossman," the oldest guard replied. He nodded to two younger men who stood up and began dressing in raingear.

Smolderhof said, "Good, get in my jeep. I'll drive you to the processing shed where you're supposed to be. You can hide from the rain in there." He was frustrated with both Harry's team and these local guards. He ran through the rain to Ollie Shifflett's ten-by-ten-foot tent.

The nerdy little chemist was asleep on his cot but awoke as Smolderhof called in through the screen.

"Don't let the damn mosquitoes in!" Shifflett said in a moan. It was a ridiculous comment; the insects had free rein of the place. Smolderhof ducked inside.

"No bugs. See?" Smolderhof turned on the lantern that hung from the center pole. The lantern lit up a five-foot-wide plastic table littered with diagrams—detailed drawings of the machine, Ollie's brainchild. "What are you still doing with those things? I told you to burn them."

Shifflett held a hand between his face and the bright lantern. He coughed. "I need them, in case something breaks. They have all the fitting sizes and parts. I told you that."

"Well, something *has* broken. The plasma arcs look like they're on the fritz."

"What do you mean?" Shifflett came fully awake then, but his eyes were angry at the light and he squeezed them closed.

"Looks like a goddamn fireworks show going on in the processing shed. Flash flash flash!"

"Shit. A damn rat ate through a wire again."

"Glad I got here when I did. Containers uncovered, plasma arcs on the fritz, guards slacking off, you sleeping…. What in hell is going on around here?" Smolderhof affected the grimace of a long-suffering saint forced to deal with an idiot.

Ollie did not see the expression and disregarded his tone. "Give me a minute and drive me there, will you?"

Smolderhof replied, "My car's outside."

24

An Explosive Rumble
in the Jungle

SHIFFLETT scrounged for his pants, socks, and boots. His stomach twisted in a knot.

Supposedly, Canadian mining camps, particularly those in Francophone countries, served excellent food. Here, a local threw together unsavory canned meat with some rice and plantains in an unsanitary mess tent. The only good thing about the heat and humidity was that they killed most of his appetite.

West Africa had a well-deserved reputation as a graveyard for white men—the diseases, the snakes, the unfriendly natives, the brutal heat. His attention focused on his right leg, which sported a nasty-looking bright-red rash. Spider bite? Fungus? He didn't know, but it was spreading, and the overwhelming itch was making him crazy. And the risk of something going wrong, getting caught, and spending years in jail irritated his psyche even more than did the rash spreading up his thigh. Ollie contemplated the advantages of being dead. At least that, arguably, would be nothingness; life here was actively miserable.

He climbed into the front passenger seat of the SUV as he put on his raincoat. A narrow 9 mm Glock pistol that his brother had mailed to him—disassembled and in several packages—weighed down the right-hand pocket. The weapon was his constant companion in this harsh country. No secret society was going to amputate any of Ollie Shifflett's limbs.

Smolderhof nodded and drove off, spinning mud from the tires all over the front of the tent as he turned and accelerated.

Shifflett held on tight to the handle above his head and said, "Dan, I'll fix it, whatever it is. Don't worry."

"How many more cycles?"

"Almost done. To get to 150 grams per tonne will take five more cycles. No problem. I've been running it twenty-four hours a day. I don't sleep much."

"You need to rush it. We need that result."

It was the grand finale. A 150-gram ore—nearly five ounces per ton—over anything but a short, anomalous width, was off-the charts rich. How had Smolderhof described it? Spread like butter. What crap.

Ollie had lived in this business long enough to know the truth: mining was a high-risk, low-return business. Massive quantities of gold, silver, copper, nickel, uranium, and all the other elements and their compounds were critical to an industrial civilization. People seemed to think that refined metals appeared magically, the way chimpanzees thought bananas appeared. Actually, the chimps had the better grip on reality—bananas appeared naturally, whereas mines had to be built.

Ollie couldn't suppress a half smile at the perversity of it all. His breakthrough invention out in the processing shed, not the efforts of geologists and engineers, would at long last guarantee his fortune.

His pride in his invention kept him sane in this horrible place. His machine created colloidal gold, not just dissolved but actually in suspension, in nanosized particles. High voltage ran through gold wires submerged in diluted aqua regia—a mixture of nitric and hydrochloric acids—propelling atoms of gold off the wire and into the aqueous mixture. And then his machine infused this gold-rich colloid into the naturally porous rock by using high pressure. Subsequently, a vacuum speedily evaporated the water, leaving behind the nanoparticulate gold scattered diffusely, invisibly, throughout the rock. The concentration of gold that the fire assays would report depended entirely on how many cycles of pressure and vacuum Ollie applied with his machine to each set of cores. Of course, the creation of higher-grade ore required a lot more cycling of his colloid infuser, and therefore a lot more time to prepare. Smolderhof never seemed to get that simple fact through his thick, impatient skull.

Smolderhof's thick, impatient voice cut into Ollie's thoughts. "Last time that bloody machine broke it took three weeks to get the parts. We don't have three weeks."

"I know, I know, I know we're in a rush.… This place is an outer circle of hell now, but it's going to be the center of hell in less than two weeks!"

"Shut up!" Smolderhof's sharp command was unexpected.

As the SUV approached the colloid-infuser shed, Ollie looked up at the open space above the metal wall in the overhang of the zinc roof. Smolderhof was right. He shook his head, bewildered about what malfunction could cause the intermittent flashes—and why Smolderhof was so particularly short-tempered just then.

Shifflett did not become aware of the guards sitting quietly in the backseat until the jeep pulled up in front of the machine shed and the back doors of the car unexpectedly opened as the two men climbed out. Ah, that explained Smolderhof's angry outburst. He reflected back on the conversation a minute earlier. Had he said anything dangerous? Maybe. "Center of hell in two weeks."

"I didn't know those men were back there. Sorry."

Smolderhof shook his head. "Just fix the machine."

Steeling himself to brave the rain again, Ollie stepped out onto the mucky ground, ran to the door of the long shed, inserted a key, and started working it. The Chinese lock was recalcitrant, as usual. Most of the imports to Gondwana, and all of Africa, seemed to come from China. The price-sensitive Africans could only afford cheap stuff. The Chinese unloaded their lowest-quality product, but the Africans were glad to have any product at all. The Japanese used to sell cheap stuff to the Americans; now the Chinese sold cheap stuff to Africans. What might be the next great trading pair? Water poured down on him. With a vicious twist of the key that risked breaking the lock, the mechanism finally rotated.

Shifflett cracked open the door and—as if cued by his comment to Smolderhof moments before—all hell broke loose.

*   *   *

Heavy raindrops pounded the zinc roof, making it reverberate as if an earthquake were shaking the building. Charles leaned against the big torpedo tube. Through the deafening noise, only the headlights of the car shining through the scattered cracks in the shed wall offered any clue that they were about to receive a visit. Xander kept flashing away with his camera, oblivious, standing with his back to the door that would open in a moment.

As he cursed, Charles ran toward Xander. He grabbed him in mid-picture, barked "Car!" in his ear, and dragged him back down toward the entrance they had created in the corrugated-zinc wall at the back of the shed.

"Go!" he said, as Xander dropped to his knees to crawl through the bent piece of metal wall. Xander did as he was told for once, ducking down to work his way through the tight passage. Charles doubled back to the door end of the pressurized machine. He'd had time to figure out the contraption but had not anticipated the need for what he was about to do. He grabbed a thick rope from a peg on the wall as he ran back. He looped it around the massive handle that levered the tightly sealed tube door. He tossed an end over a convenient rafter, stood as far back as he could, and waited. The long tube aimed directly at the building's door.

He did not have to wait long. The car headlights beamed directly in through the widening gap of the opening door. Three human silhouettes, and the classic, unmistakable shadows of two AK-47s held at the ready, projected onto the back wall as if it were a scene from Plato's Allegory of the Cave. Xander tried to free his pants, which had caught on a bent bit of metal as he finished wriggling through the flap under the cast shadows. Someone yelled, the words unclear but the meaning certain. They had seen Charles. Charles hit the dirt. Before Ollie could yell "Stop, you idiots!" first one guard and then the other reflexively fired their weapons at the shadows, in full auto. Charles winced as the bullets blew apart glassware throughout the shed.

Charles leaped up after the five seconds it took them to empty their magazines, grabbed the rope up high, and sharply jerked down on it with his whole weight. The rope, with the added leverage provided by the turn over the rafter, had the power to lift free the lever that latched the machine's door.

The men coming through the door had no expectation of such a violent greeting. As the tube door crashed open, propelled by pressure equivalent to being under 3,300 feet of water, it twisted off its hinges and tore through the wall in a shriek of ripping metal, smashing through a series of bubbling glass jars on the way. After knocking more than half a dozen rubber trees to the ground, it rolled to a stop over a hundred yards into the bush.

More damaging was what concurrently rushed out from the now-open end of the long tube. Fifteen three-inch-diameter cores of hard rock lay inside that tube with compressed liquid and air, all under profound pressure. Some of the core was cracked and broken, and some pieces were only a foot or two long, but two were fully intact eight-foot-long spears. When that door opened, with an almighty roar, a colossal blast of purple-brown water exploded forth; the highly pressurized acidic liquid carried a full ton of ammunition in the form of the cores, blasting out like a mixture of missiles from a silo and grapeshot from a cannon. The effect on both the shed and the men about to enter was devastating.

The air where the B-F guards stood filled with water, steam, and droplets of corrosive aqua regia. The pressure change assaulted Charles's ears and muffled the brief agonized shrieks of the men who had tried to enter. Had the shed been either smaller or airtight, the instantaneous pressure change would have deafened Charles. Instead the pressure dissipated through the newly created destruction.

Charles held his breath against the toxic mist, his eyes burning as he realized that the far wall, the one with the door, had vanished. And so had large portions of the men who had been standing there. The headlights of the SUV no longer shone directly toward the shed either. The blast had thrown the SUV sideways and one of the rock-core spears had skewered the engine block.

It was a horrifying, apocalyptic scene. Billions of sparkling flakes of elemental gold, violently torn from the walls on the inside of the machine, fell slowly through the mist. Like microscopic snow, the gold particles reflected the eerie light of the arcs still leaping across space within what was left of a dozen shattered glass containers.

Despite the ringing in his ears, Charles heard more than saw what happened next. The roof of the poorly constructed shed, no longer supported at the far end, started folding down—slowly at first but gathering speed. Intermittent sharp popping of wooden beams as they fractured punctuated the screeching and groaning of tearing metal. Charles ran.

Everything got louder as the roof collapsed faster. The light from the plasma arcs burned brighter now that the jars lay in shards, leaving the electrical arcs unblocked by the colored liquid. It was just enough illumination for Charles to see where his makeshift back door stood open, now finally freed of Winn's bulk. He dove to the loose piece of metal, his hands ahead of his head, and, clawing into the mud outside for traction, pried himself through. He ripped his pants on the same piece of metal that had caught Winn just a moment earlier. The disintegrating roof pulled the back wall inward with a twist as Charles jerked his feet out and started to stand. Then the base of the wall kicked up and smashed Charles on his backside, propelling him, spinning, through the air.

He landed mostly on his shaved head, next to Xander, and together they scrambled away from the collapsing building.

As Charles wiped his eyes clear to gaze back at the scene of destruction, Xander regarded him, questioning.

Charles said, a little too loudly, "Oops."

25

Conversations in the Jungle

"RUPERT. You de bossman. You tell us what we to do and when we to do it."

Rupert, like his brother Harry, stood large, solid, and strong as an ox. But the black man in front of him, with bulging and bloodshot eyes, was bigger. Rupert was JohnJohn's *bossman* only until JohnJohn got what he wanted, and killed him.

"JohnJohn, I respect your concerns, and those of your men. I know you are ready. But the time is not right just yet. There has been no war here for a few years. You can wait twelve more days before starting the next one. Only twelve days. That's a lot sooner than we originally intended. We are doing this to make you happy."

"My men are hungry, hungry for blood and treasure. Tha' gold is ours. Tha' gold is ours, not for selling to Canadians for nothing, not by the corrupt government that has stolen control of Gondwana. We are ready. It is our time now."

"You are right, JohnJohn." Rupert had stoked those fires and fed that propaganda to JohnJohn often enough during these past many months. Dealing with this psychotic narcissist exhausted him. It was delicate work negotiating with an emotionally unbalanced, developmentally arrested thug with an automatic weapon and a bloodstream full of testosterone. JohnJohn had extensive experience with violence—and no conscience that might curb it.

Notwithstanding the fact he might be clinically insane, the man in front of Rupert was as charismatic as any he had ever met. When

JohnJohn stood in front of the men and spoke, he had the impact of a Mohammed, a Hitler, or a Gandhi. Or a Jim Jones. He could work the two thousand young men into a religious fury. And religion motivated the masses even better than politics, especially when intertwined with sex, drugs, and violence—all of which were on offer, along with the promise of money and power. The combination proved a package few young men could resist.

By the end of a thirty-minute performance by JohnJohn, the cheers and chants of this new army could be heard echoing for miles, almost to the border with Gondwana. JohnJohn was as right for Gondwana as Idi Amin had been for Uganda, or Pol Pot for Cambodia.

Rupert knew his own limitations, among them the fact that he—like his three ex-spec-ops guys from Zimbabwe and South Africa, and the ex-Legionnaire from Poland—was white.

Their whole plan hinged on JohnJohn and his growing following. Rupert first met him as a young rebel leader more than a decade earlier. At that time, white men, mostly drifters from the declining conflicts in southern Africa, came to Gondwana to support whichever side could afford them. Payment was provided in uncut diamonds—so-called conflict stones.

Diamond exports from Gondwana were tightly regulated by means of the Kimberley process, a scheme concocted by DeBeers and meant to guard their monopoly even while it disguised them as selfless do-gooders. New wars had to be financed with conflict timber, conflict gold, conflict fishing and mining concessions, and conflict promises, in addition to diamonds. The biggest beneficiaries of the conflicts in West Africa were established diamond producers elsewhere. That was because the regulatory control of diamond exports imposed on Africa, on the pretext of defunding the wars, persisted long into the peace. The self-righteous hysteria about conflict commodities manacled the productivity of the West African diamond mines and kept diamond supplies under centralized control even years after the wars had ended— just as the world's big established diamond producers intended.

There was little difference between this rebel army and the government armies, except the government soldiers were generally equipped with better, UN-supplied gear and had had more time to pick up bad habits. JohnJohn could just as well have been part of the government military, as he had in fact been while his faction intermittently controlled Gondwana's capital city.

After years of peace, JohnJohn was back where his persona demanded—in command of a mob, and on his way to commanding a country. It allowed him to ambush, rape, pillage, kidnap, cut off arms and legs, and recruit boy soldiers with impunity. Boy soldiers have many advantages from the viewpoint of a psychopath. They're morally malleable. They're brave, because the young believe they'll live forever. And they'll do as they're told.

Some of the men had followed JohnJohn in the past, and they would follow him now. Child soldiers of the last war became his lieutenants today. One lieutenant caused particular concern for Rupert. He was intentionally troublesome. He had the ability to be charismatic when he chose but lacked JohnJohn's enormous size. In fact, Flomo Kebele was diminutive and overcompensated accordingly.

Flomo was a scam artist. He conned old ladies out of their phones and their money. He encouraged little boys to deliver stolen goods. He borrowed cars and sold them. He worked the NGOs by speaking English with great clarity while quoting Bible verses and claiming to have been an orphan. If true, he had probably killed his own parents.

Flomo had a core following within this army—a small fraction, perhaps one hundred men who felt a connection not just to JohnJohn's power, but also to Flomo's methods. Rupert had watched Flomo quietly cultivate these men, culled mostly from the older, more experienced soldiers. If JohnJohn succeeded in taking over Gondwana and becoming the nation's leader, Flomo would angle to become chief of the secret police. That would be an ideal platform for Flomo to betray and kill the Big Man in order to replace him.

JohnJohn kept Flomo close to him because Flomo had an important talent: he had an ear permanently glued to the ground. He was JohnJohn's data collector. A Third World version of the NSA, monitoring the chatter not of the airwaves but inside the tent flaps and around the charcoal fires—a spider hanging on the walls, ever listening.

Rupert carefully considered his words whenever Flomo was nearby. The little shit was nearby a lot.

Only two hundred of the men were armed with AK-47s so far. Sharing these few weapons back and forth among them, two thousand men had been trained to field strip and clean their weapons. Not that cleaning was critical with an AK: the gun was nearly foolproof and would operate under the worst conditions imaginable. Reliable, cheap, and available in quantity, no wonder it had become the icon of peasant armies the world over.

Rupert and his colleagues had taught these young men how to aim and fire the weapons. Each had fired one thirty-round magazine, one shot at a time, carefully aimed at a target only ten yards away, even though the aiming was likely irrelevant. Most casualties they would inflict would be at ranges of a few feet to a few yards, when pointing the weapon in the general direction was good enough. In the heat of combat, however, these boys and men could be counted on to fire enthusiastically until the bullets were gone and the juju had left the gun. Then they'd likely throw it away and run. Such was the dedication of men fueled by puffed-up rhetoric supplemented with a sheaf of ganja. The drug didn't encourage aggression, like coke, meth, or PCP. But it did put those who imbibed it in an altered state, and since it grew everywhere, it was free.

Rupert's men went through the motions of teaching, despite the shortage of supplies and the lack of student discipline. Now, after the training, the ammunition supply had almost run out. The few men with guns had very little to shoot through them, exactly as Rupert wanted.

And he was alive tonight because of that planning.

Ten minutes earlier, JohnJohn's eyes had revealed a desire to tear Rupert to shreds. The big man with the red eyes wanted the rest of the guns and ammunition delivered here to the camp, and he wanted them now. It had taken immense patience to bring the man back down. In the end Rupert had said, "JohnJohn. You will have nearly unlimited ammunition and two thousand more guns. They are not far away. I give you my word that your men will be fully supplied before they need to be. You will have the weapons and ammunition when the soil is most fertile for our expedition. And in the very near future, you will be the president of Gondwana." He added the last for good measure and to change the subject.

JohnJohn stared hard at Rupert for too long. It was the man's preferred intimidation tactic. When posturing for power over someone, JohnJohn tried to convey the message that he was reading his target's thoughts, looking into his soul, discovering deceit with a magical, god-like ability. Rupert had dealt with thugs, politicians, palm readers, and religious leaders in Africa most of his life; he was far too familiar with the technique—it was sometimes called the *sociopath's stare*. It worked well on young soldiers. They feared JohnJohn as they would a god. And rightfully so. He possessed a force of personality and physical power that inspired fear, obedience, and even superstition. And those are god-like qualities. Like most deities, JohnJohn was a fickle and jealous god. He could smile and pat you on the back one second and stick a shiv in your kidney with an evil grimace the next.

Rupert kept control of the money B-F Explorations provided, but JohnJohn ran the main show, including how he gathered his army, how he motivated them, and how he controlled them. JohnJohn relied on Rupert as an experienced subaltern. Egomaniacal and unstable though he was, he was also intelligent enough to realize Rupert's value to him.

When the enormous African finally turned on his heels and walked out of the tent, Rupert let out an audible sigh of relief. One wrong word could be fatal.

Harry would ring shortly, at 11 p.m., the hour set for their nightly call. Oilskins were perfect for the cooler rainy evenings of the wet season: a rain-repellant long coat, and a hat that went with it. Rupert pulled on knee-high rubber boots to round out his getup; they provided a good measure of protection against snakes. He looked like a fisherman as he stepped out into the rain. As usual, his appearance entertained those men of the camp who remained awake—the drinkers and gamblers.

No wind moved through the camp. Only the steady pelting of an infamous rain. He looked around in all directions, making sure that the little worm, Flomo, wasn't about. A handful of small generators still rumbled, but the main generator was turned off at 10 p.m. Scattered battery-operated lights and the glow of small fires shone like dotted lines through seams of green tents. A few men braved the rain, heading for the latrine; others sat under hastily made wooden structures roofed with palm leaves to keep the sky at bay. Men waved to him and smiled, with their teeth being the most visible feature in the eerie night.

Behind him, a trace of light from the moon through the clouds in the east provided just enough diffused illumination for him to safely walk the three-hundred-yard path to an odd-shaped enormous rock that capped the highest hill above the camp.

The nearest cell tower, thirty-five miles to the northeast, was powered for long-range transmission. His own phone had a good antenna, but it often failed to connect through thirty-five miles of rain. However, he could usually pick up the tower's signal from the top of the huge rock on the hill.

Rupert walked along the path between four fully graded soccer fields, complete with goals and orange cones, where only scrub brush existed four months before. The fields lay dark and deserted at the moment, but they were always busy during the day with eager young men smiling and laughing and tearing across the packed dirt fields like dancers, kicking and heading the ball with intensity. When the young men weren't playing soccer, the rebel leaders drilled them in order to acclimate them to following orders, had them practice military maneuvers in the hills, run the obstacle courses, and learn to aim on the rifle ranges hidden in the woods.

The place was decked out as a soccer camp to conceal that it was actually a place where rebels were massing, while the soccer itself served as an enticement for more boy soldiers. The promise of military adventure, the regular food, and the privilege of being part of JohnJohn's kingdom come were an added attraction for them to stay. For four months no outsiders raised any concerns, but a naive group of missionaries shipped a whole container-full of soccer uniforms and cleats through the difficult terrain all the way from the port in Conakry, through Nzérékoré, and down the beaten N-1 dirt highway, and then up through the almost impassable road to their camp. The young men loved the black shorts and green and white shirts of their new soccer uniforms, and wore them in preference to their olive military fatigues, which they used only during drills and for crawling through the mud. Although neither JohnJohn nor Rupert planned it, the soccer attire became the primary uniform of this little army, and the clothing served well to keep the army a secret. The soccer outfits were more comfortable, and the boys imagined themselves as heroic soccer stars rather than rampaging bush soldiers. These rebels were soccer rebels.

Yet the camp was now taking on a different tenor. Dozens of vehicles had arrived that were out of place in a soccer camp: jeeps, panel trucks, troop carriers, and two fuel trucks with the look of military surplus. If the missionary soccer supporters came by again, they would wonder at the extent of the motor pool that lay directly under the protective rock outcropping of the towering hill toward which Rupert now walked.

He trudged in the dark and rain, past the fields, between the fuel trucks upon which the perimeter guards sat watching, and along his worn path up the hillside. He climbed and looked back over the motor pool and down on his camp of over two thousand men. There were no women. JohnJohn's lieutenants—his enforcers—made sure of it. They could only generate jealousy and dissension, while creating a security risk, telling stories of what else was going on at the soccer camp.…

The path got steeper and more difficult as he climbed. At various points it became nearly vertical, but after several months of this nightly trek, he knew the holes in the rocks and could find them blindfolded.

Rupert mounted the massive capstone, something of a geological oddity. The sausage-shaped green-black mass, over a hundred yards in length and eighty feet thick, had buffered the hill underneath against erosion for eons, and now provided similar shelter to his motor pool. It would not provide such protection forever. Even now it seemed to teeter on the top of the steep hill, which, despite the capstone's presence, was slowly eroding from the wind, pounding rains, tendrils of vegetation, and the general action of the second law of thermodynamics. Perhaps in another ten, or a hundred, or a thousand, or ten thousand years that rocky horizontal cylinder would yield to gravity and roll into the valley, leaving the hill unprotected and accelerating its final erosion. For now, the odd-shaped rock was the only reason the hill was still there, and the only way for Rupert to have cellular contact.

Rupert acknowledged the rock once again for its service to his cause, as he clambered up its side on his knees. He pulled himself up using the weathered rope that hung there, attached to a rusty eight-inch steel eye-bolt inserted into the rock face by someone whose history and reason for doing so were lost to the past. Perhaps it was a remnant of small-scale mining during the colonial era fifty years earlier, back when economic activity in this country was still possible, before everyone's efforts were diverted to political entrepreneurship.

He stood atop the giant rock, and, as the alarm on his digital watch signaled 2300, he aimed the cell phone in his right hand toward the clouded heavens and beckoned the gods of electromagnetism to favor the device. A flash of lightning in the distance behind served to highlight his silhouette to the camp below. From the viewpoint of a dozen or so men looking up from the camp, for just that moment, Rupert was a prophet, collecting energy from the heavens.

The phone buzzed. He pulled it to his ear, unconsciously lifting his heels to assist the tenuous signal, and listened.

"Rupert, are the skies clear where you are?"

"Fog and Fire here," he replied. It was their code, confirming that they could speak. Sometimes Harry couldn't hear his response, and the call would end without information exchanged. Tonight, despite the lightning and the rain, or perhaps even because of it, the bidirectional connection held.

"Good. We have not found Charles Knight yet. He snuck off the hospital ship. We'll try to intercept him at the airport tomorrow."

"Good luck with that."

"Barney's dead."

Rupert was accustomed to hearing of the deaths of his friends. The moment of silence on the phone was the only tribute Barney would receive. But the surprise persisted. Both men recognized they'd been living on borrowed time for years.

"Look, Harry, if we can speed up this operation even more, let me know. I am having a difficult time keeping JohnJohn calm here. He is ready to roll out at any moment. The sooner we pull this off, the better, yah."

"You know I agree. We're moving as fast as we can."

"That's great. But JohnJohn is starting to posture, demanding the weapons be delivered. I'll try to keep him under control. What about anti-aircraft? That's what he's pissing about most. The bastard's relentless."

"Good news. Good news. I got hold of those Anza MK-II MAN-PADS. They were flown in from Malaysia via Abidjan."

"They should be perfect. Anything that even *looks* like MANPADS will be fine. Well done."

These particular manually portable air-defense systems—basically small missiles that could be carried on a shoulder—were developed jointly by China and Pakistan. They weren't the latest technology, but they were available at the right price because the Malaysian prime minister was currently in financial hot water. After all, in a world where the Russians had a hard time accounting for the number and whereabouts of nuclear weapons, a few dozen little missiles sent from one nothing-nowhere backwater to another weren't even a rounding error.

Rupert said, "Twelve more days in this hellhole before I can release this mob into the wild."

"You can make it. What's your number now?"

"Fifty new recruits in the last three days. Total is over two thousand now."

"Enough?"

"I don't really care. But yes, it is enough to get the job done."

"Good."

"Now, you get Charles Knight, Harry. From what you told me, that one kid could derail the whole thing."

"I know. Believe me, I know. We can't find him. He hasn't come back to his hotel. Our chance is at the airport tomorrow. He'll be there. He's got to be desperate to get out of this country."

The phone crackled loudly now. Rupert knew from experience it would beep its spontaneous disconnection any second now.

"He's probably scared witless, hiding out as far away from us as he can possibly get."

26

Discoveries

CHARLES and Xander slid back into the darkness together. A demolished shed lay on top of the machine and chemistry lab that had successfully pushed the market cap of B-F to over $5 billion. Buyers wanted B-F shares because they were supposedly backed by a hundred million ounces of gold. It was a huge irony that the dollars quantifying B-F's value were themselves once backed by gold, but were now backed with lies, just like B-F shares.

Through the rain, Charles saw a man prying himself out of the SUV on the far side of the collapsed shed. As the man staggered in front of the headlights, Charles saw who it was. Smolderhof took a few tenuous steps, then the remnants of the roof and walls blocked their view. Xander tugged at Charles.

"This way," he whispered. "There's something I want to check out back near the path. We have to be quick. It won't be long before other guards are out looking for us."

They moved through the jungle and the rain. Charles, unsure of how far or how long it would take, followed as Xander limped along the path. They arrived at the dirt road, and hurried across it into chest-high growth.

Xander turned to him. "Look. There. See that? Just over there." Xander pointed and pushed through the undergrowth, Charles close behind.

Charles wiped the water off his face and searched through the darkness. He approached two shipping containers, set back fifty feet off the path, camouflaged with palm fronds and piles of brush. He pushed back the vegetation as best as he could to access one of the doors. It was locked.

"No problem!" Xander said. He reached into the small fanny pack that he kept attached to himself at all times in Gondwana. It contained the essentials for surviving in a place where they were most needed but least available. A fat Swiss Army knife, an LED flashlight, a butane lighter, a Space Pen and writing pad, a space blanket, a bandana, some parachute cord, a small first aid kit, and a small fishing kit, among other things. The only tool that was any good was the one you had with you when it was needed. He extracted a thin vinyl wallet containing implements like those in a surgeon's kit, but designed to operate on locks.

"Some light, please," Xander said.

Charles held the light as Xander worked the lock. This was not a cheap Chinese lock. It was a solid American device that would be nearly impossible to saw through. He worked first with two metal picks inserted into the key slot, and then a third. It was intricate work that required patience—three long minutes of patience—before Xander persuaded the mechanism to release with just the right combination of placement and motion. With a few heaves Charles pulled the door back against what was left of the concealing wall of palm fronds and squeezed through the gap. He shined Xander's flashlight into the darkness. It was moist, hot, and smelled of wax, petroleum, and something else.

The bottom half was packed with palettes stacked with cardboard boxes, five inches high by about fifteen inches long and ten inches deep. They were all marked with Cyrillic letters and labeled "7.62 x 39." On top of them were much larger cardboard boxes. Charles opened one of these. It had a carbine inside, wrapped loosely in waxy paper, along with two magazines, a cheap cleaning kit, and a single page of paper— an instruction manual for a gun that was so entirely easy to use and maintain that it didn't really matter that the instructions were in Cyrillic script.

"AK-47s, and their ammunition," Xander said.

Charles nodded and added, "And lots of it. Each box has almost a thousand rounds." Charles did some quick math. "I'll guess there are a million rounds plus about a thousand guns here. Then there's the other bad boy next door...."

Xander posed a rhetorical question: "What do you think B-F is planning on doing with millions of rounds of ammunition and all of these guns?"

"Fuck" was the only word Charles could think to say. Coarse and shocking, perhaps, but the word's immense flexibility and directness made it a most sincere and honest emotional intensifier.

"Fuck," Winn replied.

*　　*　　*

Sabina wracked her brain, trying to integrate what she'd previously researched about Elliot Springer with what she'd intuited from her interview with him. For all that his IRS records had revealed about his income and investments, they told her nothing about who he was or what he believed, his philosophies about life and money.

What would his definition of wealth be? It was his big interview question, and her answer, if satisfactory, just might rescue her from her so far dismal performance. Time was short to pull together an answer.

She knew wealth when she saw it. The dictionary on the office's bookshelf defined it as "a great store of money or property." Simple enough. Why then would he ask such a simple question? Clearly, the man was looking for something more than any fool could find in a dictionary and parrot back in a sentence.

She tried to put herself in Springer's shoes, considering what she'd learned about the man. With no time to spare, she came up with a possible answer. If it worked, it would be a victory snatched from the jaws of defeat.

She wore an outfit that was sexy, yet fully acceptable for business: the classic little black dress with a jacket and pumps. When she took off the professionalizing jacket, it was simply sexy.

So she took off the jacket as she walked back into Springer's office. She stayed standing longer than she needed to, pretending to examine the pictures of horses on the wall, assuming he was looking her up and down while he went back behind his desk. When she did turn around, she saw that he had turned his chair to the side, distracted, reading some papers.

She walked over to the chair by the desk and sat down, crossing her legs carefully.

"Yes, your dress outlines your figure very well, Ms. Dresden. Of course I noticed. You need not provide me so much time to do so in the future."

She had no response planned for that, but she quietly exhaled a deep breath, like a balloon deflating.

"So, do you have an answer to my question?"

She nodded. "I do. Wealth is accumulated money, as I first stated, but there is something I forgot. Wealth also includes everything you need to use your money well—your health, your freedom to spend it as you wish." In her mind it was no more than a platitude, but it might appeal to a man like Springer.

It seemed to work, because he smiled after a moment. "Well, Ms. Dresden, you have reached farther than the standard dictionary definition, and although yours is not yet my definition, at least it's a start. Perhaps there's still hope for you."

Sabina shrugged. Her pretending to be a Harvard grad had been counterproductive, which was surprising, since the place was notoriously hard to get into. Having an Ivy League degree was like carrying a little badge saying "I'm smart!" Or at least "well connected." How could she have predicted that Springer would see it as evidence that she'd spent years swimming in a cesspool of political correctness?

"Do I have the internship?"

Springer didn't answer immediately. He looked at her; she figured he could go either way. Then she saw his eyes soften. Maybe she'd won.

"No internship, Ms. Dresden. Instead we'll play it day by day. Let's see what you can do. Come back tomorrow morning."

"What will I be doing?" she asked. At least she had her foot in the door.

"I'll have some further research for you on what we've just been discussing. Plus some more to do on companies we're considering. In particular I will want you to look into a company called Burke International Mining. We know it well but have to freshen up on it. Coincidentally, it's for a project Charles Knight is working on. He's probably the man you met who first mentioned us to you."

"Charles Knight? Maybe that was his name. I don't remember." It was best to hedge. "Will I see him tomorrow?" This would be perfect. Graves would be thrilled.

"That would be difficult."

"Oh, is he away?"

"Actually, he's missing."

"Missing?" Unlike everything else about her, the surprise was real.

"Yes. Somewhere in Africa. I'll see you in the morning, Ms. Dresden."

Springer picked up his telephone and waved Sabina out of his office.

*   *   *

After she left, Springer shook his head. His frustration with the world was constantly justified. He was never surprised by, but always disappointed in, the shallow thinking of most people.

This woman—this Sabina Dresden—was so heavily programmed. So conventionally schooled. She was so perfectly horrid that she might be perfect for his needs.

Could you ever pull someone like that back from the brink?

One of the defining events of his life, one of the best things that had happened to him, was leaving school before the process of "being schooled" was completed. It wasn't intentional, but dictated by circumstances.

He and Charles Knight shared both a relative lack of schooling and a great appreciation of learning, and maybe that was why they shared so much else. He expected that was why Maurice Templeton had introduced them. Maurice connected people who could benefit from knowing each other. It was a risky habit. Perversely, most people attributed all the good things that happened to them to their own virtues, while bad outcomes were the fault of whoever else they could blame. Therefore Maurice vetted his associates thoroughly, especially before he put them next to one another, and he had developed excellent judgment in doing so. As a result, Springer was not surprised that he greatly enjoyed his new friendship with Charles.

Maurice Templeton would never have introduced him to a woman like Sabina. But that did not mean that their meeting would be unproductive.

Springer had incubated a hypothesis for years, adding to it as he accumulated more experience by delving into evolutionary biology, a field about which, at the beginning, he had little knowledge. During his interview with Sabina it had occurred to him that this might provide an ideal platform to test his ideas, to put the theories he was forming into practice.

The question he wanted to answer was whether destructive ideas and evil ideologies arose as the consequence of infectious brain diseases, and whether they, like other diseases, spread most aggressively when people congregated in large groups—revival meetings, sports events, political rallies, college classrooms, and the like. But ideology didn't need direct contact to spread. It also could spread virtually, as a meme. And large groups served as its Petri dish.

The notion of ideas as infections was not too far a reach, really. Bacteria were thousands of times larger than viruses. And viruses were enormous relative to prions—those smallest of proteins familiar to most as the cause of mad cow disease. Some suspected tiny prion infections to be the cause of Alzheimer's disease as well.

Even smaller than prions were *ideas*.

No one questioned that ideas—complex conglomerations of thoughts—could change the brain connections, alter cellular signaling, and even activate genes to modify cellular function. Some of those genes were derived from, or indeed still were, primordial infectious organisms that originally parasitized the bodies of our remotest evolutionary ancestors by invading DNA, inserting themselves within the coding of what eventually became the human species—sometimes beneficially to the human, but sometimes purely as a latent opportunity for revival of the infecting organism. Springer's hypothesis was that somehow an ancient parasitic infection—reactivated in the brain by the electrochemical interactions of an idea—destroyed parts of a rational brain's function so as to make the infection able to multiply and spread.

Objective evidence exists that learning alters the brain in much the way that exercise forms the body. Ideas, by their very nature, are sum totals of substantial biologic brain alterations. When the ideas are bad, the concomitant brain alterations are—whether through a viral or parasitic reactivation or not—by definition destructive. Ideas can, in this manner, lead to true disease. As with more conventional diseases, like measles or cholera, as the population density increases, the risks of contagion grow. Conceivably, that was why small, isolated bands, like the

Australian aborigines or Kalahari Bushmen, seemed to have little social pathology. They weren't exposed. Wars, pogroms, persecutions, envy, indignity—all, perhaps, were the insane products of psychological aberration caused by the spread of an infection.

The infection caused the brain to change, and human rationality suffered while the collectivist infection spread from place to place. Hundreds of millions had died from the collectivist epidemic in the last century, and it had diminished the dignity of billions more. Yet the idea thrived. It was the defining essence of a parasite.

Diseases are subject to evolutionary pressure too. If a parasite kills its host, the parasite usually dies as well. But an infectious disease has no intelligence. It lives or dies not by thought but by accident. If an evil ideology is indeed a parasitic disease—a disease whose only purpose is replication—then its unchecked expansion could very well kill its host in the end. Indeed, the collectivist idea already had sickened its host for centuries. From the point of view of such a disease, individual humans were not the host—they were just expendable cells that could be killed off with little harm to the parasite itself. No, it was the entire human species that was collectively its host. Was this host at risk? Certainly. Not long ago, one danger to the species from collectivism had been evident to all: nuclear holocaust. Now that meme had retreated to the back of the collective consciousness, semi-forgotten, while the parasite spread nearly unchecked.

Springer wanted a cure. Could the latent genes that derived eons ago from parasites be turned back off? Could collectivism be cured?

There were occasional case reports of people seeing the light and breaking out from the mental confines of the failed paradigms.

So, yes, it could be cured in individuals, occasionally. To Springer, individualism was the only rational antidote.

Collectivism needed to be cured one person at a time, if it could be cured at all. As Charles Mackay wrote in *Extraordinary Popular Delusions and the Madness of Crowds*, "Men, it has been well said, think in herds; it will be seen that they go mad in herds, while they only recover their senses slowly, one by one."

He would test his hypothesis on this Sabina Dresden. Fully inculcated in collectivism and statism by her schooling and her life experiences, she was evidently infected with a huge inoculum of the parasite. She could be a wonderful person; she was simply ill at the moment.

If Sabina Dresden was the woman that her resume and references described her to be, she would make for a perfect case study.

*　*　*

"Wake. Wake." Nyahn whispered into his brother's ear. "Wake!" The sound of his voice, as quiet as it was, echoed against the corrugated metal of the shipping container that served as the back wall of their makeshift shelter of palm fronds.

Saye was far down in sleep. He groggily pushed his hand into Nyahn's face, groaned, and rolled over.

"Jeep here. Jeep here, Saye." But Saye did not respond. A flash of light shot past their shelter—the headlights of a vehicle turning on the path nearby. Nyahn stuck his head out from under the palms, the rain hitting him and soaking his face. He kept his eyes open, though, and watched the red taillights of the jeep as it disappeared around a turn in the path.

Nyahn turned onto his back, listening to the pounding rain. Saye rolled over again and reached out a hand, laying it across Nyahn's shoulder, patting him before snoring faintly, once again in his deep sleep. Nothing more happened then for a time. The jeep did not return.

But Nyahn could no longer sleep. His heart bounced in his chest, and he breathed fast. He tried to listen through the rain but could hear nothing. He rolled so he could look out under the edge of the shelter. His eyes darted around, seeking anything, but all was completely dark.

Time passed, he knew not how much. But then he heard noises from deeper in the bush. A muffled roar, gunfire, brief screams of human agony, and the twisting of metal. Nyahn knew it was a monster, a giant night monster, and it was on its way toward them.

He couldn't keep his voice down now. "Saye… Saye. Wake! Wake, Saye!" he cried, desperately trying to get his brother to rouse. "Wake, Saye!"

Finally, Saye moved, and then suddenly he became alert. "What is it, boy?" he rubbed his eyes and spoke angrily.

"Monster. Big monster."

"No monsters, Nyahn."

220

"Yes. Big monster. Listen."

Saye pushed his brother away, but he listened. There was nothing but the pounding rush of rain.

But then there was a voice. Or was it the monster, coming near? No, it was men, out late at night in the dark and rain.

"Shh. No talk," Saye whispered in his brother's ear.

Some more voice sounds, deep, uncertain. Scuffling around, not far away. A groan. Nyahn's eyes opened even wider and then closed tightly. He leaned toward his brother, who held him firmly.

They listened to more muffled talk, and then the creaking of a door opening. It was the door to the container that served as a wall to their shelter. There was more talk inside the container, echoing from their wall.

A voice that was familiar.

"Stay still." Saye crept out under the palms in complete silence, his bare feet disappearing into the darkness. Nyahn remained, alone and afraid.

Suddenly a noise and a light. "Is me," Saye softly said to his brother, pulling himself partly under the palm fronds. "Come out. It okay. Friends!"

* * *

The rain let up some as Nyahn emerged from the boys' dark shelter into the faint light of a flashlight partly covered by a man's wet shirt.

"Hi, Nyahn! How de body?"

It took a moment for Nyahn to recognize his friend Charles with his newly shaved scalp. But he saw Charles's blue eyes and his smile soon enough. "Body fine-oh!" Nyahn's smile emerged, his teeth reflecting the light.

Saye said to Nyahn, "We go wid Charles, small-small. No safe here."

Charles added, "That's right." He closed the door to the container and replaced the lock, then started moving some fronds back to cover up the front of the container. Saye moved around the edge of the container and came back with a pile of palm in his arms, a big part of their tempo-rary roof. Nyahn did the same. Together they worked to cover the front of the container.

Partway through, Saye said, "No. Do like dis," as he threw more fronds to the top of the pile, re-creating the way it had appeared before the boys had pilfered the material for their own shelter. "Now fix."

"Good job, boys. Let's go," Charles said, and the two men and two boys moved off through the darkness, flashlight off.

Nyahn did not understand what the white men were doing. "Who is dis?" he asked Charles.

Charles whispered back, "This is Xander. Xander, this is Saye and Nyahn. These are the boys that gave me directions to this place. They're on their way to a big soccer camp up north, up past Banga Sioquelle, I think in Guinea."

"Free uniforms and shoes!" Nyahn added, a bit too loudly now that the rain had let up.

"Quiet, boy," Saye said to him.

Charles said, "Come to our jeep with us so we can all be safe."

Almost running, the men led them two hundred yards up the road and onto the path where they had hidden their car. They climbed inside. Nyahn breathed in the smell of fresh plastic and clean carpet, so different than the human scents that filled the crowded cabs he occasionally rode in.

"Let's go north for a while," Charles said. "Give these kids a little help."

Xander backed the Land Cruiser off the path and then turned it north on the Guinea road.

"Nyahn, what were you doing sleeping by those containers?"

He replied with a typical Gondwanan expression. "What else *would* we do?" It was a good answer. Why would these men ask such a silly question?

Charles nodded and reached back from the passenger's seat to show a thumbs-up. "We'll take you a little ways up here, okay?"

Saye nodded quietly. After a bit, Nyahn asked, "Water?"

Charles gave each boy a bottle, breaking the seal on the cap.

Nyahn reached for it. White men always had new bottles filled with water, and threw the container away. Didn't they know that the bottle is worth more than the water?

Charles spoke to Xander quietly, but he was audible to the boys in back. "Do you want to take them up an hour or two, then get some sleep in the car?"

Xander replied, "Sounds like a plan. It's time to lie low. Time to get out of this country. We can go up through Guinea anyhow, and then over to Sierra Leone."

Nyahn's mind raced. What if these men were not what they seemed? What if these men were white bandits, delivering them to traders who would take them north into Muslim lands, where they would be slaves? Auntie warned them that these things happened.

Saye and Charles talked a lot during the next hour, laughing and making fun. That white man seemed to understand Saye's jokes. Laughter put the dark thoughts out of Nyahn's mind. He tried to stay awake, but his eyes would not stay open. As the jeep crossed the rickety bridge over the Bangu River, he drifted into a troubled sleep, his head falling on his brother's thigh.

27

Doing Well by Doing Good

THEY had slept in the car, pulled over on the side of the road just north of the border in Guinea, the boys leaning against each other in the back, completely comfortable.

Xander wished he had a real breakfast to give the boys. Perhaps they'd get three hots and a cot at the soccer camp, which was clearly more than they were used to.

They dropped the boys off at a lonely intersection about a dozen miles into Guinea just as the first glow of the sun appeared.

Nyahn said, "We can walk to the soccer camp from here."

The two men shook the hands of both boys, in the complex Gondwanan style, with a snap at the conclusion. Xander shook his head in amusement as the boys started bounding up the side road—really just a path through the bush carved by many vehicles crushing the foliage. He experienced the faint melancholy of recognition that he would likely never encounter these two boys again. Such transient but important encounters had occurred many times in his life.

With a long trip still ahead, Xander insisted on taking the wheel: knowing just when a tire would fall into the next pothole allowed him to brace on the steering wheel and minimize damage to an increasingly sore buttock that wasn't healing well. Unexpected bouncing had steadily stressed Xander's wound, tearing apart the tissue adhesions that were attempting to mend. His butt cheek was the front line in trench warfare between his cellular biology and the miserable road that took them into Guinea.

At least his head ached less.

"I could be sitting on a comfortable airplane, nursing a bourbon on the rocks, on the way to Brussels," Charles said with a short laugh. "But no. I'm bouncing along this road with a crazy man, driving away from one broke-ass African country through another one, heading to a third, where we may not even be able to cross the border, much less be able to get a flight out."

"At least you aren't dead and your butt isn't bleeding like mine is," Xander joked.

"Most of our relationship so far has consisted of you being unconscious, suffering in pain, or being shot at. So I don't know much about you," Charles observed.

"You first," Xander said.

"No, you first."

So, Charles was going to insist. The kid was growing up fast out here in the midst of all the recent excitement. He'd throw Charles a little information.

"I'm fifty years old, and in all that time only once came close to getting married. I rarely return to Holland, and ignore anybody who tries to tell me what to do. I'm a PT—a *perennial tourist*, a *perpetual traveler*, and a *prior taxpayer*."

"A man without a country."

Xander replied, "Not really. My country is wherever I find freedom. I'm simply not going to be ruled by any particular government. I don't spend more than six months in any one year in any single country, so I have no obligation to file a tax return anywhere. In the whole world, only Americans and, believe it or not, Eritreans, are obliged to file taxes even if they leave the place and never set foot in it again. I'm no government's milk cow. If you let them treat you as a milk cow, they might decide to turn you into a beef cow at some point."

He glanced over to see if the young man would laugh at that. And Charles did.

Xander wanted to laugh along with Charles, but right now, laughter risked making his head hurt more.

He looked again at Charles, who appeared totally alive. His eyes glowed with intent and his smile broadened. He had survived danger in an exotic country, pursuing a mystery and a fortune. In fact, he could be living a scene from an action movie, and he even looked the part. What more could any young buck want?

It didn't appear that Charles had yet absorbed that he had certainly killed the men at B-F's Frankenstein laboratory. It would trouble him after the fact sank in. But this wasn't the time to push the issue. Charles would find a way to come to terms with it. The men had been shooting at them, after all.

They rode in silence for a time. After a bit, Charles started talking, and Xander listened. At some point, Charles would bring up the deaths of the men.

"My father is a good man, but he's always been bound by conventional thinking. He's *reflexively* patriotic. It's one of the things we argue about. He grew up in the US when it was still America, when it was probably more free than any other country. That's changed, though, and he won't acknowledge it. The reality of the United States and the idea of America are now two different things. My father insists on conflating America with the United States government. The first is an idea. The second is an organization that now has a life of its own, with its own interests and agendas, and what amounts to an unofficial royal class that the population has to carry. He doesn't see it. His country is the best country, because that's where he was born and that's where he lives."

"It's a form of atavism," Xander offered. "Do you think your father might have been equally patriotic if he'd grown up in Russia in the '20s, or Germany in the '30s, or China in the '60s, or even North Korea now?"

"God, I hope not, but there *is* a bit of that in him. *My country, right or wrong.*"

"Don't judge too harshly, Charles. It's what your father was taught, and therefore believes. All governments, in all eras, drum that concept into their subjects."

"Yeah. My father isn't stupid. He's conflicted. He grouses to the empty atmosphere about stupid regulations, wasted taxes, corrupt politicians, destructive welfare, high inflation, silly foreign aid, and a hundred other things."

"Let me guess. Your father sees them all as mistakes made by earnest politicians, however misguided, rather than the revealed essence of the state itself?"

"That's probably right. And it frustrates me. My father writes strongly worded editorials decrying the national debt, and blames the politicians like everyone else does. But then he invests in Treasury bonds."

"That *is* frustrating."

"Yes. He's helping the US government take on more debt. Now, I know it's not *my* debt. It's not the debt of America, nor that of future generations. But the US government assumes America is going to service its debt."

"Yes, it does. That debt not only finances all manner of destructive things, but it's turning future generations into serfs who'll have to service it. Until the government eventually defaults, wiping out the savings of scores of millions. The US government is a parasite feeding on America. Or maybe a fungus trying to eke out its final existence by digesting America's fallen remains."

"My father was raised thinking it was everyone's patriotic duty to buy US bonds. That's ridiculous. I'm getting a little jaded about the whole idea of patriotism. It seems to me more patriotic to never buy their bonds."

"Just let it go bankrupt?"

"It's already bankrupt. And I don't see the point in throwing good money after bad. Or being complicit in what amounts to a swindle."

Xander smiled. "So, the US government should default on its debt.… It's a radical idea, but lots of governments do it, all the time. It would bring down the current financial structure, of course. But that's a house of cards anyway. And if a structure is about to collapse, it's better to have a controlled demolition than wait for it to fall unexpectedly. It's a good idea, really. Doing so would keep future generations from being turned into serfs, wasting their lives to pay for the high living and foolish spending of previous generations. It would punish those who'd foolishly loaned the government money, allowing it to grow bigger. And, it would make it nearly impossible for the government to borrow again for a good long time."

"I know! That's exactly right!"

"Beef cows." Xander stopped, eyeballing what amounted to a newly created river in front of them. A wash of water cut diagonally across the road; he had to gauge whether the Land Rover could successfully cross through the muck and climb the other side. He made his decision, backed up thirty yards, and pressed his foot down. The car tore forward and dove into the mud, losing all traction while the tires were half submerged but racing through on momentum alone. Yellow mud flew everywhere, occluding the windshield as if sprayed from a paint gun. It took more than a minute of running the wipers to clear most of it away.

Xander continued the conversation without any comment on the muck and road conditions, as if nothing had happened. "The US used to be something special, something different. Now it seems to be just another of the over two hundred nation states that cover the face of the globe like a skin disease. Well, I guess nothing lasts forever...."

"That's exactly right! My father can get it briefly, but a few days later he slips right back into the old perspective."

Xander felt no need to critique a man who could raise someone like Charles—a young man who, he was excited to find, shared his philosophy of life. But Charles had more lessons to learn, and they wouldn't come from his father. "It's not unusual. Nor is it a moral failing. Like most people, it's likely his mind has just been programmed, Charles. Most people fly their lives on autopilot. Leviathan depends on its subjects to act predictably and with little insight, in order to keep its power."

Xander steered the car around, through and over a series of holes in the road sufficient to swallow a smaller vehicle. He drove mostly at less than ten miles per hour, making ridiculously slow progress.

But it gave him plenty of time to teach. "America is a concept that transcends time and space and borders. It's a name brand, however corrupted by its current management. America means pursuing your version of happiness, as long as you don't hurt anybody in the process. It means the freedom to make the most of yourself, and not have to answer to so-called authorities. It means that you have the right to do what you ought to do, and most importantly the right *not* to do wrong even when someone commands it. America exists wherever individualism thrives. And it isn't just in the US. It can be anywhere. Look at me."

"And where are you?"

"Not in the US. I'm here with you. Right here in America."

"America is right here bouncing around in a Toyota Land Cruiser in Africa?"

"You got it, kid."

They inched along in silence. Xander sped up when he could. It wasn't long before Charles fell asleep.

Xander drove in silent contemplation as the morning wore on. The sun climbed to its zenith, the heat built, and the gasoline-filled mayonnaise jars vended here and there along the road became increasingly infrequent. Xander topped up their tank at every opportunity; every small thatched roof shanty that had gasoline offered their entire supply, usually no more than a few gallons kept for the motorbikes.

Later, there was no problem crossing the border from Guinea into Sierra Leone. Two white men in a white SUV could get through with a twenty-dollar bill stuck in each passport in lieu of a proper visa. But things were tightening up all over the world.

Even up until the late '70s you could cross most borders in small countries with as little as a World Service Authority document. Garry Davis, a World War II bomber pilot—disgusted with the recently ended carnage and blaming it on nation-states—burned his US passport in Paris. He found, however, that he needed a document to cross borders. So he formed the WSA and printed some very official-looking documents that resembled United Nations passports.

Xander got one. To make it look more official, he went to a grocery store and asked the butcher to stamp it with the device he used for indicating meat grades, and then scribbled a signature over it. What a charade the whole process was!

In what was then still Rhodesia, and also later in Switzerland, border agents became angry, and sent him to the back of the line, like a naughty schoolboy. In both Egypt and Morocco, he was taken to a back room and questioned before he produced his Dutch passport. But it worked in a number of countries—Peru, Honduras, Costa Rica, French Polynesia, and even Iceland, among others. Today, with computers interlinking immigration services everywhere, it was no longer of much use—except perhaps to give a desk clerk when a hotel required you to hand in a document. The world was changing.

As they came into the small border town of Buedu, a cell phone rang. It was Caroline's phone, loaned to Charles in place of his own, to avoid tracking.

"Yes?" The signal was weak.

Charles nodded. "Yes, Captain. Yes.…"

His face darkened. "I'm so sorry. Have your men recovered?… Yes, I'll let him know. We're both very grateful.… Thank you. We'll be careful."

Xander's concern had increased with every word he heard Charles utter on his side of the phone call. He eyed Charles after he disconnected.

"Captain Freberg said that two men came on the ship last night and assaulted a bridge officer and a crewman. His crew killed one of the invaders, the other got away. A big blond man with a crew cut. Sound familiar? The captain said they were armed and they were looking for me."

"No mention of me?"

"Not directly. They asked about an old man, though."

"My other persona; they won't see him again. Are the crewmen okay?"

"Yes. The captain said they'd be fine."

Xander relaxed. "I'm glad we decided not to fly you out of Gondwana. You would have been intercepted before getting inside the airport."

The men talked as they drove through small villages and past ruined plantations that had been prosperous in the 1950s but had gone into rapid decline as the country trod its own glorious path to socialism. What little had survived had been completely destroyed during the civil wars that ensued after the first president-for-life died. The histories of African governments were remarkable in their similarity.

Xander's thoughts came back to the shed in the jungle.

It did not surprise Xander that Charles's mind was back there in that shed as well.

Charles asked, "Is there any reason you can think of why it would be there? That machine?"

The kid was still avoiding the real issue.

"Any honest reason? None. It looks like they were making a colloidal suspension."

Charles nodded back.

Xander nodded. "Submicroscopic particles suspended in a liquid. Nanosized, the size of individual atoms and molecules."

"Like the gold B-F reports in the cores. Nanoparticle deposition. They were making gold colloids, and then using that machine I destroyed...."

Xander interrupted him. "The machine *we* destroyed! They used the machine *we* destroyed to generate high pressures to infuse the colloidal gold from those big jars into the rock." Xander studied Charles's face. "Then they could dry out the cores with the vacuum pump, making the gold deposit in the rock as the water evaporated. Over time, that coated the inside of the machine with gold, too. I suppose that machine can create whatever gold concentration they want in their cores. In nature it would take superheated volcanic fluids percolating through barren rock millions of years to do that. This machine gets the job done a whole lot faster. Maybe a few weeks."

Charles's spoke in a voice that was too quiet. "That would explain their increasing delays in getting assays from cores, too. It takes them weeks to infuse the gold, and it takes them longer when they want to fake higher-grade ore. In the end, the ore would end up looking a whole lot like hydrothermally deposited gold, but as high grade as they want it to be."

Xander wanted to tell Charles that he had done well. But he had to figure that out for himself. Instead, he said, "It's a whole new kind of salting. It's the salting scam of the century! We could write a book about this one."

B-F's scheme would take millions to perpetrate, but the return was in the billions. And all the money to fund the fraud, as well as the payoff, came from the investors.

Charles nodded. "It's a depressing thought."

The immediate and direct consequence of this fraud would be the transfer of wealth to a very few, with perhaps a half-dozen insiders set to live like kings, while thousands of individuals would lose their savings. Perhaps they deserved to lose their savings for failing to investigate before investing. Still, it grated against Xander's sense of karma to see sincere—if naïve—investors taken to school by criminals. Successful fraud, whether perpetrated by an individual con man or a central bank, led to the transfer of money from lots of good people, in general, to the few unethical people, in particular.

The indirect and delayed consequences of a fraud were much worse. It would destroy a certain amount of capital, making the world slightly poorer, and it would also turn many against what they perceived to be the free market. Regulators would point to the fraud to justify more regulations and a bigger bureaucracy, supposedly to protect investors but mostly just making it harder to create wealth. This B-F episode would, at a minimum, make it much more difficult for companies in the resource business to raise money.

Xander judged fraud more harshly than force, since it lay hidden and covert. Dante put the violent in only the Seventh Circle of the Inferno; the fraudulent occupied the Eighth. The Ninth was the very bottom of the pit, reserved for betrayers.

"Don't forget why you came here—to see if there was still a good speculation to be had."

Because they had gone to the effort of getting boots on the ground, they would be two of the very few to keep their fortune, by selling before the fraud was discovered. But much bigger money could be made.

Xander glanced again at Charles. It wasn't a bad start in the world of speculation if he served a moral purpose while reaping enormous financial rewards. Speculators were friends and benefactors to society.

"Xander, we should sell all we have, don't you think? It's Sunday today. Tomorrow the markets will be open. What do you plan to do with B-F?"

Xander laughed. Charles had plenty more to learn from him. "I'm going to watch the stock price rise further! Then I'm going to await your results from the assays of those rock samples you took. If those pilfered rocks have zero gold, nada, then after I've sold my long position, I'm going to buy cheap put options that are *way* out of the money. The returns on a fraud going to zero are vastly more certain than the likelihood of even the best deal working out, and it happens more quickly. Investing is like a ball game with no called strikes. So you don't swing until you get a perfect pitch. This, I suspect, is that perfect pitch."

"Don't you think we have an obligation to go public with our findings sooner, rather than later?"

"I don't think so. People come out with hypes and lies, misinformation and disinformation, all the time. We wouldn't have any credibility. And B-F will counterattack. They have a publicity team, lots of believers, and a ton of money. And, since we would be alleging fraud, they'll sue us for slander. And likely convince the authorities to go after us for market manipulation. It's happened plenty in the past."

"With all their ability to neutralize us, maybe we don't need to worry too much about them trying to kill us."

Xander raised his eyebrows. "I think they're just trying to kill *you*, kid." He pointed at Charles for emphasis. "And from their point of view, killing you makes sense. The marginalizing, lawsuits, and threats from the SEC will not be their best defense against us. Our information would still put downward pressure on the price, and they don't want that. They'd rather not risk anything coming out yet. No. They don't want us talking. They don't want *you* talking. Killing you is a no brainer. No big leap over any moral hurdle, not for these guys. One death? Hah! From what I saw in those containers, just before Burke gets any drilling going, B-F is going to make sure that the whole region goes up in flames. There is going to be a lot of blood in the mud here. Yours would just be one more body. With all of Gondwana lighting up, Burke won't come in with their team. Without Burke, it'll be years before there is any evidence of fraud, if ever. B-F is committing the perfect crime: the victims will believe they just had the bad luck of getting caught in another African revolution. To keep *that* a secret, Smolderhof will kill you."

Charles said, "Except you'll still be alive to tell the secret."

Xander stayed silent for a moment, sighed, and then replied, "I'm looking forward to both of us cashing in after this thing blows up."

"So, then from our point of view, all we have to do is lie low, wait for the rebellion and the share price of B-F to collapse. And we get super wealthy from our new short positions."

"Yes. That's right. Except that you also have to stay alive."

"Yeah, for sure. But there are some other problems...."

"What don't you like?"

Charles's eyes squeezed closed. "Let's suppose Burke gets their people here as planned, and they find no gold. Then, with the aid of our explanation for how they accomplished the salting, B-F will be clearly exposed as a fraud. The share price will go to zero and any short position we have taken will be stellar. 'Out of the money' put options will become very much *in the money*. And we can have lots of those put options. At these levels each of them could return to us one hundred or two hundred times our money, depending on whether we buy at 50 percent margin or not."

Xander smiled. Charles had figured out just how big the profit opportunity was. He said to Charles, "Right now, the pros will write those options for us every day and twice on Tuesday, figuring there is essentially no chance that the puts selling for pocket change will end up in the money in three months. They'll think it's easy money. We could have options for millions of shares, Charles."

As a general rule, skilled speculators didn't buy options, they sold them. The buyer always has the time clock running against him as the premium expires. The seller is acting as the house in a casino, or an insurance company. To make money, he doesn't have to be very right—like the buyer has to be. Instead, he just has to not be very wrong. On the other hand, when you were dealing with a sure thing, it made sense to be an option buyer. And B-F's impending doom was as close to a sure thing as anyone was ever likely to find.

Charles went on. "But if a rebellion prohibits Burke from drilling and there are no other assays to work from, the share price of B-F will go down, pretty far perhaps, but nowhere near zero, and possibly not even below the strike prices for our cheap puts. The market would still believe that Banga Sioquelle is the world's largest gold reserve, and that B-F will still control it once the rebellion dies down. Investors will think their return on investment has just been postponed. So the fraud won't be exposed for years. That's B-F's plan. And then it will gradually fall out of everyone's minds, and the news cycle will move on. Maybe B-F will bribe the government to keep everybody off the property. Our put options will have long since expired without ever getting in the money. And we could wind up with zero."

Xander said, "That's a real risk."

Charles added, "So, we can confidently buy a lot of dirt-cheap puts at low strike prices that expire soon only if we really know the stock is going all the way down to zero. Look, I've made a couple million dollars so far, from almost nothing. I can walk away from the table now, and it would be a great win. Still, there are already people out there who want to kill me over this. And I figure my life is worth more than a couple million bucks. The way I see it, I've got a real shot to turn that couple of million bucks into a hundred million." Charles's voice became adamant. "I've gotta take that shot!"

Xander looked at Charles closely. "Chances like this don't grow on trees. But it's not just about the money for you, is it? You really don't want B-F to get away with this, do you?"

"No, I don't." Charles's jaw was firm. "I appreciate a revolution as much as the next man. But this one isn't right."

Xander agreed. The tree of liberty now and again does need to be refreshed with the blood of patriots and tyrants. But no tree of liberty was going to grow in the forest of this revolution. Whatever B-F's plan was, it wouldn't involve patriots and wouldn't promote liberty. It was unlikely to do anyone any good, other than the fraudsters of B-F. The Big Men running Gondwana now weren't even tyrants, just criminals who got lucky on a grand scale, and it was better than even odds that anyone who took over would be much worse. And there was a 100 percent chance that thousands of innocent locals—maybe including Nyahn and Saye and TJ—would get killed.

"Well," Xander said, "I wouldn't mind seeing Smolderhof and B-F bite the dust. And I think you're right: we make more money, more quickly and more certainly, if Burke comes in and exposes B-F as a fraud."

Charles stayed quiet.

After a bit, Xander prompted him. "So, where does that leave us, kid?"

By then, Charles had had time to conclude where it left them, and he said it slowly and clearly.

Charles scratched at his two-day stubble. "For us to make the most possible money the fastest, we have to stop this rebellion."

A part of Xander had hoped Charles would not reach that conclusion.

The two men remained silent then for a long time, each in his own thoughts.

Trying to start a revolution in Africa is tough enough. Trying to stop one would take it to a whole different level. It would be like trying to keep the tide from coming in, or an earthquake from happening. It was a fool's errand, an effort to stop nature itself. However, on top of the effect on B-F, and in addition to the magnificent effect on their own wealth, exposing and stopping such a rebellion might well save more lives than every NGO in the country could in a decade.

And, as a bonus, what an adventure it would be.

28

Springer Shocks Sabina

"So, you're interested in the world of resource speculation and investment, Ms. Dresden. And you have the beginning of a clue about what wealth is."

She looked particularly alluring today, according to her mirror.

Springer added, "But I want to be sure you understand my intentions."

Was he going to have *intentions* for her, she wondered? Had she won him over with her figure, her sensuality, her beauty? Maybe he was succumbing, after all. That would certainly make matters easier.

"Do I have the internship?"

"As I said, we'll take this day-to-day."

She pouted. That sometimes worked with men.

Not with Springer. He just shook his head.

And then Springer said, "I was about to kick you out of my office yesterday, soon after you walked in and started talking."

Sabina had cultivated her own form of thick skin when it came to any critique or lack of response to her charms. Her defense wasn't the hard shell of a turtle in which she could bury her head and close off her ears. No, hers was the skin of another cold-blooded creature—the beautiful but poisonous dart frog, which secreted one of the most toxic substances on earth, batrachotoxin; South American Indians used it to tip arrows. She verbally and psychologically overwhelmed whoever dared to critique her with a disproportionate attack, before the critic realized what hit them, or even why. Hers was an ego protection gone nuclear. In response to Springer, her skin started secreting.

Springer added, "But I've changed my mind, for the moment."

Sabina contained her scowl.

"It's my intention," he continued, "to try to rescue you from convention."

She stared at him, aloof, with a slight frown, somewhat insulted, and quite unconvinced of any need for rescue.

He said, "To be clear, I wish to experiment upon your brain."

What bomb was he about to drop?

"But it's not ethical to experiment on someone's brain without informing them and giving them the chance to opt out, is it?"

Sabina shook her head slowly, her brow further furrowed. Where was he going with this?

"Ms. Dresden, I am sure you have many strengths. You are beautiful, as you know too well. And you have a certain type of intelligence valued by most firms in our business, evidenced by the schools that accepted you and your accomplishments to date.…"

Which were fake, she thought, but at least he was right about her intelligence.

"…but your brain has either been poisoned or infected, probably repeatedly, and I want to see if it can be detoxified and cured. If you are willing, that is. Only if we succeed might you be truly useful to my firm."

Was this allegorical? Was he a psychopath? Her father had warned her that agents occasionally had to deal with potentially dangerous people. She flashed her gaze around the room, checking for a clear path to the exit, while scanning for items she could use to defend herself. Her brain stayed always hyper-alert to threats, just as it also sought out opportunities. But it gravitated toward the worst case as being the most likely. She lived according to her version of the Golden Rule: do unto others as they would do unto you… but do it first. She lived life aware, expecting the worst from anyone and everyone; it was hardwired in her personality. But she pushed aside horror-movie images of experimentation in dark root cellars, and brought her full attention to bear on the man seated in front of her. What, exactly, was he driving at?

Was he a sexual pervert? After all, sexual excitement was actually more cerebral than physical.

Maybe Springer saw her confusion and the flash of unexpected fear.

"Oh, Ms. Dresden, my experiments will involve only words, I assure you. I am hoping that some very select words—a rare opportunity for you to consider some fresh ideas—might be the antidote, the beginning of a cure."

She found her voice then. "What do you mean?"

"I mean," he said, as his face and entire demeanor took on the appearance of a college professor settling into his pace, "to determine if you can stop lying to yourself, after years of being taught to do so."

How did he know she was lying? And why did he imagine she was unaware of it? Sabina became utterly lost in this unexpected conversation. She grasped for something to say, and came up with, "I think I should feel insulted."

"No more than someone who catches the flu during an epidemic."

"What?"

"Ms. Dresden, you are still here in my office because you have a combination of gifts which could be used for producing great value, or, alternatively, for destroying it. For good or for evil."

She couldn't sit here stupidly saying nothing. So she said, "Do you mean, like Dr. Jekyll and Mr. Hyde?"

"Not at all. Totally different."

Had she been a normal job applicant, she would have walked out of the office, cut her losses, saved her skin. But she had a specific mission. This was a very weird bump in the road to completing it.

She shook her head in confusion. She couldn't help herself. Hesitantly, she asked, "Just what do you want me to do?"

"It is my hope that you can help teach me."

"Teach *you?*"

"Yes. Teach me whether there is a chance to cure some distortions of the mind that arise during schooling of the type you have received. Let me clarify this. The mind, I think, relates to the brain much the way software relates to a computer. The problem seems to be how minds are now programmed. I want to see if we can cure your mind. You seem to have a perfectly operational brain. Your mind, however, appears to compute that two plus two equals five while being very confident that it is right. Denial of obvious contradictions is one of the symptoms of the disease, but it is only visible to someone not suffering from the same illness."

Her skin secreted some of its reflexive poison. She spat back, "Had you gone to school longer, they might have taught you that no cure is necessary, don't you think?"

Springer deflected it with ease. "I doubt it. Had I gone to school longer, I might have been infected too."

Sabina controlled herself. Why did she care what this whacked-out guy was trying to accomplish? What was important was that he still wanted her around—whatever insane reason justified it to him.

So she said, "Just words?"

"Yes. Words and day-to-day exposure to people who think differently than your professors."

"No hypnosis or séances?"

"None."

She looked deeply into his eyes—her method of making him think he was being weighed and measured, although actually it was just a stare. He didn't seem to care. In the end, she said, "Okay, I'm in. *Tentatively.* I'll be your guinea pig." But her muscles were ready to bolt.

"Okay, then. This will take some time. But let's start. I want you to spend a few minutes writing down a list of ten disreputable occupations." Springer revealed a bit of excitement in his voice, the first since she had met him.

"Disreputable?"

"Yes. Occupations that society despises and judges harshly. Careers and activities that you consider indefensible, corrupt, morally repugnant...." Springer stood up from his desk, the minimal change in the height of his head again reminding her of how short he was. He walked over to her and handed her a pad and pen. "I'll give you ten minutes."

He walked out of his office and left her to ponder. It didn't take her long. She wrote her list.

*   *   *

He would give her ten minutes exactly. His excitement grew. He was about to enter a race. Not for the beautiful woman inside his office—and she certainly was stunning—but a race for a cure.

240

Her infection, if truly an infection, was severe. It wasn't a cancer: a DNA change in her cells that had spread out of control. It couldn't be cancer, because cancer won't spread to others, and the disease that this woman had was highly contagious.

Springer called his wife because he wanted to hear her voice. She was sick, but this time perhaps the most recent round of promising new medicines might work. They had to. Then he checked in with his secretary. Using a corner of her desk, he signed some of the weekly paychecks, a task he never delegated. He felt it important to remind himself what his people were earning. And to remind them who made their earnings possible. He glanced at an envelope from the IRS and tossed it in the trash.

He returned with two glasses of water and handed one to Sabina and then sat down at his desk. He didn't care about his height, but his tall chair kept visitors from obsessing about it. He preferred his colleagues and employees to focus on matters of business rather than matters of cultural stupidity.

"So, Ms. Dresden, tell me the first disreputable occupation on your list."

Sabina glanced at her list. "Gun dealer."

"And why is the gun dealer considered disreputable?"

"They provide weapons used in mass murders and wars."

Springer nodded. "Ah yes. The provider of the tools gangs use to intimidate citizens; the equipper of crazy psychopaths, so they can rampage through schools. But then how about the knife merchant? Or the baseball bat manufacturer? What of the man who sells wrenches or ropes or lead pipes or candlesticks, or any other device useful for murder? Are they all despicable? No one suggests banning knives. Knives are useful for food preparation, which keeps us alive. Doesn't the gun supplier provide tools especially suited for self-defense? And self-defense is certainly a basic right, and even an obligation. Doesn't a gun give a petite woman the power to defend herself against a much larger aggressive male, and is that not a worthy purpose in your mind? A pistol makes a big person and a small person equal. I would expect you'd endorse equality...."

Sabina shrugged. "But they make no effort to avoid selling to murderers."

"How does one identify a potential murderer?"

She shrugged again. "I suppose you're going to bring up that argument about the 'right to bear arms' in the Constitution's Second Amendment, too?"

"No. The US Constitution can't give anyone rights. It's just a legal document. And, in any event, it's essentially a dead letter. Its important elements, those defending the individual's life and property, have been disregarded, watered down, and interpreted out of existence. Historically, one of the main distinctions between a free man and a slave was the possession of weapons. You have a right to weapons by virtue of being free. Gun dealers give you the means to defend yourself effectively. They're the friend of the common man."

Springer leaned back. "The next occupation?"

Sabina consulted her list. "Used-car salesmen."

"Of course. A term used to describe any greasy, underhanded, untrustworthy liar."

"Exactly."

"The profession of selling used cars didn't develop a slimy reputation because it's ignoble or inherently evil. They said the same thing about horse traders in the old days, for exactly the same reasons. In fact, used-car salesmen provide a valuable service by making a market. They stand ready to buy your car if you want to sell it, and sell you a variety of low-cost vehicles when you need one. You could probably sell your car to a private buyer for more money, of course—but that takes time, it's inconvenient, and involves advertising and other costs. Likewise you might get a better bargain from a private seller—but that's even riskier than buying from a dealer.

"A used-car dealer takes a lot of risk when he buys a car. It's expensive for him to carry inventory. And he has to spend time and money to find buyers for them. Why the bad reputation? The used-car salesman may lie to a customer about the quality of a vehicle. But that is true in most any sales position; salesmen tend to overemphasize the positives and under-emphasize the negatives of their product. *Presumptive* fraud is the main problem here. A customer makes a bad purchase, based on no misrepresentation by a seller. If a car goes bad, the buyer tends to blame the seller, not the previous owner who might have abused it. Or his own ignorance. Of course, some used-car salesmen are slimy, taking advantage of an illiquid market and the fact most buyers are unknowledgeable. But it is not a quality of the profession itself. There is no compulsion involved in used-car sales. If you don't think a dealer is honest, visit the one next door. People anxious to assign blame for their own bad decisions generally get what they deserve. Next?"

Sabina smiled. "The prostitute."

"Of course." Springer smiled back. "The person who exchanges sexual services for money or barter. I ask you, Ms. Dresden, does the prostitute force her clients to buy her product? Or defraud them? She does neither. Barring intentional or neglectful spread of disease, she commits no offense against any other person. If she has voluntarily entered the profession, we can assume she sees it as better than the alternative of cleaning hotel rooms, waitressing, or, in really bad times, of starvation and homelessness.

"Of course, her choice of an occupation may offend some people's moral sensibilities. But what right do they have to impose their values on someone else? The primary possession of anyone is their own body. They should have a right to dispose of it as they wish. The problem doesn't lie with the hooker, but with busybodies and bluenoses who'd impose their values on everyone else."

"I'll have to agree with you about that." It wasn't as if Sabina hadn't previously thought about the differences between trading her sexual favors in an informal, unspoken way as opposed to a strict quid pro quo manner. Many of her girlfriends did the same. She'd just never previously confronted the issue directly.

"Good. But I'm not expecting you to agree." He preferred her to be completely candid, although that was probably impossible for her. "What's the next occupation on your list?"

"How about the pimp?"

Springer nodded. "Ahh, a slam dunk, you might think. Someone without any redeeming graces. It's true, of course, that most pimps not only lack the Boy Scout virtues but usually suffer from a host of vices. But that's largely because his occupation is illegal, his workers are often troubled, and his clients are taking risks. It's not a function of the business itself. Presuming he uses no force or fraud to engage his workers, he is simply an agent. Should a book agent, a sports agent, or a real estate agent be considered disreputable?"

Sabina shook her head. "No, but those are legal activities."

"By that you mean they are easy to tax and regulate?"

"No, I mean that government has declared prostitution illegal, and therefore pimping is illegal, and certainly disreputable."

"So, to you, legality and morality are the same thing?"

Sabina paused, evidently weighing the potential right answers to the question.

Springer continued, "Why should morality be determined by whoever controls the government?"

Sabina shrugged again. "I have 'drug dealer' next."

"Ahh," replied Springer. "This has been a real hot button in the US for several generations. Certainly since Nixon declared the War on Drugs, and even move so since Nancy Reagan decided we should all *Just Say No*. The same issues arise. A drug dealer is simply the middleman between a producer of a product and the willing consumer of the product. Nobody is forcing any side of that transaction."

"Addiction forces the consumption."

"Fair enough. But there is no human force involved. Natural forces are always relevant to decision-making. Hunger, for instance, *forces* you to eat. That's not, however, a moral issue. Why the different treatment of so-called illegal drugs?"

"Because they harm the user and they harm society."

"Some do. Some don't. The addict has a choice regarding taking more of a drug, which he knows may be harmful, and does so because it feels good. There's not a great deal of difference between being addicted to caffeine, nicotine, or alcohol and being addicted to heroin, cocaine, or meth. All of them are harmful in large quantities—as is food, for that matter. But there are many voluntary activities that risk harming the user, such as extreme sports, or that harm society, such as voting socialists into positions of power. We don't ban those activities.

"The fact is that many productive people enjoyed drugs regularly. Freud loved cocaine. Carl Sagan was a regular marijuana user. Richard Feynman liked ketamine. John Lilly and Francis Crick enjoyed LSD. It's a very long list."

"Maybe. But most drug addicts steal."

"That's largely because their drug of choice is illegal; that's why it's egregiously expensive. But more importantly, when the drug addict steals, it is the drug addict committing the offense, not the dealer. There's nothing immoral about providing a product voluntarily sought by another individual."

Sabina sighed. "You are going to spin all of these on their heads."

"Not necessarily. Some occupations are completely reprehensible by their very nature. Let's see if you stumble on them. What's next on your list?"

"Tax cheat," she replied, without looking at him.

Springer shook his head. "Let's say a man approaches you with a gun and demands the money in your purse. Out of fear, you give it to him. Should you also turn over the cash you have hidden in your hatband? If you don't, are you *cheating* the thug?"

"You're equating the tax collector with a thief."

"What's the difference? Does it really matter who the man demanding your money works for? The moral thing is to deny funding him and defend your property. Your property represents the hours of your life you spent to earn it; in a way, property is concentrated life. The successful tax evader, even if he doesn't fully understand the righteousness of his actions, is a hero. The unsuccessful ones are at least trying to be."

"But then everyone else has to pay more tax!"

"The way to say that in a moral context is that the tax collector—the thief—has to go rob someone else of more money. Should that compel you to hand them your hard-earned money?"

"If everyone abided by that, the country would go broke."

He couldn't help but smile at that. "Not the country, Ms. Dresden. The *government* would go broke. But then the government already is broke. And it's broken. We're all idiots for thinking it has a right to tax. Or, for that matter, that taxes are even necessary for an orderly society."

"You better be careful, Mr. Springer. The IRS may come after you someday."

"Very likely. The IRS is the strong arm of what amounts to a giant protection racket. People have come to believe that unless they give half of what they earn to the state, society will collapse. The reality is more that society is going to collapse *because* they flush so much wealth down into the septic system of government. What's your next?"

Would she actually find one of the real evil professions?

Apparently not, for she had nothing more on her list.

She said, "I know I stopped with only seven. But why don't you tell me the occupations you consider reprehensible, Mr. Springer?"

"Fair enough." He sat back again. "First, I'm surprised you didn't mention the slum lord, the monopolist, the sweatshop owner, the pawn broker, and the loan shark, among others. But I would have redirected you in regards to all of those as well. One of your assignments will be to read Walter Block's *Defending the Undefendable*. Will Rogers was quite correct when he said that the problem wasn't so much what people don't know, but what they think they know that just isn't so.

"First on the list of reprehensible professions is the politician. They seek to acquire the legal power to enforce their will on others. Success in politics requires being a superb liar, a willingness to betray trust, and no compunctions about initiating force. There's a greater concentration of narcissistic sociopaths in politics than any other occupation. The whole object of politics is to gain power over other people."

"But, Mr. Springer, isn't that kind of an unfair generalization? Just as you said with used-car salesmen, not all politicians are like this."

"You are right to correct me. Some very few politicians are trying to decrease the power of their colleagues. And fraud is not always required to succeed. So your critique is fair. But the objective of a used-car salesman is only to sell cars and make money. The objective of a politician is power over others, enforced by men with guns. It necessarily attracts the most morally ambiguous types."

"So you would rather have the government make no plans?"

"Correct! When the state plans, it obviates the plans of its subjects. But let's keep on the topic at hand. Next on my list is regulatory lawyers. There's nothing wrong, in itself, with being a lawyer. Lawyers are trained at arbitrating disputes, defending the accused, drawing up agreements, and the like. But some just live off the unnecessary, arbitrary, and confusing rules that they lobbied for. They're parasites. They're paid by one group to create a problem, then, again, by another group to mitigate it."

Sabina chimed in, "And most politicians are lawyers themselves."

"Excellent point," Springer replied. "Tax collectors might be next on my list. What kind of person is willing to force another human to hand over much—sometimes all—of what they have to the state? How is a tax collector any different from a Mafia shake-down enforcer?" Sabina

246

disguised the fury she felt welling up inside her, and responded with an honest answer: "I've never thought about it before."

"I want you to start thinking, Ms. Dresden. That's what this is about. The next on my list is central bankers. The Federal Reserve is sold to the public as a clearinghouse for the transactions of commercial banks and a lender of last resort should any of its members become temporarily illiquid. This was problematical to start with, but we don't have the time to engage in a long discussion of banking."

Sabina breathed a silent sigh. Springer picked up on it but ignored it.

"But central banks, all over the world, are actually just engines of currency inflation. They're in a position to create trillions of currency units. When they create new currency units, that dilutes the value of all the currency already in existence. Worse, some people—those who are politically connected and close to the fire hydrant of new money—get it first, and get more of it. Worse yet, their manipulation of interest rates and creation of new money cause the business cycle. That was the direct cause of the Great Depression. At some point they will cause an even greater one."

Springer noticed that the woman in front of him made no effort to respond.

"Closely related is a group we might call crony capitalists. These would include what President Eisenhower once called the military-industrial complex. They feed off the state's wars, regulations, taxes, and inflation."

"I always thought," Sabina said, "that we needed a public-private partnership to get things done...."

"It's strange how a meme like that, once it's created by some academic, can be parroted and taken seriously. Crony capitalists need the so-called private-public partnership because it gives them access to the government's legal power of compulsion. Cronies use a PPP to force others to comply with their plan. A real capitalist would never turn to coercion and connections with the state to provide goods and services people want."

She said, "The average person doesn't know what he wants."

"So they need to be told what to do, by other people who *think* they know what is best for everyone?"

He waited for a moment for her to respond. She didn't.

"And how about the do-gooder who lobbies and writes editorials trying to pass laws to force everyone to do, or pay for, whatever he thinks is a good idea? So-called 'public-spirited' reformers are often just busybodies with an authoritarian mindset.

"And beware of professional charity hustlers. 'Give us your money, and you will feel less guilty about being successful.' Very little of the money that flows to the charity industry actually does any good for the supposed beneficiaries."

"How can you be opposed to charity, Mr. Springer?"

Springer studied her. Was she displaying righteous indignation, in an attempt to recapture the moral high ground?

"Charity tends to destroy the recipient by, in effect, rewarding him for his misfortune. I understand that accidents happen, and people often both need and deserve help. Such help should be from one individual to another, which encourages responsibility to both the giver and the receiver, and cuts out the middleman. Throwing money at a big organization, where much of it goes to advertising and administration, destroys capital, absolves the giver of the risk of direct exposure to the downtrodden, eliminates the possibility of developing true empathy, and makes the recipient feel and behave like a mooch."

Sabina sat forward like a clever prosecutor who's detected an opening. "So, taking all of what you have said, it seems that the people in suits, people who are part of the establishment, are usually the bad guys?"

Springer wondered if she had learned anything. "You seem to have missed the basic point I'm trying to make. The issue is not whether someone is rich or poor, weak or powerful, but whether someone initiates force or fraud against the innocent. Increasingly in our society, people have come to accept that the ends justify the means, and therefore government should be allowed to do pretty much anything. This is, of course, the road to socialism and fascism, leading to a society like those under Stalin, Hitler, Mao, Pol Pot, and a hundred others like them."

Sabina nodded her head. "I get it. I'll think about it more."

"Good. Perhaps tonight you can read an old paper I wrote that goes into a lot of this in more detail." Springer reached into his bottom drawer and pulled out a glossy reprint. He slid it across his neat desk toward her.

"I will!" she replied, picking the document up.

248

This young woman spoke with such enthusiasm that he started to believe her. But he wouldn't expect much. He had planted some seeds that might incubate in her mind and, just perhaps, might slowly start a change in her neuronal connections. It was only the beginning of a long process. Did he have any reason to hope for success?

Then she asked, "What started you thinking this way, Mr. Springer?"

"Did you ever read comics when you were a child, Ms. Dresden?"

"I was never really into them."

Springer continued. "Then perhaps you never encountered Scrooge McDuck, one of the great heroes of literature. He was famous for his wealth, and some people thought that was all that mattered to him. But once, on an expedition to Alaska, he had to choose between keeping his fortune and rescuing his sled dog, Barko. He chose his dog."

Sabina nodded.

Springer said, "Money is a storehouse of value that can be used to help us pursue happiness. But it's not happiness itself. Although I value money, I find money less and less important the older I get. I would trade money for happiness. But there is no one who is selling happiness. At least not sustainable happiness."

"Everyone knows that," Sabina added. "We're taught as children that you can't buy happiness."

"That's essentially right. But money provides things like food, shelter, clothing, and some level of security. They allow you to better *pursue* happiness."

"Mazlow's hierarchy of needs."

"Right. You probably heard that phrase in a Harvard sociology class. Physiological needs come first. And money lets you cover that base. My most enjoyable times weren't obtained by spending money. Like a couple of times in the past when I hopped freight trains with a friend. Each trip took three days and nights, each was full of adventure and weird experiences, and neither cost anything. It was liberating."

"Because you had no money?"

"Even though money is also a high moral good, because it represents the life you spent to earn it, I don't take money too seriously. It's just something you *have*. It's much less important than what you *do*, and trivial in comparison to what and who you *are*. This is a question of your character, your actual essence. I could be happy as a hobo, or a

Taoist monk, for that reason. Certainly, during those trips, I was not distracted by the pursuit of money. But, at the same time, I don't kid myself. I couldn't have taken those trips if money didn't exist. Somebody had to buy the food that we ate at the missions, and build the tracks and provide the fuel for the trains. My impoverished train trips were not the equivalent of fighting scarcity in the Stone Age."

"That's what I was thinking," Sabina purred.

Springer said, "So we would all like more money, for the same genetic reason a squirrel wants more nuts to store for the winter. The one common denominator of all living creatures is one word: survive! Money enables that."

Springer sipped some water and spoke. "The very concept of money has been degraded over time. That's one reason why kids don't save coins in piggy banks anymore—coins are no longer minted with valuable metals, like gold or silver. They're now just worthless slugs, tokens manufactured from base metals, no better than the top off an empty soda bottle. Maybe kids have figured that out even though most adults haven't.

"There used to be a common saying, even when I was a kid: 'As sound as the dollar.' Nobody says that anymore, for obvious reasons. When I was a kid, and somebody was asked to stop doing something annoying, the standard response was: 'Hey, it's a free country!' That phrase too has dropped out of use. In the '70s they used to say, 'The US will never have concentration camps… they'll call them something else.' That, I think, is turning out to be true."

Sabina looked at him quizzically and laughed. "You are entirely cynical."

"Hmm. Cynical. You know, you're right, Ms. Dresden. I am cynical. Should I, instead, be unjustifiably enthusiastic? Which is more honest?"

Sabina only shrugged.

He said, "There's some cause for optimism, however, because *most* people are *mostly* honest, *most* of the time. The problem is that as the infection—the one that you have—has insinuated itself into society, the definitions of what's right and wrong, good and evil, ethical and unethical have mutated. People are now considered 'generous' if they vote to compel *other people* to subsidize a welfare program. Entrepreneurs are called 'selfish' and 'greedy' if they become rich working their tails off to provide what people want and need. You are called 'caring' if you demand the government to raise the minimum wage that *others* have to pay. And you are called 'mean' if you fire employees because you can't afford to pay them anymore, or if you try to avoid having to fire your employees by speaking out against a minimum wage that leaves unemployed and destitute anyone whose skills simply aren't worth that minimum wage.

"When the people allow the meanings of words to be twisted, often without realizing it's happening, the moral fabric of society decays. It's impossible to think clearly when the meanings of words are improperly defined."

Sabina interrupted. "You keep making it sound like the government is a bad thing...."

"Yes. That's because of what it is. The government has a legal monopoly on the use of force. Contrary to the meme they like to promote, the government is not 'we the people.' There's nothing voluntary about it. It's based on coercion. In the real world, anyone who initiates force is a criminal. But the government has excluded itself from that standard. So, the government naturally attracts a certain type of person to itself. This is true of all organizations—the priesthood, the military, investment banks, the Mafia, the Lion's Club, motorcycle clubs, or chess clubs—they all attract their type. Birds of a feather flock together. Who is the government's type?

"There are many ways to categorize people. Categorizing people based on skin color is one of the stupidest ways. And by stupid, I mean *an unwitting tendency toward self-destruction*. But a valuable way to classify people is to ask whether or not they think it's proper to initiate the use of force. Their answer to that question tells me whether they are essentially good or evil. The government has always acted as a magnet for criminal personalities, people who have no compunction about using force and would love to do it legally. As a result—and I know this will shock you—governments *are* criminal organizations. I'm not just talking about notorious ones, like those of Caligula, Hitler, Stalin, Mao, or Pol Pot that we mentioned earlier. I'm talking about the institution in itself."

The view that governments were, in effect, *bad*, would be a preposterous notion to this woman in front of him, schooled by those very people that consider it *good*, and who thought it fully acceptable to force anyone to do whatever they wanted done. From her perspective, subtly or blatantly ingrained by her teachers and college professors, the people—the individual citizens—misbehaved and failed to do their civic duty. It was the job of the best and brightest, as they called themselves, to control them.

He suspected that it required a mighty act of will for her to sit quietly and not argue with him every step of the way.

Springer stood up behind his desk, leaned his hands on it, and spoke down toward Sabina. "One more thing is the issue of selfishness. Are you familiar with Ayn Rand?"

Sabina allowed that she'd heard of the author. "My professors didn't respect her, and we never talked about her work."

"Read Ayn Rand, Ms. Dresden. One of her major points is that self-ishness is a virtue, and altruism is a vice. It's just the opposite of what everybody is taught. It's unfortunate that some of her followers have taken on the aspect of a religious cult, treating her like an unerring godhead. Rand herself might never forgive me for saying this, but if you take the two concepts—ethical self-interest and concern for others—to their logi-cal conclusions, they are actually the same. It's in your selfish best interest to provide the maximum amount of value to the maximum number of people; that's how you become wealthy."

*　*　*

Springer's effort at curing her couldn't possibly work. It wasn't that she failed to understand what Springer said; she understood every word. And indeed he opened her eyes to new concepts, just as she supposed Springer wanted. But in contrast with Springer, Sabina did not sympathize with the victims of force and fraud; she identified with the perpetrators.

She understood but hadn't paid much attention to the concepts he broached. Except those about the Federal Reserve, which piqued her interest. She had never grasped its role as a "money maker." In a semi-nal moment, Sabina's path changed. She was her father's daughter, and as such she was cunning. She would redirect her efforts. With an inner smile, she thought: Why just make money, like these fools, when it was possible to literally *make* money?

She looked up at Springer and said with complete honesty: "Mr. Springer, you have already opened my eyes. I am going to launch into understanding everything you have just shown me. I would very much like to work with you."

Springer nodded. "You're bright. Very much like Charles Knight. But Charles avoided the infection. I will take a chance on you, on a trial basis. You'll work for me, as a researcher, on a short leash. Whatever I want to know about, you will research and report to me. And as you do that, I want you to think, always think: how will this piece of data help us turn one unit of capital into two units? Is such a position agreeable?"

Sabina nodded.

"Good. We'll start you as an intern, with a basic stipend. If your work progresses, we'll be pleased to put you on reasonably generous salary. From there it's up to you. There are no limits." He slid a piece of paper across the desk on which was scribbled the stipend. "We offer no contract, nor any benefits whatsoever other than this pay. Acceptable?"

"No health insurance?"

"Of course not."

She nodded.

"You can quit anytime, and we can fire you anytime."

Sabina sat silently, already feeling exploited.

"And we expect you to do the right thing. No lying, cheating, or any sort of fraud, ever. I expect you to keep investment opportunities we discuss confidential. We like to keep things simple by observing Boy Scout virtues."

"Of course," Sabina said, and although she had no idea what the Boy Scout virtues were when he had mentioned them before, she viscerally reacted against the concept.

Springer expounded on them. "The concepts of being trustworthy, loyal, helpful, friendly, courteous, kind, obedient, cheerful, thrifty, brave, clean, and reverent are rarely taught to a young person these days, even by the Boy Scouts." Springer himself had reservations. "And, before you say it, I don't agree with all of them. If I were in charge, I would convert 'obedient' to 'observant.' And I would change 'reverent' to 'respectful.'"

"When do I start?" she asked.

"Tomorrow. Here in my office. You can expect to be very busy."

*　　*　　*

Sabina left the office of Alchemia Resources and made the two-hour drive to her new office in the step-pyramid fortress of the IRS at Laguna Niguel.

"Frank, I'm in at Alchemia." She marched into his office without knocking.

"Already?" Frank Graves's face revealed that he was impressed, even if a little suspicious. "How did you pull that off?"

"I had to listen to an hour of philosophical voodoo, pretending to agree with Elliot Springer's every comment. You've trained me well."

"I've trained you not at all. You only got here a matter of days ago. Are you in a position at Alchemia where you'll learn something? Or are you hired on in the mail room?"

"I'm in at the top."

"With Knight?"

"No. Better. I will be working directly with Springer. He runs the operation."

"What about Knight? He's your target."

"He is. And I will get him. I have no doubt he's skipping out on his tax responsibilities. I just have to prove it. The fact that he's currently offshore is an indication. And I also have no doubt Springer's whole company is doing the same." It wasn't a leap of logic on her part. The implications of Springer's presentation on money and occupations, and his disrespect for the very concept of government, made it entirely obvious. "This could get big pretty fast."

"Okay. But stay legal, do the right thing." Frank returned to the papers he was reading before she had barged in, but he looked back up for a moment. "And above all, keep your integrity."

"That's pretty much the same advice Springer gave me."

"It's good advice."

Sabina had never heard this advice before at either the SEC or at the IRS, certainly never from her father; it impressed her as the kind of bogus truism to which people reflexively pay lip service, but that nobody could possibly take seriously. That kind of advice became the pathway to victimhood. To the mind of Sabina Heidel, worshiping a weakness like honor was both stupid and counterproductive.

She did not like Frank Graves. He was a fool.

29

The Person in a Hot Tub

"I'M staying here, kid."

They stood together in a line to purchase airline tickets at the Lungi International Airport, just west of Freetown, Sierra Leone. It had been a long drive.

Charles turned to look at Xander. "Here? As in Sierra Leone?"

"More or less. Back to Gondwana, I expect. I have stitches to get out, and a scheduled CT scan to radiate my head. I promised the doctors on the *Africa Grace*. TJ's jeep needs to be returned. Plus, a few days or weeks working here, now, playing this right, and you and I could make a hundred times as much money."

If they sold all their shares and used the proceeds to buy put options, they would risk 100 percent of the trade but with gigantic potential gains. With the stock now trading toward $240, an option giving them the right to sell shares they didn't yet own at, say, $140 anytime in the next six months might be purchased now for $4. Better yet, an option to sell at $50 in three months would cost perhaps fifty cents, and they could buy eight times as many. With that put option, if the stock went to zero in less than three months, they could make 100-to-1 on their money without even relying on margin. A double is wonderful, but a 100-to-1 shot in a few months—especially if you could be certain of the outcome—was worth some serious trouble.

Xander added, "I've played these games on this continent before. *You* need to be in the United States for your own safety. I'll be on the ground here. I'll get local intel. The first step is always to get accurate information. We have nothing but a guess and a container full of munitions. We need more good input. So, I'm going to get it."

"So you're heading back to Gbarngeda?"

"Soon enough. These African rebellions typically start with massing troops in a neighboring country. As often as not the neighboring government wants to see chaos next door—sometimes to profiteer, sometimes to install a more friendly regime, and sometimes just because one thug is sleeping with the other thug's wife. In the past, the troops have amassed here in Sierra Leone, or over in Côte d'Ivoire."

Charles said confidently, "This time it might be Guinea."

"Maybe Guinea. B-F's mine is only a few miles from their border."

Charles said, "So, it sounds like a plan. You stay here and risk your life collecting information on an impending rebellion, while I sit in a hot tub in the States, sip a Rum Collins, buy B-F put options, and contemplate how to spend $100 million."

"That sounds about right. Specialization and the division of labor are good things."

"Seems fair to me."

Xander said, "Want to trade jobs, kid?"

Charles pretended indecision for a moment. "Nah. I like hot tubs."

"We'll need someone in North America. Someone moving the money, maybe using the government, keeping track. You need to work closely with Springer to put on the trades. He's better at that sort of thing than I am, and you might as well learn from the best, huh? Also, you need to get all the information we have together in a packet. Make the media and brokerage connections so we know to whom, and when, to release it for optimum effect. I don't know how we're going to do this quite yet. I just think we'll need to divide in order to conquer."

"You just flipped Caesar on his head, Xander. He meant we have to divide the enemy to conquer them, not divide ourselves."

"Most likely I'd have joined the crew that did him in. There are some people that just need killing. A lot of assassins end up getting a bad rap, like Brutus. Not every assassin is a bad guy."

The line moved forward. Charles whispered, saying quietly what his heart had been shouting to him. "I killed those men, Xander."

Xander nodded. "And why did you?"

Charles knew why. Survival. Defense. Because he could.

And then it was Charles's turn to talk to the airline staff. "Let's see if I can even get out of this country. If not, I have a friend in America who can always help."

An hour later, they went their separate ways. Charles had not needed Uncle Maurice's help. He carried nothing but his rocks from Banga Sioquelle.

Xander limped away, using his cane for real, not just as a prop. Leaving Xander made Charles feel uneasy. It was guilt for letting his new friend go into danger without a wingman. Xander might be going into a combat zone.

What neither imagined was that it would be Xander happily ensconced in the hot tub, and Charles who, safely back in the United States, would come face to face with death.

*   *   *

Caroline stood with her back to the sea, leaning against the rail that protected crewmen on Deck 8 from slipping overboard. Vacationers on a cruise ship would have availed themselves of sundeck chairs and shuffleboards up here near the bow. On the *Africa Grace,* however, the space was reserved for storing vehicles and shipping containers filled with medical supplies: a hybrid between an outdoor storage lot and an automobile repair facility. Heat filled the narrow gaps between the containers on the deck, which provided a wonderful place for the medical staff's three-dozen children to play tag and hide-and-seek. A bunch of them played there right then, hooting away like chimpanzees.

Charles had been gone for two days without a word to her. Captain Anders reported that Charles was well, with his friend Xander, somewhere, but he knew not where. Hopefully the men chasing him didn't know either. The black SUV and the watching white men had left.

Caroline had not slept much for the past couple of nights; she thought about Charles day and night. It wasn't often that one met a man who was running around Africa involved in a multibillion-dollar deal, with people trying to kill him. Although her parents might wish otherwise, Caroline had never been drawn to the normal type. Just as well; Africa wasn't the best place to find normal.

She had told him so much about herself, but managed to avoid mentioning that she was the daughter of the queen of Denmark. Both her parents and Captain Anders had warned her to keep that confidential, and only a few on the ship actually knew. The Danes on board were aware, of course, but they were proud to be in on the partial secret and enjoyed treating her—mostly—just like anyone else. Normalcy provided a degree of protection. So she had hidden some truth from him, sure. But then he had kept even his name a secret for days. Quid pro quo.

Caroline had led a fairly sheltered life so far, at least for a Scandinavian girl. Charles had not. His mother's early death must have influenced him deeply, but it would take a lot more time to understand that part of him.

He was important to her, even though they had spent barely four days together. She had liked Charles from the first moment they met, even though she hadn't known what to call him. Whatever he did for a profession, it assuredly offered neither security nor a consistent income. But that was okay, for she had both.

She caught herself. Why was she thinking about a future with him, and of visions of security and income? Some sort of female instinct? A runaway imagination pointlessly fabricating nonexistent castles in the air, when her family had real ones in Europe? With a man she had just met and hardly knew?

Foolishness!

She pushed herself away from the rail, walked to the other side of the ship, and looked down the hull, back toward the gangway deployed down to the pier. Unwelcome people supposedly could neither get aboard unobserved, nor bring weapons through the metal detector. But somehow, two nights ago, two men had indeed boarded the ship. Her family would have heard about this. Did Captain Anders reassure them that she was not their target? Would it matter? They would call her home, or at least send bodyguards to confine her and observe her. All against her will.

She sucked in her breath so rapidly that her heart indeed skipped a beat. A white SUV, covered with mud, stopped just past the end of the gangway. A man climbed out of the driver's seat. A man with a shaved head.

Xander Winn! And that meant…

She wanted to run aft, down the deck, inside the superstructure, and down to Reception as fast as she could go. But she stood frozen, waiting to see Charles get out of the car. She waited as Xander began ascending the gangway, walking slowly, limping slightly.

Then she broke into a run, her heart in her belly, suddenly afraid. Why was Xander looking so beaten and dejected? Where was Charles?

Ship's crewmen greeted Xander in the reception area when Caroline came bursting in, her momentum carrying her stumbling into Xander's arms.

"Hey, girl! Slow down! It's good to see you too, Caroline. Charles won't stop talking about you." He gently slid her back as she recovered her balance.

"Where is he?" She searched his face, both anxious for and apprehensive of clues.

"He's fine, young lady. A little worse for wear, but nothing a day or two of rest and relaxation won't cure."

She stood up straight, regaining control of herself, and looked at Xander, still waiting for the answer she hoped to hear.

He then said, sheepishly, "He's not with me, though. I'm sorry. He's probably long out of Africa by now."

"What... Where?" Loss replaced fear.

"Best not to tell you where he's going or how he is getting there."

"I understand," she said, although she didn't fully. It was for her safety, just like her mother would insist. Instead of pushing, she accepted the reality and said, "Are you okay?"

"I'm fine. Just coming back for the follow-up CT scan of my injured brain." He pointed with his thumb to Louise, who sat behind the reception desk. "And I'm afraid I've tested the sutures in my buttock a bit too aggressively...."

"What happened?" Louise asked, with no attempt to conceal judgment.

He looked at her and winked. "Had to do a little running through the jungle and a little crawling in the mud. The usual. Nothing major. Not a marathon or anything. The real problem was sitting on my sore buttocks in a car for more than nineteen hours."

Caroline asked, "Where have you been?"

"All over, young lady. All over. And I've got to go back out, too."

"Well, let's get you settled in first, and fix you up."

Three hours later he soaked naked in a whirlpool tub, the hot water from the jets irrigating his wound. It was a genuine pleasure, even absent a drink, a cigar, and a good-looking female companion.

Caroline told him, "With the depth of that wound, and the infection, I'm guessing about six weeks for it to heal."

"Hmm… six weeks of soaking in a hot tub, with you in attendance? I believe I'll survive."

"That's what you get for sitting on your ass for so long, Mr. Winn!"

"For that crack, maybe I won't give you what Charles sent with me." He carefully reached for his pants, groping in the pocket with wet hands.

"What's that?" Caroline said it as if absentmindedly. But her heart pounded and her face reddened with anticipation.

"He wanted me to give you this. I read it a few times. Very entertaining." He winked at her and shook his head, denying the very thing he had just said. Xander handed her a folded sheet of paper, wet from his fingers.

She took the note, unfolded it, and read it for the first of many times. Before she had reached the second paragraph, tears formed. But after the second paragraph, she was smiling.

30

New York and Toronto

IF flag carriers like Air India and Air China were dangerous and uncomfortable, then African flag carriers could make them seem like Air Force One. Charles arrived in New York just past dawn and had to get to San Diego to meet with Elliot, but he first needed to see Uncle Maurice. After a few robotic and impertinent questions from a surly US Immigration agent, he emerged into an area where cell phone use wasn't a felony. He called the Four Seasons to try to reserve a room, just for the day, not even a night, for he had another flight leaving in the evening. The Four Seasons would be an expensive luxury and a huge contrast to the jungle, days of driving, and Air Ghana. Was his newfound wealth already altering—perhaps corrupting—his approach to life? He was desperate for a shower and a real nap, but the hotel wouldn't allow him to check in until after 3 p.m. He hung up. Just as well. He looked like a refugee. The desk clerk would likely have turned him away when he presented himself.

His luggage and computer remained at the Zamba Point Hotel, his base of operations in Gondwana before first heading up to B-F's camp. It would take little for the men searching for him to get hold of that computer, although the password would probably keep his files safe for a while.

It was midday back in Gondwana. He sat down on a torn, grey airport bench. Two women sharing the bench chose just then to move away. He used his cell to call the Zamba Point Hotel's manager, a Lebanese as naturally bald as Charles now was artificially bald.

"Yes, Mr. Knight. I still have your computer and your luggage, as you requested. I am so sorry you ran into difficulties here."

"Any trouble?" Charles asked.

The manager, Imir, said, "A man came looking for you. He said he was your friend. He seemed very worried about you."

This prompted Charles to ask, "What did he look like?"

"Very strong-looking man. Blond hair. South African, I think. He did not give his name."

"Thank you, Imir. That is not a friend of mine. Not at all."

"I suspected not."

"I'll make arrangements for my computer, but it may take a couple of days. Can you hold it safely?"

"I will, Mr. Knight."

He called his uncle next, not to confirm his uncle's presence at home, but just to let him know he was on his way. Uncle Maurice would always be found at home, except for that one yearly trip to the doctor. It wouldn't be an imposition to crash in his old room for a few hours.

"Uncle Maurice. It's Charles."

"Charles who?"

"Your nephew Charles."

"Oh yes. Where are you, Charles?"

"Very close to making you very rich."

"That's one of my favorite destinations."

"I can be at your apartment in an hour."

"Well, get on over here and make me rich, boy!"

"You *are* rich, Uncle Maurice."

"Make me richer." Then his uncle hung up without saying goodbye. If his uncle ever followed rules of etiquette, it would be a good indication he was under substantial duress.

Charles grabbed a taxi and had it wait for ten minutes in front of a Banana Republic clothing store. The store's name now had meaning it would have lacked before his trip. Bags with new clothes in hand, he directed the driver to the Royal Towers in Chelsea.

Maurice owned the building's eleventh floor but routinely visited only the living room, the bedroom, and the kitchen. Still superb, the building had not changed in the ten years since they'd first met there. To get up to the eleventh floor he had to go through the annoying process of passing muster with the doorman—or was he a bellhop, or a concierge, or a bodyguard, or all four? He was a professional obstacle whom Maurice paid to protect himself from anybody and anything, as well as deliver the takeout Chinese, Ethiopian, Thai, and other exotic foods that Uncle Maurice lived on. The man looked at Charles with distaste, perhaps even disgust. He demanded ID and checked to ensure the video was recording before dialing Maurice's apartment to secure permission for Charles, who looked and smelled like a tramp, to go up.

It always took time for the door to open because Maurice had a substantial amount of inertia to overcome, and standing required that he do battle with gravity. Together, gravity and inertia caused Maurice to prefer the sedentary lifestyle to which he had become so perfectly adapted.

But he eventually unlocked the door at three levels after checking through the peep sight, which he kept covered on the inside so that nobody with a specially designed reverse lens might peer through it and catch him snoring on the couch.

"M' boy! It's great to see you, kid!"

"Hi, Uncle Maurice. So you're still calling me 'kid,' huh?"

Maurice stammered self-consciously for a moment as he trudged back to his couch. "Sorry, sorry about that. I need to stop that. You aren't a kid anymore, are you?"

"No, but the term is starting to appeal to me, the more it's used. A new friend of mine in Africa, about your age, does the same thing."

"Well, good. It's a term of endearment." Maurice fell resoundingly into his seat and then looked up at Charles more carefully. "It looks like you've been ridden hard and put away wet." The argot from his polo-playing days still flowed easily—even though acquired two hundred pounds earlier in life.

"Yeah, I'm pretty beaten up."

"Did you fly in from Africa in those torn-up, blood-soaked pants?"

"No. That happened when I tried to get through passport control and customs here in the US."

Maurice snorted.

Charles understood why so many people had seemed to avoid him in the last several hours. He could keep good company with a group of recently mugged homeless men.

"You're covered with bruises, cuts, and holes, and your hair is gone."

"I bought some new clothes to change into. And I need a shower."

"And a hospital, maybe?"

"I'm okay. I'll pass on the hospital." His mind flashed back to Caroline. "I came back from Africa with nothing but my passport and wallet."

"Are you playing the piano, Charles?" Maurice changed the subject without a break. It was his way. Charles expected a non sequitur every few sentences until the man started to concentrate on something urgent or complex, at which point his brain became laser-like in its focus.

"I play when I can," Charles replied, his thoughts drawn back to the ship. "I have something pending in San Diego. A concert series with the university."

"Someday I'll get a piano here. It's been years since I last heard you play live."

"I'd like that. Or, when I next play in New York, perhaps you could venture out…?"

Maurice fumbled around for something on the crowded table in front of him. He spoke in a murmur. "Well, if the opportunity arises, well, we… well, we'll see about that."

The living room remained always a mess, even after the maid's visit. Maurice concerned himself only with the availability of information. His brain organized itself in ways that his apartment could not, ways that most men would not comprehend; it allowed him to process incoming information alongside his own pre-existing storehouse in a manner that caused small details to become bright beacons showing the way to some unobvious truth. This intellectual skill set accompanied a reputation for impenetrable discretion. And so his services were sought by people who had uniquely challenging questions that required complex and illegal means to get them answered.

Such people were necessarily wealthy, for Maurice Templeton's services came at a substantial price. He required his clients to pay him both in treasure and in obligation. Those obligations allowed him to acquire seemingly impossible information, further heightening his reputation. Maurice's reputation, knowledge, and connections grew exponentially over time. His encyclopedic mind—given enough time to contemplate and collect data—would arrive at solutions and present opportunities previously unimagined. Especially regarding all things illicit, irregular, evasive, sensitive, or troubling. Maurice was a wonderful man to have as an uncle.

Maurice said, "Before we move on to your new endeavors, we need to clean up some old business. You still have some equity investments that I hold for you under my name. Leftovers from when you were a minor."

"Oh, yeah. I'm sorry. I still haven't rolled that into my own portfolio."

"M' boy, I'll have to pass this stuff on to you someday. Sooner the better."

"I rather like having some wealth tucked away that no one knows is mine."

"Well, it's all right for a bit longer, but I hate doing the accounting. You gotta deal with it before another five years passes, and certainly before I drop dead of old age!"

Charles nodded. "I'm really grateful, Maurice."

"Look." Maurice rustled around in a pile of papers and handed a folder to Charles.

Charles scanned through it. The portfolio his uncle managed used to look so big to him. But now, in comparison to his current paper valuation in B-F, it seemed insignificant.

"I've got some recommends at the moment." Maurice always had good suggestions. "Including selling the companies I highlighted in yellow."

Charles glanced at those again, remembering when and why they bought them. "It's past time to sell those, isn't it?"

"Yes, Charles. You've been lazy. Or, perhaps, just distracted."

"Okay, let's sell them."

The resulting cash would amount to less than $200,000: previously much of his net worth, now trivial in light of recent events. He was in the midst of changing his perspective on relative wealth.

Maurice looked at him sideways. "Kid, this is real money. Why are you acting like you don't care?"

He didn't give Charles time to answer.

Maurice shrugged. "Well, if you don't care about your money, I have a speculation for you. If it hits, it will be a five to ten bagger. And its chances are good, either in a month or a decade."

"What is it?"

"A pharmaceutical company called Visioryme. It has an interim assessment of a Phase 1 study going before the Food and Drug Administration in a few weeks. The street expects their plan to be rejected."

"So why would I buy shares?"

"Because it's a penny stock now, knocked down from forty dollars a share, and I think FDA might surprise the street and give Visioryme's plan the nod. If so, you can sell it a month from now and make a million, maybe."

A million dollars could still catch Charles's attention.

"If FDA declines it, you'll take a loss. Sucks for you, but at least then I won't have to pay any capital gains taxes on your portfolio for a few years!"

Charles's mind remained mostly in Africa. "Sure, Maurice, can you buy Visioryme for me?"

Maurice frowned. "Whatever. Obviously, something else is on your mind, Charles. Are you learning from Elliot Springer how to *not* do your due diligence? If so, I'm gonna have to have a conversation with him."

"Elliot's great."

"Tell me what's making you feel so damn cocky, then. What new news of B-F and their rocket ship bound for the stars?"

"Much news indeed."

Maurice said, "You know, this is the first time in my memory that the mainstream media has picked up on a junior mining company and brought it to the attention of the general public. They're turning Smolderhof into a hero, if not a household name."

"It's getting out of their control."

"Yes. As is the price of their stock. Over $260 now. The crazy fools in the newsrooms are now suggesting that the Banga Sioquelle gold deposit could increase supplies so much that the value of gold could collapse! Can you believe it? How absurd is that?"

It *was* absurd. Nobody knew exactly how much gold had been mined since the dawn of history, but the best estimates placed the number at around six billion ounces. New production added another eighty million ounces a year, so the annual growth in the world's supply of the metal quite reliably remained between one and 2 percent. But every mine in the world is a wasting asset; each would be depleted over time. Though truly extraordinary deposits could last a hundred years, few mines had lifetimes greater than twenty. Most new open-pit mines were good for less than ten. If anything, gold production seemed to be headed down.

Maurice said, "A gold-price collapse because of new supplies hasn't happened since the conquistadors flooded Spain with stolen Inca and Aztec gold that had been mined over centuries."

"I can assure you that Banga Sioquelle is no New World."

Maurice nodded and replied, "Even if it was, the gold has to be produced, not stolen. Even the gigantic strikes in California in 1849, or the Witwatersrand in 1886, or the Klondike in 1898, didn't affect the price much."

"B-F may not affect gold price, but I hope they manage to jam their share price up to $300. The higher the better."

Maurice smiled. "Yes, then you plan to short. Based on the results of your trip, I presume?"

"Certainly unload what I own. Anything can happen, of course. But I'm planning to use the cash to back up the truck on far out-of-the-money puts. However many of them people are willing to write."

"When?" Maurice played with a pair of chopsticks stuck in an empty white cardboard takeout box in front of him.

"Very soon. I expect lots more hyped-up news over the next couple of weeks. Soft news only, though. I'll warrant no more core is coming out of B-F's drills. At least none that will assay for gold...."

"Why, pray tell, is that?" Maurice leaned forward.

"Look at these pictures, Maurice." He handed his uncle a digital memory card.

Maurice stuck it in his computer. For the next five minutes, Charles described what the pictures indicated: a machine designed to turn completely valueless rock into the pretense of ore worth over $100 billion.

"Charles, how is Smolderhof planning on winding this down? It'll all go south with the Burke drilling results. How's he planning to get away with it?"

"Smolderhof isn't planning for there to be any Burke drilling."

"Why not?"

"Because Gondwana is about to get very hot. The only foreigners there for the next many years are going to be heavily armed."

267

"I've heard nothing about another rebel army. Another Charles Taylor?"

Charles replied, "Can you help keep it from happening?"

*   *   *

It was a great honor for Dan Smolderhof to be chosen Prospector of the Year by the Society of Mineral Developers at its three-day Toronto conference. He accepted his award a day after Ollie Shifflett died of gangrene and exposure alone in the jungle—the result of a machine having turned against its inventor. Shifflett bled his life away one hundred yards from where his machine lay in ruins. He had managed to drag himself under a fallen palm after Smolderhof deserted him, his services no longer needed, his planned elimination no longer required. Only a few men knew about the processing site. Shifflett would be written off as another unfortunate casualty of the impending revolution, assuming his bones were ever found.

Smolderhof had flown to Toronto to accept the award, give a speech thanking all the little people behind the scenes, and hold some press conferences. It would have been sweet to report a bunch of 150 gram/tonne intersections, and then to follow those up with independent lab assays of the machine-enhanced cores. But all that heavily salted core now lay irretrievably scattered around the jungle.

While Smolderhof had been growing the value of B-F shares and fighting every day to ensure his future wealth, his partner, Ben Washerman, had been busy doing everything wrong. Washerman's unilateral move to finalize this half-assed Burke deal could be disastrous. Washerman balanced the values of up-front payments against long-term profits and royalties, acting like a responsible CEO. Of course, there could be no long-term profits or royalties, but Washerman didn't know that. Washerman's deal with Burke risked everything. Now, with the colloid infuser destroyed, JohnJohn chomping at the bit, and Burke geos rushing to start confirmation drilling, things were going to come unglued quickly. So tomorrow, Smolderhof and Goodluck would start unloading the rest of their shares in B-F through their carefully created shell companies in offshore havens. Between them they had enough shares that the price would start tumbling if they did not balance it with an absolute barrage of exciting new and absurdly positive information.

So the name of the game was hype, just to keep the price as steady as possible. They would have less than ten days to liquidate their positions before the price would fall off a cliff. The very bad news was destined to come at a horribly inconvenient time for business in any country as potentially unstable as... any place in sub-Saharan Africa.

Smolderhof smiled at the large golden plaque. They handed it to him at the conclusion of a series of platitudes recounting his vision, his recognition of pre-Cambrian hydrothermic nanoparticulate-gold deposition, his determining the likely sites for such deposition, his successful acquisition of the Banga Sioquelle prospect for B-F Exploration, and, of course, last but far from least, his care for the environment and admiration for the indigenous people. He stood in his tuxedo with his black bow tie, smiling broadly, because a smile was not only appropriate but an excellent disguise for a cynical laugh. He enjoyed the professional accolades, imagining them as something more than utterly and ludicrously hollow fantasies.

The stress built each day, and he consumed more stomach-acid-reducing medications than could possibly be safe, plus multiple doses of Alka-Seltzer. His blood pressure rose so high that he could feel every beat of his heart coursing through his neck, reverberating in and around his brain. If he had a stroke, would it kill him? Or turn him into a vegetable? His body offered proof that the psychological controlled the physical. Was the money worth it? No point in pondering that now. The die was cast.

Charles Knight, almost certainly the one who had tampered with Shifflett's machine in the shed, remained at large. Rupert had come down from Guinea and, in the daylight, discovered evidence of his tampering. He found the machine's door far from the shed, sheared from its hinges, with the remains of a rope still wrapped around the handle. Muddy footprints ran throughout the shed from boots that weren't on Shifflett's now-amputated feet. Evidence that a car had been concealed just off the road by an array of palm fronds. It was all clear. More than ever, Charles Knight had to be eliminated, and soon.

At least, he thought, Knight hadn't found the containers with the ammunition and weapons.

If Knight came forward with information about the colloid infuser—and the numerous flashes that Smolderhof had seen in that shed suggested he had photographic evidence—then the hyped stock might take an untimely blow at the worst possible time, just when they were peak selling. Sure, they could protest and combat it: present Knight as a bad actor, desperately trying to rescue a foolish short position. But Smolderhof did not have the energy to deal with the consequences of this now. Or ever. Bubbles inflated with hot air are in constant search of a pin. Even rumors of Knight's discovery risked a perfectly rational, but most inconvenient, panic in the market. It would decrease their gain and raise far too many questions. Mysteriously declining stock prices can draw the attention of the authorities.

He had one more major ploy to promote the stock, but it was a good one, long planned and orchestrated to counter the downward pressure caused by his own selling of shares. It would do the job, if Knight could be kept quiet.

Upon returning to Canada, he found very little reliable information on Knight; Charles Knight was a common name. Someone about the right age co-owned a Coca-Cola bottling plant, and another had established an Internet domain-name brokerage. And scores of others. None seemed likely to be this kid traipsing around Africa blowing the lid off both a very special machine and a very special exploration company.

After the gala presentation dinner, he called Harry.

"Yah, what is it?" Harry's voice was as if next door, though rough and slurred from a deep sleep.

"I can't find anything on Knight. There's nothing about him anywhere in the mining sector. Nothing about him as a journalist either. Nobody's heard of him. And he doesn't behave like a government agent."

"Okay." The voice emerged from a barely aroused brain. "What next?"

"You thought the manager of Zamba Point Hotel was protecting him. See what more information you can get out of him."

"Will do."

"And Harry?"

After a moment of silence, Harry replied in monotone. "Yes."

"See if Xander Winn is still in Gondwana. Maybe those two buddied up more than we thought. Rupert thinks there was more than one person messing around with the colloid infuser. Even if not, the old geezer may know something."

"It's a thought. He seemed to have experience. I'll try."

Smolderhof found himself parroting some words from a movie that he had seen a long, long time ago. "There is no try. Only do, or do not." He paused before continuing. "Billions of dollars are riding on this. Billions."

"Yet I only get millions."

"Millions is good. It beats a prison sentence."

"Get some sleep, Smolderhof. I'll do what I can from this end."

For Smolderhof, sleep was impossible as his exhausted mind raced. In frustration he swallowed two different sleeping pills, and lay down on the bed while he stared with wide pupils at the barely illuminated ceiling above him. He, almost singlehandedly, had turned B-F from nothing into something. He may not have deserved to be Prospector of the Year, but he deserved some sort of award. Too bad it all had to be kept secret. Maybe he would write a book someday that would put soft edges on some of the harder facts. For now, however, the question was how to neutralize Knight and the information he might release. How could he neutralize a man whom he knew nothing about?

He made a mental list of tasks. So much to do.

The more his fevered brain worked the problem, the more he concluded that the problem was not just Knight's information, but Knight himself. He'd taken an immediate and intuitive dislike to him back at the camp, much the way a dog, or even a horse, can dislike another on sight. It was visceral, not intellectual. Lying on his back, in the dark, something strange happened; the more he realized he hated Knight, the more settled and focused his mind became. If it went bad, it was Knight to blame, not himself. With that calming notion, his mind eased, and he slipped into a drug-induced sleep.

Fleeting dreams darted in and out of his intermittently conscious mind, blending imminent reality with meaningless fantasy. He worked his task list within this fragmentary dream state. He blocked the port in Gondwana with giant marshmallows, so the Burke transport ship couldn't dock. He reminded Harry to move the ammunition and weapons, including the photon torpedoes and phasers. His arms and legs became wings, and he flew through the hot Gondwanan sky, ducking dark clouds while red winds whistled past his ears. And finally sleep took him over entirely, until there was no rationality, no connection with reality left at all.

31

San Diego and Adamstown

"CHARLES will be here tomorrow," Springer said. "I think you'll like him."

Sabina had worried he might be away for weeks. She couldn't tolerate this blowhard jockey droning on about "integrity" much longer.

"He's in New York now, taking a late flight out."

Sabina applied her practiced affectation of empathy. "He'll be exhausted."

"We're meeting in the morning. It might be educational for you to sit in on it. He'll have information directly from the frontlines."

"Wow. Could be exciting."

Springer replied, "We'll see. I wouldn't put it past him to have something that our principals will all be interested in."

"What might that be?"

Springer explained. "Charles cottoned onto this B-F Explorations opportunity before he joined us. He already owned some shares of B-F. The rest of us missed the boat by at least a few months."

"What do you mean?"

"The horse is out of the barn. Mining-exploration stocks are the polar opposite of the Graham-Dodd value deals that Warren Buffett buys. People finance the junior mining companies because they're the most volatile stocks on the planet. Sometimes the sector moves up 1000 percent over a few years, then falls 95 percent in half that time. Some individual stocks will go up a hundred times or more in price; most will eventually go to zero. Although it's possible to pick out gems buried in the garbage, most people lose money when they get involved with exploration companies. That's the nutshell of a junior. Almost all of them end up with their doors shut."

"Sounds like a lot of people end up pissed off."

"Not usually. People treat it like gambling losses. By the time it all plays out, shareholders have forgotten their initial optimism and their plans for early retirement. They've written the money off, and end up grateful for being able to take capital-loss offsets against gains elsewhere. Nobody is hated, because they don't know the management; nobody is angry, except at themselves or the market. And they've had a little fun along the way, dreaming big."

"What's special about B-F? How did we miss the boat?" She did not use the term "we" accidentally.

"B-F's share price is over $260 today, putting its market cap at well over $6 billion. That's huge in this industry. Unprecedented, really. They've made a deal with Burke, and the mine will be under construction in a year and probably in production in three or four more." He paused for effect. "Or not."

"Not?"

"Charles said on the phone that he had a fantastic play for us with B-F. I'm pretty sure Charles knows that I wouldn't be interested in buying the stock now, not after a run-up like this. So, I figure he thinks it will go the other way."

"You mean he thinks it will come back down to earth?"

"We'll find out in the morning. It may be a short play. At $260 and climbing, it's ripe for a stock split. That won't change the fundamentals, or the market cap, but it will make it seem cheap and probably bring in a new wave of unsophisticated buyers who'll think they're getting a bargain. A premature short on a stock like this can lead to a total loss. Or bankruptcy."

"Sounds like he has a good chance of making a fool of himself." She knew it was unwise to say anything negative so early in this relationship, but she couldn't help herself. She disliked Knight instinctively; any chance of knocking him off his high horse was tempting.

"Maybe," Springer replied.

Sabina spent her evening synthesizing all the information she had obtained during the day about a Silicon Valley software startup. It was seeking new investment, and Springer had given her the company, Zixox, as her first research assignment. Zixox's founders had created nothing but vaporware in the past. Now they planned to build an array of fictitious mechanical tools that would actually sell, for real money, to video gamers trying to gain an edge over the competition in a popular online game that involved building fake factories. Their business plan obsessively detailed the wattage, weight, characteristics, colors, and useful life expectancy of phantasms that would exist only on gamers' computer screens. They had extremely high expectations about how many people would pay real money for imaginary items. The whole thing seemed outrageous. Sabina liked it. It was so ridiculous that, in this world of morons, it just might gain a market capitalization in the billions.

As soon as she had finished her report on Zixox, she went to work digging into Burke International Mining and B-F Explorations, two companies in a sector that could not be more different from online video games.

She focused on the head geologist, Dan Smolderhof. A picture, posted online only hours earlier, showed him receiving an award at a mining conference in a posh Toronto hotel. He sported a bandage covering an injury above his eye. His image was that of an active, in-the-dirt field geologist, and his tuxedo gave him a James Bond flare. Attractive enough, and about to become incredibly wealthy, he fit some of her criteria. As she learned about him, her purpose in examining B-F became less about the unknown Charles Knight and more about the unknown Dan Smolderhof. If he was as malleable as most men, then she just might include him in her long-term plans.

She caught herself debating the same old dichotomy again. Money vs. power. Which held greater sway? Money could give her power. Power could give her money. The two were fungible. At the moment, money was the low-hanging fruit. Her mind wandered into a daydream about Smolderhof's money. She considered how she might transform the daydream into reality.

The answer lay in somehow making herself valuable to him, and then wrapping herself in his golden fleece. First something to get his attention, something that would make him open the door for her. Given the opportunity, her body, guile, and charms would make the rest happen. Of course there had to be a score of women who already had their eyes on this newly minted billionaire.

She had to find a doorway into Smolderhof's world.

When that door opened, it opened very wide.

*   *   *

"Mr. Imir, I have a proposition for you, sir," Harry said, in as businesslike a tone as he could muster.

"Yes. Come this way." The bald Lebanese hotelier guided Harry up a flight of stairs, through a double door and into a restaurant with a bar to its left. He indicated a small couch and adjacent chair. "Joseph, fetch this man a drink."

The bartender dropped what he was doing and came over to Harry.

"Club Beer. Large and cold," Harry commanded. It was the only beer available in Gondwana. If any business could be relied on to prosper in a third world country afflicted by all the factors that made it a Third World Country, a brewery was it. Demand was constant and unquenchable, and the margins were high. Harry momentarily contemplated a microbrewery of his own, on the beach in Mozambique, once he cashed in his B-F shares. The prospect offered a continuing income, nice climate, plenty of women, and a place to swap war stories with colleagues. It would be much more than just another beach bar.

Imir personified hospitality. "Might we offer you some lunch? Compliments of the hotel, of course."

Since when did Lebanese hoteliers offer idle visitors free meals? The man must have sensed that Harry was about to ask him to do something distasteful.

"Food is not necessary, but thank you, Mr. Imir." Might as well get to the point. "My friend, Mr. Knight, whom we have talked about before: he is still missing, and I am worried. He may have left something that would help us make sure he is okay. Did he leave anything at all?"

"I'm afraid very little. Just a suitcase with clothes."

Harry nodded. "I would like to see that suitcase."

"I'm afraid that would not be proper. What is your name again?"

"Dietrich Bonhoeffer." It was another alias Harry kept on tap, the name of a man who had possessed an approach to problem solving rather different from his own. But Harry took some pride, and enjoyed the subtle humor, in the twisted nature of this alias. Humor was often in short supply here; a man had to bring his own.

"Yes. Mr. Bonhoeffer. I recall now. But I am not in a position to provide you access to another guest's private belongings."

"Mr. Imir. This is very important to me. I am willing to provide you with substantial compensation if you allow me to examine what he left behind. It is a matter of life and death."

"Yes, I am sure it might be." Imir stood up. "Now, Mr. Bonhoeffer, I must excuse myself. Please enjoy a meal here, as I said, with the compliments of the hotel." With that he turned away.

Harry had no chance to specify the amount of the bribe. Annoyed, but resigned to what now seemed the inevitable, he stood up and followed the man out the swinging doors into an empty hallway. He caught up to Imir as the hotelier was just starting back down the stairs. No one else was within sight. Harry, far larger and stronger than his prey, simply reached down, grabbed Imir by his collar, and dragged him back up the stairs while clamping a hand over his mouth. He pushed him hard against a wall, and then punched him with only moderate force, just enough to break his jaw, bloody his tongue, and stun him into passivity.

He dragged Imir through another door, down a hallway, and into a closet.

"Now, tell me what you know." He bent one of the man's fingers in a curl, fracturing it slowly. He kept his other hand covering the terrified man's mouth, muffling the involuntary scream. "Tell me what you know, Imir!"

Imir's friends described him as a gentle and peaceful man. Even with most of his lifetime spent in Africa, Imir had no preparation for what was now happening. And so he gave up Mr. Knight's computer and that Mr. Knight had called him from the United States.

Harry took no pleasure in hurting Imir, but prudence dictated that he be kept silent. Imir remained unconscious for more than two days after the final blow. And so Harry succeeded in his first assignment of the day.

32

Soccer and Shares

XANDER'S backside still hurt, maybe worse than it had at first. Keeping the wound clean was almost as unpleasant a task as what he was doing now: trudging in the muck of typhoid-ridden swampland, swatting insects, and picking off the leeches that so rapidly insinuated themselves under his clothes. The leeches accrued as part of the price he had to pay to get a look at this place, and, hell, maybe they would help clean his wound. If *they* didn't, perhaps the maggots would. Both the annelid worms and the fly larvae had formed part of mankind's primitive medicine chest for millennia, and were coming back into vogue.

It had not taken long to narrow down locations where a rebel army could be amassed near enough to overrun Banga Sioquelle early in the operation. Clearly it would be Guinea, whose border lay only miles from the edge of B-F's property. The border area of Guinea consisted of primeval bush, devoid of even small villages. A dismal road descended from the nearest town, forty miles to the north. It ran through 500,000 acres of wilderness, most of it a national forest reserve—a free-fire zone for poachers during the recent wars.

He'd had some help in discovering it. From someone with eyes in the sky. The satellite homed in on a place that looked for all the word like a soccer camp. The boys—those young friends of Charles—would be there.

Maybe it *was* just a soccer camp; his friend with eyes in the sky couldn't say. His friend, after all, did not have direct control over the satellites. There were no recent close-ups of the land in this region. But a soccer camp would provide excellent cover for a rebel training camp.

278

Driving seemed the only way to get there. The UN-enforced no-fly zone allowed only politicians and certain preferred NGOs to use private aircraft. So he once again took advantage of TJ's SUV. It was grueling, but nothing even remotely comparable to what explorers like Stanley, Baker, or his favorite, Richard Burton, had endured in the mid-nineteenth century. They walked for months, slashing their way through untracked bush, probably wounded, while afflicted with two or three tropical diseases as a bonus.

Nonetheless, here in the modern world, there seemed only one thing worse than walking with his sore buttock, and that was sitting on it while driving hundreds of miles on roads that had seen no maintenance for fifty years.

The rough dirt path where they had dropped the boys off cut into the bush about a dozen miles into Guinea. Perhaps he had sped those boys on the road to perdition. That road, both physically and metaphorically, was recently well traveled, no longer just a footpath that had served the poachers. As near as he could tell, this was where the satellite images directed him. It made sense.

Xander drove a bit farther north, until he found a suitable place to conceal his vehicle, which he camouflaged as best as he could with palm fronds and pixie dust. Now, two hours later, he found himself wondering what was burrowing through his swamp-soaked bandages to plant eggs in the tissues of his muscle. He had visions of a Guinea worm sticking its little head out from under the skin of his ankle, and having to pull it out a centimeter a day until the whole three-foot-long spaghetti noodle with teeth was exhumed from his flesh.

But those things came from drinking the water, not from wading through it. He was more worried about surprising a snake; he methodically thumped his walking stick so that the vibration would give warning to any resting snake and allow it time to move away. The last thing he needed was to have a Gaboon viper sink its fangs into his leg.

He climbed free of the swamp as soon as he could and continued through the bush, paralleling the road. The road itself was too risky. Although he would hear an approaching vehicle, he would have no advance warning of young men approaching on bare feet.

So he stayed parallel to the road, edging through the bush, ducking from time to time. Except for an occasional impenetrable wall of tangled growth, the jungle was generally thin here, with the palm trees keeping the undergrowth tame by denying it sunlight. He looked up at the canopy and wondered how many green mambas and cobras were moving from tree to tree through the long palm leaves, ready to drop down on his neck at any moment. Xander hated snakes.

He whacked at a bothersome series of bamboo stalks with his machete, leaving behind the notoriously sharp edge that makes unnoticed bamboo so effective at impaling careless hikers, animals, and invading armies throughout the tropical world.

During his two-hour trek through the jungle, Xander could never be completely confident that he was heading toward the correct place, or whether there even was a correct place. Evidence of a brewing rebellion included nothing more than containers full of munitions and the theoretical usefulness to B-F's scammers of a conveniently timed revolution. Doubts pervaded his mind. Perhaps the containers were left over from the previous wars. Perhaps the B-F masterminds were dullards, and actually had no clue how they would get away with such a massive fraud. Perhaps they were panicking now, trying desperately to block the deal with Burke, to put off the hour of reckoning. Perhaps he would find a real soccer camp that some missionaries had set up in the middle of nowhere in order to safeguard youth from the vices of the city.

He came through a wall of vegetation, stopped swinging the machete, and listened to the noises of humans in the distance.

Xander continued onward until the road cut between two high hills. He could either expose himself on the road, or head over the hill that rose in front of him to his left. An old military maxim dictated that when given a choice between a tough physical obstacle and an easy human obstacle, choose the inanimate and predictable one. He chose the hill, which took him a few painful minutes to climb.

A huge sausage-shaped black rock perched atop the hill, resting on and overhanging the soft rock below it. The hill rose almost vertically—indeed, it was even at a reverse angle near the bottom where erosion had worked the hardest. A thick rope hung down from the top. He tugged at it. It felt secure, and he used it to help ascend the last fifty feet. As he approached its bare top, apparently the region's high point, he realized that he would be exposed to the world below if he tried to stand.

He inched himself to the top, belly tight against the dark rock's round, smooth surface, raising his head just enough to see what lay below.

The dark color of the giant rock absorbed all of the sun's rays, reflecting none back. He crawled along this solar-heated frying pan until the soccer camp became visible below. He could spit on two dozen or more vehicles that served as a motor pool directly at the base of the hill. Men and tents filled the center of a small valley. On dirt soccer fields, hundreds of young men and boys played or watched ongoing games. Was this place truly just a soccer camp? It certainly seemed to be, but for the military-looking transports and fuel trucks below him.

Xander slid back down the way he had come. He snuck around the hill until he could just see the camp again.

He stood hidden by underbrush and watched through his small binoculars. Men and boys sat in circles, working on objects in their laps that he couldn't yet clearly make out.

Then one of the men held his project in the air. It had the universally recognizable shape of an AK-47 with its magazine in place.

Around the edges of the camp, piles of palm fronds smoldered. A slow burn dehydrated them into what was known throughout equatorial regions worldwide as *charcoal*. To the average person from the West they looked like the slightly scorched plant bits that they were. To a Gondwanan, this charcoal served as the primary fuel for cooking. In the absence of breeze, the smoke hung thickly and added familiar flavor and texture to the air Xander inhaled.

He counted men and watched their movements through the haze. He looked for Saye and Nyahn, but he had known them only as they rode in the backseat of a dark car. He couldn't recognize them at this distance, and would be uncertain even if up close. It proved impossible for him to pick them out from a crowd of a thousand or more.

He identified what appeared to be a command tent, a mess tent, and a well-guarded supply tent. Over to the south stood a clinic tent. Open latrines abounded at the edges, and a dug well stood in the middle of the place. A few groups of men cut down trees on the periphery and dragged them back to the camp. Soccer games and associated happy cheering continued. Sporadic sounds of rifle fire in the surrounding jungle sparked discordant notes, but no one on the soccer fields cared.

Darkness would arrive soon enough, and then the anopheles would be out to spread their malaria. It would take less than two hours to get back to the car if he stuck to his original cut path.

He took one last look. Just then a white man stepped out of the command tent, followed by four other white men. Heavy-set, these older men stood straight with a military air. The four moved off in pairs in opposite directions, but the lead man stood still gazing out over the camp. Xander focused his binoculars on the man's distant face. The man in turn brought his eyes slowly upward, gazing right back. And then he started walking straight toward Xander.

*   *   *

Rupert emerged from his conversation with JohnJohn more frustrated than ever. The man was a veritable library of vices; he was the antithesis of Boy Scout virtues—duplicitous, treacherous, demanding, antagonistic, bad-tempered, mean, power-hungry, nasty, profligate, brash, and disrespectful. He was also a regular user of heroin and an intermittent user of cocaine; the combination made him dangerously unpredictable. Almost all of these vices, applied to the right victim in the right way, could yield excellent short-term results, as any analysis of Shakespeare's villains would illustrate.

Flomo whispered something into JohnJohn's ear as Rupert left the tent. Rupert saw it but couldn't hear it. Flomo was a pissy little Iago, further twisting JohnJohn's bent mind in ways that Rupert could never be sure of. The little viper might reinforce JohnJohn's natural paranoia to such a degree that Rupert would wake up dead some morning.

Every day here was dangerous. Nine more days. Right up to the day the first Burke team planned to arrive. Smolderhof insisted. But Smolderhof wasn't the one sitting on a time bomb. Smolderhof needed that much time to—as quietly as possible—sell his millions of shares, even though for the last few months he had demanded that no one sell any B-F stock. Rupert had only fifty thousand shares. He was going to contact his man in London, instruct him to dump them now, and tell his brother to do the same. Then, if this whole thing went tits up, they would have cashed out at least partway and would take home something.

But more would be delivered next week, ten thousand shares at a time—or so Goodluck Johnson had told him. According to Goodluck, who visited the camp once a week, Smolderhof was sweetening the pot by transferring some of his own shares to the two mercenary brothers—to keep them dedicated during the climax. It worked. At this share price, the promises amounted to $2.5 million every day for five days, all next week. Each day would deliver a fortune, ten times more than could be gained robbing every bank in Gondwana—a thought that had previously crossed his mind. It was hard to leave even one $2.5 million payday on the table. But this red-eyed lunatic might make a choice impossible. The man got hungrier for blood every day. Rupert had felt more relaxed when he was laying minefields on the border with Zambia during the war in Rhodesia.

Unlike him, the camp stayed calm. The soccer fields had become an essential asset, perhaps the most valuable idea of all. With food, entertainment, and some regular money—things missing at home—the men and boys felt privileged. The soccer kept them happy, and the military training gave them purpose and made them feel they were learning skills to improve their station in life. Twice on most days, the charismatic JohnJohn roused them: once with his highly charged noon performance, and another in the evening—usually a liturgical follow-up to his lunchtime extravaganza. The most dangerous creature to have ever walked the earth, even more so than T. Rex, was the young, testosterone-intoxicated human male. And here were two thousand of them, with a charismatic psychopath as their leader.

He glanced at his watch. In an hour, his London broker would close his doors for the evening. He looked toward the hill and the giant boulder. He would head there now, call London, and make the trek again later for his brother's nightly call.

He looked around to make sure that weasel Flomo wasn't following him before he headed off.

*   *   *

Xander watched through his binoculars as the mercenary walked toward him. He passed the last of the soccer fields and now approached the motor pool, moving along a narrow path, one man wide in the tall grass.

The man talked to himself as he trekked toward the hill. Could he be communicating through an earpiece with a squad of soldiers? Xander didn't think so. But as he studied the mercenary's face, he also listened intently for any suspicious sounds behind him. Something about the man's gait, the angle of his head, spoke of tension, and anger.

Xander assessed where the man's path would take him. Then he retreated around the back of the hill and concealed himself in a crevice protected by brambles and bamboo. A few minutes later the man's voice came down the side of the rock face. He must be standing on top. Every word was audible, completely clear, almost shouted.

"Can you hear me, Reynolds?… Yes, bad connection. It is Rupert Pell…. RUPERT Pell! … Yes, that's right…. I need you to look at my portfolio…. Yes, I'll wait. If we disconnect I'll call you back…."

A minute passed. Xander stayed completely still.

"Yes, that's correct." The man recited a number, an account number or confirmation of some sort. "Reynolds, I want you to sell my B-F Explorations stock. All of it…. At the market price. Today if you can…. There will be more B-F stock transferred into my account next week. Every day. I want you to sell it immediately after receipt. That is a standing order…. Yes, you have that correctly…. Thank you."

For the next ten minutes, Xander heard only silence from above him. Was the man still there? No noise, no hint one way or the other. Xander could only wonder what the merc was doing, but he had no choice other than to wait. Surely the man would not stay there for much longer. Surely he would make some noise coming down from that rock.

Xander waited, and he waited. He waited until dusk. Then he took the risk. He moved from his concealed spot and gently climbed the rope up the back of the boulder. He peered over the curve, keeping his head down, moving slowly, like a cat. Soon he was back at the top, and there was no one there. He stayed low and looked out over the camp and had a thought. Maybe this was the one place in the area that received a cell signal. The merc's cell phone had worked.

He made a call, and it went through.

As he finished the call, he heard voices, young, laughing, coming his way up the narrow path. Quickly, he slid back down the rope and concealed himself once more amid the vegetation growing behind the huge rock, hunkering down in the deepest shadows below the darkening sky.

The mosquitoes would be out in force very soon. And his butt hurt.

33

The Spider Meets the Fly

CHARLES awoke midmorning, finally in his own bed, where he had collapsed after failing to sleep on his evening flight.

His house in San Diego stood high up on Point Loma, with a broad view over Mexico to the south, as well as San Diego Bay and North Island Naval Air Station to the east. The climate, a constant seventy-two degrees with clear skies, remained perennially perfect. The political climate in the US suited him less well, but the fortune he was making could insulate him from the worst of what the politicians could throw at him.

He had moved here seven weeks ago, so the walls were bare, the three oil paintings he had so far acquired in his life still in boxes. He had only used a few of the four sleeves of red Solo cups he had brought the first night, when he slept on a naked mattress, drying himself off with paper towels after a shower. Interior decorating and housekeeping weren't among his strongest points. Despite his visit to Walmart for linens and the rest of the basics, the place needed a woman's touch: someone who would help him turn this sterile accommodation into a home. He thought of Caroline without even being aware of it. She also appeared in his mind sporadically as he navigated the traffic to his new office at Alchemia Resources. Her presence in his consciousness provided a partial inoculation against what he was about to confront.

Elliot awaited him in the conference room. As he entered, his eyes were automatically drawn to the unexpected addition to the meeting: a woman who would stand out in a room of hundreds. She wore a white blouse over khaki pants tailored to her trim figure. Her platinum hair fell not quite down to her shoulders. Her face was symmetrical, faultless, extraordinary. She stood as a photorealist work of art and smiled at him as he walked in.

He immediately felt uncomfortable.

What triggered that feeling? A sixth sense?

He would understand it much better as he grew older, when it would both protect him from harm and help him find allies so regularly that it was, he would decide later, a key component of any successes he had. But, for now, it remained immature, in process, a hint of uncertain meaning.

He suspected one of two things affected him today. Her attractive smile appeared rapidly, but her eyes failed to express the same emotion that the smile attempted to convey. The eyes came alive a moment late, out of sync, as if the smile were automated, trained for effect, and the eyes an afterthought. Those eyes were less adept than the smile at concealing something underneath.

Or perhaps he felt off-kilter because he was intimidated by this beauty. The woman could have stepped from the pages of a style magazine. In an earlier era, she might well have been selected from the masses to be a princess, a queen. Even her scent, which reached him just then, served as a powerful attractant. That one first breath, the scent coupled to that first vision, would forever connect him to this moment—and to her.

"Charles, I'm Sabina Dresden." She spoke as if trying to score a win, as if Elliot did not exist and she and Charles were sharing a private moment. She stared at him, eyes attempting to penetrate into his, and held his gaze for far too long.

Other than with his uncle, Charles had not had any personal contact since returning to the States. Was this woman's not-so-subtle aggressiveness impacting him abnormally because of jetlag and fatigue? Were his perceptions slow in readjusting to America: a culture shock after the brief alternate reality of Africa?

"Pleasure to meet you, Sabina." He pulled his eyes away from hers, and shot a quick glance at Elliot full of meaning, before reaching across the table to shake hands with his boss.

"Charles, it's good to have you safely back, with or without your hair. Sorry to not give you a heads-up about Sabina. She's coming in as a new mentee, following in your footsteps in a way. I'm experimenting. You two come from entirely different places, as it were. It will be interesting to see how"—he caught himself as he was about to say "if"—"you two synergize."

"I'm sure we will synergize," Sabina interjected.

By the way Sabina spoke, he knew she had intentions beyond work. His body responded to the possibilities. His brain, from which blood flow was now diverted, failed to remain in control, confounded as it was by the release of adrenalin and testosterone.

Charles swallowed as he sat down. He wanted to physically shake his head to clear it. Caroline flashed in his mind. It wasn't a sexual thought, nor a romantic concept. Just her face. An echo. An image that prompted him to stand back up.

"I'm sorry. Can you excuse me for a moment?"

Charles walked out the door and headed for the bathroom. No doubt he appeared flustered, to both this woman, and to Elliot. No doubt they both knew Sabina had caused it. He splashed cold water on his face and his scalp. He did it again. He breathed slowly. He let his brain have time to gain control over his physiology, which was thrown off by basal instincts. But when he inhaled her scent again, reacting to her penetrating pheromones as if he were an insect, would his mind remain in charge?

His cell phone buzzed then, and he fumbled for it with wet hands. It was the overseas call he had been hoping for and a voice that calmed him.

A few minutes later, as he returned to the conference room, he found Elliot and Sabina chatting about something innocuous.

"Sorry about that. I'm still nine time zones off." But that was disingenuous. Why avoid the elephant in the room? So he added as explanation, "Apart from that, Sabina, your beauty threw me off balance. I don't recall experiencing anything quite like you before." And with that blunt and honest statement, he felt like himself again.

He looked at Elliot, who beamed back at him proudly. He looked at Sabina, who suddenly seemed smaller and lower in her chair—and more manageable. The candor of the compliment defused the bombshell—or the bomb—that was the core of this Sabina Dresden. Balance was restored for a time.

Elliot said, "Well, let's get on with it, then. I'm keen to hear both your news and the proposal you mentioned."

"First," Charles faced Sabina, "I'm a naturally trusting person. What I'm about to tell you both is, not to be overly dramatic, top secret. It does not leave this room until I say so. You need to know this is a matter of life and death, perhaps many, many lives. You need to explicitly agree to this secrecy until I say otherwise. Do you agree?"

"Of course. Not a word." Her voice was less confident than before, her eyes less persistent in their gaze; yes, she was indeed defused for the time being.

"Good. You will understand shortly." He turned to Elliot. "At yesterday's close B-F Explorations traded at $284, and the aftermarket was higher yet. I think this is an excellent time to short this stock, and more than that, to buy put options, because I believe they're salting their cores."

Elliot sat back in his chair and simply asked, "How?"

Charles replied, "I know that this has been evaluated before: the assays repeated in duplicate and triplicate by completely separate labs whose reputation relies on their accuracy. We've all been told this plenty of times. Independent mineralogists, including two academics with no conflict of interest, have examined the ore and found only support for B-F's nanoparticle gold-deposition theory. There was no evidence of misplaced placer gold or shaved bits of bullion, or any other typical salting method. A clean bill of health from a fraud point of view, right? But then there is this." Charles handed Elliot some printed pictures.

"From what I can tell, those violet bottles contain colloidal gold. B-F was manufacturing it on site using vapor arcs between gold electrodes, powered by a generator. I'm confident that the liquid in those bottles is pregnant with atomic gold."

"Did you obtain some of this liquid?" the woman asked.

"No." He wanted to say they were lucky to get away alive.

Elliot slid the pictures over to her. Charles handed Elliot some more. "This machine here is, for want of a better term, a pressure cooker. It was loaded with recently drilled cores and filled with that liquid, and cranked up to high enough pressures that simply opening its door—at, let us say, an inopportune moment—caused it to self-destruct, and collapse the building it was in."

Elliot smiled questioningly. "Are we to assume that you had something to do with that?"

"It was necessary at the time."

Sabina's fragrance caused him to close his eyes to help suppress the response that built in him once again.

She asked, "How does a machine like that work?"

"The drill cores are naturally saturated with water when pulled from the ground. This big machine alternates between a vacuum and a pressure chamber. I think they expose the cores to extreme vacuum to evaporate out almost all the initially present water, and then they infuse gold-saturated water from those bottles into the ore by cranking up the pressure in the chamber. This spreads colloidal gold throughout the porous cores. Then they evaporate the water off again under vacuum. As the water dries away, the gold colloid stays behind and deposits as nanoparticles in the rock. Then they repeat the process as many times as necessary to get the grade they want. Most of their cores are silty limestone conglomerates of high porosity. This process allows them to control the deposition, and therefore the final ore grade, based on the number of cycles they run the cores through. I think this is how they kept getting higher and higher ore grades."

"That's a unique methodology," Elliot said.

Sabina asked, "Are you sure that's what the machine does?"

"I suppose it's possible they were experimenting in some way totally unrelated to fraud. I can't be 100 percent sure. But why would they perform science experiments in the middle of the jungle, under horrible conditions?"

The woman interrupted. "But isn't that area rich in gold?"

"Much of West Africa, especially Ghana, has gold, and there is a lot of placer gold around in the south of Gondwana, although no one has ever found its source. There's likely gold in the north too, where Banga Sioquelle is—that's B-F's prospect. While I was on-site, I picked up some rock samples from their richest formation. Yesterday I sent them for assay." He handed a sheet of paper to Springer. "This is the lab, here in California. The results should be available shortly and should be at least remotely similar to the B-F core assays—that is *if* B-F is real. It's the only physical data I can offer."

Sabina nodded. "So, you're saying the whole thing may be a fraud?"

"I think so. Maybe there *is* gold there somewhere, but if that machine I bumped into is what I think it is, then Banga Sioquelle is nothing like what B-F has made it out to be."

Elliot said, "I don't know, Charles. That's a lot of ifs. Let's say that machine really is being used to salt their drill cores. How on earth do they think they'll get away with it?"

Charles looked at Springer and then at Sabina. Again, he decided to simply face the stunningly beautiful elephant in the room. "Sabina, may I bother you to step out so I can talk to Elliot in private?"

Springer nodded to Sabina, who stood up to leave. Neither man missed the change of her smile into an expression approaching petulance.

After the door closed, Charles said, "I'm sorry, Elliot, but I don't know her and what I am going to tell you next needs to stay quiet for now. I think you know Xander Winn."

"Xander! Hah. Sure, I know him! He used to drink me under the table."

"I met Xander at Banga Sioquelle."

"What are the odds? How *is* that wild man?"

"A bit beat up right now. He and I snooped around and found thousands of rifles and at least a million rounds of ammunition in shipping containers concealed on a piece of B-F property near that machine."

"Sounds like they're preparing to defend their $100 billion stake."

"Maybe. But the arms weren't in Banga Sioquelle itself. They're over an hour away on a different property. And B-F doesn't have the men to carry twenty guns, to say nothing of a thousand. If, as we believe, B-F is a giant fraud, then it's much more likely they're trying to cover their tracks. We suspect B-F may be intentionally fomenting a revolution so that Burke never drills new cores."

Elliot stared at Charles for a moment. "That's a lot to suggest. To start an entire war over money?"

Charles looked back at Elliot. He probably didn't need to say anything verbally. His face said enough, but he spoke anyway. "It happens all the time, Elliot."

"Okay, you got me there," Elliot admitted. "But it's still an outrageous claim, don't you think? Do you have any other evidence?"

"Yes. Just a few minutes ago, when I stepped outside the conference room, I had a phone call from Xander. There's a rebel camp, with two thousand soldiers. As the crow flies, it's fourteen miles away from the B-F tract, just across the border in Guinea. They have a group of mercenaries training them."

"Charles, to me that sounds like a good reason for B-F to be stocking up on guns and ammunition, no?"

"Not without men to use them, Elliot. No, B-F is going to supply the rebels with the arms."

Springer shook his head. "Still only circumstantial evidence, Charles. You think this army is ready to move?"

Charles said, now completely suffused with confidence, "So much so that one of the mercenaries in charge there is panic selling all of his substantial stake in B-F stock as we speak."

Elliot lost any expression of skepticism.

Charles's smile, almost always present, broadened. "*Now* you're getting it."

*   *   *

Frank Graves had only joined "the Service," as its employees liked to call it, because he felt he had no alternative. Burdened with loans from college and more debt accrued while studying to be a CPA, he had been under pressure as he worked to build his accounting practice. The pressure mounted when his wife gave birth to a child with a list of unexpected diagnoses that made the billing department of the neonatal intensive care unit salivate with anticipation of the financial windfall. The medical insurance company responded by quadrupling the premiums for his small practice. He felt guilty joining the IRS—the organization he'd been fighting against on behalf of his always-struggling clients. But the Service's regular paycheck and, most importantly, the rich medical benefits, forced his hand. He rose through the ranks stoically. Not as high as he might have with conscious backslapping and backstabbing. But as high as someone who was competent, reliable, and basically decent could expect to in a bureaucracy.

It was worse for the younger folk now. Billions of dollars of government loan money pouring into the system allowed university administrators to double and triple tuitions, and name new buildings after themselves. New graduates, immersed in debt, took government jobs in exchange for forgiveness of loans they should never have needed. Foolishly grateful for the government's beneficence, they didn't realize that they had just become indentured servants.

"I understand you want to make a trip to Toronto?" Frank Graves looked up from his work to see his recent assignment tapping her fingers on the table next to his desk.

"Yes. Today," Sabina said. "I would like to go there today."

"That's a bit out of our jurisdiction, Sabina. What's up there?"

"The head geologist from B-F Explorations is there."

"Canadian company. What's it to us?"

"I met Charles Knight this morning."

"Yeah? That's fast." Graves closed his eyes for a moment, and tried not to imagine exactly how this woman had arranged that. "But I had no doubt you would accomplish it. What's he like?"

"Actually, he's a bit beaten up, bruised and cut up all over, and bald. But he's a sharp guy."

"Sharper than you?"

"He's pretty sharp.… Anyway, he just came back from Africa last night. He's been to B-F's digs there. And he's very involved in B-F. He apparently has a lot of stock that he's selling, and he's putting on short positions. He's concocted a tale about fraud, put together some blurry pictures, and will try to actively make B-F shares tank soon and make money by denigrating the company."

Graves looked thoughtful and concerned. This sounded like something other than a tax case. "He's trying to manipulate the share price of B-F with lies—is that what you're saying?"

"Maybe. I want to get to the truth. That's why I want to talk to B-F's head geologist."

"The guy in Toronto?"

"Yes."

"Sabina, what's wrong with the phone?"

"This needs the personal touch. Stock-market players talk to CEOs and other corporate officers all the time. But when the government calls, his guard will be up. I need to see through the fences. This was my territory at SEC. I need to talk to Smolderhof. That's the geologist. I need more information. This is a perfect crossover case between SEC and IRS."

That did sound true. Graves stayed silent.

She dropped the bomb. "The vice president will insist on me having a great deal of latitude. Do I need to call him?"

Graves had been here before, with subordinates trying power plays of one type or another. The Service had always been something of a snake pit, but it seemed to get worse as time went by. Veiled threats, often about imagined discrimination or sexual harassment issues, were standard fare. Name-dropping was generally a bluff used by those transferred in, as Sabina had been. Rather than putting her in her place, Graves thought to use this as an opportunity to see what this young woman could pull off, so he gave her more leash. "Okay, Sabina. Go for it. But fly coach, and stay clean, okay? Everything you do might become part of some prosecution of Charles Knight someday, you know. Everything you do will be scrutinized by whatever defense team he puts together."

She picked up her approvals and her itinerary. She would be in Toronto by 9 p.m. By 10 p.m., she would be having drinks with Dan Smolderhof in his hotel bar while extensively discussing Charles Knight and his evidence of B-F's fraud. By 11 p.m., she would be inside Smolderhof's hotel room, and by midnight, he would be inside her.

She doubted Knight's future legal defense team would ever scrutinize that.

34

Transoceanic

XANDER fell asleep against the base of the giant boulder, waiting for a group of young men to leave their party on the hill above him. Twice, an empty beer bottle rolled down the rock face, bouncing through the vegetation to land in front of his partial cave under the rock. When he awoke, it was black. He looked at his wrist, pressing a button on his watch. It was 22:50. Thank Shango, the local storm god, it wasn't raining. He pried himself up from his concealed position.

From around the southern end of the boulder he peered into the valley. Campfires and a few flashlights glowed, providing the only light in the overcast night. Some occasional laughter trickled up the slope from the camp. But the generators were off, and most of the camp slept after another day of playing soccer and preparing for mayhem.

He watched in the darkness for guards on the periphery. Elsewhere in the world there would also have been the telltale sign of cigarettes being lit. The flare of the match, the flame of the lighter, or just the smoldering red of the butt as a man inhaled would serve as obvious indicators of the guards' locations, visible from more than a mile away. But few Gondwanans smoke.

He planned to take the road back to his car. Hopefully, no one would be out on that road tonight. It was a risk that extreme darkness and the pounding pain in his buttocks compelled him to take.

Before he turned to feel his way down the slope, he heard a crack. He froze and listened. Footsteps and breathing. Tracking up the slope toward him.

He heard the man scramble up the boulder and, a few minutes later, the sound of a mobile phone ringing.

It was the same male voice as earlier with the same accent from southern Africa: Rupert, he recalled.

"Harry. Yes, no change…. Very dark here. Terribly unstable situation…. Any luck finding Knight?… Really? Well, it is a start. Are you following?… Oh, clearly you are!… Yah, and how're you going to figure that out?… That's a long way to travel with so little to go on…. Finish him as fast as you can and get back to Africa, yah? I tell you, this is going to get very hot…. Look, I have informed our broker to start selling what I have already got…. Yes, all of it…. You should also— What? I can't hear you. Repeat…. Good. About time…. Correct…. I know. I will…. Good luck with Knight. Get back here fast."

Xander heard the man trundle his way back down the boulder and head down the grass path. He exhaled fully for the first time in five minutes.

He waited for thirty more minutes, immobile as a rock—or a sniper. Then, slowly, he moved behind the boulder, away from the camp and down the hill, and, with stealth, made his way through the darkness several miles back to where his SUV was concealed.

The border guards slept as he re-entered Gondwana, saving him some bribe money. He drove south as fast as the road and the darkness allowed, glancing at his phone now and then, checking it for a signal that did not exist except on that rock. The signal appeared when he approached Gbarngeda at 2 a.m. He tried to dial Charles, but got no answer, so he left a message.

It rained intermittently during the next five hours of his trek. The red fuel jugs strapped to the top of TJ's SUV were US models, and suffered from the new EPA rules on fuel-container design. The jugs emptied their contents slowly, and had to burp constantly, and when they burped, gasoline sprayed all over everything, including himself. Just enough went into the car's tank to maybe get him back to Adamstown. Of course, the rain god chose to void his bladder just as he refueled. He was quickly soaked through with both rain and gasoline. He launched Dutch expletives at whatever bureaucratic asshole had mandated this stupid intervention into the fuel-jug market, no doubt to protect the environment, but with the opposite result.

He drove straight back to the *Africa Grace*, desperate for Caroline's ministration to his wounded rear. He assumed Charles would not be jealous, and grinned as he considered how he would tease him. But there was a man named Harry on the way to the US to kill that kid. He tried calling again, to no avail.

*　*　*

Harry banged Charles's laptop computer on the airplane foldout table, an action that served no purpose but to draw attention to himself and perhaps to damage the machine. Harry was overspecialized, with military skills that far exceeded his skills with a computer. Should he start by typing "password," which he heard was, rather ironically, the most common password? It would be an exercise in futility, certainly here on the plane, with the machine's limited battery life. The damn thing was useless to him until he could find a competent nerd to break the password.

Imir's revelation that Knight was back in the US provided a second avenue of attack. Imir, while unconscious, had kindly lent Harry his cell phone, which contained Knight's US number. Smolderhof claimed to have contacts who could track the cell phone's location. Harry doubted it. If the geologist did not succeed at that, then this trip was going to be a waste of a whole lot of travel time, each way. Time was especially valuable now.

At the layover in Ghana, he had contacted Rupert. Then he slept for most of the overnight flight from Accra to New York. He connected to Toronto and arrived unkempt and wrinkled at Smolderhof's hotel in time for lunch. Smolderhof met him in the lobby, smiling broadly, and suggested they talk in a back corner of the restaurant.

"You look like the cat who ate the canary, Dan." Harry hoped Smolderhof had some news that would both make his life easier and add to his retirement nest egg.

"And you look like a rat the cat dragged in." Smolderhof's face bore a cemented smile, in sharp contrast to the stress it usually presented. He told Harry about his unimaginably fantastic night of sex—hours and hours of sex—with the most amazingly lithe and attractive woman he had ever experienced. After two months in Gondwana, it was a welcome change from the whores available at hotels in Adamstown.

"Good for you, Dan. Hopefully that's just a taste of good things to come. But right now I'm more interested in Knight than your sex life." Harry smiled, with slightly exposed teeth. Only the right side of his mouth contracted, a smile that indicated danger more often than satisfaction.

"That's because you don't have my sex life, Harry."

Harry wanted to hit him. "Look, I need to move rapidly on this issue with Knight. Has he released anything?"

"Not a thing."

"Not that you know of."

"Nothing. I'd know. Turns out that my recent sex life comes with dividends."

Harry let it slide. The guy had been an academic geologist for a long time, living a university lifestyle, and had the cocky narcissism that came with that academic territory. He would figure it out later.

For now he just asked, "Maybe the kid is sitting down right now with NBC's evening-news anchor?"

"He's not."

"Why not?"

"Because he's planning to make money, and lots of it."

"How about you tell me something I don't know."

"Knight needs to have a tragic accident, and there is another man who needs to die with him, also tragically."

"Xander Winn?"

Smolderhof's face went blank for a moment. "No. Not Winn." He shook his head. "Where *is* Winn?"

"I don't know. I only know he hasn't flown out of Gondwana. At least not on a scheduled carrier."

"You know this how?"

"I'm sleeping with a booking agent for SN Brussels Airlines."

"Sounds like you're benefitting from a sex life with dividends too."

"Just part of the job."

Smolderhof held his thumb up. "We have good jobs."

"Now who is this other man?"

Smolderhof handed him a card with a name and address.

Harry read it quickly. "Why him?"

"Knight's boss. The only other person who knows what Knight has figured out."

"How much did Knight figure out, actually?"

"He figured out that we've been salting the cores, and knows exactly how we're doing it. It was definitely Knight who destroyed the colloid infuser."

"Have you been in touch with him? Is that how you know this?" Then it came to him. "The bastard is extorting you, isn't he? Now I get it."

"Actually, he could extort us all if he chose to. And then he would be easy to manage. But he's made no effort to do so. We've heard nothing from him. From what I understand, he's taking the high road."

Harry waited.

"He has a reasonable position in the stock, which of course he's already starting to sell. While *we're* selling, I prefer everyone else be buying. If that was it, though, we could let it be. He makes his money and walks away happy. No harm, no foul. Sadly, he's not letting it lie with just his profits from being long. He's a greedy bastard, it seems. He's starting to short us, including buying as many puts as folk will write for him. Some of those will expire soon, and that means he has a deadline and is going to be very motivated to make sure that B-F shares collapse. As soon as he's staked out his short position, he'll be hungry for our failure. And his boss and his partners have a lot of resources and may travel this route with him. If Knight succeeds in starting a wave of selling, the whole game collapses too fast and may take us down with it. Anybody who sells hurts us. Anybody who shorts hurts us more." Smolderhof's face darkened.

Harry caught the meaning. "I haven't sold a share."

"Your brother has, and he wasn't supposed to yet."

Harry quietly considered that. Rupert's shares, like his own, had been transferred through two brokerages and a holding company. It would take at least a week before the ownership paperwork would get to the B-F company books, and then, with all the shares changing hands constantly, it would not be noticed. How did Smolderhof know his brother was selling?

Harry played it cool. "I know nothing about that."

298

"Your broker is spreading the word. His clients are unloading our stock. You see how fast this can happen? You might as well sell your current shares now too. But don't short us, Harry. And don't let Rupert, either. If you short us, so will your broker and his whole firm and all their clients."

Harry shrugged. "Okay. I hear you."

Smolderhof continued, "Springer has some real financial firepower. He didn't have any shares on the way up, but he's planning on taking an aggressive short position now."

"He's placing a winning bet."

"I'm doing everything I can to hype this thing and bring in new buyers for the next eight days."

Harry said, "Knight could land us in jail if he talks."

"You needn't state the obvious. That's more important than the millions he'll cost us." Smolderhof shrugged. "Although your brother and that psycho JohnJohn damn well better make sure that there's no evidence against us, okay? No chance anybody's going to venture to Banga Sioquelle for years, right?"

Harry nodded. "How far can Knight and his boss take down the share price?"

"If he gets the attention of CNN or MSNBC, and they do a typical snarky half-assed story, there could be major damage. Most people who own shares won't believe his story, of course. Hell, most won't even hear it. Still, he could cause a substantial drop—fifty dollars, maybe more. At this point the price is strictly a matter of psychology...."

Harry calculated quickly the effect on his own ownership. It would be about a $2 million hit to him, also to his brother, just from the promised shares not yet received. More than enough to justify the effort. The price one could put on other people's lives was rather arbitrary. You might kill somebody out of drunken rage in a bar or an alley for no money at all. When he had signed on to the Rhodesian Light Infantry during the war he had been knee-deep in gore for what amounted to a thousand dollars a month. Now, as a freelance professional, his market wage was about ten grand a month. But for the next few days he would be paid an outrageous $2 million *per day*. Now, cut in on the stock profits, he was truly running with the big dogs.

"There's a lot of money at risk here, Dan, on top of a jail sentence."

Smolderhof nodded, slowly.

"I want another $10 million." Harry said it not as a desire but as a demand.

"I expected you might be thinking along those lines. It's a deal. But only if you take out both Knight and Elliot Springer before they release any information publicly. And make sure they don't leave any proof behind."

"How am I supposed to find them?"

"I've taken the liberty of booking you on a flight to San Diego in four hours. You will find them both there. I booked you in business class. You can afford it."

*   *   *

Sabina boarded the plane in Toronto eager for a chance to sleep on the transcontinental flight back to San Diego. Last night with Smolderhof had been exhausting and not half bad. She reveled in her prowess—and her progress. Based on the care she had taken with Smolderhof, there was a good chance the man was already in love with her.

Whatever the hell love was.

She closed her eyes as she settled into her business-class seat, defiant of Graves's orders to travel back in the cattle car. She had come to Toronto and conquered. Worst case, even if she had not yet quite conquered, at least she had made a conquest with substantial potential. Those faceless cubicle-dwelling accountants at the IRS who would review her expenses could take that and shove it.

Who cared what the Service thought of her travel arrangements when she had a billionaire on the line? The issue now was, who would be a better conquest? Smolderhof, to whom she had supplied sufficient information about Knight and from whom she had received certain promises? Or Knight himself? Knight would be a sexual challenge, but she knew her effect on him, culminating in his having to leave the conference room just after meeting her. Her face cracked with an unintended smile as she considered the degree of impact she had. She had not sensed, however, any weakness of being. None of those little hints that, as a skilled predator, she could intuit, although not always define. In contrast, Smolderhof exuded those tip-offs, in droves. Her smile disappeared as her forehead furrowed. She suspected, from the hour she

300

had spent in Knight's presence, that he too was an apex predator. But, paradoxically, one that didn't take pleasure in hunting.

As a bonus, Knight was far younger and altogether more attractive than Smolderhof; even his shaved head titillated her. Knight attracted her in the way men once did, years before. He was no male swimsuit model with the perfectly toned build so necessary among the men of that profession. Rather, he was attractive in a more rugged way, projecting self-confidence. Such self-assurance had once attracted her as much as power and money, back in her naïve youth. But she grew to see it as a sign that someone would be harder to manage.

Two men. Each with huge financial potential. She wanted money. But she also wanted power. Money. Power. Money. Power…. Her head fell to the left as she slipped away toward sleep, but then she jerked awake again.

She stretched her long legs, reveling in her own control and power. Her legs were perfectly tuned to do what she needed them to do, to communicate what she needed them to communicate. Right now, she did not mind in the least that her legs were communicating rather stridently to the tall, blond, military-looking older man who sat across the aisle. She gave him a brief smile, enough so as not to discourage him, but not enough that it was an invitation either. She bet she could get him to fall for her in two minutes or less.

She needed to sleep.

* * *

"Uncle Maurice, have you got anything for me?"

"What the hell time is it, Charles?"

"It's 11 a.m. here in California. And 2 p.m. in New York. Why? Are you sleeping?"

"Of course I am. What else would I be doing this time of the day?"

"What do we do about Gondwana?"

"Charles, people have been trying to start, stop, prolong, and prevent wars in Africa for forty years. These things have a life of their own. There's always some charismatic narcissist itching to set off the next cataclysm."

"Yes, but this one is being instigated by Canadian fraudsters, not African psychopaths."

"And it's your problem why?"

"I told you. I can make more money if it doesn't happen."

"Well, maybe. And maybe not. Sticking your nose into that meat grinder makes no sense from the point of view of preserving your life; just grab the low-hanging fruit and FIDO.... I fear, however, you have ulterior motives, beyond money."

Charles long ago had absorbed the meanings of Maurice's military acronyms. A SNAFU meant Situation Normal, All Fucked Up. From there a situation moved to FUBAR, Fucked Up Beyond All Recognition. At which point experienced operators will FIDO—Fuck It, Drive On.

"Ulterior motives, huh? Why would you accuse me of having any?"

"Admit it, Charles. You like taking the moral high ground. You always have. It may be psychologically appealing, and even spiritually satisfying, but it causes complications."

"It was you who put me on this path."

Maurice sighed. "I know what you're thinking: never initiate force, never initiate fraud. Keep to that, and all the rest is good. And the absence of evil will allow the good to come through. It's an attractive philosophical conceit, something like when Michelangelo said it was just a matter of removing unneeded marble to reveal the hidden essential."

"Uncle Maurice, I know that would be true of you, if we could just get you on a bit of diet and exercise...."

Maurice laughed. It was funny because it was true.

"No, Charles, I agree with you, I really do. The difference is that I think the whole world is filled to the brim with force and fraud, so it's rare that you would ever have to *initiate* it. Someone else already has."

"It's a sad testimony to the state of the world if that's true, Uncle."

"It's true enough, Charles. As Gibbon said, history is little more than a register of the crimes, follies, and misfortunes of mankind."

Maybe Maurice read ancient history because he was already a cynic. But seeing how little things had changed since the days of Rome could certainly incline someone that way.

"Well," Charles said, "I try to stay positive, just because it feels good. I want to keep it simple: if another hasn't started it, neither will I."

"So who started it with you in regard to this rebellion? What have they done to you? You've made a few million dollars on B-F if you sell now. You're only twenty-three years old. It might be wise to grab your money and run."

"Yeah, I hear you. But no."

"Watch it, m' boy. You're sticking your nose where it don't belong."

Charles could not just ignore what his uncle was saying. What *had* this rebel force done that would justify his trying to thwart them, other than potentially interfere with the amount of money he could make? And that provided insufficient cause to stick his nose, perhaps violently, into somebody else's business. So what if the rebellion was the artifice of some stock promoters committing a fraud? Most rebellions in Africa, no matter how tarted up with rhetoric about freedom and justice, were just contrivances of someone willing to do almost anything to get money or power or both. That was nothing new. What made this one different?

He was aware of this one.

And, Xander planned to join the fray in a big way and needed backup, and Charles couldn't tolerate the idea of deserting him. Getting involved in an African revolution would provide a rare adventure.

And he just might save two young boys from the psychos. That continent was full of young boys in chronic danger of all sorts. Perhaps it was as futile as trying to save a couple of stray dogs from execution at the pound. To the world at large, saving those boys wouldn't make any difference. But it would matter to those two boys.

Stalin is quoted as claiming that if one man dies, it's a tragedy, whereas if a million die, it's just statistics. If he really said it, and believed it, then one of history's great mass murderers might agree that the deaths of Saye and Nyahn—and maybe Xander Winn—would be tragic. Charles doubted that Stalin would care at all.

"Uncle, I need to know how to stick my nose where it doesn't belong. If I can, I'd like to prevent a tragedy."

"Okay. I hear you. I've never been able to change your mind once you've made it up. And I just heard you make up your mind."

"It was that obvious, huh?"

"Yeah, like gears grinding."

"So, what's the answer?"

"I don't have a clue."

"Can your connections in Washington do something?"

"Look, m' boy, I haven't been sitting on my hands. I talked to guys I know, some of them clients, in the CIA, the DIA, the State Department, the Pentagon. The Pentagon isn't doing anything in Gondwana; probably have a couple spec-ops guys there, though, mostly hanging around bars. If anything, they'll like the idea of a war; it justifies their existence. The DIA and CIA don't have a relationship with any of the players there, although that can change; maybe in a couple months the CIA will be cozy with the government and DIA friendly with the rebels, or vice versa. The State Department, even if it cared, has no power to do anything. It's not like they'd have contact with the rebels, and the regime is on their naughty list. At the most they might release an update to their travel advisories, but they're always the last ones to know anything."

That last certainly made sense. One of Charles's best-traveled friends used State Department advisories as a tip-off on where to go, as opposed to not go. They told you where security was on red alert, so a place thought to be dangerous was actually very safe. With tourists acting like scared kitties, State Department advisories provided better guidance than travel agents regarding where to find fantastically discounted high-class lodgings while assuring that no reservation would be needed even at the finest restaurants.

"Our tax dollars at work, Maurice."

"It's the government, kid. You don't like how they screwed you in your businesses. I thought you of all people would appreciate their absence."

Indeed, Charles felt the words from his uncle just like a punch in the nose. Maurice was right. This whole thing was no business whatsoever of the United States government. Why had he even asked? Simple answer: it was easier to evade responsibility than accept it, and pass the buck to Big Brother, who was smarter, larger, and wiser and could kiss everything and make it better. And, more importantly than all the rest, was more powerful and better protected from the consequences. Charles felt a wave of unease travel from his head to his stomach, along with a surge of self-disgust. It was a feeling he hoped to never again experience.

Charles spoke quietly. "Thank you, Maurice. A moment of weakness, and I feel like an idiot."

"It won't be the last time, m' boy."

Charles pursed his lips and slowly closed his eyes. "Yes, it will." He said it to himself with a determination intended to last a lifetime.

His uncle sighed, with the experience of years behind him, and replied, "No. It won't."

*   *   *

Harry glanced over at the legs across the business-class aisle, drawn by the scent delighting his olfactory nerve. He glanced at her face, at her faintly provocative smile, her platinum-blond hair: a ten, even an eleven out of ten. He thought of the old understatement used by so many in his circles: "I wouldn't throw her out of bed on a cold night."

It was not cold; in fact, everything was heating up fast. He should have caught up to Knight in Africa. The best place to commit a successful murder was in the most backward country available. It went without saying that the police and the courts were corrupt, but that mattered only as backup. The first line of defense consisted of their terminal incompetence. As he flew into the US he knew it was going to be substantially harder, not necessarily to kill him, but to make a clean getaway after the fact.

His mind ran through scenarios for killing Knight and Springer. Harry had worked almost as much with knives as guns over the years. Close-in work was his specialty. Avoiding being identified posed the greater challenge. Government computers would document his presence in the US and arrival in San Diego. That he had flown from Gondwana could be tracked if anybody thought to look. The police would uncover Knight's recent trip to Gondwana. Would they think to see who else in town recently came from Gondwana? Probably not. Unless they found papers in Knight's possession that led them to consider a connection, but even then, his name would not be found on any document Knight would have in his possession. Tying him to Knight would not be easy. Someone would have to care very much, or identify him at the scene. No one would care.

But just in case, there had to be no physical proof. No fingerprints, no security-camera images. No GPS tracking in rental cars. He had to kill these men so that the B-F fraud would never be detected. It was pointless to end up with so many millions of dollars just to spend the rest of his days on the run from international police.

So, do not get caught. Do not be stupid. Clean these men with simplicity and intelligence.

He glanced back over at the legs. The woman who owned them appeared asleep, so he kept looking her over. Some nerd of a man, a wealthy geek or a soft corporate type, was sleeping with her. Maybe she was sleeping with him to ensure her own security. Maybe *she* was the wealthy corporate type and was sleeping with a male model. Who knows. Who cared?

If she offered, he would volunteer to show her a good time during his brief stay in San Diego.

Making love and making war. Perhaps the two most primal activities of the human animal. He shut his eyes and focused on sex and killing.

35

The Six *P*'s Vindicated

CHARLES had to unpack the moving boxes eventually, but there was an urgent reason to do so now. Somewhere, useless while packed in those boxes, were a couple of handguns and a couple hundred rounds of ammunition.

Uncle Maurice made jokes about failing to observe the six *P*'s—Proper Planning Prevents Piss Poor Performance—but this was no joke. Charles liked the Boy Scout motto "Be prepared!" but the urgent often triumphed over the important. Those weapons should have been immediately accessible, cleaned, loaded, and in suitable holsters. In his life so far, the US had always seemed a safe place. And his activities had remained normal enough that he could view guns as fun toys or occasional tools, but hardly as imminently needed essentials. That, however, was an invasion of groupthink into his mind, and he recognized it only now. The fact that the US was a generally safe place did not mean that *he* was safe.

Hell, he had even chosen, for a time at least, to live in California, a state so confused that, although they seemed to appreciate the liberty to smoke marijuana, they rejected the liberty to protect their own lives. If the political class had their way, all guns in California would be illegal and the soccer dads and cubicle moms would confidently rely on the police to protect them and keep them safe. It was a state where group-think and doublethink melded into a collective internal contradiction.

Stop beating yourself up, he thought. At least I *kept* the guns.

Southern California: a place where almost everything, from the life-style to people's lawns, from the friendly smiles to starlets' bodies, was perfect and artificial. Or perhaps it seemed perfect *because* it was artifi-cial. But everything needed maintenance; the second law of thermody-namics—entropy—eventually conquered everything. Like, for instance, the whole region's water supply. The Colorado River Aqueduct provided the region with billions of gallons of water, without which it would revert to desert, and its lawns to sand, and its starlets to waitresses in Omaha. The race was on to see which would dry up first: the Colorado River or the California state treasury.

In California the open carry of a gun was illegal and concealed-carry permits hard to obtain. Disregarding the capricious laws did not pres-ent Charles with a moral dilemma, only a practical one. Today it was an easy choice. He would simply carry concealed by packing under a blousy shirt and a sports coat. And he would take extra care to avoid police.

Lavrentiy Beria, chief of the Soviet secret police, during a problem-solving session with Stalin, had famously observed, "Show me the man, and I'll show you the crime." Whether in the USSR or the US, police did what they were told, enforcing the laws that the politicians wrote, quite often reflexively. True, they acted as a line of defense against mis-creants. But, first and foremost, they were a brotherhood. As such, their allegiances were divided. Or at least prioritized. Cops showed loyalty above all to other cops. Next to their employers. And only then, in third place, came those they were supposed to "serve and protect." The gen-eral populace increasingly became the problem, or even the enemy, as numerous new laws criminalized all manner of things.

Cops' attitudes reflected this reality. Since the Vietnam War, more police were ex-military, which aggravated the situation. Many had picked up an assortment of bad habits while immersed in what Gibbon described as a culture of slavery and violence. The police increasingly thought, dressed, and acted like soldiers, as opposed to peace officers. There were still plenty of good cops, of course. But it seemed like more and more of them had an extra Y chromosome.

At this point, however, even good cops couldn't help him. Right now, men backed with billions of dollars wanted him dead.

They could not possibly know where he lived. He hadn't even noti-fied the post office so that they could forward his mail. No one knew his address except Tina, the accountant at Alchemia Resources, for whom he had dutifully filled out his IRS W-4 form.

He considered that for a moment. No, the IRS had no reason to pay him any attention right now. Only B-F wanted him dead, and they had no way of finding him. He kept unpacking the boxes, though, since the only useful gun is the one you have in your hand. He could think of nothing worse, nothing more foolish, than to be the target of a killer and stuck with no way to defend himself.

*   *   *

When Caroline knocked on Xander's door, it was past the 2200 curfew for the Christian-run *Africa Grace*. It was neither the first nor the last time that the curfew got snubbed.

He opened the door, smiling.

"Oh, I'm glad I didn't wake you."

"Caroline, come in. Are you allowed to be here?" He looked both ways down the passageway, making an exaggerated conspiratorial face, imitating the cartoon character Elmer Fudd. He put his fingers to his lips and whispered, "Be vewy qwiet. We ah hunting wabbits."

"For a Dutchman, you know a lot of American," she said, as he ushered her inside, proffering her the small cabin's lone chair.

"As do you, for a Dane."

American culture—the music, the entertainment, the fast food, the language—had permeated the globe. The Dane and the Dutchman could have conversed as easily in German, the second language for both, or even in French, but English had become the world's new lingua franca.

Caroline said, "The captain has been concerned for you. You feel perhaps a little better?"

"Antibiotics are beginning to work."

Caroline shook her head. "You need to rest and to sleep. You're pale and more ill than you'll admit."

Xander shrugged. "I'll admit it. I'm not at my best."

Caroline urged him to sit back on his bed, and asked, "What do you hear from Charles?"

"He's not been answering his phone. I'm going to try calling him again shortly. Would you like to join me?"

"If you don't mind my hearing your secret plotting."

"I think you have earned our trust, young lady. But there *will* be secret plotting."

"I believe you."

Xander could see the lights on the cell tower that rose above the Freeport through his porthole, and its signal penetrated through the hull sufficiently. He dialed Charles's number. Caroline watched Xander's face light up with evident relief. She found her heart pounding as she heard Charles's voice through the speaker.

Xander said, "It's good to hear your voice. Caroline is here with me too."

"Caroline! How are you? Are you well?"

Charles sounded tentative and formal, as if he felt guilty about something. Her heart sank as fearful thoughts floated to the surface of her mind, a bit of jealousy. He was home. What was there? *Who* was there?

She replied, "I'm well, yes. I've been worried about you, though."

"I'm safe in the US. You're the one on a ship that's been invaded and its bridge shot up. *I'm* worried about *you*, Caroline."

That was the source of his guilt, she realized then: he felt like he had deserted in the face of the enemy.

"Charles, did you hear my message earlier?"

"Yes."

"Good. Is our business proceeding?" Xander asked.

"Yes. In some ways, at least. I've dumped my long position, and I'm using the proceeds to buy puts."

"Good for you. I'm doing the same. Shooting the moon, I think you call it?"

"With everything I have. Betting the farm."

"This is the first time I've thought doing such a thing might be wise. This is one of the cleaner plays I've ever seen."

"Maybe not so clean. It got you shot up pretty bad," Charles said.

"Yeah, but I've hurt worse," Xander replied. "And now I am doing great," he added.

Caroline mouthed the word "Liar."

He should have been in the hospital ward, but the doctors let him have a guest cabin to better recuperate after his nearly sleepless night somewhere in the bush. Her defiance of curfew was therefore, in reality, a highly appropriate professional visit. And it was ridiculous anyway. People playing for billions of dollars, trying to kill one another, while she was worried, like a schoolgirl, about an arbitrary curfew.

Xander went on, "I said it's one of the cleanest plays I've seen. But everything has some degree of risk. Put options are a wasting asset. We have to be very right, and our timing perfect. The whole stake can get lost if the share price doesn't actually collapse in time. Even shooting the moon and losing shouldn't cost you the entire game."

"I understand. I'll keep a backstop. But how can this go wrong?"

"Those sound like famous last words. It can definitely go wrong, Charles. Burke could delay their drilling for a few months longer, or who knows, a year? The gold isn't going anywhere, right? During a delay, Burke could decide that the better deal will come from buying out B-F entirely, right now, rather than paying royalties. Or maybe the government of Gondwana will demand that B-F sell entirely to Burke. Then, with B-F stock solidly supported with a valid offer for buyout on the table, the price of the shares will stay high until the stock is no longer traded and is engulfed entirely by Burke. All our puts will expire, worthless, by the time the fraud is finally exposed."

"Right, Xander. Nothing is for sure."

"Unless you're the dealer in three-card monte," Xander replied. "So you keep your backstop, kid. And don't cheat that backstop; you can't be a capitalist if you lose all your capital. Oh, and remember, even without the danger of B-F being bought outright, even with a sure thing and full exposure of the fraud, the market can stay irrational longer than you can stay solvent."

"You already taught me that. And Springer uses the same line."

"Springer is smart. Like me."

With no delay, Charles followed with a question. "Are you smart enough to stop a rebellion, Xander?"

Caroline gasped. One did not lightly discuss rebellion in this region. The first object of the people who controlled the government was to stay in power. That was evident everywhere, of course. But the politicians here genuinely played a blood sport, and a rebellious opposition, and even those sympathetic to them, could expect to spend years in an unappealing prison, assuming they escaped immediate death.

311

Xander looked over at her, with a face at once reassuring and concerned.

"I don't know yet. I counted four other white men, probably mercs working with the man from Zimbabwe whose phone calls I heard."

"Zimbabwe?" Caroline interjected. "The man who escaped from the bridge came from Zimbabwe."

"Could be the same gent, I suppose. But my man was talking to our B-F friend Harry, or someone of the same name. It's Harry who is coming for you, Charles."

Charles didn't reply.

Caroline shook her head in horror.

"Sorry, young lady," Xander said. "If there's any chance that you're going to hitch your wagon in any way to Mr. Knight, there should be no secrets, good, bad, or ugly."

She nodded, but her eyes teared up.

"I'll keep an eye out," Charles said.

"And lie low."

"And I'll lie low," Charles confirmed. There was a sound of metal on metal audible through the phone. "You know what that is, Mr. Winn?"

"I hope that is the action racking a round in a large-caliber semi-automatic pistol."

"It is indeed, sir."

"That's reassuring. But don't get cocky, kid."

Caroline grabbed the phone from Xander. "Charles, why don't you leave wherever you are and go to the mountains where you can't be found?"

"I'm pretty much there already. Nobody knows where I am, Caroline."

"I hope you're right. Keep your head down. I like your head."

There was silence on the phone for a moment, and then Charles came back with a chuckle. "And I like yours, Caroline."

The phone disconnected, and Caroline let her head drop.

"Young lady, there's nothing more you can do. He's a big boy, and he's smart. Let him be the man that he is. And he'll need to let you be the woman that you are. No controls. They're emasculating."

Caroline wiped her eyes. "I do not support castration. That would be entirely against my best interests."

"Good girl. Now, I'm going to send you back to your cabin before you get thrown off this vessel for unchristian behavior."

"What could be more Christian than helping a friend?"

Xander broke a wry smile. "Jesus didn't say anything in the Gospels that should discourage your visit here after 10 p.m., but for some reason churchgoers pay heed to Paul's puritanism, not Jesus's liberal spirit. This is a puritan ship. Like so much else in organized religion, it's more about appearances than reality. Let's appear to obey the rules in reality, shall we?"

"You're crazy, Xander."

"It's a private vessel, funded by private individuals. They have the right to make their own rules, and I have the right to choose whether I want to accept them. But I don't have the right to demand that they change. Right now, it's in my better interest to adhere to archaic rules about women visiting men's rooms after curfew, so I'll see you in the morning, Caroline."

She left with no fear about her position with Charles, nor fear about the sudden loss of her potential salvation, but substantial fear for Charles's safety in this world.

She wasn't there to hear Xander call back to Charles a few minutes later. The topic was stopping a rebellion.

The two men talked for thirty minutes, and came up with about ten questions, but only a couple of answers.

* * *

There is some communication system in the fabric of the cosmos that causes one received cell phone call to induce a second, and that one a third, in a series of overlapping intrusions followed by hours of quiet in which the cell phone is ignored by the universe. No one has discovered the reason for this phenomenon; maybe it's just another way the mind can trick itself. But whatever the truth, Charles's cell phone rang again the moment he got off the call with Xander, and somehow he expected it to.

"Charles, it's Sabina."

He wasn't expecting *her*, though.

"Hello, Sabina." He felt the rush of adrenalin combined with a feeling of dread.

313

She asked, "Are you free? I was hoping we'd get a chance to talk some."

Charles rubbed at his shoulder. "I'm not sure that's wise." He recognized the risk to anyone who might be around him now. A gun rested on his lap.

Her voice indicated that she had taken a different meaning. "I'm not going to seduce you."

That cleared his mental fog, and he came back to the moment. "That's not what I meant, Sabina. I was thinking about something else. I phrased that poorly."

"Not poorly at all, Charles. I still would like to get together with you."

Charles had wondered about this woman since yesterday's meeting. Had she been sufficiently vetted to be in on that sort of conversation? Elliot vouched for her. But he knew Elliot took gambles on people. Was Sabina a safe gamble?

"Okay, Sabina. I'm free for dinner. How about Dick's Last Resort? Right in downtown at 6 p.m.?"

"I'll be there."

He disconnected, and the phone rang again within thirty seconds.

"Mr. Knight?" A man's voice.

"Yes."

The phone disconnected. Cell calls fail in San Diego just as in Africa. Maybe more so.

But this time he wouldn't ignore its implications. He called back. The woman who answered was a librarian at a public library in the city, near the airport, but she had not seen anyone use the phone just recently.

36

A Dinner and a Death

CHARLES spent the late afternoon away from his house, down on the waterfront, sitting on a wall and thinking. He put his .32 caliber pistol in his jacket pocket, its outline obscured by a folded piece of chamois he kept in his gun-cleaning kit. He had his .45 caliber 1911 in his backpack. The difference in power between the two weapons made him chuckle as he thought of the joke about the lady who was talking to a Texas Ranger at a party, and said, "Ranger, I see you're carrying a pistol. Are you expecting trouble?" The Ranger answered, "No, ma'am. If I was expecting trouble, I would have brought my shotgun." Charles wished he had a shotgun, a rifle, and a few grenades.

His guns hardly solved the impending problem, but they made him more comfortable. Armed, he could defend himself against even a stronger and better-trained opponent. Without them, he was a walking victim, the prey of his own fears.

The salt air and the gently lapping waves against the rocks calmed his mind. The soft breeze from San Diego Bay kept him cool. He sat there, undisturbed, confident in his anonymity. He listened to the waves, slowly extinguished his emotion, and brought himself as best as he could toward a state of rationality so as to consider his options.

Option 1: Release all the information he had right now. Let the world know the scam B-F was pulling. But why should the market believe him? Burke would begin drilling in less than two weeks. So the market would wait for that. But Burke would never drill, and therefore no results would ever be released because a rebel force would take over the land before Burke arrived. No, releasing the information now would not have the impact he wanted. The B-F thugs had billions of dollars to protect. Preventing him from testifying in court would become their priority. The rebel army at Banga Sioquelle would destroy any physical proof. So he would be B-F's only threat, the only loose end. Their logical choice would be to quietly kill him. Option 1 had marginal upside and seemed likely to end in death.

Option 2: Make a deal with B-F right now. Extort them. Become part of the fraud. Run a protection racket against them. Cash in. Be Danny to the B-F lemonade stand. Most governments consider blackmail a crime, perhaps because most politicians are easy targets. Charging a fee for not making a miscreant's actions public is perfectly moral—no force or fraud is involved. The fact that a blackmailer could charge a miscreant money might serve as motivation for a segment of the workforce to stay on the lookout for blackmailable offenses. The increased risk of exposure by a roving fee-for-service professional blackmailer would act as a financial disincentive to committing such offenses. There were really many positives to blackmail; the crime had an undeservedly bad reputation. No moral qualms made this choice unappealing. However, blackmailers tended to have short lives and suffer violent deaths. Blackmailing B-F would be a perennially dangerous game, dealing with unsavory, angry, and risky people. Option 2 therefore also seemed likely to end in death.

Option 3. Keep quiet. Wait for the rebellion, play the short gently, with much less opportunity for leverage, and miss out on tens of millions of dollars of opportunity. There would still be a risk of ending up with nothing, for the reasons that Xander had described. But once again, B-F would be trying to eliminate any risk of exposure of their fraud, and they knew he was the risk. Option 3 seemed likely to end up in death too.

Option 4. Prevent the rebellion. It would ensure that Burke would get in and drill. Then let Burke expose the fraud alongside him. His shorts risked his whole $10 million profit. But they could be worth almost $200 million if the stock went all the way to zero. It was incredible. $10 million he would consider to be a huge victory, but $200 million was what it might amount to now. That would be astounding. But in the meantime, he had best not be seen by any mercs from Zimbabwe.

The downside? Getting killed stopping a rebellion would limit his ability to pursue happiness every bit as much as getting killed by B-F's henchmen. Option 4 seemed likely to end up in death, but with a lot more money.

No matter which he chose, the specter of death loomed large. Knowledge can be a very dangerous thing. But he had it. And, unfortunately, the bad guys knew he had it.

The waves kept up their gentle motion, percolating across the rounded rocks below his feet as he weighed these options. There were the other reasons he'd enumerated to stop this bogus rebellion. But trying to stop a rebellion rubbed him the wrong way. Throughout history, the rebels were usually the good guys—or the less bad guys—at least until they got in office. He already felt an urge to balance the scales someday by starting a revolution of his own—something that would be a real monument to personal freedom, not just a power grab. He didn't imagine that such a revolution, perhaps the most radical in world history, would start in Gondwana many years in the future.

Charles made his decision and some necessary phone calls. He passed the next hour in contemplation of how his life had changed in the last two weeks, and how it could change even more in the next few weeks—assuming he lasted that long. The sun reflected off the bay and the shining glass of the tall buildings. The Coronado Bay Bridge dwarfed the sailboats moving on the wind that passed underneath. A skier skimmed along the cool clear water past a silently surfacing submarine. But his mind was elsewhere, in a wet, muddy, smoky, impoverished hellhole.

*   *   *

Dick's Last Resort was cleverly named to draw attention to its outré ambiance. To wear a tie in that establishment was to risk having the bartender cut it off with scissors; the wall decor consisted of hundreds of cut ties, with no regard to what the owners might have paid for them. The waiters balanced mugs of beer on their bulging, exposed bellies as they stood next to customers' tables while the bartender attempted to land three-pointers in their mugs with wads of wet paper towel, often succeeding from as many as forty feet away. There was more beer on the floor than in the glassware, the food was hearty, and the waiters, as well as the local dry cleaners, made out very well.

Charles thought this restaurant might provide a distraction from Sabina's practiced perfection, a perfection that was both enticing and disturbing. She disturbed him not because of his recent preoccupation with Caroline, whose style stood in comfortable contrast to hers, but for other reasons that he could not yet parse.

He arrived twenty minutes early, wearing a sports coat but no tie, illegally armed and watchful. Why would a killer fly to the US absent a clue where he was? How would he find such a clue? His own father could not find him right now. All rationality assured him of his safety. Yet both guns were loaded, with chambered rounds. Paranoia? No. The guns on his person simply acknowledged that his information was incomplete.

She arrived at ten past six in a short, red spaghetti-strap dress with her bright blond hair done up in a manner that defied gravity, engineered at enormous expense by a Hollywood hairdresser. As she glided in, the waiters—chosen for their comedic skills as well as their expertise as servers—followed both their male instincts and the training provided by the management of this unusual restaurant. Almost as one, they dropped every tray of drinks in a rapid-fire series of crashes and gaped at her with their mouths wide open. It was a practiced move for the waiters, and it happened at least once every night: mugs of draft beer are cheap, and customers loved the show. Some of the women took offense at this shtick, but others loved it. The easily offended were free to stay home.

As Sabina passed each waiter, the man would stand up straight, suck in his gut, and make an ogling face, and then start to follow her, falling in line behind the previous waiters; six of them vied for the right to pull out her chair at Charles's table. Two of the waiters cut Charles off as he attempted to do the same, standing arms akimbo, their substantial girths unyielding.

The place was unique and something of an anti-Hooters.

The waiters' action seemed to give permission to all the male customers to gawk at Sabina as well, even while their own dates or female colleagues shook their heads in something between amusement, pity, and, for some, a disgust born of envy. As the waiters bowed, the restaurant broke into applause.

The attention did not seem to affect Sabina much, if at all. She just acknowledged the waiters with a smile—nodded her head like a duchess—and sent them off with a gentle wave.

"I like this place," she said.

"It makes for an entertaining dinner."

She exuded an anthology of pheromones that complemented her Aphroditic appearance. Charles could consider her sensibly when he wasn't near her, but in her presence his rationality faded, his thinking inflamed. He knew it was happening, and also that it was foolish to allow it to happen. But the reptilian base of the brain can overrule the cortex. Even Albert Einstein was a lady's man.

His hormones came close to changing the direction of his entire life. His only protection—and he relied on it entirely—was his scheduled flight out of San Diego soon after dinner.

But for his earlier decision to fly back to Africa that night to join his friend to stop a rebellion, he might have succumbed to the woman's beauty and chemistry. His ensorcellment would not have lasted long, because a bewitching hold can only be maintained over people who lie to themselves to protect their own ego from reality. Charles tried not to lie to anyone, least of all himself. A tendency to self-deception amounts to a tendency toward self-destruction. It is common in people with large egos and low self-esteem. Self-deception transitions into delusion. It was drinking one's own toxic Kool-Aid.

While they talked, Sabina stared at Charles, holding his gaze, making a pretense of being able to read his thoughts or see into his soul. He found it irritating; it was the stare a snake might use on a rabbit.

He had no doubt about her beauty or her effect on all those who observed her. His doubts focused on her character and intentions: those were much more important—and much harder to assess. Through the evening, his body and mind battled against each other, simultaneously frustrated and safe in the knowledge that no consummation was imminent.

* * *

Harry was waiting outside Dick's Last Resort when Knight arrived. Smolderhof's phone call an hour before had been spot on about the time and place where the kid could be found. Smolderhof's sexual prowess had convinced his new special lady to keep tabs on Knight, or so Smolderhof had bragged.

Watch that entrance, wait for darkness, wait for Knight's egress, and then follow and act when the time seemed ripe. No careful planning. Just the simple things. This wasn't a political assassination to be performed for impact. This was a cleaning, to be undertaken with stealth and never mentioned again.

Knight rested secure on his home turf, far away from the dangers of Africa. That was Knight's weakness. Harry waited patiently, leopard-like....

He watched the door, paying closest attention to those leaving. He almost didn't notice her going in, focused as he was on the outbound males. He couldn't sense her scent as he had on the airplane, but those legs, that hair. Unmistakable. A coincidence? That seemed unlikely. This blond woman must be Smolderhof's fling. And what a catch, AAA. Lucky bastard—how had he pulled that off? Impressive.

He thought briefly back to Gondwana and to Laetitia, whose youth and vigor helped him feel young again. He rather liked her. She was innocent. That word could never apply to this blond woman.

Perhaps he could kill Knight, and then come back and find her. An appropriate reward for the evening's activities.

Come on, Knight—he thought—hurry up in there. You have an appointment with your fate.

*　　*　　*

Charles's sixth sense continued to bother him through dinner. She expected to seduce him, of that he had no doubt. She had made her intentions clear with dropped hints and expertly inserted double entendres. She possessed a quick intellect. But as they discussed the world, their current jobs, and their aspirations for the future, her social veneer wore thin. She was a package of superficial beauty wrapped around a chaotic mass of conflicting desires, conventional thoughts, and discordant views, tied up with a bow of covert hostility.

Sabina also possessed an unmatched sexual appeal. Had Charles not already made a psychological commitment to Caroline, he would have been incapable of defying two million years of male evolution and twenty-three years of cultural indoctrination.

He was no Puritan. The thought of doing a quick horizontal tango on the warm hood of her car crossed his mind. But that would remain an unfulfilled sexual fantasy. When he left her in the restaurant alone with nothing more than a platonic handshake, he just let her wonder why. He never told her that he was flying out of the country again.

He walked on the city streets to calm himself, breathing exhaust fumes far less toxic than the pheromones from Sabina. He had an hour before he needed to be back at the airport for his red-eye to New York's JFK, connecting back to Africa. Lindbergh Field sat in the middle of the city, a short way from the restaurant. The landing pattern provided an electrifying view of the planes as they descended between the high rises thirty seconds before touching down on the airstrip. A jet flew overhead. It felt as if he could throw a rock high enough to hit it.

Earlier, he had left his car at the airport with his luggage inside. He would need to leave his guns in the car when he flew off to Africa. Up until the 1970s, anyone could—according to what Uncle Maurice had told Charles—carry a discreetly concealed weapon on a plane. Or, for that matter, just put them openly in the overhead compartment. Apparently, that had even been true on many international flights before World War II. It was a mellower time then.

It took him twenty minutes to reach the fenced portion of the airfield along its extensive circumference. Three times he considered that someone might be following him, but the man far behind who raised his suspicion disappeared down a parallel street as Charles turned a corner.

This was not the best sort of place. It was a haven for the homeless, once known as bums, who were drawn to this city because here they never froze, they never needed air conditioning, and it rarely rained. The area was lit by a disorienting confluence of pink mercury streetlights and deep-blue airport landing lights. At intervals, for perhaps three hundred yards along this fence, the bums made their homes. Sleeping bags served as bedrooms when their owners slept within them, and living rooms when they sat atop them. Grocery carts offered closet space, and the spacious bathroom region was designated by a scent of urine and excrement. Men occasionally made their way to one of the kitchen substitutes across the street, stocked with junk food and the alcohol that helped keep them in these no-rent accommodations, even while it eased the discomfort of being there.

321

As the disagreeable odors wafted past his nose, he distracted himself with thoughts of more appealing aromas. The scent of Caroline was a connection with empathy—and contrasted with Sabina's evocative combination of perfumes. Even as these thoughts wafted through his mind, he scanned the people against the fence, wary, focused, his hand in his pocket. Now and again he glanced back as well. This city was so wealthy, had so many police, so much security. Why was he more wary here than in Africa, where he had been shot at and chased?

The answer lay in the full recognition of where he now stood. Never before had people wanted to kill him. People with unlimited resources and motivation. He would try to thread the eye of a needle that he couldn't see, but the chance of success in that? Nearly none. Constant wariness might be the essence of his life to come.

He turned around again, studying the street. No dark figure back there darted into the shadows. But he was looking in the wrong direction.

"Mr. Knight," an accented voice said.

Charles turned to his right as his heart beat faster and his muscles tightened, ready to leap away or counterattack. His brain and body went on full alert.

The man appeared to be just another in a long series of bums, partially covered by blankets. But this man didn't have the persona of a stumblebum; he was in control and intense. Charles recognized Harry, the Zimbabwean at Banga Sioquelle. Also probably the man who had invaded the *Africa Grace*, and who Smolderhof had sent to erase him.

Harry had found him, despite all the reasons why that was impossible. A tumble of confused thoughts ran through Charles's head as his cognitive mind struggled to take some control back from the parts of his brain that focused on immediate survival. The concept of a betrayal hit first. Xander Winn? Had Xander made a pact with B-F, just as Charles had temporarily considered a pact himself before immediately discarding the idea? If so, it would be the first time in his life that his judgment had so profoundly failed him. And the last time, perhaps. Who else? There were billions of dollars at stake, and billions could buy almost anyone. Elliot Springer? He could not imagine that. But the only man he could be entirely confident in was Uncle Maurice.

"You're not a geologist, are you, Harry?"

"Not exactly. Now, I need you to sit, right there across from me." Harry pointed with his left hand. "Please don't try anything, yah? I am very good with a knife."

There was no knife visible.

Harry said, sternly, "I am sure my knife moves faster than you can run. So sit with me, Mr. Knight."

"I wouldn't think of running... but I choose to stand."

Harry came to his feet rapidly then, his face darkening, his hand emerging from the blanket gripping the handle of an eight-inch blade. He was three inches taller than Charles, who was an inch over six feet himself. He also had fifty pounds more muscle. He was eight feet away. "Sit!" he commanded.

Charles ignored the order. "How did you find me?"

Harry replied, "Smolderhof knew."

"How?"

Harry shook his head. "It doesn't matter." There was no point in giving a dead man an education.

Charles read his tone well. He said, "Well, Harry, it does matter to me. But I don't feel like arguing with you."

"Nor I. However, I have been asked to obtain some information from you."

"What information?"

"The whereabouts of Xander Winn."

Charles did not answer, but was very pleased to hear the question.

"It will be easier if you just tell me now, Mr. Knight." The knife came up in a grip used to thrust and stab at a distance. Stabbing is much more effective than slashing, as the Roman legions well knew. The knife moved from his thigh to just above his hip, positioned, ready.

"I don't plan to tell you," Charles replied.

"Change your plans, Mr. Knight." The knife rose higher, perched to come at, and through, Charles. Harry's face was as sharp as the knife. There was no doubt about the sincerity or intent of the threat.

Charles's face now wore no smile. "Harry, I'm afraid you underestimate my resolve. Goodbye."

It was as simple and cold as that.

When the time comes to shoot, don't talk—shoot.

On later reflection, Charles was astounded at the purity of his resolve at that moment. But it was a straightforward moral calculation: the man had made a credible threat against his life, and he had the right to protect himself.

His hand, already in his sport coat pocket, pulled the trigger of the concealed .32 caliber Beretta Tomcat. Six times, to compensate for the weapon's low power.

Just as Harry poised his knife to stab Charles, the bullets entered his chest. Surprised, unbelieving, reaching his arms out toward Charles slowly, he went to the ground, to his knees first, before falling forward, dead, facedown at Charles's feet.

The spent casings from the small but sufficiently effective bullets collected inside Charles's pocket, obviating the need to scavenge them, denying investigators any fingerprints. Wrapping his hand in the cleaning cloth he had carried in his pocket to conceal the shape of his weapon, he crouched to extract Harry's wallet, passport, and cellphone from his pockets, then stepped over Harry's body and continued walking to the airport.

He looked back several times. A few of the homeless had gathered around Harry; one appeared to be removing his shoes. A car drove by, but there was as yet no other response to the gunshots. He crossed the street to walk along the waterfront. Just before he could cross back again to enter the airport through the car entrance, he pulled out the little Tomcat, quickly field stripped it into several components, thanked it, and hurled the parts as far as he could in different directions out into the bay. Harry's cell phone he skipped across the water, counting four skips before it sank in the darkness.

Hearing the phrase "Thou shalt not kill" repeated as a mantra over a lifetime ingrains a form of Pavlovian response. Though sage general advice, something was likely lost in translation. Translations, especially from a dead language, are an art, not a science. A good case can be made that the Bible does not say "Thou shalt not kill." Rather, perhaps it says "Thou shalt not murder," and that is a different thing altogether. Most dictionaries define murder as the *unjustifiable* killing of another person.

Charles had been justified in this killing. But it was intentional. And he would spend plenty of time in contemplation. Later.

He locked the .45 caliber 1911 in the trunk of his car. He double-checked his sports coat for any contents, ripped off its bullet-torn pocket, and tossed the coat, its pocket, and the spent cartridges into different trash bins outside the airport terminal. Inside, he washed his hands to remove any gunpowder residue. In two hours he was on his way back to Gondwana. On the airplane, he wrapped Harry's passport and wallet in a barf bag, added some orange juice for effect, and dropped them in the trash. It was entirely possible that Harry's body, so far from his home, might never be identified.

When he had destroyed the salting machine, he had killed men, but not by intent. In shooting Harry, he had become a rational and calculating killer.

But he was no murderer.

37

Charles, Meet Johnjohn

"SAYE, what you do!" Nyahn shouted from the sidelines.

Saye scrambled after an older boy who had just stolen the soccer ball from him. The thief was fast, but Saye put everything he had into his pursuit, building so much momentum that he slammed into the ball thief as he tried to cut the corner toward the goal. They both crashed to the ground.

There was no need for a referee. The players all knew the rules and didn't need a black-and-white-stripe-shirted authority. Peer pressure and social opprobrium kept everybody on the right side of the rules, in a microcosmic reflection of society itself. At least most of the time. Saye rolled himself up from the ground and reached down to give the ball thief a hand up.

Nyahn worshipped his older brother, and the thought of life without Saye terrified him. Death came easily, and often unpredictably, in Gondwana, especially to children. He put the thought out of his mind, because he mostly lived in the moment. And, for the moment, Saye was with him, and home was wherever Saye might be. Before their father died, home was a place where his parents loved him. Every time they went somewhere new, Saye climbed in with a bunch of people and made a home and new friends fast. It took Nyahn longer.

This place, however, didn't qualify as home, despite the free soccer uniforms, the sneakers, and the plentiful food.

Shyness afflicted both boys on occasion, but especially Nyahn. Saye had seemed shy with that white man, Charles. White people rarely stopped to talk. Older boys said the white folk were simple, lacking in smarts, and easy to take advantage of. Rich, but so foolish. They should not feel shy around them.

Saye had said only that he saw something in Charles's eyes and noticed something in his manner that gained his respect. He appreciated being treated like an adult, a person of worth. And that made him want to earn that respect and *be* a person of worth. It wasn't shyness, then. Saye gave examples of people worthy of respect. A big man, a healer, a good bossman, an elder, a forgiving shop owner, and anyone who gave Nyahn soup or let them pick lunch off their land—palm or cassava or plantain, sometimes even a breadfruit. Such people had power but also kindness. Saye saw that in Charles. Saye wanted to become such a man himself. And therefore so did Nyahn.

Saye seemed to respect some people here at the camp, like the white bossmen. But fear could mimic respect. They looked like they could never laugh, although they did laugh among themselves. They had their own tents, and they ate apart, and they would probably eat the smaller boys if they were angered. Nyahn followed his brother's lead and steered clear of them.

JohnJohn was a crazy man. Nyahn knew that right away. Perhaps the other boys knew it too, but nobody dared say so. Everyone danced and shouted when JohnJohn appeared before lunch and then usually again before bed. They went wild when JohnJohn got up on stage and spoke to them all so powerfully; they grew more frenzied with every passing minute and every word that emerged from his red face. He energized the crowd. They all settled down only after JohnJohn dismissed them to eat or sleep. Only then did each man and boy revert to being an individual rather than just part of the unthinking mob. They weren't riled up right now; they weren't crazy most of the time. But they would predictably go wild as soon as JohnJohn emerged to speak to them. Those times scared Nyahn, because then it seemed bad things could happen.

The day began with a formation, organized into squads of ten, platoons of thirty, and companies of ninety, each unit led by some of the older boys and men, complemented by the teenagers. They were taught to drill and follow orders for two hours. Some units played war in the bush, while others fell to soccer until the noon bell rang. They then all came running from wherever they were around the valley, gathering at the stage where JohnJohn would soon appear. JohnJohn spoke for about an hour, and then they would eat.

Nyahn's belly wanted food, and he wished JohnJohn would just skip the speech. It was like going to the mission, where he had to listen to the minister go on for an age before he could eat.

JohnJohn was just as crazy today as ever with his red eyes, sweating face, and screaming mouth. Everyone tried to imitate him. Even Saye jumped up and down and shouted, but when Nyahn caught his eye, Saye winked, so he knew he was okay, just playing along with all the craziness.

Saye did not respect JohnJohn, even though he was certainly a Big Man. But he feared him even more than the white men who taught them how to drill and play war. JohnJohn was unpredictable. He seemed capable of anything, and he told them that he would make them all men of respect, power, and wealth. They just must follow his plan. And they would be punished both here and in the world to come if they failed to do so.

At lunch Nyahn filled his stomach with fufu, his favorite, with pepper sauce today, fresh and hot, and fruit juice, thinned by lots of water but still sweet. A boy he just met shared some palm nuts, and they quietly chewed on them together.

Then came more training. More mud to crawl through, barbed wires to avoid. After, he sat with the other boys, and each took a turn at taking the gun apart and putting it back together again. It was called "field stripping," but he did not know why he did it. They put the magazine that held the bullets in and out and in and out over and over again. Loading the bullets into the magazine hurt his thumb. Tomorrow he would shoot it; the thought scared him.

But Saye was there with him, always.

*   *   *

Xander and TJ met Charles outside the airport terminal east of Adamstown as he walked out into the steaming heat.

"It's a damn zoo in the baggage claim."

Charles was gripped by a delayed numbness borne of the shock of what had happened in San Diego. It was a different numbness than he had experienced following his mother's death, which had been an

328

emptiness followed by a debilitating sense of loss and grief. He'd thought more about the men inadvertently killed at Gbarngeda when he opened the machine door—men he had never met but who had been shooting at him, probably for the second time. It wasn't a good feeling to kill a man.

There is a reason that almost all religious and philosophical traditions counseled against taking life. Charles never wanted to initiate violence against another person. And he hadn't, until now, dealt with the consequences of defending himself with deadly force. A lifetime of watching movies had trivialized killing in society. War movies glorified it, and video games awarded points for it. Little was spoken of the damage caused to good people who killed. He felt no glory whatsoever, no "tough guy" self-congratulatory post-adrenalin high. He wondered whether, under other circumstances, he might have liked Harry.

He asked himself disturbing questions about who initiated all this violence in his life right now. After all, he had snuck onto B-F's hidden land in Gbarngeda. It wasn't his land, except for his passive, limited-liability, fractional ownership. The B-F guards had a right to defend against his intrusion into their property. Charles had at least provoked, if not initiated, the violence.

But then, it was B-F that had initiated the *fraud*. And Charles had a right to respond to fraud.

B-F was the initiator of all this hell.

"You should shower." TJ yanked Charles out of his self-absorption. Whereas the perspiration of an African man smelled mildly bitter and sweet, the sweat of a white man smelled—to the senses of a nearby African—like curdled milk. Charles was no bouquet of flowers.

"Twenty-seven hours of accumulated sweat so far.... Hey, I thought us rich guys were supposed to always be in the lap of luxury?"

Xander said, "Well, maybe when the rain starts, you can use it for a shower."

"As long as I wash up before I see Caroline...."

TJ said, "Yes, your friend Caroline can do without seeing you like this," and patted Charles on the back. "Besides, you don't want to see her quite yet. Do not put her in danger, my friend."

Xander said, "Speaking of danger, let's get out of here. We have lots to talk about, and not much time."

TJ waved off a small Gondwanan man who offered to help with Charles's suitcase, and they moved to his waiting Land Cruiser.

Charles said, "I doubt anyone is expecting me to return to Gondwana."

"Yes, I think that most everyone would consider it insane."

"The United States isn't any safer for me."

Xander said, "Probably not. You're not a safe person to be around right now."

TJ drove out of the parking lot along with the small trail of other vehicles there to meet the day's sole international flight.

"Charles, TJ doesn't think that we can stop this rebellion."

TJ looked back over his shoulder at Charles while he drove. "Yes, Charles. The military here still has no weapons. The UN hasn't let it re-arm yet. Only the SPU has any guns, and they don't have many. And now the UN has mostly left, leaving only a handful of Pakistanis and Bangladeshis in blue hats."

Charles said, "The UN won't respond fast enough. It's a bureaucratic nightmare."

TJ nodded. "And I have good friends in the SPU; the SPU has made good friends with B-F Explorations."

"Are you saying the police are not trustworthy?" It wasn't really a question....

"They wouldn't be able to do anything even if they were trustworthy," TJ replied. "But given that they aren't, with all of B-F's friendly money around, I don't recommend going near them. It might end up with you unpleasantly detained."

Charles shook his head. "I haven't found any other way through this B-F hell. I may or may not be richer when this is over, but I'll certainly be dead if we don't stop the rebellion."

TJ said, "They would want you dead too, Xander, if you had not dressed up like an old geezer and thrown them off."

"Like I said, it's best to be underestimated."

Charles said, "I took that lesson to heart yesterday."

"Yes? How is that?"

"Perhaps I'll tell you someday." Unless there was a compelling reason, it didn't make a lot of sense to reveal what had happened to anybody. Some ambitious prosecutor could readily pervert it from self-defense into a capital crime. Charles had gained an understanding of why soldiers rarely went into detail about what they did in combat. "By the way, they *are* looking for you too, Xander."

Xander nodded as TJ turned the car around a particularly sharp turn that led onto the long, dark, straight road to Adamstown

"So, what new information do you have? You have a plan?" Charles asked Xander, hopefully.

"I've still got almost nothing, kid. Stopping a rampage by a couple of thousand heavily armed, brainwashed teenagers isn't an everyday problem."

"Well," Charles said, "we need more information. And I do have an idea that might just allow us to pull this off. It's going to involve you both."

Xander turned his head around to look at Charles. "My guess is that your idea is insane and impossible."

"It's good to be underestimated."

*　　*　　*

If things worked out for Knight and he played B-F's fraud just right, he would end up very rich. Sabina's effort to hedge her bet with him had not gone as she expected. First, Knight had blown her off after their dinner, a dinner that she thought had gone quite well. And he wasn't playing the role of an anachronistic gentleman. It was as though he did not want her. And then he disappeared altogether. No sign of him, and no response on his cell phone for over a day now. No man had ever treated her in that manner. This was clearly Knight's fault. Just proving himself the lowlife cad that she had figured him to be when she first started researching him.

In contrast, Smolderhof behaved predictably, and perfectly, having already called her six times today. She answered only the first. Let him hang. Sink the hook deeper into his droopy gills.

She spent some hours formulating her attack on Knight, assisted by access to his office and his files. It shouldn't be hard to accomplish, using his naive colleagues at Alchemia.

From an IRS perspective, she had found no evidence of tax evasion. But she knew Knight would never willingly pay over half his profits in taxes. She would look harder. From an SEC perspective, she had him dead to rights. He planned to profit from inside information regarding B-F. She had contacted her old boss back at the SEC. The woman claimed interest while choking back a yawn. "Very good, Sabina. But, as you know, we're overloaded with cases here. Let me know when the crime has actually been committed, when you have something that will result in a conviction. Something big enough to be worth our time."

Knight had worked with Springer to chart out exactly which put options to buy on B-F's stock. Their cost and the profit potentials varied tremendously, based on their strike prices and expiration dates. Their plan of execution lay with Springer. As to where Charles was, Springer only said that Charles would "be away for a while." Springer gave her a list of Charles's desired puts, with instructions to work with the trading team to execute them.

The phone rang again. Smolderhof. Okay, she would answer it. Her sugar daddy to-be was almost a billionaire, after all.

"Hi, Dan!" she said, with her well-practiced, most excited voice.

"Sabina. Where have you been?"

"Very busy. But not too busy for you!"

"Have you seen Springer today?"

"Of course." She dropped her voice. "He has the next office over."

There was a pause before he asked, "How about Knight?"

"I told you I would call you if I ran into him again. He seems to be off the radar entirely."

"Maybe that's good."

"Good? Not to know where he is?" After all the appreciation the man had shown her when she told him where Knight was, where he lived, where he worked, and what restaurant he would be dining at, she would expect him to be concerned if Knight went missing again.

But then a thought struck her. "Dan, *what* have you done?" Maybe Knight was dead.

"Done? Nothing, sweetheart." He said it like a Chicago gangster, an imitation of James Cagney from an old movie. "Nothing. But I sure as hell want to do something."

She picked up on his innuendo—and his effort to change the subject. She said, with a playful lilt, "I was just with you less than forty-eight hours ago. Wasn't that sufficient to last you for a while?"

"Just an appetizer, Sabina. I need more, much more than that."

332

"Well, what are your plans?"

"Me? Beyond just with your body? Well, I have to make sure I get every one of my billion dollars, that's all."

*　*　*

Smolderhof called Harry's cell phone immediately after hanging up with Sabina. Once again there was no answer. Springer was supposed to be dead, preferably alongside Knight. Springer wasn't dead, Knight was missing, and Harry was incommunicado.

It would be hours before he could expect to get in touch with Rupert at his nightly moment of connectivity on top of that giant rock above the camp in Guinea. Perhaps Rupert had heard from his brother. If not, then the situation was probably bad and heading for worse.

*　*　*

In the capital, TJ, Xander, and Charles swung by the Zamba Point Hotel so Charles could shower—which, at this point, he insisted upon—and pick up his laptop computer. The computer was gone and Imir, the manager, had been hospitalized after being assaulted. The staff were shocked by the attack. Gondwana had become a relatively peaceful place after the horror of the wars.

Perhaps the wars had purged most of the violence from the culture for a generation. Perhaps people who had seen and heard and done terrible things never wanted to see or hear or do them again. Perhaps the worst of the perpetrators had been killed, or committed suicide, to the benefit of the gene pool. Perhaps, with the passage of time, some of the people who'd done those things were starting to feel remorse. But most of the people who had committed heinous crimes during the wars were still alive and in Gondwana. And they looked like everybody else.

Most people in Gondwana now shunned any thought of war. But the younger men, children during the bloody conflicts, would over time forget their hatred of war, and some would once again find hatred for others. Someday war would be very possible here. The wrong sort of leader would rise and recognize mass violence as the most effective way to obtain control of the government, the fountainhead of wealth and power.

So war would return, sooner or later.

TJ could not go with them on this trip back up to Guinea. He had another mission, so Xander and Charles set out alone. The sun worked its way down to the horizon as they bounced for hours along the road. Xander winced as he so frequently did. Inadequate rest, sporadic medical care, and constant reinvasion of his open wound by various pathogenic denizens of the bush all took their toll.

"The turnoff to the camp road is just ahead," Xander told Charles. "From there, we walk."

After more than an hour of grimy, uncomfortable hiking along Xander's rough-hewn path parallel to the road and through the swamps, Charles found himself lying at the top of the rock-capped hill Xander had described, looking out over the camp about a quarter mile below, prying off leeches. In the otherwise dark night, lights illuminated a stage in the center of the camp. Men and boys stood mostly by their tents. The sounds of laughter echoed out of the small valley, above the hum of generators. Xander pointed out a round tent behind the stage.

"That's where the mercs live."

"How many?"

"Five."

"How many men do you figure overall?"

"At least two thousand."

"But not all armed?"

"I see them handing guns around among them, but few. I'll guess a couple of hundred AKs, and not too much ammo."

"I wish Saye and Nyahn weren't here."

Hundreds of boys, with stories like theirs, mingled in the mob below them. Like Saye and Nyahn, each was worth caring about as an individual, but as part of the mob they lost that essential nature—transformed into the human equivalent of a couple of grains of rice in an afternoon's lunch. The collective hive of humanity was not humanity at all; that was a misnomer. Once they lost themselves to the hive or immersed themselves in the collective, it became the purest sort of inhumanity. The people became a pack, a herd, a swarm, a mob.

"Maybe they aren't here anymore; maybe they deserted."

That was unlikely. Deserters from such a setting would be hunted down; a successful desertion destroys unit cohesion.

An hour later the loudspeakers adjacent to the stage squawked, and the men and boys started moving to the center of the camp. Charles and Xander turned their binoculars to the stage. After all had gathered, a muscular African jumped onto the platform; he leapt across the stage and with a final bound landed behind a podium. The crowd started chanting "JohnJohn" over and over when he appeared, and they burst into cheers when he almost flew through the air.

JohnJohn then strode back and forth across the stage, like a British naval commander on the quarterdeck, or a Bible Belt preacher at a revival. The men cheered as if he were a famous soccer star. When he wished to speak, he put his hands up above his head, palms out, and lowered them. The noise immediately disappeared. Only the hum of the generators and the occasional squeal of a monkey would be heard for the next two minutes. The gathered mob of men stood mesmerized.

JohnJohn took the microphone from the podium and spoke gently, quietly into it. The still and humid air carried the sounds clearly, all the way up the hill. Tenderly, almost in a whisper, in the English of Gondwana, he said, "Are you with me, my men." It was not a question. Enthusiasm was the only acceptable response.

That response was overwhelming, immediate, and, to Charles—who was averse to groups larger than might gather around a dinner table—both unexpected and incomprehensible. The silence was gone, replaced with the roar made by boy-men jumping in the air, as if one, landing en masse with a thunder that echoed in the valley, while shouting and hollering in a frenzy. Some waved AK-47s above their heads. This lasted until the man on stage lifted his hands again, his palms out, lowering them. His motion was met with immediate, obedient silence.

He held the microphone out to the crowd. "Let me hear you!" he commanded. Another roar, more guns above their heads. Now, with just one hand, he quieted them.

"Again!" The command, the roar of voices, and then the abrupt absence of noise with just a flicker of one hand from their leader.

"Are you well fed?" Cries of affirmation followed; the chicken and pork that had supplemented the usual rice gave the boys and men extra enthusiasm. There was no hunger here.

"Are you well paid?" Wild affirmation ensued.

Charles could not know the financials of this operation, but he could speculate. The equivalent of $100 per month per man wasn't a fortune even by local standards, but would be enough for these men, few of whom otherwise would have any income at all. It was more money, every month, than they'd ever seen at one time in their entire lives. So, perhaps B-F was spending $200,000 a month for the soldiers, maybe another $100,000 for the mercs plus some company shares, and maybe another $100,000 for food, fuel, JohnJohn, and the odd soccer ball. It was a bargain price for what they were trying to achieve. The ordinary shareholders of B-F would hardly approve of such expenses at an annual general meeting, but then a certain degree of latitude must be accorded the management of a five-billion-dollar company.

"Are you hungry for righteousness?" JohnJohn cried out to his followers with an English more educated than most.

JohnJohn focused on a simple but credible ideology.

"Gondwana is a rich land. Why then are you poor?" he asked, calmly. "Why all the white men who come here go 'way rich? Do they take 'way wealth from our country? Why do Big Men in Adamstown give them *our* riches? Why do the Big Men—the president and his dogs of ministers—why they take our riches for themselves? It is time for *you* to be the Big Men!"

In essence, it was the same line that educated European adults had bought into for well over a hundred years. It was a very easy sale to poor, ignorant African youth.

"Men, my men...." With a sincerity that made each of them feel like his best friend, JohnJohn spoke into the quiet that was guaranteed by the palm of his hand. His accent shifted to one akin to the boys in front of him. "We wait da time da we once again live at home, rule only by ourselfs. We will be Gong, our own nation!" The cheers rose higher. "Kpelle, Mandigo, Mano, all of us togetha!" he shouted above the crowd. "We will take da mines back from da Chinese, from da Canadians, from da corrupt government!" The crowd roared and his accent returned to that of an educated man. "We will be swimming in gold, rolling in iron, living as real men, no longer under anyone's whip. No longer slaves!" He smiled then and added conspiratorially (although through a microphone to thousands), "Da women will be lovin' you, plenty of dem."

336

How so much noise could emanate from any-size gathering of humans challenged the laws of acoustics. Here in the open air, even hundreds of yards away, it was so loud as to be nearly intolerable.

Charles observed, at once astounded, intrigued, fascinated, and appalled. He knew plenty of historical examples of one man controlling many just with words, but he'd never witnessed it in person. Control was obtained by means of psychology. Money, prestige, and the threat of physical force were all elements, of course. But what the Chinese termed chi—the life force—trumped all else. The ability to express it verbally came to some as a rare and innate gift, in much the same way that a select few developed into top athletes or world-class physicists. Even though almost always put to a destructive use, demagoguery itself was morally ambivalent, like the arts of seducing a woman, or gun fighting, or litigation. All could be put to good use or bad. The person possessing the skill made the choices. Charles studied every intonation, every movement the man called JohnJohn made. He watched a master at work. He would learn from this moment—and remember.

JohnJohn's hands again went up, and the men instantly obeyed with silence. The hands stayed up as he said, in a low voice, "Gong County has the best university in the country. The education will be ours. Shh now. Shh. For free. Shh now. Shh."

"Gong has the best people in the country. Shh now, shh." The hands stayed up, the men stayed quiet.

"Gong men have the most beautiful wives! Shh now, shh." The implicit promise was not lost on the boys.

"Gong has the biggest gold mine in the world!" His hands came down as he shouted this, and the men exploded, jumping up and down, guns waving. He let the energy grow even further before shouting through the loudspeakers. "And God is wid us! God is wid us, we men from Gong County. We have de God wid us."

The men in the periphery, who could move freely, started dancing, bringing their knees up and down, hands waving in the air, heads tossed back, and shouting at the sky, "God wid us! God wid us! God wid us!" The man on stage watched, smiling, nodding, stirring the uproar while bowing to one side of the stage or the other, holding his arms wide as if embracing his entire army.

JohnJohn's hands came up, and the tumult subsided in moments. "You ask me when we do this thing. We do this thing soon. The moon she not go small before we see this. I will tell you when de time come, but know dis. De time come soon and when it come you men be heroes, every one, wealthy and powerful, and with many women, so many women, one and all." And then in a voice inconceivably deep, he shouted, "And proud to be from Gong County!"

After that, it took ten minutes for the noise to die down. The man left the stage to the cheers and gesticulations of his followers, crying "JohnJohn" until the name itself defined them. He would give them everything they could want, clothed in the mantle of patriotism—a historically proven formula for scoundrels to gain and keep power. Slowly men and boys started filtering out of the group, back to their tents, all dancing more than walking now, energized, ready to go at the man's command.

Charles sat amazed and disgusted. The man had the verbal power of a Hitler, the spiritual certainty of a megachurch evangelist, and the body of a heavyweight champion. He dominated them psychologically, emotionally, physically, and intellectually.

"Charisma and criminal insanity," Charles whispered.

Xander replied, "All these rebel leader types share that. If he were transplanted to California he'd be top dog in a biker gang. Color him white, put him in Alabama and he'll be the top Kleagle, or whatever, of the Klan. Give him a suit, put him in Illinois, and he would be elected governor."

"I've got what's likely a stupid question. How violent is he?"

"He's capable of almost anything. Sure, he's a stone killer. Look at Idi Amin, Jean-Bédel Bokassa, and Charles Taylor. They might smile at you one minute, and the next chop off your limbs and put them in a freezer. It intimidates their followers, and it impresses them too, to think their leader is a demigod, not limited by things that constrain ordinary humans. They have to believe their leader is capable of absolutely anything. JohnJohn is a textbook psychopath—not to be trusted, ever, in any way."

Charles absorbed Xander's words. Whether it was because of his innate character, his lemonade-stand experience during his formative years, or what had happened since he came to Africa, Charles was developing profound disgust—and lack of toleration—for criminal personalities. It would last for the rest of his life.

They watched for another hour as the camp activities tapered off. Then Xander pointed down at the path that came up through the soccer fields. "Look there. That is the leader of the mercenaries. His name is Rupert Pell."

"It looks like Rupert is coming our way."

"Come back down here with me." Xander led him to his vegetation-covered crevice under the back face of the rock. "Be quiet now. He's coming to use his cell phone. This is better than having the NSA record his calls. Wait for it. It's a spy's wet dream."

They waited, and at 11 p.m. Rupert's cell phone rang, clearly audible from above them.

"Harry?... What? Oh, Smolderhof. I was expecting my brother.... No.... Not last night nor the night before.... Yes, it's not uncommon to miss several nights in a row.... I'm not worried. Harry can take care of himself."

Not always, thought Charles.

Rupert's voice came down from above after a minute-long pause. "JohnJohn wants all the guns and the ammunition. He wants them *before* he marches his men south. It's dangerous enough for us here already.... This bastard Flomo is always up JohnJohn's ass. Needs killing.... These hyped-up kids still have some ammunition left here, unfortunately.... What?... Yes, a million rounds at Banga Sioquelle, or it might still be in Gbarngeda. Hell, I don't know. Depends on if Harry moved it yet.... Yes, I know.... He damn well better have. I'll contact you when I hear from him. He should call tonight.... Eight more days. I know. I will try to delay it that long, but it's not easy. JohnJohn is not a patient man.... I am earning every bit of my money, and don't forget it.... Well, yeah, have a safe trip back. Good night."

The phone call was over, but every few minutes an impatient obscenity interrupted the silence. The curses grew louder, and despite the swearing, Rupert received no other calls. The hoped-for contact from his brother Harry would never come.

They heard him slide down the far rock face. Soon after, Xander slipped around the rock to watch the man walk away, already far down the path toward the camp.

"They don't have much ammunition here," Charles said to Xander.

"But they have some. And they'll get more. If they moved those containers from Gbarngeda up to Banga Sioquelle, then their little ammunition dump is going to be less than thirty miles away by road."

"Then they're going to move down to Banga Sioquelle and meet up with their guns and ammo there. And it sounds as if our friend Rupert is tasked with keeping JohnJohn waiting for eight more days. I guess that means that Burke International Mining plans on being on the B-F site in little more than a week. The guy is walking a tightrope. I don't envy the job of delaying JohnJohn."

Xander replied, "Not one bit. I expect JohnJohn may well kill all the mercs, just to show his men who's boss."

"And JohnJohn sure looks like the boss. And the buck stops at the boss."

Xander shook his head. "No, Charles. The buck stops at us."

38

A Secret between Old Friends

THEY collected intel in Guinea for most of two days, living off supplies in their backpacks, Xander struggling ever more with his wound. They perched, hidden, near the massive boulder that sat on its partly eroded base. They observed the little army in their daily exertions: calisthenics, running, firing weapons, field stripping them, crawling in the mud, and, of course, playing soccer. Its members were happiest playing soccer. They smiled and laughed and hugged on those fields. Twice each day, noon and night, JohnJohn gave his men a pep talk, feverishly stoking their emotions. Then, after an hour or two, the hype settled, and the young men who would be savage killers next week were once again just boys playing soccer.

Now and again Charles could pick out Saye and Nyahn from among the throngs on and around the soccer fields. The boys also spent time in the training areas, heading off in the woods to fire guns, and working in small groups on camp chores. There was no way to make contact with them. And, if he did, who was to say the boys hadn't become JohnJohn loyalists who would turn him in?

They watched JohnJohn move around the camp. He was treated with awe, as a godlike figure. Or at least as a father figure, something that many—perhaps most—of the young men lacked, if only because of the wars. He in turn patted them on their backs, sat down with them, laughed with them, and made each one feel, for that moment, that he was the most important person in the world. Occasionally he would suddenly become stern, shouting loud enough to be heard on the hill, voice becoming pitched, stamping his feet, pushing someone to the ground. But those episodes were not common. Whether or not JohnJohn had ever read Machiavelli, he clearly understood his principle that, although it was ideal to be loved, it was paramount to be feared. He would be an effective warlord.

It was just before midnight, and, according to what they could determine from the swearing that floated down from the top of the rock, it had been too many nights in a row that the merc named Rupert had failed to receive his hoped-for call from his brother, Harry.

The heat, the humidity, and the dirt made an unholy alliance with the insects. Xander's pain increased. In the faint light, Charles caught a glimpse of the open and pustulant wound as Xander changed a dressing. He shook his head.

Anticipating that Xander wouldn't want his wound to be the cause of scrubbing the mission, he said, "We need supplies."

"Frankly, I wouldn't mind Caroline ministering to me again," Xander said. He was not going to argue.

"Nor I. We have a plan. Why don't we bug out of this popsicle stand?" He glanced at Xander with a smile.

"You've seen enough?"

Charles nodded. "I think so."

"But we're not ready. We're not done here."

"You're done here, for now. TJ and I will come back and finish the preparations, Xander. But let's get you back to the ship. You have to heal. We're going to need you in fully functioning condition within a week, right?"

Xander twisted and looked down at his injured buttock. "I'll do what I can. But the best I may be able to offer is pretty, shall I say, half-assed."

*　　*　　*

It was a busy day on the *Africa Grace*. There were surgeries scheduled, personnel changing, and new volunteers flying in from Europe. But Caroline left all the activity and flew into Charles's arms when he unexpectedly arrived at lunchtime.

Then she pulled back almost as fast as she had come toward him. "God, you're a mess!" She squeezed up her face. "A stinky mess."

"I'll clean up, all right, but Xander needs some attention."

"We'll fix up Xander again. He keeps working against all we do. Now to the guest cabin you go. I will be waiting right here."

"You better be. I don't have much time."

"Don't you sneak off this ship."

"Trust me, I'd rather be on this ship than anywhere else I can think of."

Caroline smiled, but her face darkened for a moment in thought. Then she smiled again. "I like your short hair, Charles." She reached up and ran her hand along the increasing shadow.

"What about mine?" Xander asked from behind her.

"Yours too." She turned and rubbed his scalp, as if he were a middle-aged puppy. "I am so glad to see you both safe."

Four hours later Charles was on his way to physical and psychological renewal. His clothes were in the laundry while Caroline examined the rapidly mending wound on his shoulder by placing her cheek on it as they lay together in her cabin. They had broken the ship's rules.

"Look at the bright side. At least it isn't after curfew," he quipped.

"It is good to know that you abide by *some* of the rules," she replied.

Xander knocked. "Sorry to bother you kids," he said through the door, "but TJ is here."

Charles smiled warmly at Caroline. She was real and natural and competent, and entirely more desirable than the artificial, plastic creature in San Diego. He came out of the cabin a minute later, dressed in scrubs, to find Xander grinning suggestively.

Charles caught the smile and said, "None of your business."

"Righto." Xander handed him a heavy duffel. "Food, fluid, and other necessities," he offered, as Charles tossed it up on his shoulder. "Get properly dressed. TJ's waiting. The fun's about to begin."

"Won't be more fun than I've just had, but I'm always up for excitement."

They found TJ on the pier, in the driver's seat of a gigantic flatbed truck loaded with a container. With wheels five feet high, the vehicle was meant to travel slowly over horrible roads with heavy payloads. An identical truck idled immediately behind it. High up on top of the second truck's cargo container sat five men enjoying what appeared to be a picnic. One of them waved and then slid off the top of the container like a gymnast, bounded off the cab's roof, and slipped feet first through the window into the driver's seat. The maneuver was so smoothly accomplished that the truck's engine revved even before the man had his head fully inside.

Shovels and a pick ax occupied the passenger's seat of TJ's truck. TJ pushed them into the space behind the seat, reached down to grab Charles's hand, and with a grunt pulled him up into the giant truck's high cabin. He pointed backward toward the other truck and said, "Those men are my friends. All of them Djenne men, from my hometown, Djennetown."

Charles nodded in appreciation. Rationally, he now conducted an orchestra, and many would have to play their various roles. But physically, he felt on edge, as if he were approaching the exit point for a parachute jump. He had to rely on the people who packed his chute, and their failure would mean his death.

Xander looked up and said, "You two are on your own for a while. I need to stay off my ass, plus I need to pick up all those items we talked about. And I need to make a phone call. Stay safe!" He turned to walk up the gangway.

Charles called back. "Take it easy while you can! Remind Caroline to keep the lights on for me."

And with a wave they were off, two huge lumbering diesel trucks with a gang of men sitting atop. With a top speed of thirty miles an hour, they had a long way to go. TJ and Charles had a lot of time to get to know each other better.

*　*　*

"It's declined just a bit, now at $270, down from its peak at $290." Maurice Templeton recited the data. "Sellers are coming into the market, and there's a small but growing number of short positions. But I expect most of the shorts are the guys at Alchemia Resources—plus ours, of course. At some point, trend-following traders are going to pile in."

"Yeah, and once the B-F people are through selling their shares, you can bet they're going to join us on the short side through their offshore companies," Xander said, holding the phone near a porthole where he would have a signal. "That selling is what's holding the share price down."

Maurice added, "That makes sense. Otherwise the price should have gone up a ton today. They are hyping this like crazy, emptying the company's treasury on publicity. Recasting old data and old stories in a new light to suck in new buyers. The only actually new news is that they just released an internal scoping study, based on the cores and the structural geology. It's pegging your place there at *300 million ounces*, far more than they've ever before suggested. With every gram of it profitably extractable."

Xander shook his head. "How much crap can get incorporated into a scoping study! I'm sure Smolderhof saved this study for exactly this moment to keep the price at least a bit stable as he sells. I wouldn't be surprised if he puts out an entirely forged feasibility study in a couple of days that looks so impressive that he draws in major institutional buyers with it. The man is bold. It's *incredible*, and I use that word in its literal sense. When this thing comes unglued it's going to kill the mining-exploration sector for a decade." He added, "Any luck with the UN?"

Maurice responded with a sigh. "Not a peep. It has to work its way up the channels. It will be six months, maybe six years, before it even gets in front of the right committee. Xander, you know you're not going to get any help from those people in this. Nothing past those satellite images that I scrounged up for you.

"I didn't expect much."

"My nephew's naive hope the UN would help is proof that he's still got a lot to learn. Don't forget that, Xander: Charles is sharp, but young."

Xander replied, "I won't, my friend. He reminds me of us thirty years ago. I like that he's an optimist. He looks at all the angles and alternatives. He's trying to live in the world as it is, but he doesn't discount that the world could actually transform itself into what he believes it *could be*. You were right about the kid, Maurice."

"Of course. He's my nephew, after all. He's as close to a son as I have."

Xander didn't respond for several seconds. "I know, Maurice." He took a breath and added, "I can't see you mating and reproducing at this point."

Maurice chuckled. "Why should I? I've already got to deal with the 50 percent stake the government seems to think they have in me. I don't need another fifty-fifty partner. That would only leave me with 25 percent of myself."

"You might as well incorporate and give away shares of yourself for free."

"Sounds like a great deal—for somebody else."

"It's said that if in marriage you give away 50 percent of yourself, at least you are getting 50 percent of somebody else in return."

"Let them say that. To me it sounds like a mutual slavery pact. Anyway, Charles sure took to you fast. That's no surprise. He's protective of you too, you know. He's not even mentioned your name to me. Not even to me! That's amazing. He just occasionally slips and says something like '*we* found something' instead of '*I* found something.' Other than that, he keeps you a secret."

"And I'm grateful for that, Maurice. He's a good kid and he's helping make me a fortune."

"Me too."

Xander added, "Thanks for hooking us up."

"Who could be more trustworthy than you? I told you it would be worth traveling to that hellhole to meet up with him. Now for God's sakes don't let that boy get killed. He's got an important life ahead. You know I can't get out in the world. I need the vicarious entertainment of watching him from my ringside seat."

For the moment, Xander could do little to prevent Charles, or even himself, from getting killed.

39

Sabina Comes Into Her Own

SABINA did math as the bubbling jets of the hotel's poolside hot tub massaged her body. She calculated money and opportunity. Of the many positive outcomes that lay ahead for her, which would be the *absolute* best? It was a pleasure to choose between options that could best be described as "spectacular" and "extraordinary." Which word implied the better choice? Springer liked to define words. Perhaps she'd have a chance to quiz him on that while the US Marshals handcuffed him.

Through Springer, she knew Knight was alive. And she assumed he was in Africa again. By her calculations, if the B-F stock price collapsed to near zero, Knight's put options could be worth about $200 million. Knight must already be in a fool's paradise, anticipating all the friends, luxuries, and happiness that such wealth would bring him.

Either Knight wasn't as infatuated with her as he should be, or he simply didn't trust her. It was hard for her to contemplate that he would not be interested in her, at least sexually, and possibly even romantically. That just didn't compute. Even if he were gay, she should have succeeded! So it must have been his plans to fly to Africa that prevented him from insisting they extend their evening through the night and into the morning. At least that made a little sense to her bruised self-image.

If he became very wealthy, many women, even some of her own caliber, would target him. The question was how best to play her cards. Should she try harder, at the risk of seeming weak? Or play hard-to-get, at the risk he would simply direct his attention elsewhere?

The thought that he had spurned her clung to her mind and narrowed her mental bandwidth. The idea of being rejected activated some hardwired defense mechanisms that countered any threat to her ego. The greater the ego, the more powerful, irrational, and even ridiculous the defenses could be. Sabina reflexively shifted her thinking away from the threat presented by Charles Knight and redirected her attention to Smolderhof.

Smolderhof was seriously in lust. But lust has a fairly short half-life. Especially so with all the choices available to billionaires. She had ignored his repeated calls over the last few days, partly from a lack of immediate interest, and partly because it was a standard way to make sure that her fishhook stayed secure.

The hundreds of millions that Smolderhof had already taken in should compensate for the fact that he might someday be indicted for securities fraud. Whenever, if ever, such a thing happened, the facts that he was not a US citizen, he wasn't in the US, and his money could buy a lot of legal time and favors meant his indictment would be nearly irrelevant. He would certainly never see the inside of a courtroom. Civil cases would also be filed, of course, but Smolderhof would be even more out of their legal reach. Maybe it was worth spending some years with the man, living large on some island safe from extradition.

But where was the upside, beyond some high living and some expensive gifts that would come her way? The notion left her empty. She knew his type: he would feel depressed and isolated when he read the news reports calling him a fraud and a criminal. He might create a fantasy in which B-F was all he had made it out to be, and he was the victim of libel. But it really didn't matter what he told himself. She believed that he was committing a major fraud that would dog him the rest of his life.

He knew it, she knew it, and he'd know she knew it. That should make him easy to control. But that same dynamic might make him dangerous if he saw her as a threat; the man was capable of anything. Plus, he was old, and he would soon become intolerably dull. It wouldn't all be smooth sailing into the sunset.

If she went with Smolderhof, her reach would only extend to him and a bunch of menial household servants. Nor would her access to the money be guaranteed. It would certainly end her process of climbing the ladder in global-power-brokering circles through US government agencies. She would be isolated too, on a beach, somewhere. Smolderhof was essentially a dead end, in terms of real influence.

She congratulated herself for the foresight. Her mind flipped back to Charles Knight, her ego defenses shored up.

Living with Charles Knight would be much more exciting. He was young, energetic, and, if she allowed it to be so, he would have no indictments hanging over his head. He would be free to travel the world. If the facts were presented with the right spin, he might be hailed as a hero by the media, and maybe the US government would give him an award for exposing the giant fraud. There was power to be had from being a hero. Charles would bring wealth, very possibly fame, and no hindrance to her opportunity to climb the ladders of power. An alliance with the very presentable Charles, and all that money, would help open the door to a political career. And through politics, she would gain introductions to those who controlled the world's money. A thought started to crystallize. She couldn't articulate it, but power over people—anybody, anytime, including people such as Charles Knight—was her ultimate prize. Her sexuality provided a convenient steppingstone to power and money. The nexus of both was government.

As she thought about this, something sparked in her brain, pinpointing a conflict. On the surface it seemed clear that she should focus her energies on seducing—and subduing—Knight more than Smolderhof. But what of the remote possibility that, for reasons beyond her understanding, she might not be able to win Charles Knight? What if he spurned her more definitively next time? Her ego quickly rationalized that if she couldn't win him, then he was profoundly broken and could serve no useful purpose; she shouldn't waste any more time on him. Unless that time could still pay off big. And that was possible. Perhaps he was worth more as a target of prosecution than of matrimony.

She climbed out of the hot tub then, in a rush. Her skin-tight, skin-colored one-piece bathing suit became essentially translucent when wet, just as its designer intended. She looked around, but, so late at night, there were no other hotel guests to gaze upon her, neither males in whom to incite lust, nor females to cultivate envy. So she wrapped herself in a towel and headed back to her room. Feeling underappreciated, she dourly noted there wasn't even someone to share the elevator with.

In her room, too impatient to finish drying off, she flipped open her laptop and searched for a legal case that an old pro at the SEC had once told her about. Back in the 1970s, a securities analyst named Ray Dirks had exposed systemic fraud in a company called Equity Funding. He dug up hidden facts on the company, some from disgruntled company employees. Although he reported what he learned to major newspapers, the company's auditors, and to the SEC, no one chose to do anything. So, in order to draw attention to the impending disaster, he advised some large shareholders to sell their holdings in Equity Funding. This caused the share price to drop suddenly. And that, not the evidence of fraud, drew the SEC's attention. What's more, the SEC decided to prosecute Dirks. Even though he was proven right, and Equity Funding subsequently went bankrupt, at a cost of $300 million to the defrauded investors—a lot of money in those days—the SEC nailed Dirks for aiding and abetting insider trading.

The SEC reasoned that any use of insider information deserved prosecution, even if the information was used to expose a fraud. Since Dirks advised others to trade on that information, he was guilty. As a matter of legal precedent, the SEC would nail anyone who reaped any benefit from such knowledge.

Ten years and millions in legal fees later, the Supreme Court found Dirks innocent of all charges, although the reprieve came only because he had not personally profited. Charles Knight, in contrast, would profit on an enormous scale from his inside knowledge of B-F.

She realized then that if she handled the case one way, with the correctly placed nudges, the SEC would treat Charles Knight as a criminal, for insider trading. If she handled it another way, the government would treat Knight like a hero, for exposing a fraud. The arbitrary nature of it all would have thrilled Franz Kafka; it certainly suited her.

It came to her in a flood. Her career so far was only a prologue for this moment that would put her in the limelight. Her position at the SEC, her time with the IRS, her father's power, the attention of the vice president of the United States, the usefulness of his Government Efficiency Enhancement Initiative and its intention to increase revenues, and of course Charles Knight: they all fell into place.

She got dressed and drove to Alchemia's office. She would surely be the only one there this late at night. On the way, she finally answered one of Smolderhof's calls.

*   *   *

Smolderhof called Sabina from Gondwana. He still lay in bed in his suite at the Zamba Point Hotel, not yet having had his morning coffee. Today would be a long day: meeting after meeting with the advance team from Burke, which had flown in from Lomé. It was bad luck that they had just closed down their drilling operation in Togo, and all the equipment became available for immediate redeployment at Banga Sioquelle. Last night he learned that a ship loaded with Burke equipment would arrive at the Freeport tomorrow. They planned to start their parallel drilling and would ship core immediately. They already had their initial drill sites plotted out. The fuse on this keg of dynamite was getting short.

He still had more shares to blow into the market. But he was out of time. He needed to activate JohnJohn soon enough to prevent Burke from drilling their first hole. Or at least to make sure that anyone from Burke who got to Banga Sioquelle left the place in a box.

"Danny!" Sabina purred languidly in a pretense of ardent passion. "God, I'm so glad you called."

Smolderhof said nothing. He had not expected her to answer. He hated being called Danny. He preferred Daniel, or Dan if need be, but Danny wasn't a name for a globetrotting geologist such as himself, even when Sabina breathed it in her sultry manner.

"Where are you?" she asked.

"Back in Gondwana, of course."

"Without me?" she said, with suggestive petulance.

"I thought...." He paused. He wasn't feeling strong. But he wanted to present his most vital face to Sabina.

"Thought what?"

"Never mind. Where are you, Sabina?"

"In San Diego, trying to help you out with Charles Knight."

"Is he there?"

"No. I think he's back in Africa."

He had hoped Knight would be dead by now. Counted on it, actually. He stayed silent for a time, and then, accepting that something had gone very wrong, said, "I figured."

"Tell me you have put some money aside," she said.

That sent a shiver up his spine and made him sit up in bed. What the hell did she mean by asking that?

He said, "I don't know what you mean, but I have plenty of money, as you know. Come join me."

But a moment later she hammered the next nail into his psychological coffin.

"Dan, there is no gold at Banga Sioquelle, is there."

He responded with silence.

"Charles Knight's stolen rocks will speak volumes."

He was silent again before he finally said, "So he stole the wrong rocks."

"Don't bullshit me," Sabina said. "I'll ask you again: have you put money aside, safely?"

He had what he hoped was untouchable money. "I've got money, Sabina. Hundreds of millions. Absolutely safe as can be." It should be enough money to convince the young beauty to follow him wherever he wanted to go. At least for a while.

Then she said something he couldn't possibly have anticipated. "I'm going to need you to obey me carefully, now." Her tone had shifted completely to deliver this statement with an authority that expected compliance. She was no longer teasing, and her voice offered no pretense of concern.

Even without his coffee, he came fully awake. "Obey?" he asked.

"Listen closely. We're going to need to work together on this, and there's no room for error. You have to let me call the shots."

He listened to what she said over the next few minutes with mounting anxiety. He scribbled a couple of notes at first, but then he stopped and just listened. When she was done, he said, "Why should I do any of this?"

"Because that's the way you're going to neutralize Charles Knight."

His mind hung, frozen.

She added, in an unmistakably sultry voice, "And if you do exactly what I ask, Danny, and you do it well, then, when I get to Gondwana in twenty-four hours, I will in turn do exactly what you ask, and you *know* I will do it well. Do we understand one another?"

Of course he understood her. His groin stirred as if he were a teenager.

She hung up without another word.

He stared at the phone for more than a minute. Sabina knew more than she was saying, or she wouldn't be asking about money offshore, or asking for all this shit she was telling him to do. What was her angle?

*   *   *

Sabina pulled up to the Alchemia offices a few minutes later.

She went straight to Knight's essentially unused office and to his fax. It was there: the results of the assays from the rock samples he had pilfered.

She was right, of course. Charles Knight was right. There was not a microgram of gold in any of them. Smolderhof had essentially admitted it with his responses on the phone.

But to Sabina, that fax she held in her hand—a single piece of paper—was worth a billion times more than its weight in gold as one component of her plan to elevate herself by taking down Knight.

Special Agent Frank Graves would never approve of what she was doing. He would be horrified, stuck as he was in his antiquated notions of integrity and the way things should be done. The man was a dinosaur who had no business working for the government. He would probably chastise her and in his strange reality even have *her* arrested, when she should be getting a promotion and a commendation! Obviously, he would have to be kept out of the loop. She had to get out from under a superior as confused and ineffectual as Graves: the man had so much power, yet lacked the guts to use it to accomplish what was needed. It sickened her more than a vegan meal might disgust a leopard. It would make sense to transfer back to the SEC soon in any event, since this was, at least at the moment, a securities, not a tax, matter. Her father would make it happen.

Sitting at Charles's unused computer, she signed in as a guest and changed its date and time to fourteen days earlier—a time when she knew Charles was in the office. She opened up an email program and sent a series of messages to Smolderhof at B-F Explorations, all dated incorrectly. She typed a few memos. She planted a few clues. It wouldn't hold up to even minimal forensic evaluation. But it didn't have to.

Springer's office was unlocked. That made it easier. It took her ten minutes to find what she wanted.

40

A Double Reversal of Fortune

AT 11 p.m., Smolderhof called Rupert.

"Have you heard from Harry?"

Rupert's voice came back through the phone in segments, barely enough to make out. The occasionally heard word was not encouraging.

Unable to make out any more of the response, Smolderhof spoke. "We need to let JohnJohn do what he was designed for. Three days from today. Are you ready?"

One syllable came back. "No."

Smolderhof said, "What do you mean, 'no'?"

Of the response, Smolderhof heard only syllables and word fragments.

"Rupert, Rupert. I can't hear you. Speak louder." That made no sense, but he said it anyway.

The refraction of the signals off the clouds steadied, and Rupert's voice came through cleanly. "The munitions are gone."

Smolderhof made Rupert repeat it, even though he heard every word.

"I've just returned from Gbarngeda. The containers are still there, but they are empty. The ammunition and the weapons are missing."

Thoughts tore through his mind, but the only thing Smolderhof said was "Where?"

The signal cleared entirely. Rupert spoke as if to an idiot. "If I knew where, then they wouldn't be missing, would they?"

"Harry moved them?"

"Possibly. But I don't think so; he would have informed us."

"Have you looked up at Banga Sioquelle?"

Rupert said, "I stopped by. The tract is two hundred square miles. Harry could have hidden them anywhere. Goodluck has no knowledge of it. I don't think Harry moved it before he went to the US. There were fresh tire tracks from very big trucks by the containers, probably from last night. And they turned south, not north."

"You have to get in touch with Harry!"

"Hell, my brother's off the grid when he should be calling nightly. To me, that means Harry is dead."

"If so, Knight probably killed him."

"Killed by the kid? Not likely."

"Knight's alive and shouldn't be."

The men stayed silent for a moment.

"Fuck!" Smolderhof screamed into the phone.

"That's the right word, Dan. How about me? I'm up in Guinea with a psychopath and two thousand crazy piranhas. JohnJohn wants his munitions. Flomo wants me dead. Flomo wants everyone dead. I told JohnJohn I would bring him down to Banga Sioquelle and show him the containers. What do I offer him now? A bunch of machetes instead of AKs and MANPADs?"

"Can you get more guns?"

"More? What's the matter with you? It took Harry months to bring that stash in."

"Then we gotta find the munitions!"

Rupert said calmly, "Then find Charles Knight. He must be the one that took them. Find him now; JohnJohn is about to go critical."

"I'll find the cocksucker," Smolderhof stated.

With each passing hour, he despised Charles Knight more.

*   *   *

The next morning, Smolderhof walked out along the pier toward the water. To his left, Burke's ship offloaded containers filled with pre-fab buildings, supplies, and the smaller vehicles. A crane lifted one of the drill rigs out of the ship's central cargo hold. It dangled in the sky. He wished it would break free, crash through the center of that ship, hole the hull, and sink the rest of Burke's equipment.

He looked to his right, where the *Africa Grace* lay, bordered by a line of patients waiting for the gangway to open. He felt genuine antagonism toward that ship too, for fixing up and protecting Knight. Smolderhof strode out toward the gangway resting on the pier. Adjacent to it stood a canopy tent, offering shade for triage or check-in or something. An older woman in a white coat and a young woman dressed in scrubs worked together registering patients and logging their medical complaints. Mother Teresas, racking up gold stars for heaven, he supposed.

His white skin made it clear he was not just another sick and penniless native, so he disregarded the line and stepped into the tent.

"Hello," he said, by way of getting attention.

The older woman, with "Louise" embroidered on her white coat, looked up as she stuck an armband on a young child's wrist and patted him gently on the back. "Can I help you?"

"Perhaps. I'm looking for a friend," Smolderhof replied.

"Aren't we all," Louise said. She handed the boy's mother a clipboard.

Smolderhof said, "His name is Charles Knight."

The younger woman jerked her head toward him, and then lowered her eyes just as fast.

Louise shrugged. "Is he Gondwanan?"

"American."

"Ship's crew, you mean?"

"No. A guest. A patient."

Louise smiled a partial smile, insincere certainly. "Well, I can't tell you anything one way or another about patients, of course. Confidentiality and all."

"I understand." Smolderhof read the other woman's name tag: "Caroline." "Well, if you happen to run into Mr. Knight again"—he spoke directly to the silent Caroline and stressed the word "again" just slightly—"will you give him a message for me, please? Tell him that Dan Smolderhof suggests an urgent meeting." He pulled out a business card. He wrote on the back of the card: *This is your one chance to win.*

Caroline stuck a stethoscope in her ears, but her eyes followed Smolderhof's hand as he placed the business card on the table.

Louise nodded and said, "I'll pass it on to the captain to see what he knows, okay?"

"That'll be just fine. Thank you."

Smolderhof bowed faintly to Louise, who smiled again, just slightly, and then to Caroline, who appeared to ignore it altogether. But she kept her stethoscope on the same spot on the child's lungs for far too long.

He walked away, confident Knight would get the message.

He strode diagonally across the pier to Burke's container ship, dreading the day's meetings. He'd treated yesterday's meetings with unprepared disdain, because at that point he assumed the rebellion would close off northern Gondwana for years. But now everything was different. Would, indeed *could*, JohnJohn invade, and take over Banga Sioquelle, with only a promise of future weapons? Rupert would have to convince JohnJohn, replacing the AKs with lies and assurances.

More than likely, JohnJohn would kill Rupert.

The rebel army did have *some* ammunition, albeit not much. They actually could round up a couple thousand machetes, and they would do almost as well as guns for a while. If Rupert stayed alive, he would get the rebellion going. He would arrange for JohnJohn to overrun Banga Sioquelle. He would ensure that Gbarngeda was sacked and left burning. And that plenty of horrific pictures and videos became available to keep Burke scared and at bay.

They could rampage through the area, committing mayhem and taking over police stations and government buildings. But after that it would likely be game over. Without the munitions, the rebellion would be brief and too soon quashed. Far too soon.

Burke would then come back. And as soon as Burke reported data from their first drill core, Smolderhof could count on his travel being forever limited to a few small islands and some unpleasant former Eastern Bloc countries immune to extradition by the US and Canada. He recalled the unhappy history of Robert Vesco, who stole $200 million from a mutual fund group in 1970. The money allowed him to hide out by bribing politicians in the Caribbean and Central America for years. But reality caught up with him. Authorities imprisoned him in Cuba, of all places. Smolderhof didn't want to wind up like Vesco.

Right now his perfect crime looked about as perfect as that of a drunk robbing a liquor store on a Saturday night.

He needed the munitions. Or he needed that dangling drill rig to break free and sink Burke's ship, preferably killing everyone on board.

He faced another day of cooperative planning for Burke's expanded gold explorations. Yet he had much more important matters to attend to.

*   *   *

Charles smiled through an unshaven face smeared with dry mud. He had been out tramping in the boondocks for days, and looked the part. Alive and safely back on the ship, albeit only for a moment, he luxuriated in the simple pleasure of soap and water. A thickening brown fuzz of new hair covered his head, giving him the appearance of a younger version of the mercs back at the soccer camp. After a long shower he joined Caroline at their special place at the ship's bow, secluded from view by containers, machines, and tarpaulins.

Mostly they just sat in silence, holding onto each other. He wanted to stay there forever.

He nuzzled the top of her head, and then leaned down to kiss an eyebrow, an eye, and then her lips. She melted into him, his arms pulling her close as she let herself fall forward, pressing herself ever tighter to him.

Maybe he shouldn't go. Maybe he should just let it all happen. What was he doing? Stopping the rebellion might make him exceedingly wealthy. Was it worth putting his life on the line? But his life was already on the line.

And it wasn't just about money.

The moment of doubt and weakness passed.

"This is all going to be over soon, Caroline."

"What else has to happen?" she asked, quietly, hopefully.

"A lot or a little. I hope a little."

"You aren't being candid with me, Charles."

"No, I'm not."

"Just like when we first met. You would not even give me your name."

"Yeah. It's definitely not the way I'd like it."

"Just what are you planning to do?"

Charles shook his head, "Nothing foolproof, I'm afraid. I'm not trying to be cryptic. There are just a lot of factors pretty much beyond our control."

They spent the rest of the morning together, and at noon in her cabin they once again broke the ship's rules. Thereafter, they returned to their special place on the bow.

"Why does Dan Smolderhof want to meet with you?"

Charles replied only with a "hmm."

"Is he one of the men who shot at you?"

"He's their boss."

"Oh, Charles, then you won't meet with him! You know it's a trap!"

"Perhaps. But I think not. I think he wants to make a deal."

"What deal?"

"He wants to buy my silence."

"And Xander's?"

"Maybe. But I can't speak for Xander, and Xander didn't receive an invitation."

Sounds of the port surrounded them. The throbbing engines of a tugboat, the offloading of a ship in from Côte d'Ivoire, the basso profundo horns of regional freighters, the port authority speakers calling out commands. Seagulls laughed. A crane clanked. Men shouted, angrily sometimes. A moist wind steadily rose, flapping tarpaulins and carrying the smell of fish, salt, and oil. Africa was starting to grow on Charles.

What information could Smolderhof have that was worth risking a meeting? Would he go so far as to threaten his family? Charles should have used an alias when he first came here to view B-F's operations. But thoughts of fraud, murder, and rebellion had not crossed his mind then, when he had been an innocent man on an innocent mining tour. And one cannot live one's life assuming that every business and every person is out to lie, cheat, and kill.

"Kids?" Xander's voice came from behind. "Don't let me interrupt anything unchristian, huh?"

Charles replied, "Too late!"

Caroline turned and smiled. "You aren't interrupting anything, Mr. Winn."

"Please, Caroline, you've been so intimate with my wound that it seems inappropriate to address me formally." He came around in front of them as Charles stood. Charles's grin could not conceal a degree of consternation.

"What's wrong, Charles?"

Charles replied, "While I was away, did you succeed at acquiring what we need?"

"I cleaned out the country's entire supply. It should be enough, but we won't know until we try, will we? Now, what's wrong?"

"Smolderhof stopped by the ship and left a message." Charles handed Xander the business card. "He wants to meet."

"Trap?"

"I suspect he wants to offer me a deal."

"I don't think he has anything that we want or need."

Charles said, "That's what I thought too. But he seems to think he does. What harm can come from meeting with him?"

"Not much," Xander said, and then leaned close and whispered into his ear, "Just death."

Charles said, "Shall I call him?" Smolderhof's men had tracked him through his cell phone before. But at this point tracking him to the *Africa Grace* required no particular skill. Smolderhof's business card testified to that.

"What the hell. Go ahead. We might gain some information. Even if it's in the form of a lie."

Charles pulled out a cell phone.

Caroline sat on the bench. Xander brought his head close to Charles to listen to the call. Smolderhof answered on the second ring.

"Mr. Smolderhof. It's Charles Knight."

There was silence for a moment, and then "Ah, Mr. Knight. Thank you for calling."

"What do you want, Smolderhof?"

"Direct to business, I see. I propose we meet."

"Why?"

"I assure you that it is in your best interest to do so."

Charles replied, "Well, you asked me, so we *know* it's in *your* best interest to meet. I'm not convinced it's in *my* best interest."

There was another long pause. "Mr. Knight. You have purchased put option contracts. Forty thousand contracts at various strike prices and expiry dates. What if I were to tell you that your options will all, every one of them, expire worthless? And those that Elliot Springer has bought as well, and those of all his partners and clients. You will lose everything you made from when you were long on B-F, all you gained from the time while you were a loyal shareholder."

How did Smolderhof know details of his put option contracts? Was that information available to the company? Charles wasn't sure; there was so much he still had to learn about the markets. Confusion coursed through his veins; his face flushed. He felt much the same as when he had first met Sabina in Springer's office— he needed a break to compose his thoughts.

"Mr. Smolderhof. I will call you back in a moment." And then he disconnected before there was time for a response.

"You hung up on him?" Xander's eyes were wide—in amusement, not surprise.

"I have to get my bearings for a moment." Charles frowned. "He knows my trades."

Xander considered this. "Smolderhof knows the market makers and maybe folk at the options exchanges. Probably wined and dined them all, and now maybe they give him intel. It's a possibility. Although not likely. The trades would all have been done in the name of your broker, not *your* name."

"How else would he know about purchases I just made in the past few days?"

"I don't know. It's concerning. Call him back."

Charles did.

"Mr. Knight. You rang off so quickly. Are you well?" Smolderhof's tone implied no sympathy.

Charles replied honestly. "Your knowledge of my trades bothers me."

"As it should. Let's meet today. Are you in Adamstown?"

"Near enough."

"Good. The bar at the Zamba Point Hotel. Shall we say one hour?"

"See you then."

Caroline took Charles's hand after the call ended. "Are you two going to *meet* with that man?"

"I will. Not Xander."

Her expression conveyed more than just a mild concern.

*   *   *

The Zamba Point Hotel stood high above the beach, near the US Embassy, on a loop road in the nice area of the city. The hotel had served briefly as Charles's base, when he had first arrived in Gondwana. It now carried a specter of malevolence in his mind not just because of what had happened to Mr. Imir, but also what might happen next. The open ocean, with no islands for a hundred miles, dominated the view from its hillside location.

Charles bounded up the stairs and through a vinyl-padded swinging double door into the restaurant's bar. The air-conditioned space held the aura of a modest hotel bar anywhere in central Europe, except that there was no cigarette smoke. When inside, one could forget the run-down buildings and torn-up streets that lay outside, as well as the beach itself—used as an open air bathroom by the locals and populated by what they appropriately called *bandits*.

Smolderhof sat on a couch against a wall, facing the bar. After a moment of delayed recognition because of Charles's short, cropped hair, he acknowledged Charles with a nod, and then stood. He held out his hand, in a standoffish way. No pretense of friendliness this time. The last time he had seen the man was on the tour, when Smolderhof had embraced him.

"Charles. May I call you Charles?"

"Most wouldn't ask, Mr. Smolderhof." It was no answer, but all Charles felt like supplying.

"Well, you may certainly call me Dan."

Charles nodded as he sat in an adjacent padded armchair. A plate with hummus surrounded by bread adorned the table in front of them.

Charles waited for Smolderhof to speak. It was his meeting, his request after all.

"Would you care for a drink?"

"No."

"Are you enjoying your time in Gondwana?" Smolderhof asked.

"Shall we get to the point, Dan?"

"Very well. Charles, let's put a small matter out of the way first. I believe you have something of mine."

"And what might that be?"

"Certain materials taken from one of B-F's facilities recently."

Charles could have asked, "And what materials are those?" but there was little point in such silly games, so he stayed silent.

Smolderhof next said, "Come now, we're both men of the world." He added a nearly imperceptible grunt. "You've taken something that's mine. I would like it back. Again, a small matter, but a necessary first step to generate mutual respect and trust."

Charles studied the room. The bar to his right had chairs for only five patrons. One seat was taken by a patron who looked a whole lot like local muscle Smolderhof might have brought along. A television showed a soccer game. To the left was Smolderhof's couch, and in front were more couches and soft chairs; a glass wall and then a seating area on the broad patio lay beyond. The main restaurant was off to the left.

TJ sat on one of the soft chairs, his back to the glass wall, looking at the televised soccer. Charles's eyes passed by him without acknowledgment.

"I want what you took. I want it back. In fact, I want it delivered to the B-F tract at Banga Sioquelle." Smolderhof lowered his voice. "Two shipping containers of defensive munitions."

Charles reached forward, dipped bread through the hummus, and chewed on it longer than he needed to. "What use could you possibly have for two containers of guns and ammo?"

Smolderhof's thin smile was the primary response. He repeated, "As I stated. It is for defensive purposes."

"Should I be able to determine their whereabouts, what would that be worth to you?" It was an insincere question, in that any number would be inconsequential compared to his payday when B-F went bankrupt and the put options matured.

"For the materials, I'll pay you nothing. They're mine. You took them. But I am willing to compensate you for other matters. Value for value. And Charles, the amount is substantial. It's more than you will achieve from your plays with B-F shares—that I assure you."

"I think you underestimate the value of my positions."

Smolderhof cracked a smug grin. "Charles, the average strike price for your put options is fifty dollars. Your positions, if B-F were to go bankrupt in the next few months with complete loss of all share value, will be worth $200 million. Less brokerage fees. The math is simple."

Charles kept a straight, unemotional face. Inside, his heart hammered.

"So you see," Smolderhof continued, "I know precisely the value of your position. But of course your ability to realize this impressive return requires two things. The first is that B-F's price needs to fall soon, and very substantially."

Charles was fully aware of how much money was at stake, but Smolderhof should not have been. He breathed in slowly and exhaled, trying to control the pounding of his heartbeat, and asked, "Mr. Smolderhof, don't you think B-F will fall?"

"Oh, it *will* fall. But not low enough to get you in the money. I think not."

Slowly, Charles asked, "Why not?"

"The market can remain irrational for longer than you can remain solvent."

Charles nodded. He had heard his mentors state the same exact phrase at least three times in the past two weeks. It was an important lesson to hear reinforced. But not by Smolderhof. He said, "You admit it would be irrational for the price to stay anywhere near where it is now, at, I think, $250 today?"

Smolderhof replied, "Oh, I think your rational analysis has been fairly spot on, Charles."

Charles dipped his head faintly, acknowledging but not thanking the provider of the compliment.

Smolderhof added, "But good analysis and right thinking don't necessarily mean the market will agree with you, do they?"

Smolderhof waited.

Charles probed him. "And the second?"

"The second?" Smolderhof's flare for the dramatic was not limited to his outrageous speeches about the lucrative nature of the B-F tract.

Now Charles waited with a blank face.

"Ah yes, the second. Charles"—he took on a patronizing tone—"the second thing required for you to achieve value from your strategy is more important than the collapse of B-F. The second is that you have to be *allowed* to exercise your options."

Charles looked at Smolderhof. There was an axe ready to drop, and Charles knew that now. His mind hastened to crystalize what he intuited would come next. Not a murder threat. No, Smolderhof had something even more sinister, and less overt, up his sleeve. Something in the air had just taken on the scent of injustice. Echoes of his lemonade stand intruded on his thinking.

"What are you saying, *Danny?*"

Smolderhof's anger at Charles became apparent in his tone as he answered. "I'm saying that you will not be allowed to exercise your put options."

"Who won't allow it?"

"We'll get to that, *Charlie.* But first, let me assure you that despite the total loss of your investment on all those put options, you can still make good money on B-F. Had you just sold your long position and been satisfied with that, you would have earned over four million dollars. I am offering you ten million."

"That seems rather small compensation for the loss of my upside."

"Mr. Knight, it's all you're ever going to make on B-F. And it can be ten million untaxed dollars, if you so desire. Value for value."

"Tell me what value you want in return."

"In exchange for the ten million dollars, I want your silence."

Charles, rather appropriately, stayed silent. A minute or more passed.

Smolderhof repeated, "Ten million dollars of silence."

"Versus two hundred million?"

"Ten million real money, versus two hundred million that will never materialize, Mr. Knight."

"Tell me why you say that, Dan."

"Ever hear of Ray Dirks?"

"No."

"You will soon enough."

Patronizing bastard. "Mr. Smolderhof, I think I'll just see how things work out in the irrationality of the rational marketplace." Charles started to stand. "Thank you for the hummus."

Smolderhof coughed. "Charles, before you leave, why don't you take a look at these." Reaching into a briefcase at the side of the couch, Smolderhof extracted a small sheaf of papers. "I hear you are learning to be a speculator. Consider this part of your education about risk."

Charles stayed standing as he began to read through them. After the second page he sat down. Five minutes passed. Smolderhof nibbled at the hummus and sipped at a glass of water. Charles maintained an unreadable face. Inside, his rage ignited.

What else could he expect? Fraudsters commit fraud. It's what they do. The papers were copies of a series of emails from his own email address to Smolderhof. And a contract signed by Smolderhof, and, yes, that did look like his own signature on it as well. And other incriminating correspondence too.

"So Smolderhof, you've manufactured emails and documents that make me appear complicit in *your* scam."

"Yes."

"They're blatant lies. Completely manufactured."

"Yes, they are." Smolderhof maintained his thin smug smile.

"They won't hold up in court. Documents and emails are tracked."

"Oh, Charles. These documents are for the politicians and bureaucrats! None will ever be seen by a judge. I have something else for that purpose."

Charles couldn't imagine how *any* of this fraudulent material could hold water. No one would accept this. How could they? He said, "You can't use these unless you're outed as a fraud yourself."

"Again, you're correct, Charles. If I go down, you go down. But I will go down wealthy and live my days in a paradise from which I can't be extradited. You'll go down broke and imprisoned."

"So we're both going down, regardless. Burke is here. You *will* be exposed."

"I think you mean that *we* will be exposed, Mr. Knight. But you should trust me. We are on the same team now, you and I. Do you think I would have no plan for Burke? Let me take care of them."

"Not yet, Smolderhof. This is all so thin, so clearly falsified."

"Are you sure? Look at this." Smolderhof handed him another sheet of paper. It was Charles's assay results from his pilfered rock samples. "Were you ever going to release this information publicly before you finished staking your short position? The government will of course depose Elliot Springer under oath to obtain the truth."

"I have simply discovered your fraud, Smolderhof. That is no crime."

"Ahh, but you're planning to profit from it, and that *is* a crime. This piece of paper is all that is needed for your government to indict you."

Charles didn't know the Ray Dirks case, but he knew that insider trading was one of the hobby horses government agencies liked to ride until the steed died. Someone always got information first, even when it was publicly announced. The people in the room hear an announcement before anyone else, and then the people they call to tell hear it next. The last guy to hear anything is the little guy who, if he's going to be in the market at all, has to realize where he stands.

From an ethical standpoint, only shareholders, not the public, have a right to corporate information. In the event of any impropriety, it should be addressed as tort action between them and the person in question. Trading on insider information is only an actual crime—as opposed to a violation of an arbitrary regulation—when the person who uses it violates a trust. Perhaps a CEO and the company's CPA, who have fiduciary duties not to put themselves ahead of the shareholders. But applied in any other sense, making insider trading a criminal offense only quashes the free flow of information and chills the functionality of whistle blowers.

But it does give regulators a reason for existing and law firms a massive source of income.

Charles was ill prepared for this turn of events. He didn't understand the rules of the game or even the shape of the playing field. The man in front of him was not only a swindler but a full-fledged sociopath, and one who may well have outfoxed him. He felt his face grow red both with anger and humiliation. Having any contact with criminal personalities, talking to them, even being in the same room with them—not to mention getting into a contest with them—almost always ended badly. It was time to leave.

"We'll talk tomorrow, Danny."

As Charles rose, a woman came through the swinging doors into the bar.

Shock coursed through Charles's body, and he involuntarily sat back down.

She sashayed, displaying her perfectly symmetrical smile and equally symmetrical body, and stood over Charles. Had he looked at TJ, he would have seen TJ's jaw hanging open in the same manner adopted by the waiters at Dick's Last Resort. But Charles didn't look at TJ. He looked at Sabina.

"Charles," she said, sitting down even as he stood. She crossed her right leg over her left with practiced grace. Her faint scent ascended from her flawless skin. She wore a white skirt in a country where dust and red mud were ever present. But the white skirt remained spotless.

Charles attempted to center his mind, but the situation was moving too rapidly. He had too much to contemplate, and they didn't intend to allow him the time to do so. He willed himself to calmness.

He looked at her closely and said, "Sabina Dresden, let's start by you telling me who you really are."

She told him with the pride of one who had captured a difficult prey. "Allow me to introduce myself. My name is Sabina *Heidel*." And then her story emerged, with a reasonable peppering of truth.

She told him that the SEC had just obtained an injunction and would be freezing his stock-trading accounts. She told him that, based on extensive documentation obtained during her investigation, he would be indicted for insider trading. She was the Very Own Special Agent of the actual vice president of the United States, and the name Charles Knight would be in the history books, alongside some of the biggest historical scoundrels of Wall Street. Sabina smiled consistently during her recitation of facts that were not facts, presenting a newly manufactured reality, a clever merging of truth and falsehood that Charles had never contemplated.

He felt like saying, "But it's *all untrue*." But to say so was pointless. It was a carefully crafted frame-up.

Smolderhof said, "If B-F goes down, Charles, you go down."

Charles looked at Sabina. "You are going to let this happen? You, a government agent?" Charles himself did not know whether his question was a grasp at some naïve hope or a sarcastic quip.

She smiled back. "The bottom line is that you are unlawfully using material nonpublic information for personal profit. The SEC will take action against insider trading no matter where or when it occurs, or who is involved." That was true enough, except for the "who" part. That pretty much depended both on the attitude of the "who" that was pursuing the action, and the exact identity of the "who" that might be accused.

Smolderhof raised his hands, palm outward, calling for calm. "It doesn't have to be this way, Charles. Ten million dollars. Clear and clean. Think about it. You have tonight to consider. I will call you at 8 a.m."

"Don't call me, Smolderhof. I'll call you. When I'm ready."

Smolderhof shrugged. "Okay, Charles. But one more thing." Smolderhof's face could not possibly have appeared more smug. "We have good evidence that you killed Ollie Shifflett, our chemist, as well as two of our Gondwanan security men. I plan to report the crime to the Gondwana police tomorrow at noon, and I will tell them all that I know. And that I understand you are in possession of an enormous supply of weapons and ammunition. You know how seriously this government takes its gun control laws. If they find those weapons—and very likely even if they never do—they'll throw away the key to your cell. I don't recommend Gondwanan jails, Mr. Knight. Although, neither do I recommend US prisons, where you might find yourself should we follow up on the disappearance of Harry Pell during his recent visit to San Diego. That might further complicate your situation. I suggest you make your decision before noon tomorrow."

Charles left the hotel bar feeling like an oil-soaked rag, physically weak, mentally dazed, and highly combustible. If this was a chess game, he was looking at an impending checkmate.

But he still controlled the moral high ground, for what little that was worth. The battle seemed lost. But Napoleon said that in conflict, the moral is to the physical as three is to one. He had to find the way to build on his strength.

As he drove back to the ship, the obvious solution flashed in and out of his mind: in this country anybody could disappear without a trace. Xander, TJ, and their friends, who'd been watching the perimeter of the hotel, knew people who could make Smolderhof and Sabina vanish in an hour. But Smolderhof had surely considered that possibility.

A trail of breadcrumbs, indeed whole loaves of bread, would lead right up to Charles whether Smolderhof was alive or dead.

41

A Hole in the Jungle

ON the foredeck of the *Africa Grace*, Charles, Xander, and TJ discussed the angles and alternatives. Charles attempted to draw Maurice into the mix by phone, but Uncle Maurice couldn't stay awake. His comical but disabling sleep apnea might prove to be a fatal flaw, and not only for Maurice himself. Fortunately, enough information was exchanged to permit Maurice to confirm, an hour later, that Sabina Heidel was in fact a government agent.

Charles called Elliot, who, overcome with remorse and mortified by his extraordinary lapse of judgment, repeated, "I was taken in. I was taken in, Charles. I'm so sorry." If the situation got out of control, Elliot would have his own troubles with the SEC, with even more to lose than Charles.

At one point, Xander said, "I can't get a grip on the woman's position, Charles. She's a government agent, but working with Smolderhof?"

"Yes," Charles replied. "That's exactly what's happening. I'm not surprised the government would work with the bad guys. My question is whether Sabina is playing both ends against the middle. If she's working with Smolderhof, and we prove B-F is a fraud, it could turn into a huge embarrassment for the vice president. Maybe that risk of embarrassment could be useful, somehow."

Had Xander been an old lady instead of a middle-aged man, he might have clucked just then. "Charles, you understand the nature of governments well enough in theory, perhaps, but you're missing the way they work in practice. If the vice president might possibly be embarrassed, he will do everything he can to prevent it. And in practice, that means redoubling their efforts to nail *you*, not outing his poster girl."

TJ glanced aft toward where the hospitable captain had welcomed him on board for this meeting. No one was about. He took a long swallow from one of the beers he'd smuggled onto the ship, then sat back in his chair. "He's sleeping with her."

"Who? The vice president?"

TJ said, "Probably him too. But I meant Smolderhof."

Xander said, "Likely right on both counts."

Charles opined, "The whole government's against me. Am I paranoid?"

"It's only paranoia when what you fear is not true," declared Xander.

"So I'm up a creek."

"Yes, up the creek you are. They'll try to convict you of insider trading, plus throw a bunch of other charges in, just to see what sticks and to shock and awe the judge with the number of counts you're accused of. Truth doesn't matter in the world of a federal prosecutor trying to rack up another conviction, Charles."

"But when this goes to trial, a jury will decide. They'll see what's happened. The facts will come out...."

Xander looked at him for a moment. "That's the way it works in television dramas. But in the real world, 95 percent of indictments get settled before trial, after a whole lot of pressure and threats. If you do go to trial, remember that juries are mostly composed of people who aren't motivated enough to get out of jury duty, or who want to collect the per diem and get time off from dull jobs. No one on your jury will have a clue about financial markets. The prosecutor will make sure of that. The prosecutor will push their envy buttons because you're a young guy who's become wealthy through his own efforts. It subconsciously makes them realize how little they have achieved for themselves, so they'll dislike you. And, anyway, in the US, nowadays, it's trendy to eat the rich."

Charles shook his head and clenched his jaw until his face was red. His fury at *their* world mounted. At the same time he wondered where *his* world was. It didn't exist.

But it should be, and could be, built.

Xander said, "Charles, you can make $10 million. It's not $200 million, but still, it's not a bad take for a few weeks' work. You're playing high-stakes poker. You've got a straight flush draw, but they've got four aces. What do you do? Well, you fold your hand and cut your losses."

Charles had a hard time accepting that analogy.

"Why would Smolderhof believe that once he's paid his ten million, I would stay quiet?"

"He figures no one will listen once you're indicted, and the government has you painted as a criminal. So he wins now even if you try to speak up."

TJ added, "What he wants for his ten million is the ammunition. He can't get new munitions here fast enough, not even for $10 million."

Charles agreed. "Burke is on his doorstep. Ten million dollars is nothing to him. But time is everything. Still, we can't let him arm JohnJohn."

Xander replied, "They're not your guns. They're his."

"Not really. He got them with money acquired by defrauding me and all the other investors."

"Fair enough. You find yourself on the slippery slope. Who started what, and against whom."

"It's not that slippery. Smolderhof committed the fraud. We're fighting back."

"Okay, Charles. Obviously I agree with you this time. But in your life, make sure to watch how far down that slippery slope of justification you drop, okay? An emotionally laden human brain can justify a whole lot of evil."

The three men were silent for several minutes.

TJ leaned forward. "Does he know that we know about the soldiers in Guinea? Did you tell this Sabina woman about that?"

Charles shook his head. "No. We discussed B-F in Elliot's conference room back in San Diego. But I kicked her out of the room during that part. "

Xander smiled. "That was prudent. Unless she also had the room bugged."

TJ smiled too. "If so, then we're cooked. Let's proceed on the basis that she did not. You swear to be silent, take their $10 million, and give them their munitions back."

Charles almost shouted, he was so exasperated, but he controlled himself just enough to not be heard around the ship, "And let the rebellion happen? Right here in your backyard, TJ? What about the lives at stake? Or even your put options, Xander? And Elliot and Maurice?"

"We'll be fine, Charles. The value of our options will increase as the price falls. Maybe not from one to a hundred. Maybe just up to five bucks each. So it could still be a win for me—if the decline happens fast enough. Your life, your future, and your freedom are at stake here."

"And I didn't say to let the rebellion happen," TJ clarified. "I said to give them their munitions and promise silence. We can still stop the rebellion. It takes both guns and people to make a rebellion in Africa. We can sell them back their guns—"

"And then simply enact part two of your insane and impossible plan, Charles." Xander interrupted TJ with an ease of a long-time friend.

Charles turned to Xander. "What a goddamn mess."

Xander patted him on the knee. "Lying, cheating, stealing, and war make big messes, kid. It's why I try to avoid them."

*　　*　　*

"Ten million dollars." Charles spoke into the phone, peering over the great rock and down at the rebel camp. "You have two hours to wire it to the following account." He provided Smolderhof with the numbers for an intermediary bank account Xander used in the Caribbean. It was on an island nation that, under threat of sanctions, had recently signed a tax treaty to help the US tax authorities garnish US citizens' money wherever they were on the globe. But since Xander wasn't a US citizen or resident, it would matter little if Sabina learned about that particular bank account. And Xander and Charles would immediately begin to rewire it through trust accounts and bond trades to its final destination in the account of a different company, in another country, and thence onward to Charles.

Charles continued giving directions to Smolderhof. "While I verify the money transfer, you can get someone on the way to a GPS location that you will receive in a text message. There will be two trucks there, with your munitions. You will find them outside Gbarngeda, down a side road. If the money doesn't arrive shortly, the trucks... well, the trucks just won't be there."

"You're making a wise decision, Charles. I'm sorry about the loss of your put options. If it's any consolation to you, you made some brilliant trades."

"No consolation at all, Smolderhof." He disconnected.

But there would be *some* consolation. TJ and Charles had spent far too much time—miserable, uncomfortable, hot, and sweaty time—in those trucks, with no air conditioning, no effective springs, no shock absorbers, bouncing agonizingly along the old roads. Xander's butt would never have survived sitting in them for even an hour. Charles had learned to hate those trucks. He would gladly blow them to kingdom come, if that was destined to be their fate.

The containers secured to the trucks' beds contained all of B-F's ammunition and weapons, loaded three days earlier—one box at a time—by TJ, Charles, and TJ's five Djennetown friends. A five-hundred-dollar bribe proved sufficient for each of the two remaining African guards, who had little heart to protect B-F's only real asset. The two guards, pleased with four months' wages in hand, even helped them load up.

Some said weapons were more valuable than gold, if only because they would allow you to steal gold. These weapons were certainly more valuable than B-F's gold.

And all of the munitions within those two despised but useful trucks would explode if the $10 million wasn't transferred as Smolderhof had promised. "You can't trust a liar," Xander had said. So, among all those boxes of guns and ammunition, they hid two additional boxes, each wired to cell phone triggers that Xander had carefully constructed. He relied on skills acquired in the days when he solved problems with direct action, rather than strategy and words.

The five Djenne men, whom Charles had first seen picnicking on top of the second truck on the pier beside the *Africa Grace*, had guarded the hidden trucks for the past three days more effectively than B-F's hired men, that's for sure. They were by now stationed far enough away to be safe if, indeed, the trucks' fates consisted of explosions followed by inferno.

The day moved fast. Charles, Xander, and TJ had slipped off the *Africa Grace* hours before sunrise. TJ had driven, the back of his SUV packed with a half ton of supplies. After stopping off to complete their preparations on the inside of the munitions trucks and station the Djenne guards safely, they continued up to Gbarngeda, then further north, past the road that led to the now-destroyed core-processing facility with the remnants of Ollie Shifflett and his machine. Then on past the dirt path that entered the B-F property where Burke would soon arrive, and then along up into Guinea toward the rebel soccer camp.

TJ had made the driving time go quickly, telling jokes and anecdotes, and reminiscing with Xander as Charles listened, laughing when he could keep his eyes open. TJ made the best of this time, the last chance they would have to speak above a whisper for a long time.

They drove the SUV as far as they dared up the access road toward the soccer camp. While Charles ran off to climb the giant boulder for his ten-million-dollar call to Smolderhof, TJ and Xander offloaded their supplies into the bush in a silent, rapid burst of action to minimize the time the vehicle would be at risk on the access road, then covered them thoroughly. TJ then drove back to the main road fully five miles north of the access road, spent an hour thoroughly concealing the Land Cruiser, then walked two hours back to rejoin Charles and Xander.

The men lugged their water, food, and hundreds of pounds of mission-critical supplies on their backs, fifty pounds each per trek, securing it all near the back of the hill that rose above the valley with its massive capstone. Charles logically christened it Bunker Hill. There was a bunker, and there might be a battle.

Charles again climbed the rope back to the top of Bunker Hill and made three more phone calls, being careful, as always, to stay low and out of sight of the camp.

The first call assured him of the success of the $10 million transfer. He followed Winn's instructions to activate its immediate onward transfer to another account at a different institution that shared the same diminutive Caribbean office building with the first, and then off island altogether with a second phone call. For his third call, he dialed Smolderhof.

"Dan. Money received."

Smolderhof responded, "And we found the trucks just where you indicated they would be, Charles. We both seem to be good to our word. Let me ask you, what would you have done if the money never made it to your account? You already told me where the trucks were."

"I trusted you, Danny."

It was a lie, of course. But it was a morally acceptable lie, in that one doesn't owe the truth to everybody. He certainly didn't need to tell Smolderhof their contingency plans.

Two hundred feet down—behind Bunker Hill, entirely concealed from the camp, and far below the great rock—stood a twenty-foot-diameter thicket of tall, dense bamboo, sprouting among the palms and undergrowth. Charles and TJ knew it well, for while Xander started to heal on the *Africa Grace* the week before, they had spent a whole night there very quietly digging, fending off mosquitoes, preparing for this current phase of the mission. Inside the bamboo thicket the two men had molded a lining of dirt—a rampart of earth four feet high in a circle around a deeply dug central hole that they covered with bamboo and palms. The walls of the secret fortification would block the view of any peering eye.

Xander examined the primitive but meticulously built nest. If he had even a twang of guilt about resting in bed while his friends stole ammunition and built this fortress, Xander didn't let it appear on his face. Perhaps any guilt was displaced by another feeling: shooting pain emanating from a wound that he had once again stretched too far.

When Charles and TJ had first started this excavation, the dirt moved with ease. But bamboo roots go straight down for the first foot or so, until their rhizomes shoot out to the sides, creating a tight interlacing horizontal structure. Whacking through it efficiently required a heavy mattock swung repeatedly—a rhythmic noise that would carry to the camp. So Charles and TJ had worked inefficiently, with quiet handsaws and metal sheers, silently excavating several cubic meters of the material, piling it all in between the stands of thick bamboo. It provided insulation for sound as well as sight in the process of building the hideout. Even after TJ had decided it was plenty big enough, Charles kept digging deeper and wider, making more space. He knew something that TJ did not.

It had taken them nine hours of preparation, but once stocked with water and food, the little fortress appeared livable, if not luxurious. It would serve as their keep, when the critical time came.

"You and TJ should be in the construction business," Xander told Charles as the three men sat together inside the hole.

"I think the market for this product is quite limited, even in this country," TJ quipped.

They would test it very soon. Insufficient preparations would result in two thousand angry young men tearing them to shreds. There was no room for error.

"We have no idea if this is going to work," Charles admitted.

After assessing it with the eye of an engineer accustomed to jerry-rigged projects in backward countries, Xander said calmly, "It will work. Maybe you need to do something better about your drainage." Four inches of muddy water lay in the bottom. "Let's build a floor with some of the bamboo. The thought of marinating in a pool of swamp water doesn't appeal to me."

Charles looked down at the water. "Hey, that's our Jacuzzi...."

Xander said, "Well, let's pretend we're going to enjoy it, because there's a good chance we'll end up jungle fertilizer. Life is a terminal illness, Charles."

TJ corrected Xander. "Life is a *sexually transmitted* terminal illness."

Xander continued, "Nobody gets out of this life alive. And I'm much more aware of that than you guys are. Past a certain age, you know, these things cease to be merely academic observations...."

TJ said, "Terminal now, or terminal later.... Let's hope for later."

Charles installed the bamboo flooring—an insignificant task that would relate to his later life in a manner he could not, now, possibly anticipate.

Xander examined their preparations once again. "Okay, gentlemen. I think it'll do. Let's get the rest of the supplies. We'll need some sleep. We'll wake at 2 a.m. to do the work on the camp side of Bunker Hill in the dark, as quiet as church mice. This is prime time, no dress rehearsal. Tomorrow at JohnJohn's lunch speech, we'll see if we can change the course of local history, for fun and profit."

TJ said, with a serious voice, "Xander, I'm confident you'll do it right the first time."

"If I don't, there won't be a second time, and we're all dead men."

They tested out their newly constructed accommodations that night. TJ and Xander slept well on Charles's platform of bamboo in the deep hole in the ground, their bunker so thoroughly surrounded by the thicket of bamboo and brush that they imagined even the mosquitoes had a hard time getting through.

Charles kept watch until, at midnight, he roused Xander.

"It's time for my excursion," he said softly.

"Okay, kid. I hope to see you alive again."

"I'll be back by 0200. You can count on it."

"I *am* counting on it," Xander whispered.

Xander patted Charles on his arm. Charles climbed up out of their fort.

TJ's voice came from the blackness below. "Be careful, Charles. Xander may not care if you come back, but I do."

Charles crept out the twisting pathway through the bamboo walls of their keep. He mentally rehearsed where to go and exactly what to do. He had to sneak right up to the edge of the hornet's nest. This excursion was a moral imperative.

The clouds blanketed the sky and ensured that the night remained as dark as his clothing. He could not see the ground beneath his feet. Faint wisps of illumination snuck through the fabric of some tents in the camp, and he used them as guides. He paused to plaster his face and hands in mud, then moved down the hillside like a cat, stopping still for minutes at a time when a noise intruded anywhere. The camp slept, for the most part. Occasionally someone arose and headed to a latrine, but the latrines stood mostly on the far side. Charles skirted more quickly around the soccer fields, in easier terrain. He peered through the night, trying to identify landmarks that looked so different in the near blackness than they did by day.

The two boys slept under palm fronds at the edge of one of the larger open tents on the periphery of the camp. He hoped they were still there, as he moved toward it, careful with every step. If they had changed location, then he would abort the mission and return empty-handed. If he were caught, JohnJohn or the mercenaries would torture him. But he believed, with certainty borne of naiveté, that he would die before revealing any information to his inquisitors.

Just ten yards away now. He crawled through the damp dirt and slid up next to the shadowy lump that was the sleeping Saye.

Nyahn slept at his feet. Charles felt it would be safer waking Nyahn first. He moved toward the boy, and softly stroked his arm. Would he scream?

"Nyahn, it's Charles." He whispered it a dozen times as he gently helped the boy rouse. No sudden motions. Be soft.

Nyahn awoke slowly, calmly, and unafraid, saw Charles, and reached around his neck with an embrace and tears that couldn't be seen.

Any fear of being exposed by the boys evaporated at that moment.

Nyahn knew how to awaken his brother quietly. Saye reached out for Charles's hand and held on tightly.

The three slipped away together as silently as wraiths.

42

Rally

"SABINA, my dear, how is California treating you?" Theodore Lichen's voice did not reflect the irritation he felt at the current interruption. He lay on his couch, alone in his apartment, after eating a solitary gourmet dinner he'd just microwaved. It was one of the half dozen he selected weekly from the frozen-foods section of the supermarket near his apartment.

He was immersed in a brief about a high-profile case in which the taxpayer not only failed to cooperate but now was posturing stupidly, asserting constitutional issues that the courts had long since dismissed. The taxpayer was a fool, but she was a prominent fool—the host of a nationally syndicated radio show with a loyal following of silver-haired women. It had to be handled deftly. She'd have to be convicted decisively to discourage imitation by her listeners. He would initiate a PR campaign painting her as a mentally unbalanced criminal. He would allow no martyrdom.

"I'm not in California, Dad." Her voice sounded sleepy.

Did that silly old radio bitch have the smarts to hire the right attorneys, as well as enough cojones to take the battle public? A counterattack, launched simultaneously on both fronts, could risk his hundred-percent conviction rate. Most taxpayers just used their family attorney, as they might for any other legal matter; those people were easily steamrolled. Others used specialized tax attorneys, whose future livelihood depended on playing by the IRS rules; the result was usually a heavy fine and a suspended sentence, which both sides could count as a victory. But she might find a legal mad dog who would want to simultaneously fight the case in court and in the media.

"Where are you?" he asked his daughter, not really paying attention.

"Oh… Africa."

"What?" Lichen's mind engaged.

"We special agents travel, Dad. Don't you know that?" She added a kittenish lilt to her voice to defuse any serious objections.

"No, I don't. I don't know that at all. Certainly not to Africa. Did Graves authorize you to go?"

"Not exactly. This required initiative on my part."

"Sabina, what the hell are you up to?"

"You asked me to chase down Charles Knight. So I have."

"Who's Charles Knight?"

There was a pause. "Charles Knight, Dad. The young guy you wanted me to track down and make into a poster child. I've done it."

"Oh, right." He remembered now, and his attitude softened. The tax rebel. "It's only been, what, ten days since I sent you out to Laguna Niguel? What have you got that could possibly take you to Africa?"

"I've got him by the balls, Dad. And there are hundreds of millions of dollars at stake."

This also took Lichen by surprise. Big money could mean big risks. Suddenly concerned, he considered the possibility that his daughter had gone off the reservation, and he didn't like it when *anybody* went off his reservation. And if she got into serious trouble, the word would get out that they were related. That was a problem. He went into damage control mode.

"You tell me where you are, Sabina. Exactly."

"I'm in Gondwana. At a hotel right near the embassy in Adamstown. Safe as can be."

Lichen diverted his attention from a possible political misadventure, and allowed his paternal imagination to take charge for a moment. He envisioned his platinum-haired daughter in a seedy hotel that looked like something from wartime Beirut, windows broken, buildings burning on every block, the streets coated with spent AK-47 cartridges, and thousands of black men chasing after her with machetes.

Of course, the capital city of Gondwana hadn't been like that for some years. But images flashed from news reports stayed in people's minds forever.

"What the hell are you thinking? Or are you even thinking?" he demanded.

"This is where Knight is. He's working a scam on a mining exploration company called B-F Explorations."

"I've heard of it. B-F is front-page news—lead story. Tell me more."

"Sadly, Dad, it's more of an SEC matter now. I got him, solid, on insider trading."

"You don't work for the SEC right now. You work for me!"

"I know, but isn't this what the vice president wanted? To cross-pollinate the agencies so that we're more effective, right? To get the bad guys? But there are bound to be tax issues too; we don't have a million words of statutes and four million words of regulations and seventy thousand pages of case law and explanations just for fun...."

Lichen cherished all those words and pages, many of them conflicting, and many more unclear and arbitrary. Those words offered the prospect of making anyone he chose into a criminal.

Lichen's imagination reoriented itself from downside risk to upside potential. The vice president and his Government Efficiency Enhancement Initiative might yet prove useful. Sabina might be standing on the sort of platform that could get him just the exposure he needed for his final move: from *Deputy* Commissioner for Enforcement to *Commissioner* of the IRS.

Politicians had notoriously better memories for slights done *to* them than favors done *for* them. But still, with the vice president the front runner to be the next president in six years, an opportunity presented itself. If Lichen could help make one of the man's programs a PR success, the VP would have to see him as an ally.

"Just what do you have on Knight, Sabina?"

"I've got him with extensive inside knowledge of an ongoing fraud perpetrated by B-F's head geologist, a guy named Smolderhof."

"Smolderhof—is he American?"

"Nope. He's Canadian. So I'm staying focused on Knight."

"Good girl. How sure are you that there's an actionable case here?"

"From an SEC perspective, just about certain."

"Have you talked to your old SEC boss?"

"Barely. I wanted to talk to you first."

"Again, good girl. But give them a hypothetical, and make sure they'll act when the time is right."

"Oh, I did *that* already. I didn't bother calling my old boss, but *her* boss said he would be very interested. I called him directly."

"You bypassed your boss?"

"Sometimes the chain of command can get in the way, Dad. You know that. This way, *I'll* be my boss when I go back to SEC."

"You think it's that big?"

"Dad," she whined like a teenager, "Knight is twenty-three years old and could clear over $200 million from this! So, yes, I think it's big."

The reptilian base of his brain's limbic system activated, and Lichen didn't need to think at all: "I'll catch the next flight over." He should be on the spot, to ensure the recognition and forfeited assets accrued to his budget at the IRS.

It was time to take a page from the PR book of J. Edgar Hoover. Even after he became the head of the FBI, Hoover loved to insert himself in the middle of a big crime bust. He liked to pose, tommy gun in hand, for the benefit of the cameras—and his reputation. Theodore Lichen could do the same, with boots on the ground in Gondwana, heroically safeguarding the taxpayers' money. Lichen could be the bureaucrat's version of "In the room, in the deal; out of the room, out of the deal."

"Don't you steal my thunder, Dad!"

"I just want to ensure you maximize the opportunity."

"When was the last time you were in the field?" She thoughtfully coated her words with a patina of concern.

Lichen's anxiety rose, and he admitted, "I hate the field. But I'm a father and I'm coming to protect my daughter."

There was a limit to maintaining the ridiculous pretense. "Bullshit, Dad."

"You don't want me to come to Africa?" He hated to even leave Washington, and his daughter knew it. The thought of placing his soft, sedentary body in a position of discomfort, much less possible danger, distressed and humiliated him.

"Dad, I'm heading back tomorrow anyway. The mission here is accomplished."

"Good, Sabina. I suppose it's not really appropriate for a man in my position to be running through the jungle.... And I know you understand the importance of the IRS getting its fair share of that money. We want this to be a win-win situation."

Sabina's smile, prompted by his last words, was almost audible through the phone line. "I don't expect any of it's going into my pocket. So sure—not least because you're my father—it's share and share alike between the IRS and the SEC."

She would rack up brownie points with the top management of both agencies, plus the VP's office. Beautiful, ruthless, and effective: she had hit the super trifecta of virtues. But she was also naïve.

"The details of this sort of thing are way above your pay grade, but I'll hold your hand. Prepare a full briefing. Accessing Knight's money for the benefit of this agency will require real finesse, Sabina. You don't have a clue about the politics, about the turf. So I want everything you've got, in my email, by day's end, got it?"

"It's already all prepared for you, Dad."

"Really?"

"Well, I owed a report to the vice president anyway. He's been keeping tabs too. I'll just send you a copy."

So much for his thunder. "You bypassed *me?*"

Sabina repeated herself. "Sometimes the chain of command can get in the way. You know that."

What a clever little bitch. He couldn't help feeling proud.

*   *   *

The night passed, the sun rose, the camp awoke, morning activities ensued. But the activities had changed. This morning the boys and young men broke most of camp, carrying their bags and supplies and tents and weapons across the soccer fields to load into the waiting vehicles of the motor pool, which sat under the protection of the giant boulder on the hill. The mess tent, latrines, some generators, a third of the other tents, and the stage from which JohnJohn exuded such charisma remained. At noon, it was again time for JohnJohn to speak. No rain fell, but the overcast sky kept it just a bit cooler, a welcome reprieve from an oppressive heat unmitigated by even the faintest puff of wind.

Two thousand young men gathered in the center of what had been the camp. JohnJohn remained on target, his speech often like the comforting hypnosis of a church liturgy, but each time with a twist, each time moving the mob's programming one notch forward.

This time, he expanded the mob's awesome energy to a new high. So loud, so irrational, so dangerous.

Rupert stood to the side with his mercenary friends. Old mercenaries only achieved their age because they knew when to fold their tents and hike out of harm's way. These old Africa hands would have all departed with half-hearted apologies and fond farewells, but not a moment of delay, had he ever told them that the promised munitions had gone missing. All four men would have "made the chicken run." The term referred to what 250,000 Europeans had done when Rhodesia became Zimbabwe. In those days it was used as a pejorative, until it was recognized as a sign of intelligence: to get the hell out of Dodge while it was still possible. Bart, Robin, Randy, and Bazyli stuck around to protect their payday, never aware that the plan had gone off track.

Had Rupert told JohnJohn of the disappearance of the ammunition and weapons, the man would have killed him instantly. Had Flomo learned about it first, Rupert's death would have been much slower, controlled, and painful.

But Roscoe had arrived that morning from Banga Sioquelle, where he had left the two ammunition container trucks recovered from Charles Knight, a man Rupert had never seen, but whom he despised. Until this rebel army arrived there later in the day, only locals would guard the munitions. Roscoe told him that in two days Burke's drilling teams would depart via truck convoy working their way up from the Freeport to the B-F prospect.

JohnJohn's army would be there to greet them, fully armed and in total control of the region.

Today would be the day that JohnJohn would lead his men into Gondwana, to Banga Sioquelle. To the guns. And to all that gold. The B-F property, as planned, would be the epicenter of the rebellion. Whether JohnJohn understood gold mining or foolishly expected Banga Sioquelle to be a glittering paradise of gold coating everything didn't really matter. This army would make a mess of Banga Sioquelle. The design of this whole operation was brilliant. The best fraud was one that was never discovered to be a fraud.

This would be Rupert's last venture in Africa. Grab the money and run. The white man was through in sub-Saharan Africa, in any event. The writing was on the wall long ago, starting with the Mau Mau in Kenya back in the '50s, and the trend had only accelerated from there. The Congo, Rhodesia, Mozambique, and Angola had also suffered bloody expulsions. The whites had basically lost everything, all over the continent.

West Africa was best left for the Chinese and the Africans to fight over. Their battling it out on his wide screen on a quiet beach would provide free entertainment.

But that came further down the road. Right now there was little time to take cover before a most unpleasant shitstorm—with intermittent bullets and showers of blood—descended onto Gondwana. It didn't take a weatherman to see which way the wind would blow during the decades to come—and especially the next couple of days.

Rupert tallied his take. After today's stock sales he would have a total of over $15 million—plus the promised bonus. Not bad for twelve months of work—far, far better than his entire lifetime to date. In a day or two more, it would be mission accomplished. He and his men would grab an SUV, hightail it to Conakry, and disappear. Everything here was now beyond his control. The rebellion might well succeed, and Banga Sioquelle might stay under rebel control for years. Rupert had already planted in JohnJohn's head the seeds of a long-term strategy. The man could not be considered a great geopolitical thinker, but he saw the merit of consolidating for some months in Banga Sioquelle and Gbarngeda. Then, only later, would he march on the capital.

Geopolitics. Strategy. Rupert couldn't repress a guffaw. The level of sophistication was like doing a deal with a prostitute back in Adamstown.

"Will you follow me?" JohnJohn shouted into the microphone as he danced across the stage like a prizefighter. "Will you follow me to hell? Will you follow me to heaven?"

Each question elicited cheers, louder and louder, rising to a raging pitch.

"Will you follow me to Gong County? Will you follow me to Gbarngeda? Will you follow me to Adamstown? Will you follow me to the president's mansion and strip Gondwana from his thieving hands?"

JohnJohn, like a master chef, blended the ingredients of religion and populism with the spices of presumed injustice, serving an appetizer that even well-educated, middle-aged Americans would eagerly swallow. Its effect on the poor, young Gondwanans was explosive. JohnJohn could generate an unmatchable furor in these young men. But an even louder cheer emerged when he cried in a voice more booming than ever before, *"Will you follow me to Washington!"*

It was not a question.

The crowd bellowed, guns waved high above their heads, residual ammunition discharged in the excitement, bullets flying haphazardly toward the sky. Sweat and energy and mass insanity charged the atmosphere. JohnJohn bounded about on the stage. This time, he had worked himself, not just his army, into a crazed frenzy. His face contorted; his red eyes bulged. More coked up than usual, JohnJohn rejoiced in the fact that today was the day.

JohnJohn froze then, his body a statue. His voice and words took over as the sole agents to incite the next level of hysteria. He bellowed, "Gondwana will have hope again! We will change this country! We, we men of Gbarngeda, we will change. They will hope. We will change. They will hope. We will change. They will hope! We will change! Hope! Change! Hope! Change!" The words made no sense, but they didn't have to. The roar of the men got louder still, as they screamed the meaningless words over and over again, hypnotizing themselves with the well-proven mantra.

"We leave today for our guns and our gold and our destiny! We strike today! TODAY!" The mob went completely berserk.

Rupert shook his head, awed at what men will believe. Simple words stated with confidence, filled with fluff and vinegar, were all it took to change the course of history. He had no expertise in moral judgment, but he felt a mixture of amusement and disgust at what stupid sheep people could be. Rupert stared at JohnJohn on stage, doped to oblivion each night, coked to the sky all day, wanting only power and control, unpredictable and dangerous; this man on stage might be the devil, or maybe the antichrist himself. He tried to recall his Sunday school classes many years before: was the devil higher than the antichrist in the ecclesiastical pecking order?

JohnJohn shouted. "Men of Gondwana! Today we embark on our path to heavenly glory! Glory in the highest!"

The mob howled in delight and affirmation.

After that line, Rupert knew what was coming next. He had expected JohnJohn to say it and to even believe it. JohnJohn, at his most outrageously narcissistic and at the most grandiose peak of his life, finally said it.

JohnJohn shouted to the masses of his people in the most potent voice he had ever used, louder than the combined intensity of two thousand men, cracking at the strain of the volume that emerged. "Men of Gondwana!" he cried out. "Men of Gondwana!" He paused before screaming, "I AM GOD!"

And then, perhaps appropriately and certainly poetically, in the midst of this mighty proclamation of his infinite power, JohnJohn's head exploded.

The side of his skull erupted in a mass of blood that sprayed across the stage. JohnJohn's powerful body stayed upright for a moment, held vertical by the rousing energy of two thousand men and a huge amount of cocaine. And then what was left of JohnJohn slowly fell to the stage in an immodest heap.

43

The Two Daughters Attack

THE three men atop the giant boulder watched as JohnJohn's words heated the rebel army into a fury. The air vibrated as two thousand individuals morphed into a single thoughtless collective—regulated, directed, and presided over by a psychopath.

Charles watched Xander closely as he set up the weapon, made measurements, turned dials, padded and supported his elbows, loaded a round in the chamber, and slid the bolt forward and down.

"Change! Hope! Change! Hope!" the words echoed up the hillside.

Charles said, "Don't shoot until you see the reds of his eyes."

Xander snorted in amusement, not stirring. The 12× riflescope was powerful enough to allow him to see those eyes. Xander had heard quite enough of the crazed man down there in the valley. The time was now, as he hoped JohnJohn wouldn't move, nor the wind come up. He gauged the nonexistent wind one more time based on the motion of smoke rising straight upward from the piles of palms being processed into charcoal.

Many skilled snipers might prefer a higher-velocity, more modern cartridge such as the .300 Winchester Magnum, but the .30–06 in Xander's Savage rifle made for substantially less recoil. Others might opt for an AR-10 or an M-14, which would offer quicker follow-up shots should the first be off target. But Xander was, at heart, a traditionalist. His Savage, fitted with the custom Mannlicher stock he preferred, won the day for simple joy of shooting. Experience had made him comfortable with it, and he knew its capabilities and quirks. He had learned the skill of a sniper, on the job, in a different chapter of life, long ago. It was a chapter of a book he thought he had closed and put down forever, never to be reopened. It was the chapter that had cost him his family.

"Red eyes," Xander said. He halted his breathing and gently squeezed the highly sensitive trigger just as JohnJohn shouted, "I AM GOD!"

The three men on the long rock at the top of the hill crouched low, invisible to the army below. Xander watched the effect of his one perfect shot.

The sound of the rifle arrived at the stage a fraction of a second after JohnJohn's head exploded, and two seconds before the mass of men realized what had happened. No one could have localized the source of the rifle shot over the clamor and screaming.

*   *   *

Rupert knew that the shot came from a high-powered rifle from a distance, a planned hit by an expert marksman. Two thousand men, razzed up by rhetoric, had just lost their charismatic leader. They would momentarily finger him and his white colleagues as scapegoats.

He looked at the crowd of young Gondwanan soldier-soccer players, jaws dropped, staring at the stage, standing up on their toes to see, even though they must have known. They stayed quiet for the moment, but that would change, ferociously. He saw Flomo, nearer to the stage. Flomo turned slowly and looked back at Rupert. The man's face changed from disbelief to suspicion to anger over the next few seconds. He would soon recognize the opportunity.

Rupert could think of only one thing to do that had any possibility of success. He had to get on the stage before Flomo filled the power void with his own rabid brand of charisma.

Rupert bounded up on the stage. He didn't need to check if John-John had a pulse. He did, in fact, for blood pumped out of the demolished skull; his heart still beating, even though his brain lay scrambled and spread out on the planks. Rupert stood in front of the men, all completely quiet for this one moment. He had only a second or two more before a very special kind of hell broke loose among the now leaderless mob of energized young males. He grabbed the microphone from John-John's clenched fist. Thick blood dripped off of it down his hand and forearm.

391

"Men! Gondwana men! JohnJohn has been killed! Officers all come here to me. The rest of you go to the hills!" He swung his arm, pointing all around. "Go to the hills, and find his killer! Go, men from Gondwana. Go, all of you! Leave no stone unturned, spread out, spread far out, to the hills and beyond. Spread to the seven seas! Do not come back until you have found JohnJohn's killer!"

The mass of men, programmed for months to obey an authority whose orders were shouted loudly and who gave no quarter to anyone who defied him, quickly transferred that programming to Rupert, the man who had trained them, and who now stood over JohnJohn's body and claimed his authority.

One of the men shouted, "Yes. We go! We all go! We find John-John's killer!"

Rupert wanted this place empty. "Go! All of you! Find the killer before he gets away! Money will be your reward if you bring me this killer! Hurry, before he can escape!"

Roscoe and his other mercenaries shouted at them all, "Go! Go!" and threw their arms around, as if pushing the mass of humanity away.

The crowd moved, the men spontaneously spreading out from the camp, running from the center to the periphery, some with guns in hand, screaming like Banshees, without even the control of their unit leaders, scattering out in an expanding circle at amazing speed, in all the directions, including a contingent of them running toward the giant boulder on the tallest hill.

*   *   *

"Big trouble this way comes," Charles said, calmly, as he watched the crazed expanding circle of men tearing toward them. It would take them, at a run, about two minutes to reach them.

"Shit. Get ready for part two," Xander said, also calmly, despite the expletive.

TJ counted the men running toward them, four hundred yards and closing. "Fifty or more."

Xander pressed a button on a box next to him. "Sixty seconds, gentlemen. Go!"

The three men slid down the rounded dark backside of the boulder. This was no occasion to be careful, no time for a studied descent to avoid abrasions. Go, go, go!

Each landed clumsily in the dirt below. They knew exactly what they had to do in the next fifteen seconds. The three men tore through the bush, Charles in the lead, threading his way through the small orifice in their bamboo hideout. Xander dove in second, and TJ squeezed through, pulling the concealing bamboo up behind him. They jumped on top of their murky Jacuzzi, TJ again taking up the rear, sliding a covering of palm leaves over the top of them. They were in a deep wet hole, covered with foliage and surrounded by a thick wall of bamboo with a tight, camouflaged entrance. The time had come to learn if the keep was adequately prepared.

"Hi," Nyahn said, as TJ sat on him.

Charles replied, "Get ready, Nyahn. Get ready, Saye. It's about to happen!"

The boys crouched down lower in the covered hole.

This would be their cramped home for the next… who knew how long. But right now, they all covered their ears and heads and hoped that the damn thing would fall the right way.

* * *

Rupert watched the men tear out of the camp, moving away from him, away from his own men. Some of the unit leaders, the equivalent of officers and NCOs, stayed behind, moving hesitantly up toward him and the fallen JohnJohn. That was okay. He could handle them. But a group of a hundred soldiers ignored his orders to spread out. He knew these men: Flomo's chosen guard. And that was unacceptable. Cut from Flomo's cloth, their minds molded to match Flomo's, they were each of them natural-born criminals. They hesitated now only because they saw that Flomo appeared as a tiny rat, and Rupert as a ferocious war dog.

So Rupert maintained his physically commanding position over JohnJohn's bloody corpse, put on his boldest face, heaved out his chest and looked as big as possible.

He had no idea where the shooter was, but that giant boulder would have been his own first choice. A sniper often has to choose between the best place—generally the highest point with the clearest field of fire—and the safest place, the one that will give him the best avenue of escape. The rock was both.

The two most senior, most feared—and therefore the most respected—of JohnJohn's lieutenants looked at each other, and then they turned toward the little worm Flomo. Rupert knew what was going through their minds, and that he couldn't deal with one hundred men. Flomo was seeking the right moment to make his move and the right words to say in that moment.

But Rupert still had the microphone, something only JohnJohn had used. It gave him extra authority, as might a judge's gavel or a king's scepter. Or—a better analogy in this place—the conch in Golding's *Lord of the Flies*. He shouted to the one hundred, before Flomo could say anything. "You men. Go! Go to the hill there! That is where the man is who killed our leader! All of you go! I promise a huge reward to those who find the assassin!"

Half of the men turned with little thought, and started running toward the hill, now following Rupert's orders. But the others remained, looking at the lieutenants, waiting for their orders from men to whom they gave more credence.

Rupert turned to his four friends on the ground below the stage. Each knew what would happen next. The only question was which one of the lieutenants would give the order, and thereby take command.

The inevitable quickly became the imminent. The time had come to observe the Golden Rule of conflict: do unto others, but do it first. Rupert was not quite fast enough.

Flomo pulled his sidearm, fired at Rupert, and shouted, "Kill the white men!"

Guns came up fast, aimed at the mercenaries, who hit the ground immediately. Rupert watched as twenty AKs targeted his friends, most of whom had been his colleagues from wars over the last forty years. Experienced soldiers, he and his colleagues fired into the mob as effectively as they could from the ground, while squirming toward cover. But a handful of men firing into dozens aren't likely to hit all of the twenty who are armed. Those twenty weren't marksmen, but spray and pray on the part of the many overcame the accurately directed fire from the few. Thirty of the mob went down, but the mob's bullets in turn found each one of the mercs—in a limb, an abdomen, a chest, a head. Roscoe succumbed to more than a dozen bullets in his torso.

Time seemed to slow down as Rupert felt three bullets hit him, two in his legs, one through his belly to his spine. He collapsed on top of JohnJohn's body, firing his own sidearm repeatedly to make sure that at least Flomo would die then and there. His aim was true.

The bullets flew for the next few seconds, although it felt to Rupert like minutes. He lay on JohnJohn's warm body. It was nice, because he himself felt cold. His eyes faced the hill from the top of which he had last talked to his brother. His legs were both shattered. Odd how one rarely considers what happens when a bullet hits bone. It never seems to happen in the movies.... Blood pulsed out from a torn artery. He couldn't move either leg, but nor could he feel them; his mind lingered on the bullet that had severed his spinal cord. While his intellect involuntarily assessed his injuries, his emotions damned his luck for getting killed just before the big payoff. Nobody wants to be either the first or the last soldier to die in a war.

As he looked at the hill, the giant rocky mass that sat on top of it jumped.

The top of the hill leapt upward. Blast after blast of dirt shot out from under the rock outcrop, initially on the left, then moving almost instantaneously toward the middle, and then to the right, as six hundred pounds of explosives serially converted the partly eroded hilltop into an expanding mass of pulverized dust and gas, no longer sufficient to hold the many thousands of tons it had supported for so long. Rupert lay there watching, astonished, while a few more bullets flew wildly by. The echoes of the explosive charges arrived then, like the broadside of cannons from a British frigate. Bang, bang, bang, bang, bang, bang, thundering and shaking the earth. The men stopped shooting and turned toward the explosions. They stared as the huge rock was freed from the perch on which it had rested for eons. Rupert watched as the men running through the motor pool fell to the ground. He watched as dirt and smoke obscured the top of the hill in an impermeable fog of gaseous grime. He watched as the men stood back up, and as they started running, most to the side, some back toward the camp. He watched as doom emerged from that thick cloud of dust. The sound followed behind it as the three-hundred-foot-wide top of the hill crashed down onto the vehicles in the motor pool.

Rupert thought of the American planes at Pearl Harbor, lined up on runways, making convenient targets for the Japanese bombers. It was an intelligent way to position them—unless they were about to be attacked. His fleet of vehicles stood at the foot of the hill ready for the army to board on their way to Gbarngeda and glory. Two gasoline trucks sat ten feet apart, each filled with ten thousand gallons of incendiary liquid. Along with almost every other vehicle of the rebel army, and all the important supplies, they were crushed into metallic pancakes by the mass from above, while showering out their inflammable contents the way a water balloon might as it smacks a brick wall. It took one spark to ignite the expanding fuel vapors, and then the explosion came, blasting flame and dirt in all directions and causing the moving mass of rock to leap again. What had been the crown of the hill then burst its way out through the cloud of dust and fire and down into the valley, men running to the side and out of its way as it relentlessly gained speed.

His status now reduced to that of a spectator, Rupert could only watch as the massive rock raced downward toward him. It obliterated the supplies not yet loaded into the now-burning trucks, and leveled the remaining tents as it tore along toward the center of the camp. Another few seconds, and he would not die from the bullet wounds but rather from the unstoppable mass of rolling death—a steamroller as long as a soccer field. He looked at his men, who lay dying nearby. And at Flomo's flock of sociopaths about to be crushed. The sound was overwhelming. The rush of air that preceded it gusted into his face.

He felt the bloody mound of flesh below him. JohnJohn.

Rupert's last thoughts were that his own body would merge into that of the dead man below him, crushed together into a soup of flesh and blood and drugs, and that his body would be one with JohnJohn's, for all eternity. What would future archaeologists hundreds of years hence, or even paleontologists millions of years hence, make of it?

He had no opportunity to consider it further.

The hundred-yard-long sausage-shaped boulder rolled and bounced through the camp at thirty miles per hour, mashing everything in its path, like a primitive bulldozer. Then it climbed the steep hill on the other side of the narrow valley, pausing there for the strangest moment of peace. Two thousand men—now minus perhaps 10 percent of their number slain by bullets and the great boulder—silently watched the rock come to a stop and almost settle.

Inertia held it stationary for a few seconds, and then faintly at first, ever so quietly, the boulder started rolling back down toward the camp, making more and more tumultuous noise as it increased speed, unobstructed by the trees that had slowed its progress on the way through before. It bounced over a small hillock and cracked in two, the progeny now returning to the camp independently. The two rolling bludgeons plowed through the parts of the camp previously missed, flattening everything in their path and, as if coordinated and planned in detail, destroying every last standing structure, every tent, every generator, everything, before turning back toward each other to crash together, a noise louder than all else that day, as the two individually unhaltable masses finally stopped each other in a grinding, pulverizing, collision.

Forever after, the Two Daughters, as the two great masses of stone became known, would lie there, so close, but never touching again.

44

Arms at Rest

CHARLES whispered in the dark, "Xander, I believe the rock fell in the right direction. Good job."

"It was a better than fifty-fifty bet," Xander replied.

TJ whispered indignantly, "I thought you said it was eighty-twenty."

"You've always admired my optimistic outlook...." Xander replied.

"Shit," TJ said.

"I wonder what it's like out there."

Xander said, "I hope the motor pool is gone."

"At least," TJ added.

Xander commanded, "And now, it is time for absolute quiet."

Strands of light leaked through the covering of their buried keep, enough for Charles to see Saye looking at him. Charles rubbed his hand over the boy's hair, and then reached out for Nyahn with a bruised arm and squeezed him tight. After that, not a word, not a snore could be allowed.

Soon, excited voices came from above, outside the concealed bamboo bunker. But they dispersed over time. They heard a few shots, probably scores being settled in the mayhem. The three men and the two boys maintained complete silence in the bunker, uttering not even a whisper until nightfall. It was a reasonable precaution to avoid attracting the enraged young men whose leader they had just killed, and who would tear them apart.

*   *   *

They slept, they waited, they wondered. A few more distant muffled shots rang out during the night. But then only the noise of the jungle remained.

With no leader, no motor pool, no ammunition, and no additional weapons, no rebellion could happen. Soccer season was over.

They agreed to wait as long as needed before emerging from what could have been their catacomb. TJ peered through carefully aligned holes in the bamboo surrounding them. Until they finally emerged, grimy and reeking of jungle mud, the three men, and the two boys with them, had no idea just how effective part two of their plan had been.

Bunker Hill had destroyed the motor pool, just as they had hoped. But the massive rock had obliterated the entire camp as well. No part of the army lingered in the valley. Smoke rose from untended piles of palms slowing burning into charcoal and from the flattened burned out remnants of the fuel trucks.

Charles had hoped for this outcome, planned for it, but half did not expect to live to see it. The rebel leader was dead, the supporting mercenaries also dead, their compressed corpses clearly distinguished by their still-white skin, now flattened in the most grotesque possible sort of death. Their bodies lay oozing in the muck that had once been the center of the camp, their fluids attracting flies to the surface of the two titanic daughters that had crushed them.

The great majority of the soccer rebels survived. With no one to lead them and no object of plunder before them, these young men—many of them ten or twelve years younger than Charles—had no reason to fight. Leaderless, purposeless, with no food or equipment beyond what they could scavenge from the wreckage, the survivors of the rebel army had wandered off back to Gondwana and their homes.

The military training, the speeches from JohnJohn, and then the trauma of the camp's destruction made an indelible impression on many of the survivors. Some would become thugs, a few would become bandits, some would try to emulate their erstwhile leader in more subtle ways. Some would just stare into the middle distance for the weeks to come, leaving their relatives to wonder what had really happened. Most would just go back to who they were before, albeit with memories tattooed on their personalities.

Although some had undoubtedly picked up grandiose ideas from JohnJohn— plus a few rudimentary military skills from Rupert and the mercs—most just wanted to play soccer.

From what Charles could tell, the gunfight, the boulder, and the fuel trucks exploding had killed more than a hundred people, and for that he grieved. But a rebellion of this magnitude, led by JohnJohn, would have killed tens of thousands at least and left a barely functioning people abandoned to the dark ages.

Charles observed to himself, under his breath. "Death tolls in war are rationalized in just that way."

*   *   *

Caroline had no alternative but to wait.

The *Africa Grace* struggled too. It was as if the ship felt the concern of its people. The pace of the medical work kept increasing, while the physical plant kept failing—a generator overheating, a coolant pump clogging, barnacles always accreting. Captain Freberg had to comfort both of the women for whom he was most responsible: Caroline and his ship. He did not relish projecting optimism without feeling it.

Caroline worked day and night, taking breaks only for an occasional shower, change of scrubs, a cup of coffee, and the barest amount of rest. She worked considerably more than was required of her, but the long hours kept her mind off what might be happening in the interior of the country. She tried to call her mother in a spare moment. She wanted to tell her about Charles, keeping a promise to inform her parents about any men in her life before some news agency might get wind of it. But her mother was occupied with some affair of state. Leaving a message with the staff could only be counterproductive: if she said anything of interest, it would just open the door to a scandalous tabloid article sometime in the future. She trusted Captain Anders implicitly. He was enjoined to be her guardian angel on this cruise. But he was no substitute for her mother.

Although there had been no direct word from Charles himself, some news trickled out from Gbarngeda: young men and boys returning home after a long time away, some staying, hundreds more walking on further south to wherever their homes might next be.

The information drifting to the capital was unclear and confounded by language and culture: a rebellion planned, an army gathered, an army disbanded. Or was it decimated? Many dead. No war coming. That was the good news. But word also circulated that some foreigners were among the dead, and still she had not heard from Charles.

Waiting was a lousy allocation of her time. She cried some. But mostly she worked harder and longer. Occasionally, out of exhaustion, she would collapse on her mattress, the mattress that she and Charles had lain upon, naked and in love.

* * *

Burke's team was slated to leave momentarily for the B-F prospect in Banga Sioquelle. Jumbled reports of what had happened at the soccer camp in Guinea might put that on ice until the air cleared. Those same reports emptied the B-F camp of the last of the foreign staff. No one from B-F would be there to greet Burke, ever.

Using GPS devices hidden in them, Charles tracked the munitions trucks to exactly where he hoped to find them. They sat at the B-F prospect, unconcealed in anticipation of JohnJohn's imminent arrival. Another few hundred dollars was sufficient to divert the attention of B-F's local guards, none of whom wanted to stick around in the face of the frightening stories they kept hearing.

TJ and Charles each took the wheel of a giant truck. They drove south from Banga Sioquelle in convoy, along the road Charles knew all too well. Xander pulled far ahead of the slow-moving trucks, alone in the SUV, making a beeline back to the *Africa Grace*. He ran a fever again and needed its ministrations, hot soaks, and dressing changes.

On their first trip in these trucks, a week ago, TJ and Charles had spent two whole days together. Then more time traveling by small motorbike, by jeep, or by foot, talking, laughing, and calculating, while lumbering up the road. They worked side-by-side, undertaking hard physical labor in the most grueling conditions. They had spent nine hours—in dark silence and under persistent threat of discovery—digging and concealing their bamboo and mud keep at the now-decapitated Bunker Hill. Another long ride, a day and part of a night acting as pack animals, a morning climaxed by an assassination and the destruction of a camp and a rebellion. Then a day living in a hole in the ground, hiding from throngs of angry teenagers. And now another nine hours driving two giant diesel trucks packed with weapons down this craggy and eroded road, chatting over two short-range radios.

If there is a basis for friendship in the first place, then the sort of time that TJ and Charles had spent together is sufficient to transform a mere acquaintance into a loyal friend for life. TJ was now not just Xander's fixer, but Charles's fixer as well. They shared the bond formed among men facing death.

TJ could accomplish whatever was needed in Gondwana, and do it with skill and promptness, as long as sufficient money was available. Had agents of the US government not conspired to confiscate Charles's securities, TJ's skill and Charles's new capital might have combined to provide a resounding economic boost to the war-torn country.

But it was not to be. Not yet. Political risks were intrinsic to speculation. Indeed, politics largely created speculative opportunities, and therefore politics could take them away. The odd thing was that the fatal political risk did not arise in the backward, unstable little African country. It arose in the US.

Charles's backstop, encouraged by Xander and insisted upon by Maurice, consisted of the small trading account that his uncle still held for him, containing a few highly speculative holdings in some publicly traded companies here and there. But he had that backstop at least. Charles had come out of the whole B-F affair dead even.

Except, of course, that he had $10 million of Smolderhof's money secured in an offshore bank. Tax free. Charles would convert that money into a vast array of experiences, skills, knowledge, and connections in the next few years.

Salt air from the nearby ocean permeated the bush. It was 1 a.m.; no village lay within miles. Only the occasional giant truck traversed this remote jungle road far southeast of Adamstown. They had come hundreds of miles from Banga Sioquelle, where the Burke International Mining men would construct their new prefab buildings as soon as they were assured no rebel force loomed nearby. It wouldn't take long. UN flights over the region eventually came across the demolished camp.

TJ drove the lead truck. Charles followed behind. Their five picnickers—loaders and guards and now friends—once again perched on top of TJ's roof for this, their ride back home. TJ turned off the road and onto a path far too narrow for the trucks. But their giant tires simply broadened the path over the next kilometer as they approached their destination.

Charles thought about the men killed at the soccer camp. Then about Ollie and the two guards. Then about Harry. He was the cause. His rational mind and even his emotions could justify his actions. Each was a case of kill or be killed. But neither his mind nor his heart were at ease.

Charles shook the images of the carnage from his thoughts as TJ stopped his truck ahead. Together they walked the remaining path in the night lit by the truck headlights, Charles stretching his legs and slapping at mosquitoes. TJ examined the side path to be sure both trucks could get in. And, just as important, get out. The getting out would become difficult to impossible after it began to rain. The clouds, although not entirely blotting out the moonlit sky, warned of an impending deluge.

TJ started pulling back camouflage at a site set back in the bush about one hundred feet off this barely passable side trail. Two old, mildewed shipping containers, almost entirely buried into the side of a low hill, gradually appeared.

"They are my father's. He kept things here during the wars, and no one ever found them. It takes little to bury them completely. They are empty now."

"Let's fill them up."

TJ went back to bring the trucks further on while Charles continued clearing away the debris that had accumulated in front of the containers over the years. He had no tools but a flashlight and his hands.

Two of the five men who rode on the top climbed down as the trucks approached, quickly assessed the situation, and waved Charles aside. Some might say it was evidence of cultural atavism from colonial days, when blacks worked while whites watched. In this case, it was a display of friendship and respect. Certainly, the fact that they had their own machetes helped speed the task along. They finished the work, and TJ opened the locked doors. Within two minutes they had crafted brooms from palms and dry grass, and swiftly swept the containers clean of the debris and vermin that had infiltrated them over the years.

TJ had everyone moving fast. They knew what they were doing because they had done the same thing earlier, in reverse, when they loaded the trucks from the containers near Gbarngeda. Inside the massive trucks lay two thousand cardboard boxes, each weighing about forty pounds and containing just shy of one thousand rounds of ammunition. They set up a chain of men, as before, and the system operated efficiently. Passing two thousand heavy boxes took hours of aggressive effort, and Charles felt like he'd spent the whole time pumping iron at a gym.

All of JohnJohn's ammunition filled less than the back half of the first cargo container. Yet its combined weight was double the allowable amount for the entire forty-foot container were it to be shipped. But this ammunition was not going anywhere.

They needed the extra space, for now the men had to offload box after box of Bulgarian-made AK-47s, two thousand of them, one at a time, out of the trucks and into the containers. And then there were fifty more heavy crates, of a different shape. Each contained a shoulder-mounted anti-aircraft missile.

The task finally complete, the men locked the containers and started shoveling the mud from all around and beside, covering them with layers of dirt, then rocks, and then palms to protect the dirt from erosion by the rains until the jungle could shelter their spoils with new growth. The containers again became part of the side of the hill. They would remain invisible, but watched over by TJ.

The trucks, unburdened of the heavy payload they had borne for almost a week, buoyantly trundled the kilometer back down the pathway and onto the larger, but rarely traveled road that snaked through this small section of Djenne County, TJ's county. It was almost dawn. A hard rain started. In a week, the effects of the rain would obscure the tracks left by the trucks, and the path they had trodden would be well on its way back to obscurity, overtaken by the jungle.

Charles thought of Caroline, relishing the fact that in a day or two she would be soothing his aching body.

Sore, exhausted, covered with sweat, mosquito bites, and dirt, he felt entirely satisfied. Someday these successfully transplanted armaments might serve good purpose. In the meantime they could rest here, near the seashore just outside of Djennetown, safer than money in a bank.

The munitions would remain untouched until the day came when Charles would need them all.

45

$200 Million to the Bad

IT took longer than Burke would have liked to get their drilling teams on site; it was a balancing act between the risk of moving into an area that looked like trouble, and hanging around in the port, paying gigantic daily fees. A team sent to the site gleaned that, yes, there had been some kind of disaster at a soccer camp in Guinea, apparently one with religious and political overtones. But it didn't seem like a threat. The United Nations concurred.

After three days of preparing their giant trucks and drills, and then a long day of overland convoy travel from the Freeport to Banga Sioquelle, the Burke team arrived on site. The locals perceived Burke as a whole new level of operation, and word spread with the speed of a mamba, from Gbarngeda all the way north. A hundred new foreigners and ten container carriers filled with supplies materialized, just for starters. Upon their arrival, they began constructing new buildings designed to withstand years of Gondwana's miserable heat and pounding rains.

The Burke team dug in, getting the lay of the land, positioning their rigs close to several of the holes identified for their previous high-grade core samples. They inventoried the stored drill cores, no doubt laden with nanoparticulate gold, but moved them aside for the moment.

A couple of local teenagers—brothers who spoke English clearly enough to be understood—made their way into the fledgling Burke camp and, as the entrepreneurs they were, made themselves useful. The boys were interested in the American money that Burke brought with them but apparently not the gold that they would be mining. The boys directed them to another site, far off the property, hidden down a side road near the town of Gbarngeda.

"Are you sure? All the way down here?" the man who wore an orange jumpsuit and a hard hat asked. He and the two boys rode in the front of a pickup truck.

"Yes, Mr. Woody," the older one replied. "Near Gbarngeda."

"But the B-F team didn't tell us about another place."

The younger boy said, "It is there too. We know. Gbarngeda is our home."

The man shrugged. He needed to get to know Gbarngeda anyway, since it was the nearest source of supplies.

When they arrived at the place, he first saw two containers set back in the bush.

"Saye, you were right," he called back to the boys who walked a bit behind on a path that was all muck and water and deeply cut with heavy-vehicle tracks. He looked at the shipping containers in front of him, still partly covered with palm fronds as if someone had haphazardly tried to conceal them. The doors swung free in a gentle breeze that found its way through the trees. He stepped into one. The container stood empty.

The boys caught up and entered. The man put a hand on the smaller boy's shoulder. "Another empty one, Nyahn. Nothing in these either."

The younger of the brothers nodded and grinned as he popped back out the door to investigate the side where once palm branches formed a makeshift shelter. There were no night monsters anywhere near.

This container was not entirely empty. Two small boxes lay forgotten in the darkest, far corner of the sweltering place. The Burke man looked back toward the light from the door as he picked them up. Each held twenty 7.62 × 39 mm rounds. He winced with surprise. This was Gondwana, after all. Maybe he should not be so cavalier; the country was a tinderbox. For all he knew, they might have a whole rebel army right at their doorstep.

"Did these containers used to have stuff in them, Saye?"

Saye smiled a little and shrugged.

"Okay. Thanks. Is there anything else down in this area worth seeing? Any more B-F stuff around?"

Saye nodded. "My bossman want you to see something. Just up de path here. A big machine in broke up building. He say you want see it. He say if you see it, maybe you save yourself money and time."

The Burke man said, "Who is your bossman, Saye?"

Again, Saye smiled a little and shrugged.

Saye didn't need to say anything about the dead bodies Charles had quietly mentioned to him—two local men and a white chemist. Mr. Woody would discover them.

Saye would keep Nyahn away from all that. Nyahn didn't need to see any more monsters.

*   *   *

Wind blew through downtown Washington, DC, briskly tossing Sabina's hair and skirt as she walked up the stone steps of what Harry Truman once unfairly described as the "greatest monstrosity in America." A doorman stepped aside to let her into the Eisenhower Executive Office Building—the home to some of the excess staff that couldn't fit into the West Wing. Her hand clasped a briefcase that she hoped she would not have to open. It was stuffed with faked documents and lies about Charles Knight.

Her case held printed emails along with signed and stamped selections of official B-F documents. When examined all together, the documents would confirm to the casual observer that not only did Charles Knight have insider knowledge from the B-F team, but that he participated in the scam. As if that wasn't bold enough, Knight had extorted the B-F insiders. The documents suggested that in the end Knight had double-crossed Smolderhof and the B-F team, essentially taking over the B-F deal with threats not only of extortion but also of violence.

She had documents purporting that Knight had killed a chemist named Ollie Shifflett. And even that he had tried to foment a rebellion. In Washington, a city in which tidbits of distorted truth adequately justified full-scale wars, it was easy to twist partial facts into outright condemnation of a twenty-three-year-old speculator. She had only to tell a receptive audience what they wanted to hear.

This material, and the money involved, had sufficed to get the attention of the VP's chief of staff, who invited Sabina—instead of her father or her SEC boss—to the VP's office.

This angered her SEC boss, but that hardly came as a surprise. Her boss was an envious, uptight, and ambitious woman who correctly diagnosed and feared those same traits in Sabina. Her boss's boss considered Knight to be a scofflaw and a dropout: a miscreant who served no useful purpose beyond earning favorable press coverage for the SEC if his case went to trial—and the same favorable press plus a fat settlement if it didn't.

Smolderhof, as a Canadian, was harder to reach legally, plus his whereabouts were unknown: the news said he was hiding out in a cave. In fact, he had settled on a private beach in Malaysia, basking in the sunshine, guarded by lawyers, guns, and his newly acquired money. Washerman proved to be a clueless stooge who had been used as a frontman. Smolderhof never made him part of the scam. He rode all of his huge stock position to zero as sincere atonement for his unwitting complicity.

The SEC needed to nail someone within their jurisdiction. A five-billion-dollar fraud had occurred under their noses. Someone had to be punished, to prove they were on top of the situation. Knight provided an ideal target in every way.

Sabina had to move that target. The evidence she had manufactured had served all the purposes that it safely could. Her father had examined it at length. Trying to use it in any court would be suicide. Well-paid, and therefore well-motivated, defense lawyers would discover her deceptions, the case would sour, and she could wind up as a defendant herself. That was unacceptable. She wasn't the criminal here.

Actually, the SEC needed none of the faked documents for a prosecution. They had Knight dead to rights according to the way the laws were interpreted by those who enforced them. She could honestly attest that she had seen Knight's perfectly timed sales of his long positions while everyone else was buying. Subpoenas of his brokerage records would provide incontrovertible proof. His nonpublic assays performed on purloined rock samples, combined with his purchase of put options so soon before B-F collapsed, clearly showed he had inside knowledge of what was going on in the company, and certain knowledge of the fraud. She had no doubt that the SEC could obtain a conviction for insider trading, just on that alone.

But what might Charles Knight say about *her* in court? A cynical judge might grant a defendant substantial leeway. Why take a chance on any blowback at this point? It would embarrass her father, the SEC, and even the vice president. And it could be disastrous for her.

Her father worked to figure out a deal with the SEC to ensure a proper share of the credit and financial proceeds came through him to his agency. But with this tangle of agencies, even *he* struggled.

He had told her, "There's a deal here, Sabina. The problem is that once the bureaucracy gets into motion, stopping it is like trying to stop an avalanche. If this goes to court there's a risk the IRS will lose and not get any of the money. And the SEC won't either. That's on top of the fact you don't exactly have clean hands in all of this—which is a major concern if it gets public. This is best handled out of court."

He was so right! Why risk court or his excellent conviction rate? Nowadays, the discovery of a marijuana plant on a farm didn't result in a criminal case but the confiscation of the farm. To avoid risk, someone with too much cash in his car would accede to having the money confiscated, as well as the car. Few people could invest the additional time and money required to contest the government, especially when doing so increased the risk of a prison sentence. So most citizens simply allowed what amounted to a giant legalized extortion racket to shake them down for their property. The power of this system infused Sabina with admiration for its creators.

Her father ordered her to make sure that no defense attorney ever laid eyes on the documents she now carried. Her mission today was to do something that surprised even her: to ensure that there would be no trial of Charles Knight. That meant convincing the vice president of this, without in any way damaging her own credibility. For the first time ever, Sabina felt nervous.

She went through another security check before a guard escorted her to the office of the vice president of the United States. She had to wait in the anteroom. The VP always made people wait; it sent the right signal.

Finally his private secretary ushered her in. The VP looked regal sitting behind a desk the size of an aircraft carrier. The inside of the top drawer bore the signatures of decades of vice presidents. It was tradition. Sabina stood in front of one of the diminutive chairs reserved for visitors.

"Ms. Heidel. I'm Dick Stafford, chief of staff." Stafford had entered directly behind her and introduced himself as he walked past.

Vice President Cooligan said, "Your recent exploits are going to make you a hero, Sabina."

"Well, I don't know about that." She curtsied faintly and felt foolish for so doing. But she knew it was a good move. It made her seem demure and vulnerable, and therefore more trustworthy—all rare attributes in Washington.

The vice president chuckled at that, titillated at her acknowledgement of his position. "Tell me where we stand, Sabina."

She looked up at him. "Mr. President—excuse me, Mr. Vice President"—a clever faux mistake—"B-F will be bankrupt soon. Trading has been halted in both New York and Toronto based on the evidence I put together of the fraud. Burke has just today announced the results of their first drilling efforts. No gold. None at all."

"And the company's value? B-F's value?"

"It's hard to say since any trading is now informal and off the exchanges. But it's going to be zero."

"Amazing. Five billion dollars. Scam of the century!"

Sabina held back a scoff. She had embarked on her personal education about the monetary system, ignited by her somewhat one-sided conversation with Springer. The fractional reserve banking system could and did create out of thin air billions of dollars of new credit-based money every day of the week. In comparison, the B-F scam was hardly a rounding error. But this was not the time to mention this reality to the VP. She needed the VP in money-scrounging mode.

"What about Smolderhof and Knight? What are the plans for their prosecution?"

Sabina shook her head. "We'd like to get Smolderhof, but he is a Canadian problem, sir. Furthermore, he has fled and his whereabouts are unknown. As for Knight, it's a tough situation that's getting us stuck in bureaucratic turf wars right now. Although there is an excellent securities fraud case to be made, there is no tax fraud yet evident. The deputy commissioner of the enforcement division of the IRS suggests we refrain from pursuing Knight with criminal charges, and be satisfied with the civil forfeiture. He's good at these assessments, Mr. Vice President."

The vice president glanced at Stafford, who nodded.

Stafford said only, "Ted Lichen. Reliable man."

Sabina added, "And I have recommended the same to SEC."

"I'm not sure I understand that, Sabina," the vice president said. "No criminal charges for the securities fraud? I thought that part was pretty blatant."

"You're quite correct, sir, it is. But it's about Knight's put options, sir…."

"What about them?"

"They've been frozen by a court injunction on petition of the SEC."

"Good, good."

"Not so good, sir," Sabina offered. "They're valuable assets, but they will likely be lost to us unless you act."

"Act? How?"

"It will be much better if we seize the assets in a civil forfeiture as the IRS wants. Then the money can be used to fund future operations such as the one I have just completed."

"How much money are we talking about here, Sabina?" The vice president's voice was warm and gentle.

"When the stock completes its collapse, Knight's options will be worth $200 million dollars."

The VP's eyebrows rose.

Sabina smiled. The VP would want that money. It was far more than he had requested from Congress for his Government Efficiency Enhancement Initiative.

Sabina added, "But it's worth nothing if we don't move quickly." This wasn't entirely true, but Sabina had no difficulty lying, even to the vice president. The money wouldn't disappear. But the broker would have to round up four million worthless B-F shares and deliver them against the puts before they expired. "The SEC has frozen Knight's accounts. In a setting like this with a pending trial, the SEC will keep them frozen until the options expire."

The VP looked at Stafford.

"There is plenty of precedent for freezing the accounts of someone under suspicion," Stafford said.

The VP knew what it all meant. "We would be giving up $200 million that we could otherwise record as profit for my Government Efficiency Enhancement Initiative—"

Sabina interrupted. "That's if you don't intercede, sir."

The VP turned back to her.

"Your Government Efficiency Enhancement Initiative may provide an opportunity to improve government in a way not previously considered. You see, the SEC may be able to *freeze* Knight's accounts pending an investigation, but the IRS can *seize* accounts outright. In fact, it has been upheld in court that the IRS can seize his accounts *and*, most importantly, exercise the options in the accounts on behalf of the government."

The VP turned to his chief of staff with his eyebrows raised.

Stafford nodded slowly. He said, "The IRS has indeed seized stock options and sold them to third parties, and, she's right, it has been upheld in court."

Sabina said, "Up to now, your initiative was focused on exchange of personnel and knowledge between agencies."

"Yes."

"You might want to consider an expanded initiative. What if you added exchange of *powers*, as well?" She let it hang in the air.

Stafford said nothing, obviously contemplating.

Sabina hoped Stafford and the vice president would now be thinking just as her father thought. In the past, expansion of executive powers required congressional action at the very least, which meant a change to legislation. Congress was intended to act as a brake on the executive branch. But politicians of all stripes now recognized that sort of thing as just a quaint notion, much like the Constitution itself. The document had been interpreted into irrelevance.

Now, executive power could be expanded and rechanneled essentially without oversight, especially in the case of about a dozen praetorian agencies, like the CIA, the NSA, and the FBI, each with their own black budgets.

In regard to the more prosaic agencies, the executive branch often had to enlist the assistance of constitutional law professors to invent ways around Constitutional prohibitions. With a bit of effort, the judicial branch could be convinced to affirm almost any powers the executive chose to assume. Relative to some, this initiative seemed easy: both the SEC and the IRS fell under the executive branch already, and no new executive powers were needed. It involved only moving the agencies' powers around some, sharing them a bit, all for the purpose of government-efficiency enhancement.

413

Stafford did not have to consider long before saying to the vice president, "If you set the precedent for an exchange of *powers,* that might be part of your platform for the presidency. And capturing $200 million from a criminal makes for excellent press...."

The VP nodded. His can-do attitude had endeared him to his constituents as he scrambled up the political ladder. He figured out how to get things done, despite all barriers—legal, moral, or practical. And in Washington, the ends always justified the means. There were constant cries to "do something" from a hundred different quarters. In a town that considered shame and guilt to be signs of weakness, a man like the vice president exuded strength.

With the seeds planted, Sabina lay out the rest of her plan of attack, hoping the VP would accept it.

She captured the vice president's eyes. "Call off the SEC, sir. Let the IRS seize all of Knight's assets. It's a small deviation from SOP. But I like to believe we're all about doing the fair thing, the right thing. The reporters will be on our side."

That would make sense to the VP. No reporter would take up the cause of a punk speculator.

Stafford nodded. "No one will make a stink about it. And then the precedent will be set."

Sabina added, "Then the IRS can exercise the options, preserve that money for us, and split it with the SEC. It is a wonderful sharing of powers across agencies, exactly as you initially envisioned. It's a huge win for the taxpayers and shows the voters that the government, and your office in particular, is watching out for their interests against the bad guys." She hit all the hot buttons. And clinched it with a dazzling, slightly come-hither, smile.

"What about Knight?" the vice president asked. "He'll have something to say."

"Knight will likely be convicted if this goes to court, and he knows it. The SEC has him dead to rights, but, on the other hand, if it came to a jury trial, who knows what the outcome might be. If he's criminally prosecuted by SEC, he will assuredly fight it, simply because he's got nothing to lose, facing a long jail term. And that will take time. Assets will be wasted. And we'll have risk. I don't believe Knight will fight a *civil* forfeiture, however, because we'll guarantee to let him off with a consent decree if he doesn't fight."

"How about postponing his indictment? Have the IRS seize the assets, exercise the options, and take the money first. Take him to trial later." The VP looked proud of this idea.

Sabina had to shut down the idea of a trial. She had convinced the man so far, but could she win on this next critical point? Her nerves had calmed, and she could not let them reemerge and throw her off her game. In this next moment, these two men must believe everything she claimed.

"Sir, if he wins the criminal case, despite all the evidence against him, the courts might award him his seized assets back, plus interest. They would call it an improper taking. It would be the worst possible outcome for your initiative."

"Could he win? You said you had him dead to rights." The VP looked at Stafford.

Sabina said, "Sir, as you know, anything is possible in a trial. Bad guys get away with horrible stuff all the time. There is always the risk of a technicality he could use to get off. For instance, jury nullification is a new trend. That's all about acting in accord with what the jury believe is just, as opposed to the letter of the law. You never know when some kind of activist might make his way onto a jury these days. Why should we take any risk?" That risk in the case of Charles Knight was substantial. For Sabina.

"So the government can choose between a sure $200 million or prosecuting Knight."

Sabina replied with a cool confidence she did not feel. "Yes."

The VP added, "I'd like to have both. If we prosecute Knight, the money will just disappear, right?"

"Not really," said Stafford. "*We* wouldn't get it, though. Whoever wrote the options would get to keep their money if the options were allowed to expire."

"And who wrote the options?"

"Various citizens and brokerages."

"From our party, or the other party?"

Stafford turned to Sabina, who knew what to say even though she didn't know the answer.

"They almost all support the other side, sir."

"Voters don't much like rich financial wheeler-dealers. More like gamblers. Fuck 'em," the VP said. Then he sighed. "Well, we can't have waste in my new program, can we?" He shrugged. "Let's not waste time and take a chance we won't get the money. Dick, tell Lichen that I'll arrange the go-ahead from the president for the IRS to seize those assets. We'll cool the heels of the SEC and assure them they can cash in on the take. Knight gets a pass this time. We'll nail him someday."

Sabina exhaled. She had won. She could now relax and do what she was best at. When he looked at her, she tilted her head just so and let her breath catch in a manner that she knew would trigger the man's baser instincts. Unlike Charles Knight, the vice president would bend to her will.

He nodded his head slowly and said, "Sabina, I'm terrifically impressed with you. Taking a big personal risk going to Africa to catch the bad guy. You deserve a big vacation."

"I'm about to take a short break, then back to work...." she said, her smile broad. Her father would be pleased with her again.

"Well, Sabina, don't be gone long. I suspect there are lots of things we can do together in the future. How would you like to work directly under me?"

The VP dropped double entendres almost as easily as she herself did. It was an invitation to climb the political power ladder, starting at a high rung. He presented an opportunity to run with a political tycoon—a perfect pairing with her financial billionaire, Smolderhof. The prospect of power and money was sexually exciting, working together like a dose of Ecstasy and a vibrator. She felt the beginnings of something that might be fulfillment. She didn't have to choose between power and money. The two reinforced each other. They were like kerosene and liquid oxygen, powerful by themselves, but rocket fuel when combined.

She left the Executive Office Building fully satisfied with herself. Her taxi drove her past the Federal Reserve on her way home. She looked up at it with appreciative determination.

Someday....

Later, she climbed into another taxi. "Dulles Airport," she said to the driver.

The black man, with thinning silver hair surrounding a central bald spot, looked back and said in a thick accent, "What airline?"

She replied, "Delta."

The man kept looking at her in the mirror. "Where ah you goin'?" he said.

She replied, "To Malaysia." To Smolderhof. He had booked her in first class, and she'd make sure the trip was worth taking.

Smolderhof had fled a month ago. Hopefully he had calmed down. He wasn't quite the respected billionaire he had planned to be. But he possessed incredible wealth nonetheless, as long as he could stay where neither the US nor Canada could extradite him.

She would bounce back and forth between Smolderhof in Malaysia and the vice president in Washington.

"I have not been to Malaysia," the taxi driver said, still looking at her in the mirror. His accent seemed familiar.

She asked, "Where are you from?" She didn't really care.

"West Africa," the man replied. "Gondwana."

She laughed then, a triumphant laugh. No one could beat her. Charles Knight may have beaten Smolderhof, but it was she who had taken Knight's incredible fortune. It was she who had beaten Charles Knight.

Charles Knight had lost.

Epilogue

AND so Charles's money was stolen, and his reputation impugned and besmirched, by the very entities that were supposed to keep him secure in his person and his property. Unless, of course, that government wanted either his person or his property for itself.

Having cut his teeth on a small part of Africa, he decided to see the world and expand his horizons while hatching a plan to regain his money. And he would take revenge, when he was fully collected and able to serve that dish cold.

Xander, more conservative as befits a middle-aged man of broad experience, had made a modest fifty million dollars and was, at last word, making moves on Caroline's shipboard friend, Louise. Louise wasn't the beauty she might have been in her youth. But Xander knew pretty young women were widely available; wise ones of good character were harder to come by.

Maurice, a man who repaid with interest both favors and slights, had enhanced his fortune substantially without getting up from his couch. He was touched that Charles had succeeded in having a specialist visit to alleviate his sleep apnea. But Charles relinquished all hope of improving his diet and exercise habits.

TJ was satisfied with his take on the deal. He made enough to lend some of his brothers money to start several businesses in Gondwana, with no expectation of ever getting it back. A loan to a brother or a member of one's village in West Africa was never, ever, paid back. At least not in money. But such debt would have other value in the future.

And Elliot wouldn't be prosecuted. Sabina thought it best to leave this sleeping dog lie, for dragging him into it would require exposing her fraud, compromising the rest of the plan. Elliot Springer remained focused on finding a cure for the disease that would destroy the human race.

∗   ∗   ∗

Charles stepped out of the narrow shower and looked in the mirror on the bulkhead of the sailboat he had recently purchased in Sierra Leone with a small fraction of Smolderhof's ten-million-dollar bribe. He had lost weight, but he looked healthier. The abrasions, infections, lacerations, and punctures acquired in Gondwana had mostly healed. He shaved his scruffy face every few days, and today was as good as any. His hair thickened; he would let it grow long.

The porthole from the small head opened out onto the distant African shoreline as the craft moved southward along the currents and winds. Today, South Africa would come into view. Then around the cape, past East Africa, heading to India along the monsoon: the route Arab dhows had taken for centuries. He'd come to love Africa. But India and points east called.

The boat sailed large with the wind, so, unlike when the breeze came over the beam, only a slight relative motion carried airflow to the cabin below. But that faint breeze brought with it the smell of bacon sizzling on the hibachi on the taffrail. The bacon enticed him, but far less than the woman who was cooking it.

With a white towel around his waist, he bounded up the ladder in the companionway and into the empty cockpit. The boat was only forty-five feet long and it took no time to find what he wanted to see as soon as he turned.

She stood, her bare feet astride the anchor windlass, leaning on the bow rail. The wind from astern gusted and both her blond hair and her white skirt flipped upward. The boat, guided by its autopilot, surged forward another half a knot faster.

Charles walked along the deck until he reached the mast and then stopped. He did not want to startle her. Gently he said, "Good morning, Princess Caroline."

She turned her face just enough so he could see that she was smiling. He came the rest of the way forward then and put his arms around her. He leaned down and kissed her neck.

The sound of the bow breaking through the sea provided a pleasant and steady rhythm underlying the harmony created from the mingling breath of the two people in love. Above it all, the breath of the wind carried them further away from the evil of the world, and toward a life they both wanted.

An exotic life. A life of adventure.

This was a good life.

He held her close to him as the beauty of the ocean filled their spirits.

Charles Knight had won.

Charles Knight will be back.
Watch for *Drug Lord*, coming to
bookstores soon.

Visit **HighGroundNovels.com**
and sign up to receive the latest
announcements about book
releases and upcoming events.

About the Authors

DOUG Casey spends most of his time in Argentina and Uruguay, with frequent visits to the US, Canada, and various dysfunctional hellholes.

JOHN Hunt, MD, is a pediatrician and former academic. He is chief medical officer of Liberty Healthshare, and co-founder of Trusted Angels Foundation, Camryn Limousine, and Respiratory Research. He likes tractors.

Printed in Great Britain
by Amazon